"You can't stop thinking about getting me naked and having your way with me..." Kat teased.

Emotion settled in Jason's chest and warmed the cold spot that had formed there. "You left me in Denver, Kat."

"I had a tour to go on."

"You didn't say that."

"You didn't ask, Jason."

"Oh, no," he said, laughing, but not with humor. "We agreed to talk through a plan, but that never happened because you ran."

"I didn't run."

"You claimed this was all sex between us and that a few times in the bedroom would get it out of our systems. But you backed off when I called your bluff because you're afraid that no matter how many 'times' we have, your plan won't work. And you'll have to face what's really between us, be it good or bad, once and for all."

"Let's go."

He followed her to the door. "Where exactly are we going?"

"Your place!"

Dear Reader,

Winning Moves is the final story in my Stepping Up trilogy, and it's my favorite of the three. It's a story of love lost and love found. The type of story that always touches my heart.

The heroine, Kat Moore, is a famous choreographer and the hero, Jason Alright, is a judge from Stepping Up and a well-known director. He's now in charge of putting together a Vegas show in connection with the television program, and he sees hiring his ex as great for the production and the perfect opportunity to win back the woman he's never stopped loving. Look out, though! It's going to get wicked and wild before the curtain ever opens.

I would love to have your feedback about this trilogy. Please contact me at www.lisareneejones.com.

Happy reading!

Lisa Renee Jones

Lisa Renee Jones

WINNING MOVES

&

LONE STAR SURRENDER

HARLEQUIN®

entertain, enrich, inspire™

ISBN-13: 978-0-373-79726-4

WINNING MOVES

Copyright © 2012 by Harlequin Books S.A.

The publisher acknowledges the copyright holder of the individual works as follows:

WINNING MOVES
Copyright © 2012 by Lisa Renee Jones

LONE STAR SURRENDER
Copyright © 2009 by Lisa Renee Jones

Recycling programs for this product may not exist in your area.

CONTENTS

ABOUT THE AUTHOR

Lisa spends her days writing the dreams playing in her head. Before becoming a writer, Lisa lived the life of a corporate executive, often taking the red-eye flight out of town and flying home for the excitement of a Little League baseball game. Visit Lisa at www.lisareneejones.com.

Books by Lisa Renee Jones

HARLEQUIN BLAZE

HARLEQUIN NOCTURNE

*Texas Hotzone
**Stepping Up

To get the inside scoop on Harlequin Blaze and its talented writers, be sure to check out blazeauthors.com.

All backlist available in ebook. Don't miss any of our special offers. Write to us at the following address for information on our newest releases.

Harlequin Reader Service
U.S.: 3010 Walden Ave., P.O. Box 1325, Buffalo, NY 14269
Canadian: P.O. Box 609, Fort Erie, Ont. L2A 5X3

WINNING MOVES

To my Underground Angels
and my very special angel, Wendy.

1

KATHERINE "KAT" Moore stepped off the exit ramp into the Las Vegas International Airport with her long blond hair piled on top of her head, ready for a hot bath, cool sheets and her own bed, which she hadn't slept in for months. After globe-trotting with a couple of big-name pop stars' tours back-to-back, she'd found the escape she'd sought, but the lifestyle had taken a toll. She was done. This was it. She wanted roots, a pet, a fridge full of her favorite things. Stability.

Wearily, she headed toward the luggage area when her cell phone started to ring. Dang it, she knew she should have left the darn thing off. Kat sighed and dug the phone out of her purse to see her agent's number on the display. Of course. They'd been arguing when she'd had to turn off her phone in Italy to head to the States.

"Yes, I'm home, Michael," she said, without saying hello. "And no, I'm still not taking the new tour. I don't care if it's Derek Mercer or how many number-one hits he has. I don't need the money and you probably need it less." She needed a life. She needed… No. No, she didn't. She refused to think of what she really needed, what she'd run away from—apparently unsuccessfully.

"You're right," Michael answered. "You're not taking a tour. I have something just as big and you get to stay right here in Vegas."

She stopped walking. "I'm listening." Someone bumped into her and she quickly moved to the side of the walkway as clusters of people passed by.

"I got a call this morning from M&M Studios. They have a top secret project they're working on. They won't release details over the phone, but the pay is double your tour pay if you get the gig and you were requested by name."

"Double? You have to be freaking kidding me."

"Money isn't something I ever joke about."

"No kidding," she said, thinking that the house she'd planned to surprise her parents with for their retirement next year might just have gotten bigger. "And I'm not complaining."

"I need you at the Wind Walker Hotel in thirty minutes."

"Wait. No. I'm a mess. I'm grimy and tired. I've traveled halfway across the world. And who asked for me, anyway?"

"They want to make a decision today. They're waiting on you. I told them you'd be there. This is my reputation and yours. You're committed."

She was going to kill him. "Michael—"

"You said you wanted to stay home in Vegas. You said you wanted stability. I'm giving it to you. Get your skinny, pretty little backside over there—and do it now. Call me from a cab and I'll fill you in on whatever details I can." He hung up.

She gaped at the phone. He'd flipping hung up on her. She growled low in her throat and started walking. She'd been with Michael ten years, since she'd turned twenty and landed her first big dancing job. If she didn't like him so much, she'd fire *his* "pretty little backside." She wasn't going to an interview now.

Damn. Damn. Damn. She had to go. He told them she'd go, and her decision to put down some roots meant there would be less opportunities for work. She glanced down at herself as she stepped onto an escalator leading to baggage claim. She had on a PINK Victoria's Secret T-shirt and faded jeans with a rip down the leg. She looked more like she was hanging out at the house on a day off—not to mention that she felt like death warmed over, after a number of time changes.

She rushed onward to baggage claim to discover her bag was missing. Frustrated, she dialed Michael. She couldn't do this interview. Not now. She'd make a bad impression.

He didn't answer. She glanced at the time of their last call. She was never going to make it to the interview if she stayed and argued about her luggage. She hesitated and thought of her parents, of their dream retirement, of living close enough so she could actually see them. She hurried toward the exit and the cab line.

The interview was poorly scheduled, but it was a blessing, and if it worked out, she'd be thanking Michael for pushing her.

TWENTY MINUTES LATER, Kat still hadn't reached Michael and she was pretty sure he was avoiding her calls so she couldn't back out of the interview. By the time the cab pulled up to the front of the towering Wind Walker Hotel, one of the largest casinos on the strip, Kat had removed her hair clip, applied lipstick and unsuccessfully tried to cover her dark circles.

She paid the driver and dialed Michael again. She didn't even know where she was going at this point. *Finally* he answered, and before she could even speak, he demanded, "Are you there?"

"Yes, and—"

"I have my contact on my cell so hold on," he said, and she heard him say, "She's there." He came back to Kat. "Where are you?"

"I'm at the front door, but—"

"Front door," he told whoever he was talking to, then back to Kat, "Go to the bellman and give him your name. You'll be escorted."

"Okay, but—"

"Hurry," he said. "Kat. This is bigger than I thought. This is huge. Call me after. Go get 'em, tiger." He hung up.

Kat let out a breath and just gave up. She found the bellman and gave him her name. She resolved to do what she did in the middle of a tour when something went wrong—she just needed to roll with the punches. An employee led her to the hotel theater ticket booth and a row of offices behind it.

The woman knocked on a door. A few seconds later, to Kat's surprise, Ellie Campbell, an old friend and top-notch choreographer, rushed from the room, pulling the door shut behind her. "Kat!" Ellie's arms were outstretched, her long hair that, at least for today, was a pale shade of light blue, floating behind her.

Kat hugged Ellie, whom she'd met on a television project a good seven or eight years before.

"I can't believe you're here," Ellie said, leaning back to inspect her friend. "I wanted you for this project so badly. I couldn't believe the timing of you coming home today!"

"I can't wait to hear the details, but what happened to *Stepping Up?* I thought you were judging?"

"Oh, I am," she said. "I love it. Absolutely love it."

Kat's stomach twisted with the connection the show held to the very past she was avoiding. "I'm confused. Then why am I here? Why are you here? Surely you don't have time to work on a Vegas show?"

"The studio came up with this idea that we should organize a multi-state tour in between seasons and a Vegas show to run for a full year here at the hotel. The show will open a month before auditions start for season three of *Stepping Up.* The catch? They gave us a whole six weeks to make this happen. Thankfully though, the tour will be after season three ends. It's fun and exciting, but—" she grinned and rubbed her stomach "—I have a bun in the oven. I just dropped the bombshell on the studio. I can't travel to judge and do the Vegas show. It's too much."

Kat gaped. "A bun in the oven. How?"

They both laughed.

"Okay," Kat said. "I know how."

Ellie raised her finger. "Last season we had a new production manager for *Stepping Up.* Needless to say, we sort of hit it off."

"Sort of?" Kat teased, staring at the gorgeous white diamond on her friend's finger.

"I'll tell you the story later. But right now, we need a replacement for me on the live show and the tour. I saw your name on a prospect list and knew you were the one, but I called and got your service."

"I've been out of the country for months."

"So they told me, but I was determined to reach you. I contacted your agent. It has to be fate, honey, because you arrived today, and we really need to wrap up interviews today. Good, bad or ugly, we need to nail this down. You can make this end with good, and leave the bad and the ugly behind. I just know it."

The door behind them opened, and a sixty-something woman whose hair was dyed a dark chestnut color appeared. Ellie turned to her. "Dawn. Thanks for coming. How did it go?"

"Excellent. I agreed to take the job. I'm thrilled."

"Wonderful. I am, too." Ellie hugged Dawn before she departed, then whispered to Kat. "You'd never know from looking at her, but that woman is the hottest new costume designer in this city. I'm talking smoking-hot designs. And we aren't in prime time like *Stepping Up* is. We have to dirty up this show to make it work for Vegas."

Kat laughed, but it didn't sound completely genuine and she knew it. All she could think of was the TV show and its connection to her past. "I've learned to never judge a book by its cover in this business. I'd love to see Dawn's designs."

Ellie motioned to the door. "Let's go meet everyone. I'm excited. This is going to be so good."

He wasn't here, she decided. He wasn't a part of this. If he had heard her name, he would have said no. This was going to be okay. It was going to be good. They wouldn't see each other. "Me, too," Kat said decisively. This *was* exciting. It was a great opportunity.

Ellie rushed into the room. "I have a surprise. I made a phone call and got lucky. The perfect choreographer I've been telling you guys about is here. She's the one."

Kat felt her cheeks heat and her stomach twist. Ellie was giving her some big shoes to fill. She drew a calming breath and then followed Ellie into the room. A group of six people sat around a conference table, but she only saw one—the one sitting at the head of the table. She only saw *him*. Jason Alright, with his light brown tousled hair, his square jaw shadowed with stubble and his deep green eyes, intense as they met hers. Those eyes reached inside her and warmed her in all kinds of wickedly wonderful, and yet painful, ways, as they always did. Those soulfully sexy eyes had landed her in bed with him two years before, just before she'd left the country. And ten years before, those same eyes had spoken to her heart, her soul, the day they'd stood at the altar and gotten married.

This wasn't going to work. She had to leave now.

Jason's eyes narrowed and he shook his head ever-so-slightly, telling her not to leave, and reading her like he always did. Did he know she was coming? Surely, he hadn't known.

"This is Kat Moore," Ellie said to the group, touching Kat's arm and announcing, "Kat is the best choreographer in this business." She elbowed Kat. "After me, of course."

Kat laughed. "Of course."

Ellie grinned and continued, "She just got back from

a world tour with the pop star Marcus Knight today, which was pure luck for us." She glanced at Kat, explaining, "We're basically trying to bring *Stepping Up* to life in a musical, and the best people to make that happen are those who are a part of the television show, who understand what that means. So we're important to the creative process, though most of us won't stay involved beyond that. We just can't swing the time for both the Vegas production and the TV show."

Kat let out a discreet breath. Maybe Jason wasn't going to be involved long-term. Maybe that's why he didn't want her to leave. Maybe.

Ellie began her introductions, going around the table quickly. Kat greeted two women and a man before Ellie said, "Meet Lana Taylor and Darla Nelson, both judges for the show, as I'm sure you know. We trust them, so their help enables us to work under such a tight time crunch."

"We're arguing over casting," said Lana, a pretty brunette known for her diva attitude on the show. "Nothing new there, though, if you watch the show."

Kat didn't watch. Ever. But it wasn't like she could say, *Sorry. I don't watch because my ex-husband that I've never stopped loving, who's ripped my heart out a few too many times, is one of the stars.*

"No, indeed," Darla chimed in, shoving a long lock of blond hair behind her ear. "There's nothing new about Lana and I disagreeing." She smiled at Kat. "You'll get used to us fighting, though. Even I have. It's very nice to meet you, Kat. I'm excited to meet someone Ellie is so excited about."

"Oh, please," Lana said. "Enough with the excitement."

Darla laughed and wrapped an arm around Lana. "You'd never know she likes me."

"I don't," Lana said tightly and then sighed. "Oh, okay, I do, but that's a big secret, Kat. The audience loves our bickering."

The mention of a secret echoed in Kat's mind, and her gaze discreetly slid to Jason's, the connection tingling down her spine with shared understanding. They had a secret, too. A past they'd never hidden, but it had been so long ago, before either of them were established in the industry.

"And last but not least," Ellie announced. "Meet Jason Alright. He's—"

"Hello, Kat."

"Jason," she said softly.

"You look good. Your hair's longer now."

"And you forgot how to shave."

He ran his hand behind his neck and laughed, a soft, warm sexy sound that sizzled along her nerve endings. She loved the man's laugh. "I guess I did," he agreed, glancing around the room and announcing, "Yes. We know each other." They knew each other all right, and a few people understood how, but then, they'd been unknowns, barely getting started, always apart. He patted the table beside him. "Come sit down, Kat."

By him. She wanted to be by him. That was dangerous. She'd be so close to touching him—way, way too close. Touching him was bad and oh-so-good. She'd proven, over and over again, that not only was she putty in Jason's hands, she enjoyed every second of it.

Jason rose and, pulling the chair out for her, she moved toward him. It was official. Not only was he still tall, lean and muscular, he still made black jeans, a Harley T-shirt and biker boots look like the definition of sin in the city. And she would bet her left arm that somewhere nearby he had a leather jacket, despite the heat of Vegas in July.

"Oh, good grief," Lana grumbled. "The man doesn't hold a chair for me and I sit next to him at the judges' table for months of every year. Do tell, Kat. How exactly do you and Jason know each other?"

Jason glanced at Lana. "If I held your chair for you, you'd just roll it over my foot. I've learned to keep my distance."

Darla nodded in agreement. "Smart man."

Kat cut her gaze from Jason's to sit down and gain composure before facing the group, but it didn't help. He was close, so close, and his all-too-familiar spicy masculine scent flared in her nostrils. He still wore the same cologne, and she remembered burying her nose in his chest to inhale that amazing scent.

He helped her scoot her chair forward and his fingers brushed her shoulders, sending a shock wave of sensations rushing over her, heating her skin.

A knock sounded on the door and a woman walked in. "Ms. Moore's agent sent over her demo reel."

"Oh, excellent," Ellie exclaimed. "Please load it for us." The woman moved to the end of the table where a pedestal held a television and various electronic equipment. Ellie looked at Kat. "You're okay with that, right? I know your work, but not everyone else does."

"Of course," Kat assured her. "That's expected."

The lights went out and the demo began to play, but Jason wasn't watching it. He was watching her. She could feel his stare, hot and heavy, *impossibly* hot and heavy. It was all she could do not to turn to him, not to tell him to stop, not to reach out and touch him. She was as conflicted about the man as she'd always been.

The demo ended in seven minutes, though it felt like an hour, and the lights came back on.

"That was fantastic," Darla commented, and several of the other people in attendance murmured similar comments. "I knew you'd worked with some big names, but you've worked with a lot more than I thought."

"I've been blessed with opportunities," Kat said.

"And some big egos," Darla said. "How do you manage to teach a routine to a famous pop star who thinks they have nothing to learn?"

"I've been lucky enough to have worked with stars who want to stay stars and want to deserve their hype," Kat answered.

"Lucky is right," Ellie said. "I haven't been that lucky."

"I've had more of the power-trip ego issues with dancers who resent a new choreographer getting the job they wanted," Kat added.

"And how do you handle that?" Darla asked.

Ellie snorted. "Out-dance them and shut them up."

Kat reluctantly agreed. "I've been forced into that position but I don't like it. I try to enlist their help and stroke their egos."

Darla studied her a long moment. "You've been all over the world. Are you going to be happy here in one place? We really need someone who will stick it out at least a year. And even when we do travel, right now it's all in the States."

"Vegas is my home," Kat explained. "I grew up here. My parents are here. I really am ready to be here as well. I want to put down roots and sleep in my own bed every night."

"I told you this was perfect timing," Ellie added, and to Kat, "And girlfriend, I don't know how you did back-to-back concert tours. I did one and it almost killed me."

"You have to be at the right place in your life to do it," Kat said. "I was young and free and I saw the world. Now I'm *home*."

"So that's it?" Jason asked, his question forcing her to look at him. "No more traveling?"

"Not for me," she said, unintentionally referencing the past history between them, of demanding careers that had separated them, then tore them apart. Kat could have kicked herself for the slip, watching his eyes narrow with understanding. He couldn't have known she was coming today because he knew, just as she did, that the past was never the past. She just had to survive this interview and get out of here and let Jason deal with how he told everyone she wasn't the right choice.

"Kat," Darla said, drawing Kat's attention back to the present. Darla then led her into the first of a series of questions that seemed to come from everyone but Jason. As a former casting director, Darla was tough and detailed, but Kat liked her quite a lot and they hit if off quickly.

A good forty-five minutes later, Darla leaned back in her chair and said, "You have my vote, honey. You rock."

"For once we agree," Lana said. "I'm sold. We obviously need to talk amongst ourselves but I'm going on record as a 'yes.'" Murmurs of agreement followed around the table.

"Thank you, ladies," Kat said, feeling her stomach twist with regret. She liked these people. She could get excited about this job.

Ellie clapped, always youthful by nature. "Now we just need our director to give the okay."

"Who's the director?" Kat asked, mostly out of curiosity. She wasn't taking this job.

"I am," Jason said softly, drawing her shocked gaze. "And I know what Kat is capable of. She'd be perfect."

Kat sucked in a breath at Jason's double meaning, and the very idea that Jason was suggesting they work together. She turned her head so the others couldn't see her, giving him an "are you crazy?" look before deciding she was missing something. "How can you direct this show and do *Stepping Up?* You have auditions and filming in L.A."

"We're filming the entire season here in the hotel this year," he said, leaning back in his seat. In other words, he'd be here, with her, far more than he'd be gone. No. Not with her. She wasn't with him. She wouldn't be with him. His lips curved. "As far as I'm concerned, you have the job. We'll contact your agent with an offer right away."

She couldn't seem to form any words. Her and Jason, both in Vegas, both working on the same show. She tore her gaze from his and pushed to her feet. "Thanks, everyone, for your time and consideration. I sincerely enjoyed meeting you all. Darla—" she offered her hand to Darla, who stood up to shake it "—let's have lunch sometime soon."

Darla gave her a keen look. "Because we aren't going to be working together, are we?"

"I hope we will work together, yes," she said.

"But not now," Darla pushed.

"I have some conflicts I need to talk to my agent about," she said honestly, refusing to look at Jason, who was still seated. She maneuvered around the chair and waved at the group, telling them goodbye, and finally darted for the exit.

She shut the door behind her and raced down the hall, her heart in her throat, choking her. She made it to the ticket booth when Jason's hand gently shackled her arm. Suddenly, she was in a small hallway behind the booth, back against the wall, his hand on the surface above her head. She could smell his damnable cologne, feel the heat of his body, and it made her mad.

"Did you know I was coming?" she asked.

"Yes."

"And you didn't warn me?"

"Would you have come?"

"You wanted me to come?"

"Yes."

"Yes? That's all you're going to say? Just 'yes'?"

"It's not complicated. It doesn't require a long explanation. Yes. Yes, I wanted you to come."

"You know we can't work together."

"We work great together. No one gets my creative vision more than you."

"No," she said. "No. This won't work." She leaned away from the wall.

"Come on, KandyKat," he said sincerely. His hand closed on her shoulder, sending a rush of heat all the way to her toes. "We're good together. You know we are. We'll rock this show in a big way."

"Don't call me that," she snapped, referring to the old nick-name that only he used. "And 'good together' doesn't make us good for each other."

"The show needs you. *I need you.*"

I need you. His words shuddered through her, and she knew she was in trouble. In trouble, because she wanted him to mean something beyond the show.

"No." She stepped around him. "I'm not doing this with you again." She took off walking, and this time he let her. Just like he had two years before. Just like he always did.

JASON KNEW THE minute he'd said he needed her, he'd screwed up and sent her running for the hills like she always did. But not this time. He'd let her go before, and regretted it every day since.

He rounded the corner and entered the hallway, then walked back into the interview room. The room went silent, everyone was staring at him. He went to his seat and grabbed his notebook.

"We're done," he said. "And Kat's in. I'll get her."

"Do you need her agent's number?" Ellie asked.

"I know Michael," he said. "I'll talk to him."

He headed to the door. The minute he'd been told about this project, he knew it was meant to be. That it had come to him—to him and Kat—at the right time. They were both home, where they belonged. *Together.*

2

Two days later, on a Friday afternoon, Kat sat on her overstuffed brown couch with her feet bare, wearing blue jeans, a tank and minus a bra or makeup. The idea was to indulge in a leisurely afternoon in her cozy, too-often-unoccupied home, and to stop the constant replay of her encounter with Jason in her mind. Her current effort to distract herself had her with a book in her hand and a movie playing on her flat-screen television.

Her cell phone rang and she ignored it. She knew who it was. Her agent. Michael had called her ten times today, begging her to take the job with Jason, which wasn't making her efforts to forget her ex any easier.

The doorbell rang and she hit the mute button on the remote control. She grabbed the forty bucks she'd put on the glossy maple coffee table for the teenage sisters who lived next-door who had hit her up for their school chocolate sale. She'd made them squeal when she'd told them she'd take forty bars. Kat's mom and dad loved candy and she loved seeing the kids get excited. The bell rang again and she smiled. Eager teenage girls. Gotta love 'em.

Kat padded across the marble tiled floor to open the door, and before she even opened the screen, she flashed the money. "I have the cash."

Jason grinned and leaned on the door frame, muscles flexing under a plain black T-shirt that didn't look plain on him at all. "That's not enough to make me go away," he said, eying the two twenties in her hand. His gaze slid over her pink tank top and then lifted. "Not even close."

She growled and shoved the money into her pocket, then crossed her arms in front of her chest as she inadvertently noted his clean-shaven jaw, all smooth and ready…for her skin. That little bad girl thought made her as angry as she was eternally hot for the man. "I'm going to kill Michael for giving you my address."

"Your parents," Jason supplied.

She rolled her eyes and dropped her arms in frustration. "Oh, good grief."

"They always liked me."

Oh, didn't she know it. They loved the man almost as much as she did. "Why are you here?"

"You know why."

"Save your breath."

"Not a chance. Invite me in."

"Not happening."

"Why?"

"You know why."

He stared at her, his green eyes cutting through the screen like a diamond on glass. "Kat," he said softly, pressing his hand on the screen. "Let me in." The words vibrated with a plea, and she knew he wasn't talking about the door anymore.

"I can't," she whispered, unable to stop herself from flattening her hand against his. Warmth spread up her arm and over her chest. His head dropped to the screen and so did hers. She could feel him everywhere he wasn't touching, everywhere he wasn't—*shouldn't*—be. She wanted to rip the screen away, to hold him and to feel him hold her—to get lost in him just one last time. It was always *just one last time.*

"I can't do this again. This is what happens. The door is the only thing keeping it from happening now."

"I'm not going to tell you we won't end up in bed together," he said after a long pause.

"That's not helping your case if you want me to take this job," she said, wondering why his assurance that they might end up between the sheets was comforting rather than the opposite.

"I've never lied to you, Kat," he said, his voice thickening. "I'm not going to start now. I want you. I never stopped wanting you. And I want you involved in the show. Enough that I used my pull to double the salary offer originally sent to your agent's office."

She pulled back to gape. "What? That's an insane amount of money." She shook her head. "This isn't about money to me. You know money isn't why I do what I do."

"You love spoiling your parents rotten, and you know it. This will let you do it in a big way. This is security for them and for you."

"I spoil them because we spent a lot of years struggling when I was growing up."

"You don't have to justify it to me of all people. You know I love your parents, I know how they struggled. I was there when they were helping you through college, remember?"

Yes, oh yes, she remembered. Love, marriage and his career that started two years before hers and tore them apart.

"I admire you for what you do for them," he continued. "You know I spoil mine as well. Look, Kat, I have to get you in or out by Monday. We have open call tomorrow and Sunday and with seventy spots to fill. Ellie can handle it, but if you're in, I know you. You'll want to cherry-pick the dancers. At least come to the set and observe. See how you feel being there with me. And if it's still a 'no,' I'll let this go. Just give me one day."

"Why are you pushing so hard to make this happen?"

"Do you remember when we went to San Francisco and we got down to the pier and we couldn't get a cab back to the hotel, and the trams were shut down?"

The weekend he'd proposed. "You know I remember that weekend." She thought of that panicked moment on the pier and found herself smiling in spite of everything. "My feet were killing me and we just had to keep walking."

"I carried you."

"And fell down."

"And you pulled me back to my feet, spotted a midnight movie joint, where we ate too much popcorn, and then the cabs were free. We worked it out together, just like we'll work this out. We're older, wiser and more mature. We're both professionals." He touched the screen again. "Tomorrow, Kat. 6:00 a.m. Please. Be there." He backed up, his eyes holding hers. Her cell phone began to ring. "And take your agent's calls. He might have something to say worth listening to." He turned and started walking away.

Kat stared after him, watching his sexy, loose-legged swagger as he headed to his motorcycle, fighting the urge to go drag him back and rip off his clothes and have her wicked way with him.

With a frustrated sound, she rushed back to the living room, away from the door and the hot man on the bike. Her phone had stopped ringing, but Jason's words played in her mind. *Take your agent's calls. He might have something to say worth listening to.* She frowned and reached over the couch to snap up her cell. Jason didn't say anything without a purpose. Kat hit her voice mail button and listened to the most recent message from Michael.

"I know you're a perfectionist even when it comes to being stubborn, but listen up." Kat ground her teeth. Michael had been with her through her painful split from Jason. He knew good, darn well she was trying to be smart and keep her personal and professional lives separate. That wasn't stubborn, it was smart. *"I don't know what's going on with you and Jason, but he wants you on this job in a big way. He gave the studio an ultimatum, Kat. He insisted they do whatever it takes to get you—including doubling your offer—or he'll pay back his signing bonus and walk. I know Jason's involvement is messing with your head, but if you won't call me back, call him. Call one of us."*

Kat dropped the phone and stared at it like it was a snake about to bite her. A second later, she launched herself into action and ran for the door, yanking it and the screen open, just in time to see Jason's motorcycle turn the corner.

"What are you doing, Jason?" she whispered, at the same moment her eyes caught on something sitting on top of the porch stairs. Her heart skipped a beat as she forced her bare feet to cross the porch and pick up the KandyKat bar, all too aware of the memory it was meant to stir. *You're sweeter than candy,* Jason used to say, right before he proceeded to prove he meant it. He had no intention of keeping his hands off of her. That was the message now. He wanted her to show up tomorrow with her eyes wide open.

Kat turned and went back inside, shutting the door behind her, trying to shut out temptation, the memories, to shut out *him.* She fumbled to find her phone to call Jason, and then stopped. If she called, he'd know years hadn't erased his number from her memory any more than they had erased him from her heart. Not that he didn't know that. He knew. She didn't hide how affected she was by him. She couldn't if she tried, so she just didn't try. Still, she hesitated. Jason had threatened to quit over her. She glanced down at the Kit Kat bar. She didn't understand what was going on with him, only that she had to talk to him. She had to understand. Kat dropped her face into her hands. She was going to the auditions tomorrow.

IT WAS SIX O'CLOCK on the dot the next morning and Jason sat at a long table beneath the stage with Darla and Lana to his left, when the odd sixth sense he'd always had for Kat shot through him. He turned on the pretense of surveying the rows of stadium seating filled with hopeful dancers waiting to audition. He scanned and found her inside the entrance, off to the right of the doors, leaning against the wall. Jason smiled to himself and turned back around. He picked up his coffee and took a sip, savoring more than the caffeine. She was here, that was what counted. And he knew his Kat. She wouldn't be against that back wall for long, especially considering Ellie and her assistant choreographer for the day were calling the first group of dancers to the stage. No, she would stand back there, adrenaline pumping with the desire to be in the mix of things. He gave her an hour, tops, before she was on the stage.

He relaxed into his seat, watching Ellie take the dancers through steps. He glanced at the scorecard he and the other judges would use to rank the dancers, then compare them to Ellie's notes. Those with the top scores at the end of the day would be called back for another audition. Darla wouldn't need her scorecard. She'd know every dancer and their strengths with incredible exactness.

Ellie was about to dismiss the third group forty-five minutes later, when Kat called out, "Wait! Wait! Ellie, hold on a minute."

Jason smiled, not even needing to turn around to know she was running down the aisle. "It's Kat," Darla said, glancing behind her and then at him, narrowing her gaze. "You knew she was here."

"Yeah," he said.

"Kat!" Ellie yelled into her mic. "Well, yeehaw!" Ellie stepped to the edge of the stage right as Kat stopped beside the judges' table. She reached over him, the sweet scent of woman—his woman, or she would be again if he had anything to say about it—teased his nostrils. Damn, he wanted her.

"Can you have this group run the routine once more, please?" Kat asked.

Ellie grinned. "If it gets you one step closer to getting your backside up here, then sure thing."

Darla and Lana waved at Kat. "We're so glad you're here."

"Does this mean we get to keep you?" Darla asked.

"Yeah," Jason said. "Does it mean we—" translate *he* "—get to keep you?"

Kat gave him an incredulous look. "You didn't tell them?"

"No," Darla said. "He didn't tell us. Did you take the job?"

"No," Kat said. "I appreciate your eagerness but I'm observing while I try to figure out a bit of a conflict before the Monday deadline for me to make a decision." Her gaze touched Jason's. She still had her backpack over her shoulder, as if she was ready to bolt. "This *doesn't* mean I'm in."

"You're just a very hands-on observer," he teased, glancing at her skintight leggings and tank top, and the long braid down her back that she wore when she worked. All of which said that she'd come to dance.

She grimaced and motioned between her and him. "You and I need to talk."

He leaned into the microphone. "Give us ten, Ellie." He stood up and faced her, lowering his voice for her ears only. "At your beck and call. I always am. You should know that by now." He was all about talking, and he'd like to start with what had happened the last time they were together, but he knew better. Not only was there no time now, but she ran then, and if he pushed too hard she'd run now. He wasn't going to let that happen.

"I didn't mean this second," she said. "Later."

God, she was beautiful with her hair pulled back, her blue eyes luminous against her pale, perfect skin. "Fine, then," he said softly. "We'll talk later."

She opened her mouth and shut it, then shoved her backpack at him. "Tell Ellie to go ahead," she said, and turned away, but not before he saw the panic in her face.

She was afraid of getting hurt, and so was he. But they couldn't go on like this either. They were together, and before he let her get away, they were either saying goodbye for good, or she was putting his ring back on her finger forever. And if he had to kiss every last inch of her a couple dozen times over to get her to let down her walls—well, it was a tough job, but he was the man to do it, and do it right.

3

JASON SAT BACK down and settled Kat's bag in the empty seat next to him before he spoke into the microphone. "We're a go, Ellie."

"Do you want to sit down, Kat?" Darla asked, leaning forward. "I can get you a score sheet."

"I'll stand," Kat said, "but thank you." The music started and Kat's full attention was riveted on the stage she'd soon be on, he was certain.

The dancers began their performance, but Jason watched Kat, her expression focused on the dancers. He could see her mentally pacing the routine, analyzing, thinking and rethinking. The music stopped and Ellie turned to see what Kat wanted her to do now.

Kat squatted down next to Jason, losing her balance and grabbing his leg, scorching it with her hand. The woman had far too much control over him, but he didn't care. Not anymore. He'd done his own share of running, but it had been over for a long time.

Their eyes met and he saw her swallow hard. The touch, the connection, shook her, and it damn sure shook him. She moved her hand to the empty seat next to him.

"How did you rate number seven?" she asked.

He didn't have to look at the scorecard. He hadn't rated many in this group well. "Poorly." He leaned back so that he could talk to Darla with Kat involved. "What did you do on number seven?"

"I marked her as a no," Darla said, after glancing at her clipboard. "Cute little blonde thing that screams of sugar and spice, but she doesn't know it yet. She's just not ready for this."

"Ditto," Lana said, leaning forward to join the conversation. "I love how she looks angelic and still has tattoos. It's that sugar and spice thing, but she doesn't deliver the promise of her first impression." She sighed. "And I'm agreeing with Darla way too much. I'll have to fix that before the show starts."

Jason studied Kat a moment. "I know you. You see something in her. Go do your thing. Save her."

She hesitated only an instant. "This doesn't mean I'm in." And then she was up, heading to the stage.

He laughed. She was so "in" and they both knew it.

"Just what exactly is your relationship with Kat?" Lana asked, ever the nosy one.

Jason had no intention of hiding his relationship with Kat, but he wanted everyone to see she was so special before he explained. He already knew. "My relationship with Kat isn't what matters," he said, motioning toward the stage. "Her skill is. Watch her and you'll agree."

Jason turned his attention to Kat, watching her put on a headset.

"Okay," she said the instant she had sound, to the

group of twenty dancers, ten male and ten female. "One more time and make it good. Number seven, front row." The young girl gaped, looking stunned and frightened rather than excited by the notice. Jason didn't see what Kat saw in the girl, but he trusted her judgment.

The music started and Kat watched a minute, focused on number seven, and he smiled as she started to sway, slowly easing into the routine. Suddenly, she turned and stepped into the row of females, just slightly behind number seven. And his little KandyKat danced like she'd practiced the routine a million times. She was nothing shy of spectacular.

Darla and Lana both leaned forward to look at Jason. "What have I missed?" Darla asked.

"Yeah," Lana agreed. "Has Kat been working with Ellie the past few days and we weren't told?"

"Nope," Jason said, his words laced with the pride he'd always felt for Kat's skill. "Kat has this unreal, almost freaky ability to watch a routine and then perform it perfectly." Yet, she couldn't remember their hotel name, he added silently with a private smile. Of course, neither had he.

"Wow," Darla said. "She is just…wow."

"I'm officially impressed," Lana said. "And I don't impress easily."

Ellie stood on the sidelines and gave a thumbs-up sign to Jason.

Jason settled back in his seat to enjoy the show. "You ladies haven't seen half of what she's about yet."

"Stop!" Kat yelled into her headset and walked to number seven, flipping her mic away from her mouth and settling her hands on the girl's shoulders. The girl listened in earnest and then Kat flipped her mic back and said, "Everyone stand aside except for me and number seven." She glanced at the girl and smiled. "I mean Shannon." The dancers split half to one side of the stage and half to the other. Kat signaled and the music started again. She gave Shannon a nod.

Shannon started dancing and Kat watched all of twenty seconds. "Face me," she ordered, taking Shannon by the shoulders again, but she didn't turn off the mic this time. "If you stop now you're going home. Is that what you want?" The girl shook her head. "You're letting fear beat you. I know skill when I see it but I can't do this for you. You have to deliver." Kat stepped back and started dancing. The girl joined her and Kat shouted, "Attitude. Give me attitude."

Jason smiled as suddenly Kat *and* that young girl owned the stage, and with every step Shannon transformed. Kat was gorgeous, a goddess on that stage. No one who ever met her and worked with her understood why she wanted to be behind the camera, not in front of it. But he did. Kat loved to dance, but ultimately saving number seven defined who she was as a person. She loved mentoring. She loved helping people achieve their dreams.

Darla leaned close to Jason. "Ah, Jason?" She pointed to the male dancer making a lewd gesture to another male dancer that seemed to have something to do with Kat's stellar backside. And it was stellar. "You want to go kick that kid's ass or do you want me to?"

"Neither," Jason said, knowing his Kat all too well. "Kat can handle herself." And she'd be ticked if he didn't let her anyway. He'd barely made the confident declaration when Kat did exactly what he'd expected. She handled it. Taking the kid off guard, and proving she was ever-aware of her dancers, she stopped dancing and turned suddenly, walking up to the male dancer. She got up close, toe to toe with him.

Jason laughed, "And here comes the fun. Kat runs a tight ship. She's fair but tough."

"You see something you like?" Kat demanded of the kid with her microphone loud and clear for all to hear.

"Ah, yeah," the kid said. And he was a kid. Maybe eighteen or nineteen with dark curly hair and dark skin tones.

"Try again," Kat said.

"Ah, no?" he asked.

"That sounded like a question. I'm looking for an answer. The *right* answer."

"No, ma'am!" he shouted so even the judges heard loud and clear. "No, I do not."

Lana and Darla burst out laughing. "Oh, she *so* has to take this job," Darla insisted. "You have to sign her, Jason."

"That's what I thought," Kat said to the kid. "Because, you see, this is a professional stage. My girls have to put on skimpy costumes and trust the male dancers who have their hands all over them. This isn't a night club."

"She said 'my girls,'" Darla whispered.

"Yeah," Jason said with satisfaction. "I heard."

"Yes, ma'am," the boy shouted. "I'm sorry. It won't ever happen again."

"You're going to have to dance like Michael Jackson

at this point not to get sent home. In fact…" Kat glanced over her shoulder. "Ellie?"

"Coming right up," Ellie said, choking on laughter with her mic still on.

A few seconds later, Michael Jackson's "Thriller" started to play and Kat motioned the boy forward. He hesitated for a tenth of a second and then moved to center stage, where he proceeded to dance his backside off. The kid was good—very good.

Kat and Ellie let him dance for a solid two minutes before she held up a hand and stopped the music. She and Ellie whispered to each other, careful to cover their mouth pieces, before Kat said, "That was Michael in diapers. Give us grown-up Michael tomorrow or you're out."

"I'm returning?" he asked, looking stunned.

"Yes," Kat said. "And don't make us sorry."

The kid slid on his knees to Kat's feet and bowed. "Thank you. Thank you. I won't make you sorry. I promise."

"Get out of here before I change my mind," she teased with a smile and then turned to Shannon. "And you go home and practice being a diva in the mirror."

"I'm coming back?" Shannon asked, and yelped with joy when Kat confirmed. She raced forward and hugged Kat.

"Everyone else will get your fate at the end of the day," Ellie announced, and sent everyone, Shannon included, on their way.

Kat and Ellie both flipped their microphones aside and put their heads together in a short conversation before Kat headed toward the stairs.

Jason's cell buzzed with a text. He quickly replied to Kat's agent, telling Michael that yes, she was here, and he was working on making that permanent.

"Uh-oh." Darla laughed from beside him. "I think you're in trouble, Jason."

"You two so have a past," Lana said. "I can smell it a mile away."

Jason jerked his gaze upward at the comments to find Kat headed their way, or rather *his* way, with her gaze fixed intently on him. Oh yeah, he was in trouble. She'd apparently been thinking about more than dancing on that stage, because she was fired up. He could almost feel the heat of flames crackling off her. That kid wasn't the only one leaving here busted. Jason had to hope this ended as well for him as it had for the kid: with a second chance. Okay, in his case, maybe more like a third or fourth. But this was going to be the one he made count.

4

KAT WAS FURIOUS—at herself and at Jason. They both knew what would happen if she came here today, yet he'd baited her and she'd let him. Now it was done. She was attached to the show and she was going to get hurt again. *He* was going to hurt her again. And she'd lose him and the show in one short season. Why would he want to put either of them through that?

Jason stood up as she neared. "I'm guessing it's time for that talk?"

She gave a nod and he motioned her toward the backstage exit. "Should we keep going?" Darla asked.

Jason arched a brow at Kat. "Yes," she said. "Go ahead. I don't want to back things up." Her gaze returned to Jason. "I need to deal with my conflict once and for all."

"My exact thoughts," he agreed, motioning her to the right, to a path that led behind the stage.

Her chest tightened and she clung to her anger. If she was angry, she wasn't turning to melted chocolate in the man's hands. *No,* a voice in her head reminded.

That always came after the anger. But she always, always turned to melted chocolate.

Side by side, they walked past the stage and around it, then down to a sunken hallway that had doors. "This way," he said, indicating the rows of doors and opening one of them, letting her enter first.

Kat found herself in a small costume room. Racks of clothes pressed in on either side of her. No, it wasn't even a small room. It was a closet, and the tiny space set her on edge. Maybe this had been a bad idea. A small room, alone with Jason and a closed door.

She whirled on him the minute he shut the door. "You knew what would happen if I came here today and I told you I can't do this thing with us again. I can't. If I take this job then it has to be work only."

He leaned against the wall. "If that's what you want."

She swallowed hard and leaned against the opposite wall, still so close that only a few steps separated them. "That was too easy." She studied him. "Damn it, Jason. I know you. 'If that's what you want' translates to you planning to change what I want but not until I've signed a contract." He didn't say anything. He just stared at her with those gorgeous, intense eyes, and she pushed, "No reply?"

"I think I was pretty clear. As long as that's what you want, that's how it will be. The fact that I'm leaning against this door, when I want to be over there with you, kissing you like there's no tomorrow, should prove I mean it. This job has your name written all over it. And since we're in Vegas, I'm going to say that you coming home right when we were casting and looking for a choreographer says it's in the cards. You were meant to be here. We were meant to be here. I believe that so strongly that if I have to agree to keep this all business to get you to take the job, I will. But don't think for one minute that I won't be hoping you'll give me the opportunity to change your mind."

Her skin prickled with awareness and a part of her screamed—convince me now—while another wanted to dart for the door he was blocking.

"You think that's the answer I'm looking for? You think that makes this an easy decision for me?"

"It's the only answer I have. You know me. I'm straight up. Take the job, Kat. Do this one last thing for me, for us, and I swear I will never ask you to do anything for me ever again."

For him. His plea shouldn't matter, but it did. God, she still loved this man. And she knew he loved her. She did. Where they were concerned, love always hurt, and she didn't know if she could live through it again. But then, she never seemed to move on from it, or from him, either.

"What do we tell the cast and crew?"

"That you took the job."

"About us, Jason."

"Why do we have to tell them anything?"

"Someone will find out."

"Do you really care?" he asked. "Because I don't, Kat."

"I don't want anyone thinking I slept my way into this job. I have six weeks to get a show audience-ready. I need respect."

"One hour with you, and you'll have their respect," he assured her, "but I understand. You know I'll respect your wishes. We've known each other since college. Old friends, both from Vegas."

"The tour," she said. "I'm not thrilled with being on the road again. I need a home, a solid foundation."

"Three months and that's it," he said. "And if *Stepping Up* continues to a fourth season, we can negotiate the tour out of your contract."

"And if the show is cancelled?"

"My hope is that the Vegas show outlasts the television show," he said. "We have to make sure it's good enough to become a Vegas fixture."

She liked that idea. A steady job. A home. Stability. And how ironic that Jason, of all people, would deliver her the opportunity. "This is only work."

"Whatever you want," he said smoothly, knowing all too well, she wanted him. "I sent Michael a copy of the contract. He's already reviewing them."

"Because you knew if I showed up here today, I'd take the job."

His far-too-sexy lips curved. "It was a good bet." He pushed off the door to let her pass. "I know you're eager to get back to the auditions."

She knew darn well she was about to be too close to him for comfort, but she also knew she couldn't run from him, or them, if she took this job. Kat walked toward him and as she suspected, he didn't let her pass.

They stood there toe-to-toe, their gazes locked, until he let his hand settle on her arm, the touch warming her skin, her entire body. Her will to push him away evaporated. Slowly, he let his fingers trail downward until he laced them with hers and then brought her knuckles to his lips.

"You're going to be great," he said, the intimate tone of his voice familiar, seductive. "We're going to be great. You watch and see." And then, just like that, he released her hand and opened the door, leaving her aching with the need to touch him again, and swearing she wouldn't. Knowing her willpower to keep her hands off of him was one bet she'd never take in Vegas, if she was a betting woman, and she wasn't.

AUDITIONS FINALLY CLEARED out at six that night and Kat and Ellie immediately headed to a break area behind the stage. Making good use of the rectangular steel table sitting in the middle of the room, with the fridge and some cabinets behind them, they spread out head shots, comparing notes.

"We aren't going to be able to feature more than a couple of these dancers," Ellie said of the hundred they had for call backs. "We need sixty total dancers, and the twenty-four finalists and winners from the first two seasons of *Stepping Up* have to be your stars."

"But we're talking a long-running show, or so we hope," Kat said, the idea of a permanent gig starting to excite her. "We need people who can fill in for anyone who gets sick, hurt or drops out. They have to be just as good as the stars."

Ellie rubbed her stomach. "Or knocked up."

Kat laughed. "Yes. Or knocked up."

"Speaking of knocked up," she said. "What's up with you and Jason? Jason was quick to approve you for an interview but I had no idea you two knew each other as well as you do."

"Why does your pregnancy somehow create a connection to me and Jason?" She glanced down. "Are you trying to tell me I've packed on some pounds or what?"

"No, silly," she said. "And you know it. You're tiny. The electricity between you two is intense, sweets. That's what I'm talking about. And electricity is what got me in trouble." She smiled. "The good kind of trouble."

"I don't know what you're talking about," Kat fibbed, sliding paperwork into her folder. "Jason and I were hardly even around each other this afternoon."

"Not much," she agreed. "And that's how combustible you two are. It's how you look at each other, even from across the auditorium, especially when neither of you know the other is looking. So, what's the scoop? Exes? Almost lovers?"

"I think we are both just shocked that our paths have crossed," she said. "We went to college together. And don't go spreading the word that I'm involved with Jason. I'm not. If I'm going to take over this show, I need respect, not casting couch gossip."

"Anything you say to me, stays with me," Ellie assured her. "And I understand why you want it that way."

Kat glanced at her watch and grabbed the excuse to leave, which wasn't made up. "Gotta go. I'm late. I'm meeting my agent in the restaurant." She pointed at Ellie and then stuffed files into her bag. "You go to your room and rest. I'm glad that husband of yours is coming in next week. Someone has to slow you down."

"I'm pretty sure the baby on board is going to force that issue. I'm exhausted and I'm not even showing yet." She motioned her away. "Scoot. Go get to it."

Kat took off toward the typical twenty-four-hour

basic restaurant every Vegas hotel sported for all-nighters, complete with gambling cards on the table. A quick scan didn't produce Michael, so she flagged a hostess who immediately led her to the back section behind a wall, and that was when her heart fluttered in her chest. Jason sat in a booth across from Michael. It was not only unexpected, it was a bit awkward.

"Why couldn't you get a table?" she murmured under her breath, before inhaling and sitting down at the booth. She tried to steel herself for the moment Jason's gaze lifted. She failed. The instant those clear, knowing eyes met hers, she felt weak in the knees.

She dropped her bag on the floor next to Michael, who, as usual, looked his best, his blond hair neatly groomed, and his suit perfectly pressed.

"You were right," Michael grumbled, and slid a hundred dollar bill across the table toward Jason.

Kat grimaced. "Right about what?"

"Who you'd sit next to," Jason explained, his eyes twinkling with mischief. "He said you'd sit next to me. I said you'd sit next to him."

"You bet on where I'd sit?" she asked, gaping at both of them.

"Yeah, we bet all right," Michael admitted, pulling out a folder from his briefcase resting between them. "You know me. I bet on people, not games of chance. I thought you'd want to prove you weren't intimidated by your past."

"I thought you'd want to avoid me enough not to care," Jason added.

A waitress stopped at the table. "Coffee for me," Kat said, glad for the diversion. She didn't know what to say to his perceptive comment. Jason was right. She was avoiding being close to him.

"Make that two coffees," Michael said.

Jason held up three fingers and turned back to the conversation, his eyes dancing with amusement, seeing too much, and answering the question she had yet to speak. "I'm here because Michael invited me."

"And I didn't tell you because you didn't answer your phone," Michael said. "Which has become a very bad habit, by the way. I've drawn up the amendment you and I talked about on the phone, Kat, before you stopped answering, but Jason has been our go-to person on this. He's negotiated with the studio, in my place. I thought we should do him the courtesy of explaining what we've added. So to start…"

The waitress returned with a pot of coffee and filled their cups as Michael began ticking down a list of minor contractual changes. "The main concern," Michael said, "is travel. The contract was written in a way that could send Kat on the road to promote *Stepping Up*. She's not doing it without added compensation, and a separate contract, period. The end."

Kat poured two creamers in her cup. "It's not about money. I just don't want to think I'm here to stay, and suddenly I'm contractually obligated to hit the road again." She reached for the sweetener.

Jason handed her three packets, the exact three she always used, and her gaze went to his face, only to realize he wasn't even looking at her.

"I've discussed this with Kat," Jason assured Michael. "I can't do anything about the travel for this season. After that, we can negotiate it out."

"That's not the issue," Michael said. "The contract is written in vague language that could make her a slave to the studio beyond the Vegas production. I marked it out and added our wording to an amendment." He flipped the paper around for Jason to read.

He read the marked-out text and then the new version. "Good catch," Jason said. "I'd never have signed it as it was myself." He glanced at Kat. "I see why you keep him around."

"He's convenient," she teased, glancing at Michael.

"I look out for your money," he said. "Which you sometimes forget to make as important as it is."

"Sometimes it's hard to believe I get paid this well for something I love to do."

"Point made," Michael said. "You need me."

Kat's eyes met Jason's, the memory of him saying "I need you" settling between them.

Nearly an hour later, Michael stuffed his paperwork back into his briefcase, leaving Jason his copies. "I have to get out of here. I have a meeting with the Ricco family attorney."

"Ricco?" Kat asked, sliding out of her seat. "As in the famous designer?"

"That's right," Michael said, standing up. "They're buying up properties and negotiating with some of my talent." He turned and glanced between them. "It's good to see you two together again." He walked away.

Kat stood there staring at Jason, not sure what to do.

"Sit down, Kat," he said. "I can't bite you here. Not in public. No matter how much I might want to. I have something I want you to know."

Kat shook her head. "I really need to go."

He considered her, then stood up, tossing money onto the table. "You're in the garage?"

"Yes."

"Me, too," he said. "So I'll walk with you. I'm ready to get home myself."

"Home? Aren't you staying in the hotel like the rest of the cast?"

"Nope," he said. "As soon as I signed on for the show, I bought a house a few miles from yours."

"But...you're always traveling."

"My contract with the show is up this season," he said. "I've already told them I'm not renewing."

"Jason, there you are," a female voice called out, drawing their attention.

Heather Wright, the twenty-something, red-headed bombshell of a script manager Kat had met earlier, stopped beside them. Her hand went to Jason's arm, sliding down it as if she enjoyed the opportunity to touch him, and she quickly said, "Hi, Kat," before turning her full attention and the deep V of her red top in his direction.

Kat cut her gaze to the floor, feeling the familiar punch in her gut that she'd come to associate with Jason. It wasn't jealousy. She knew he didn't want this woman. She knew he'd never cheated on her. It was more about the separateness of their lives that became more apparent in every passing second.

She inhaled, calming her nerves, and her gaze lifted to find Jason staring at her as Heather continued talking.

"You promised we could review the script changes with you before morning. I know there aren't a lot of lines, but I was handed new contractual requirements for the number of lines per person for several of the *Stepping Up* stars that don't fit anything I have set up."

"I need to head out anyway," she said and started walking toward the exit of the restaurant and quickly cutting through the crowd to head to the garage.

JASON DEALT WITH Heather and went after Kat, only to watch her disappear into the elevator a second before he could get to her. He took the stairs, determined to catch her and hit the bottom level at the same moment she exited the sliding doors to the garage.

"Kat," he called, falling into step with her, thankful the garage had plenty of cars, but no people. "Why'd you take off like that?"

"You had work to do and I've changed time zones so many times that I need sleep desperately."

She didn't look at him and he followed her down an incline to the same rental car he'd seen at her house. She clicked the locks and opened the door to toss her bag inside before she turned to face him, leaning against the back door.

"You need to buy a car," he commented. "A rental will get expensive. I can go with you if you want."

She crossed her arms in front of her. "I expected to have time to shop."

"I'll get the car paid for by the studio until you can get to a dealership."

"I don't care about the car."

He pressed his hand to the roof beside her head, and studied her, trying to understand her. "You know there is absolutely nothing going on between me and Heather, right? I want you, Kat."

"I know. And I want you, too, and that's the problem."

"You're going to have to explain to me exactly why that's a problem, because it sounds like exactly what I want to hear."

"I don't want to want you. I don't want to feel the pinch in my chest I felt when you were talking to Heather—and I'm not talking about jealousy, Jason. I'm talking about the sense of being in a world that's yours, and I'm a visitor with a temporary pass. Another hot bedroom romp and another goodbye sure to follow. And that's what's coming. Before this is over, that's what will happen. A part of me says let's just go get a damn room and work this out of our systems now so we can focus on work."

"Let's go, Kat. I'm happy to take that challenge and prove to you that just won't happen."

"You don't know that," she said. "We haven't had more than one night together in years."

"I'm all for fixing that, starting now."

She stared at him for a long moment. "I'm leaving," she announced and then tried to duck under his arm.

He stopped her from getting past him. "If you're so confident you can work me out of your system, then why leave now?"

"I didn't say we could do it in one night and I haven't slept anyway. If I'm going to do something crazy like hop in bed with you again, I'm going to be awake for it."

He laughed. "All right then. I'll let you go—*for tonight.*" He moved off the car. "And for the record, Kat. You have had a place in my life since I first met you. I'm hoping I can convince you I deserve one in yours."

He turned and headed back to the hotel, not giving her a chance to tell him all the reasons it wasn't possible. He knew he was wasting his breath telling Kat they could make things work. He was going to show her, which meant doing far more than getting her into bed, though he was looking forward to that moment. It had to be the right moment though, and it had to be her decision.

He stopped inside the building and watched her pull away, swearing to himself that he wasn't going to watch her walk away again. Promising himself no matter how much he wanted to push, no matter how much he'd happily get that room and prove she couldn't work him out of her system, he was going to take this at her pace. He was going to prove to her he was here to stay.

5

IT WAS FRIDAY night, a week after Kat had stood in the parking garage and forced herself to get into the car, rather than wrap her arms around Jason and kiss him. A long week too, filled with confusing emotions, with wanting, needing and…rehearsals.

Kat stood in a private studio inside the Wind Walker Hotel overseeing fifteen dancers, six of whom were performing. While she was happy with the execution of the routine, she was unhappy with the sideline action. Tabitha, a pretty blonde and one of the stars from season one of *Stepping Up,* was leaning against the wall, watching her understudy, Marissa, perform. There was hatred on Tabitha's face, and her general nasty attitude throughout the several hours of rehearsals toward Marissa wasn't sitting well with Kat. It was a behavior she'd come to know over the years, a signal that the dancer delivering such nastiness saw his or her target as a threat.

Tabitha leaned in close to Jensen, her boyfriend and the dancer who'd taken home the grand prize from season one of the show, and whispered something in his ear that made him look Marissa up and down. They laughed, and Kat ground her teeth. She wasn't going to handle this in front of the group for Marissa's sake. Kat could already tell how the situation intimidated the young dancer. Kat didn't care how secure Tabitha and Jensen felt, based on their contracts. She was going to take action.

"That's a wrap for tonight," Kat said, turning off the music. "This group will be with Heather in the script room tomorrow morning. Six o'clock sharp." Everyone seemed to relax all at once and murmurs filled the room as they did a mass exodus.

Kat quickly grabbed a pink sweatshirt and tugged it down over her leggings, and stuffed various items into an oversized bag. The one remaining dancer in the room, a twentyish brunette named Carrie, approached her.

"It's déjà vu from season one," Carrie said. "Only I'm not the one getting the brunt of Tabitha's ugliness. I was hoping I wouldn't be working this closely with her when I accepted this job, but now I think maybe it's good that I am so I can help Marissa blow them off."

"That's very thoughtful of you, Carrie," Kat said, making a mental note to stop being stubborn and watch the old episodes of the TV show, sooner rather than later. "But don't you worry. I'm pretty proactive. I'm going to get everyone playing nice and quickly."

"I had a feeling you would," Carrie said, "but I plan to offer Marissa my friendship and support tomorrow. Aside from Marissa, I wanted to ask you about interning—volunteer, of course—to do some choreographing with you. I did some for season two of the show, as well as some production work, and I'd really like to keep expanding my resume."

Kat smiled. "That's exactly how I started out. I volunteered to help out on a couple shows and proved I had a knack for this work. I'd be happy to have you do the same but let's get you through these grueling weeks of rehearsals before the show opens first. Once it does, and we have things settled, come see me again, and you can help me prepare for the tour."

Her eyes lit. "Really? Oh my God. That would be a dream come true. Thank you, Kat. Thank you so much. My fiancé just got a job here at the hotel, thanks to the studio. He transferred from Los Angeles. He's made so many sacrifices for me and my career, I really want to make every second count that I'm here."

Kat felt a twinge of regret that she and Jason couldn't have made it work for the same reason. She chatted with Carrie for several more minutes before they parted ways.

Kat smiled to herself as she headed down the hallway, seeking Jason and the DVDs of the television show to take home with her. Carrie had called choreographing her "dream come true" when most of the dancers would call the show their dream. Kat related to that feeling and liked Carrie. It was going to be fun to work with her and watch her grow.

After a quick search of all the places Jason tended to dwell at this time of the day, Kat headed to the break area to grab a drink and call him. She was about to enter when she heard Jason and one of the production assistants.

"I'm trying to line up lunch for tomorrow's production meeting," she said. "We're ordering from Joe's Sub Machine. I need yours and Kat's orders but I can't seem to find her."

"Steak and cheese for me," he said. "Veggie with avocado and Swiss for Kat. No onion and no mayo or mustard."

"You know Kat's sandwich order," came another familiar voice that made Kat cringe. Lana was in the break room and Kat had already figured out she was the Queen of Nosiness. "How very interesting."

"Yes," he said. "I know her sandwich order. Just like I know that you not only drink your coffee black, but that you're a royal witch until you drink it. And you chew cherry gum that you smack in my ear all the time."

"And now that I know that gum bothers you," Lana declared, "I'll never stop chewing it."

Kat smiled at the exchange, and not just because Jason was quick witted and he'd covered her backside. It didn't surprise her that he respected her desire to earn everyone's respect and to keep their past quiet for a while. But the realization that he still knew her so well was what got to her and created a strange flutter in her chest.

The production assistant headed out and stopped beside Kat to confirm her sandwich order, which Kat gave a thumbs-up to before entering the break room. "I have a sudden urge for a piece of gum," she announced, finding Jason and Lana sitting at the the table, paperwork spread out. "And this burning desire to smack it very loudly."

Lana started laughing. "Oh, I do believe I'll stock up and pass it out before I head to Los Angeles tomorrow."

Jason grimaced, his strong, square jaw once again sporting a sexy light brown shadow. "I have no doubt you will." He glanced at Kat, those deep green eyes stirring her inside, as they did all too easily, as he added, "Just remember payback is a promise when you choose to participate in Lana's little games."

"I'm scared," Kat assured him with a laugh, trying not to seem too knowing about just how delicious she knew his payback to be. She sat down across from Jason and beside Lana. "So, you're leaving us?"

"I have something scheduled before the TV show auditions get going and my work here is done. Casting is complete and any minor things I could help with are finished." She pushed to her feet, slashing long blonde hair behind her ear. "And on that note I should go to my room. I have an early flight." She pointed at Kat. "Keep him in line. I have to deal with him in a month when we start the crazy travel for the television show auditions."

"I will," Kat assured her, but the jest in her voice was strained, gone with Lana's reminder that Jason would soon be leaving. "Have a safe trip."

Lana hurried from the room, leaving a strong wave of powerful perfume behind her. "One last traveling job," Jason said. "One more and I'm done."

He'd read her discomfort, responded to what she'd not spoken aloud. He knew her like no one else did. He had been her best friend, never replaced by another, and that reality made it hard to call what was between them just sex. But it was just sex, because people who loved each other, really loved each other, found a way to be together.

Kat slowly let her gaze slide back to his, and she felt

the connection in every pore of her body. *It's sex,* she told herself. *Chemistry. You want him. He wants you. It means nothing.* "I said my last tour was it for me, too," she finally managed. "No more travel, yet in a few months I'll be traveling with this show."

"Kat—"

"Whatever you're going to say, this isn't the time or place."

"Then let's go somewhere else."

"That would be good," she said. "I have a challenge with a couple of the dancers I need to talk to you about."

"There's a bar on the top level of the hotel. It's quiet there and I could sure use a drink. It's been a hell of a couple of weeks."

Heat pooled low in her tummy. "We both know how well I handle my alcohol," she said, cringing at her reference to their past, the past she couldn't seem to avoid. "I still have to drive home."

"Stay at the hotel," he said. "I know you prefer home. Living on the road is rough, but so are the late nights and early mornings right now. Exactly why the studio provides you a room."

She wanted to go have a drink with him, she wanted to talk to him, to touch him, to just be with him. And a part of her said to just do it, do him. Get this damnable need for him out of her system once and for all. Another part of her said he was a drug, and she had an addiction she had to break, or she'd never really live her life. And you didn't beat an addiction by doing more of the drug. You broke it by just saying "no."

Thanks to this show, their paths were going to cross. She couldn't start down a path of hopping in and out of bed with him when he was around, and really expect to move on with her life. Right. Exactly. That made perfect, logical sense. Damn it.

Kat inhaled and bound herself to mature logic, and reached to ensure temptation did not become indulgence. "How about the diner again?" she finally said. "I haven't eaten and we can talk there."

WITH KAT BY his side, Jason stopped at the doorway of the very public, very unromantic, diner. He didn't love her location preference, but after spending an eternally long week of wanting her, he'd take what he could get. And no matter how challenging it might be to give her time to digest that not only was he here, he was here to stay, he was committed to taking things on her time line. Well, with a little nudging to hurry things, he thought.

"Two?" the hostess asked.

"Two," Jason agreed, and then leaned in and whispered to her, before slipping her a large bill.

She smiled and motioned for them to follow her. "This way."

Kat frowned at him as they fell into step behind the woman. "What did you just do?"

"Moi?" he asked innocently, hoping the little French reference would remind her of their honeymoon in Paris.

"Oui, vous," she replied quickly.

He laughed at the "yes, you" in French, pleased with both her reply, and the fact that the hostess had just led them past double glass doors to a private, empty seating area.

He and Kat slid into the booth across from each other

and when they were alone he wiggled an eyebrow. "Just how much of your French do you remember?"

"If you're asking if I can still talk dirty, I'm pretty sure it would come back to me, *if* I tried. I'm also quite certain I can remember how to curse you out in French." She grimaced. "You paid the hostess to put us back here alone."

"That's right," he said. "We needed alone time. Now reward me and talk dirty to me in French." She complied with a graphic rant that was meant to be far more "curse him out" than "turn him on," but it did the job anyway.

"Naughty little thing, aren't you?" he asked, feeling his cock thicken at the sexy way she'd rolled her tongue on the words.

"Hello there," a white-haired waitress greeted, stuffing a pencil in the poof of her hair above her ear. "What can I get you two?"

"Two frozen margaritas and chips and salsa to start," Jason said. "And we'll give you the rest when you return."

"I told you I can't drink and drive," Kat argued, the instant the woman departed.

"If I don't get a drink down you," he countered, "you're going to spend this entire time we're here worried about what happens after dinner."

"I…" She started to object and then quirked her lips. "Okay, maybe you're right. And I suppose I'm safe. As you said the other day, it's not like you can bite me right here in public."

"No matter how much we both might want me to," he said, reminding her of the rest of his previous statement, his blood running hot at a vivid, mental image of just the spot he'd like to nip and tease first.

"Jason," she warned, her voice raspy, her lips parting in an alluring, come kiss me, kind of way.

"Distract me, baby, before I forget I promised myself to give you space to come around. Talk to me about work. What's going on with the dancers?"

She swallowed hard, and brushed her teeth over her delectable full bottom lip. "Right. The dancers. I need to know what latitude I have to deal with the finalists from *Stepping Up* considering they're supposed to be the stars of the live show."

"As much as you need," he said. "No one is going to hold you, me or anyone on this show, captive. If you can't get someone to do what you need them to do, there are provisions in the contracts to get rid of them."

"You don't even want to know who I'm talking about before you stand by that statement?"

"If this wasn't you asking," he said, "then yes, but I know you and I know you wouldn't do something that wasn't necessary."

"You trust me that much after all these years?"

"Yes. Do you trust me?"

Her expression slowly softening, she said, "Yes. Of course I do."

He leaned in closer. "Then trust me when I tell you I'm going to fight for you, and for us, Kat. I'm not going to let this time end like every other before it."

"Here you go," the waitress said, setting the drinks before them and then the chips and salsa. She tugged a pad from her napkin. "Now what can I get you?"

Kat glanced up at her. "Grilled chicken sandwich and salad with Italian rather than fries."

"Greasy cheeseburger and fries for me," Jason said.

Kat sipped her drink and the waitress disappeared. "You eat like crap."

"I know," he agreed, all too aware that she had just dodged a response to his vow. "I plan to fix that in the next few years."

"In the next few years," she repeated. "Well, at least you have goals." Her smiled faded, and suddenly they weren't talking about food anymore, even before she declared, "I have a confession to make."

He arched a brow. "You can't stop thinking about getting me naked and having your way with me."

She laughed and shook her head. "I doubt you need me to confess that to know it's true, which is why I won't deny it."

Interesting. He was beginning to think his assumption that she was trying to make this all about sex was still on target. "Feel free to confess whatever you need to."

"I hate to even admit this considering I've taken this job, but," she hesitated, and then blurted, "I've never watched one single episode of *Stepping Up*."

"Really?" he said, surprised by just how much her admission bothered him.

"I'm finding out that there are some conflicts that occurred between contestants that I probably should know about. Do you happen to have copies of the first two seasons?"

"At home," he said tightly, certain there wasn't a

show of hers he'd have ever missed. "I can bring them into work tomorrow."

"You don't like that I didn't watch your show."

"No," he said. "I don't."

"I don't do well on the outside looking in."

Emotion settled in his chest, as understanding took hold, and warmed the cold spot that had formed there. "Then don't stand on the outside."

"I didn't."

"You ran from me after Denver."

"I had a tour to go on."

"You didn't say that."

"You didn't ask, Jason."

"Oh, no, sweetheart," he said, laughing but not with humor. "Don't put that one on me. It killed me to leave you that morning and you knew it. We agreed to talk through a plan the next day, but that never happened because *you ran.*"

"I didn't run."

"You're running now."

"I am not!"

"The other night you claimed this was all sex between us and that a few bedroom romps would get it out of our systems." He whispered, "But you backed off when I called your bluff, didn't you? I'm guessing that's because you're afraid that no matter how many 'romps' we have, your plan won't work. And then, KandyKat, you'll have to face what's really between us, be it good or bad, once and for all."

She stared at him, unmoving, her expression intense, before she stood up. "Let's go."

He followed her to her feet. "Where exactly are we going?"

"Your place," she announced. "And I'll follow you in my car."

"I can live with that."

He tossed money on the table, finding her choice interesting, and knowing her well enough to know why she'd made it. She actually thought that keeping him outside her world, her personal space and home, would let her hide from the truth. That home was with him.

"I get a head start," she added. "I'll leave first and meet you at…the burger joint on the corner that everyone orders lunch from all the time. In the parking lot."

He reached for her and pulled her close, pressing his lips to her ear. "As long as you remember that I'm the cat and you're the mouse, and I will catch up to you. Even if it means showing up at your doorstep."

Kat had already made the decision to cave to desire. She wasn't holding back. She flattened her hand on his chest, pressed to her toes, and brought her mouth to his ear. "I'm counting on it."

6

KAT FOLLOWED JASON as he turned his motorcycle into the long driveway of his gorgeous stucco home and then into a garage, shocked that he lived only a few miles from her. Maybe she shouldn't have been shocked. They both gravitated toward the same things, as much as they did to each other.

She killed the engine on her rental. She couldn't believe she was about to have her wicked way with Jason. She watched him swing a powerful thigh over the bike to dismount and edited that thought. She couldn't believe she'd ever kidded herself into thinking she could resist this man. Seriously, that had been certifiably nuts. The man did it for her in every possible way.

She grabbed her bag and shut her car door. He'd removed his helmet and was there when she stood up. He reached for her bag, his fingers brushing her shoulder and sending chills down her spine. Her gaze collided with his and her body reacted instantly to the sizzle in the depths of his stare. They stood there, not touching, but yet her skin tingled as if they were. She resisted reaching for him when it was all she wanted and everything she needed. He didn't reach for her either, and she was pretty sure he knew what she did. If they caved in to the burn right here, right this instant, they'd end up on the hood of the car, rather than on a soft bed.

They moved at the same time, in tune even without words. Kat inched out of the way from the door, and Jason shoved it closed. She followed him to the house, and let him motion for her to enter first. The anticipation of touching him tingled deep in her nerve endings. She entered the house, the air conditioning chilling her ultra-sensitized skin in a way it might not otherwise have done if she wasn't so aware of Jason on every level. Of how tall and broad, how raw and male, he was. How easily he read her needs, her pleasure, how long she'd ached for him, for this.

Kat immediately walked up a flight of carpet-covered steps to a second level with a tiled foyer, and she continued up the next set of stairs. The lights came on behind and in front of her and she stepped to the room above, taking in a massive living area with an open kitchen and dining area to its left. More expensive tile covered the entire floor, and a brown and cream rug sat under a sleek brown leather couch and love seat.

Kat softly inhaled against the pain pinching her chest. What had she been thinking by coming here, taunting herself with the life he had without her? No. No. No. She wasn't going to think about things like that. Not now, not anymore. And maybe, just maybe, sex *would* cure all. Maybe distance and random good sexual encounters had built her and Jason up to more than they were. Tonight, a few nights, and they both could see that there was a reason they had divorced.

Kat turned at the same moment Jason cleared the top step, and she shoved him against wall, desperate to focus on him, not the house. To touch him, to feel him, to forget everything but pleasure.

He dropped her bag and wrapped his strong arms around her and, God, it felt good to have him touch her. Heat radiated from him, warming her palm where it rested, her skin where he touched, where he didn't touch but she wanted him to. Suddenly, they were kissing, drinking each other in, and Kat felt like she'd die if she didn't have more of him. Her tongue stroked his, her hands pushed under his T-shirt, feeling the flex of his strong muscles.

He twined his fingers into her hair, tugging away the band holding it at her nape, and angling her mouth to his, taking more of her, and still not enough. Kat leaned into him, the thick ridge of his erection melding to her hips, and she moaned with the need expanding inside her.

"You feel good," he murmured. "So damn good."

So did he. Too good. Scary, wonderful good. "This is sex," she panted. "Just sex."

"If you say so." His palms caressed her ribs, then cupped her breasts, and he slanted his mouth over hers, tasting her, before adding, "I'm fine with anything that means you take your clothes off and we keep doing what we're doing."

On some level, his refusal to say this was just sex pleased her, on another it scared her, but remembering why it scared her was becoming a challenge. Kat nipped his lip and shoved his shirt upward. He yanked it over his head and tossed it away, giving no resistance at all. She explored his broad, hard chest, absorbing the feel of him with near desperation.

"Sex," she reminded him.

"Great sex," he countered.

"Just sex," she said. "Say it."

"Whatever you want, KandyKat."

She stared at him, knowing he wasn't going to say it. And she was glad, which made her pretty messed up where he was concerned. Or maybe insane to think she could get over him by being with him.

"Then you won't mind if I do this," she replied, dropping to her knees, as she tugged at his belt.

He held his hands out to his sides. "Feel free to use me all you like, sweetheart."

She tugged his pants down, freeing his shaft and wrapping her hand around the width. "I intend to."

THIS WASN'T JUST sex, but Jason didn't figure he'd convince Kat of that when she was on her knees with his cock in her hand. Besides, he was pretty sure she was trying to convince herself, not him, anyway. Though when she licked the tip of his shaft and set every damn nerve ending he owned to prickling, he was pretty open to her trying to convince him, too. She wouldn't change his mind, but when she ran her tongue over the sexy curve of her bottom lip, as if she didn't dare waste one little taste of him, she damn near brought him to his knees in front of her.

She ran her tongue around the head of his cock, casting a sexy look up at him that said she knew she was in control, and she knew what he liked. Which was exactly why they were here. Because she did know him, and he knew her, in a way only two people who shared a special bond could. He'd never had this with any other woman, and he'd tried. He'd dated. And he'd remained unsatisfied in every possible way.

She sucked him deeper, and it felt good, but somehow his mind cleared when he'd have thought the opposite would occur. He replayed his thoughts from moments before, reason invading escape and pleasure. He would never convince her this was more than sex while her hand was around his cock, while *her mouth* was around his cock. He had to make her stop. Ah. Yeah. Stop. She drew him deeper, took all of him, and then started to pump her hand and her mouth at the same time.

He balled his fists by his side, resisting the urge to slide his fingers into her hair, to encourage her to keep going. Jason inhaled and then forced the air out, reaching down and pulling Kat from his body, wanting far more from her than a few minutes of bliss.

Jason wrapped his arms around her and pulled her close, twining his fingers in her silky blonde hair again. He inhaled the familiar scent of roses that was so Kat, so his woman, then lowered his lips a breath from hers.

"What are you doing?" she whispered, her hands on his chest. "You like when I do that. *I* like when I do that."

"I've waited way too long to have you like this again, to waste any of it, with your clothes on."

"Is that right?" she asked, sounding as breathless as he felt.

"Oh yeah," he assured her, "that's right." He slanted

his mouth over hers, his tongue caressing hers in a long, languid stroke that had them both moaning with the contact, with the connection, the need burning between them.

The air shifted with that kiss, swelled with past and present, pain and passion, love and loss. Until their lips parted, the air hung heavy with so many unspoken words.

Seconds ticked by, and then something seemed to snap between them, and they were kissing again—hot and wild—their hands exploring all over each other.

Jason barely remembered how his pants and boots came off, but he remembered everything about undressing Kat. He shoved her shirt upward and unhooked her bra. She tossed it aside and he filled his hands with her high, full breasts, and stroked her plump pink nipples.

He switched places with her, pressing her back to the wall, caressing a path down her arms, his gaze devouring her naked body. "I specifically remember saying 'whatever you want,' KandyKat." He trailed a finger over a stiff peak, flicking it. "And I don't think you'd argue that I'm a man of my word."

"I wanted to do what I was doing."

"Not as much as you want this." He went down on one knee, his hands framing her slender hips, his lips brushing her stomach, pleased to discover her shoes were gone, though he couldn't for the life of him say how. His gaze lifted to hers as he inched down her leggings and the barely there slip of black panties. At another time he'd have enjoyed admiring the scrap of fabric. Right now, he just wanted to taste her, lick her and hear her cry out his name. Those three things and he could die a happy man.

She kicked aside her leggings with his urging and his hands went back to her hips, his lips back to her sexy tummy. "Finally," he breathed out. "I haven't had you like this in far, far too long."

She blinked down at him and then nodded. "Yes," she agreed, her voice raspy. "Too long."

His lips lifted at her admission, and he slid his hands around her delicious backside. "Remember you said that," he insisted before he bent his head, brushing his lips over her hip, trailing kisses over her midsection, widening her thighs as he did, opening her for his touch. He explored the intimate vee of her body, his fingers teasing the slick wet heat of her sex.

She arched toward the touch, a soft sound of pleasure playing like music in the air, delicate and sensual, teasing his cock. He lifted her leg over his shoulder, lapping gently at her clit. She rewarded him with a whimper that had his cock jerking and left him craving another taste, more of her pleasure. Jason licked her, teased her, then spread the sensitive folds to press one finger and then another inside her, stretching her, caressing her. He knew just where and how to touch her to deliver her to release and he took his time, kept her on the edge, waited until she begged for more.

Her fingers laced into his hair, her breathing shallow, urgent. "Jason...I—oh..." She tensed and then spasms wrapped his fingers, intense, hard.

He licked her, suckled her, led her all the way to the height of pleasure, until he felt her muscles begin to relax. He softened his touch, bringing her back down, catching her around the waist when her knees buckled. He kissed her stomach before he stood up, scooping her off of her feet and into his arms, heading up a flight of stairs to the place she belonged for far longer than one night—in his bed.

7

MOONLIGHT SPILLED INTO the large master bedroom as Jason carried Kat to his king-sized sleigh bed. He settled her on her feet beside the nightstand and sat down on the bed, pulling her close.

She leaned into him, urging him farther onto the bed, and he didn't argue. He turned and rested his back against the headboard. Kat followed him, straddling him, his shaft pressing to her backside, thick and hard, and pulsing with his need to bury himself inside her and feel the wet, tight heat of her sex.

Jason slid his hand into her hair and pulled her mouth to his. "I missed this, Kat. I missed us. I missed *you*."

"Me, too," she whispered against his lips. "Me, too."

"Then stop saying this is just sex. We both know it isn't." He trailed his fingers down her cheek. "I love you, Kat. I always have and I always will."

Kat pressed her lips to his, slid her tongue into his mouth, the sweetness of her filling his senses, and he tasted her reply—her fear and yes, her love.

Jason wrapped his arms around her, molding her

closer, deepening their kiss, reassuring her he meant his words, understanding she needed to feel them, not just hear them. He told himself to go slow, not to push her, but she moaned, her tongue testing his, tangling with him, pushing him to give her more. More and slow didn't compute, not to a man starving for her. His hands traveled her body, and she shivered with pleasure, the way she always had in the past. It drove him wild. He palmed her breast, teased her nipple, plucking it into a tight peak. She covered his hand, molding it over her, and broke their kiss. For an instant, their gazes collided, and he swore the connection sent a rush of heat straight to his cock.

"I need—" she started. "Jason, I—"

"Me, too," he said. "Me, too, baby." He lifted her, and shifted his throbbing erection between them, the idea of finally being inside her consumed him.

Kat wrapped her hand around the base of his erection, and he could feel himself thicken with the touch, with the anticipation of what was to come. She guided him to the blessed wet, slick heat of her body and he was breathing hard, shaking inside with need, trying to resist pushing inside her, rather than waiting for her to take him there. When she reached down and parted the V of her body, touching herself, he just about snapped. He'd been hard a long time, an impossibly long time.

For the sake of his sanity, Kat noted. She pressed his throbbing shaft inside her, biting her bottom lip on a sound of pleasure when she did, her lashes fluttering as she slid down his length taking him all in.

The torture of the wait was so worth this moment.

Kat was hot and tight, and oh so wet for him, and she felt so good.

He had no idea how, but a little piece of unwanted reality slipped inside the pleasure. Damn this reality thing that kept intruding in the middle of the best and worst of moments. They weren't using birth control.

"Kat—"

"The pill," she whispered, reading his mind as she often did, and lacing her fingers behind his neck, her nipples teasing his chest.

The pill. For a second, he didn't move, feeling the blunt edge of yet another bite of reality in the part of Kat's life that he'd tried to never think about. Of course she'd had other lovers, and he had no right to even go there anyway. He'd lost her, and he'd deserved to lose her, too. Taken jobs she'd asked him not to take. Asked her to give up work she wanted to accommodate his career. He'd taken her for granted and he had to prove himself to earn her back. Worse, he had no doubt she'd seen him as unchanged, a selfish ass, when he'd left her in Denver, expecting she'd wait on him. It really had killed him to leave her and meet his obligation to *Stepping Up.*

Jason slid his hands up her back, bringing her mouth to his, planning to confess just how wrong he'd been, how much he regretted the past. "Kat—"

She brushed her lips over his. "Don't do this now. Please. I just want to be with you. I want to pretend nothing else exists for just right now." She didn't give him time to object. She kissed him, took his mouth and drugged him into a spell of her taste, her tongue and her body slowly rocking against his.

Raw hunger rose inside him, the past fading into the present. He moaned into her mouth, pressing her down against him, and lifting his hips to thrust. Her sex tightened on him, clamped down and took him hard and deep. Her fingers were in his hair, soft little touches that sent shivers down his spine. And her kisses, those delicate, sweet lips that could be so wild and wicked, and everything he wanted them to be. He was hungry for her, and she was hungry for him. It was in the air, in their every touch, taste and moan. If they could melt into each other, become one, they would have.

Kat leaned back, her hands behind her on his thighs. Jason's hand settled on her flat stomach, pumping into her even as she rode him in an erotic dance, her beautiful breasts swaying with the rhythm, her tight little nipples begging for his mouth. He wrapped his arm around her slender waist, his hand palming her breast, kneading it before he suckled one nipple, alternately licking and flicking it with his tongue, and then sucking it deep into his mouth.

She spiked her fingers through his hair, her moans turning to sexy little purrs of pleasure that were driving him wild. Jason pushed her hard against his hips, thrusting into her. "Yes," she moaned, burying her face in his neck. "So…good. I…Jaso…n."

His name on her lips, asking for pleasure and for release, drove him over the edge. Jason couldn't get close enough to Kat, couldn't pump hard enough or go deep enough inside her. Harder, faster. The room disappeared, the past faded. There was only this moment, there was only Kat, being with her, holding her, loving her and pleasing her.

He could feel the tension stiffening her body, and the tightening of her arms around him. The sweet sound of her gasp came an instant before her sex reacted, rippling with release, with her pleasure that became his.

Sensations spiraled through Jason. He pressed Kat down and lifted into her, shaking with the intensity of his completion. Burying his face in her hair, the scent of it—so soft and feminine, so her—relaxing him.

For long seconds, they clung to one another, skin damp, breathing heavy, and he felt her tense, sensed an emotional struggle in her and braced for it. Would it be regret? Anger? Something completely different?

"I love you, too," she whispered next to his ear.

So softly spoken were those words that Jason didn't dare believe he'd heard them, until she leaned back and met his stare, repeating the golden words. "I love you, too. I do. You know I do."

Tenderness and hope filled him. "We'll make it work out this time."

"You really think that's possible? That this time is really different?"

"I don't think. I *know.*" But she didn't. He could see the doubt in her eyes. He had to give her time, had to convince her that the only place he'd ever felt at home was when he was with her. He just hoped he wasn't too late, that she could still find home with him.

IT WAS NINE O'CLOCK, hours after Kat had arrived at Jason's house and she rested on his bed, on her stomach, and wearing his T-shirt. She watched him disappear into the hall, on his way to meet the pizza delivery man at the door, sighing with the pure satisfaction of being with him again. She blocked out any argument that it might be a mistake. She didn't care. It was too late. She'd done exactly what she'd promised herself she wouldn't do. Kat had fallen for Jason all over again. It was too late to run, too late to hide, because she simply didn't want to.

Kat turned her attention back to the huge flat-screen TV. She and Jason had been watching the first season of *Stepping Up.* The screen flashed from the dancers to the judges' table.

Kat sucked in a breath and sat up, her spine stiff, watching Jason interact with the other judges. It was the first time she'd seen him on television, aside from a commercial for the show, and she was hit hard with a good dose of reality. He looked good, natural and right on the screen, in the spotlight instead of behind the camera. He belonged on that screen, in the public eye, on that show. He was never going to stay here in Vegas. He would be pulled to bigger and better things, and he deserved those things.

That realization washed away her good mood, and stole the joy of minutes before when she'd been happily watching the program with Jason, pretending fairy tales did come true. She wanted those minutes back, and the hours before them. She liked here and now.

"I grabbed your bag," Jason said, sauntering into the room with it and a pizza box in hand, his hair rumpled, his broad chest deliciously bare, his jeans slung low on his waist. He set the bag at the foot of the bed. "I think your phone is inside. I heard it ringing."

"Why would you leave *Stepping Up?*" she asked, the question exploding from her lips, her urgency for the answer far more important than her growling stomach. "It's the number-one show on television. That's a dream come true. It's security. It's opportunity. It's stability going into a fourth season is hard to find in this business. You can't walk away. Even for a Vegas production."

He looked surprised by her sudden outburst. Her phone started to ring again, but she ignored it. She didn't want to pretend everything was roses without thorns, and she almost had. That wasn't good for him or her. She wanted everything out now, before those thorns tore them apart again.

Jason let out a breath and scrubbed his hand over the light stubble on his jaw before setting the pizza on the bed and out of the way.

"Kat." He settled onto the mattress in front of her. "It's a job and it's money. I don't need either of those things."

"It's a huge show, Jason," she said. "They're going to offer you big money to stay. You can't walk away from that."

"Why?"

"I told you why. Because you'll regret it later. What if nothing like this ever comes around again?"

"That's what we both said every single time one of us had an opportunity. We're both older and wiser now. We have money and we have work if we want it. We don't have to walk around in fear that there will never be another 'big' opportunity."

"Tell me you aren't doing this for me."

"For us."

She shook her head, her chest tightened. "No. No. I won't let you do this. You'll resent me, and you'll resent us, later." Her phone started to ring again and she ground her teeth, silently cursing the interruption. "Good grief, who keeps calling?" She reached into the side pocket of the bag, meaning to turn off her ringer, but hesitating when she noted her mother's number. Her mother was a former E.R. nurse who, after five years of retirement, still went to bed at eight and got up at five in the morning.

Kat answered the phone. "Mom? Is something wrong?" No reply. She had been too slow to answer. She punched the recall button and it went to voice mail, her gaze finding Jason's. He arched a brow and she shook her head. "She's not answering."

Kat stood up and grabbed her bag. "I have to go over there." She took off for the hall, dialing her mom's number again. Voice mail again. Her heart was in her throat. She could feel it in her bones that something was wrong in a very bad way.

She dropped her bag at the bottom of the stairs and searched for her pants, racing around the room, to no avail. She dialed the phone again and heard Jason charging down the stairs.

"Did you reach her?" he asked, and the urgency in his voice did her heart good. He was worried with her, he cared. She wasn't alone.

"No," Kat said, turning to him as she reached the bottom step. "I don't know what to do and I can't find my damn pants."

He handed her pants to her. Gratefully, she accepted them and started to pull them on. "Thank you."

Jason tugged a shirt on over his head. "Have you

tried your father?" he asked, grabbing his boots to put them on.

Kat started dialing, not sure why she hadn't thought of that, knowing she needed to calm down and invite a little reason into her thoughts. She tucked the phone between her shoulder and ear to shove her feet into her socks and tennis shoes. The phone went to voice mail two times in a row. She ended the call and redialed.

"Nothing," she said grimly.

"Keep trying," he said, standing up. "It's probably nothing. You're overreacting, but we'll go check to be safe."

"We'll?"

"You drive bad enough when you aren't worried," he reminded her

"I do not," she said, grabbing her bag, where her keys were stuffed. "I don't need a chauffeur."

"Good," he said, taking her bag from her, his eyes dark as they collided with hers. "Because there are a lot of things I want to be to you, Kat, and chauffeur isn't one of them."

She opened her mouth to argue, scared to count on him, to lean on him, only to have him leave again. He *was* going to leave again. But the voice of reason she'd been looking for reminded her that he was here now and she needed him.

Kat reached for the bag on his shoulder and pulled out the keys before dangling them in front of him.

8

THE RIDE TO her parents' house was ten minutes that felt like forever. "Why aren't they answering?" Kat asked Jason from the passenger seat of her rental car.

"Maybe they were fighting and now they're making up," he suggested, "in which case we could really embarrass everyone, including ourselves, by showing up unannounced."

"Please do not suggest my parents are having makeup sex," she said. "That isn't something I like to think about."

"Makeup sex is a logical answer," he pressed. "If there was something wrong when she called, then I'm sure your mother would have left a message. Better yet, she would have taken your calls. Think about it. What's the one time when you wouldn't answer your mother's call? While working or while having sex."

"Again, Jason," Kat chided. "I know you're trying to distract me, but it's not working. I have this bad feeling in my gut I can't ignore. Maybe they aren't taking my calls because one of them is rushing the other one to the hospital and doesn't want to scare me."

"Yet they tried to call you earlier?" he asked, and then gentled his tone. "Kat, baby, you're working yourself up for what is probably nothing. This isn't like you at all." He turned the corner to her parents' house. "See? No firetrucks and no police cars."

Kat let out a relieved breath before quickly fretting again. "Unless they're already gone."

"What is up with you?" Jason queried. "Do you really have that bad of a feeling or is it something else? You're supposed to be more calm now that you're home and close to them, not less."

"I know," she agreed. "I know. I do, but they don't tell me things, Jason. I found out six months after the fact that my mother had a cancer scare last year. She must have been terrified and I wasn't even aware it was going on. They're older now. I need to be here if they need me. I need them to know I'm here for them."

"They know," he promised. "And they're proud of you for all you've achieved. You know they are." He pulled the car into her parents' driveway, and put the gear in Park. "Let's go put your mind at ease that all is well."

Kat was already shoving open her door before he finished the sentence, but Jason was fast and met her at the hood of the car, falling into pace with her as she headed up the drive. It had been so long since she'd had him by her side, she was surprised by just how right he felt there. But then, maybe she shouldn't have been surprised at all. Their breakup wasn't created by cheating and lies, or even love lost, between them. It was distance that always destroyed them.

"The porch light is on," Kat commented as they neared the blue-and-white cottage-style home she'd grown up in. "They aren't in bed or they'd turn it off."

"Kitchen light, too," Jason commented, taking the first of five wooden steps to the porch in unison with Kat.

"But they won't answer their phones," Kat said, taking the final step to the porch. "I don't get it."

Jason laughed and wiggled a brow. "I told you why they won't answer."

Kat was about to knock when the door flew open, and Sheila Moore, Kat's mother, appeared before them. "Kat. Jason. I didn't expect you to come over."

Kat's brows dipped at her mother's rather stiff, uncomfortable reply, that was far from the normal, eager welcome she was used to.

"Please tell me you two aren't here because you worried over my calls," her mother exclaimed. "Because I'm really going to feel horrible I did that to you. I just wanted to chitchat and when you didn't answer I called a friend. You know how I am. Every time I click over to a call, I hang up on the other person."

"Of course we were worried," Kat said quickly, glancing at her mother's attire, which wasn't at all the robe she'd expected. No, not at all. Her mother was fully dressed, looking stylish, and as usual, a good ten years younger than her age of sixty-five, in a pair of jeans and a floral shirt, her shoulder-length light brown hair sleek and straight. "Were you and Dad on your way out?"

"I was bored and tried to talk your father into a

movie. Clearly that didn't work out. I'm sure I ruined whatever plans you two had in the process. I hate that I scared you into driving over here."

"We were about to eat pizza," Jason put in quickly. "So if you happen to have some of that home cooking of yours you love to test on visitors, I'll be happy to volunteer for the job."

"Certainly," her mother said, motioning them forward. "The least I can do after scaring you is to feed you." She disappeared inside the house, clearly expecting them to follow.

Kat faced Jason, puzzled by a number of things. "Why isn't my mother surprised you're with me?"

"I told you I got your new address from your parents," he said. "So I stopped by and had a long chat with them."

"You stopped by and had a long chat with them?" she repeated. "What the heck did you say to them?"

Her mother popped her head back out of the door. "You two want coffee or iced tea?" she asked, as if she didn't notice they hadn't come inside yet.

"Both," Kat said at the same time Jason did.

Her mother smiled, but it didn't quite reach her light green eyes and Kat could feel the tension radiating from her.

Kat turned to Jason the instant her mother disappeared again. "I want that answer. Just not now. Something is up with my mother, no matter how much she is trying to act like there isn't."

"I agree, something is up," he said, his hands settling on her shoulders before he gave her a quick kiss. "But the answer to your question is that I told them I want you back. The same thing I told you. Fortunately, they're 'Team Jason.'" He drew her hands into his and kissed her knuckles. "Now, if I could just get you on board."

Her heart skipped a beat. "I've always been 'Team Jason.'"

"Correction then," he said, his voice gentle, even tender. "I need you on 'Team Jason and Kat.'"

Oh, how Kat wished it were as easy as just jumping on board that request, but she wasn't sure she could be on "Team Jason" and still be on "Team Jason and Kat." If she held him back, if she'd held him back in the past, would there even be a "Team Jason and Kat" to talk about?

He motioned toward the door with his head. "Your mother wants to feed us. Let's not stop her. She'll be happy and so will my stomach."

"Mine, too," Kat agreed, her shoulders relaxing as she dodged the difficult topic of what the future held. "I was beyond starving when we ordered the pizza."

They entered the house, turning to their immediate left where her mother busied herself with the coffee pot in the pale blue-and-white rectangular-shaped oversized kitchen. The whole house had the same color scheme, which her parents both loved.

"Tell me you have some of that famous cheesecake of yours stashed away for dessert," Jason pleaded, making a beeline for the fridge, as comfortable here as if he had never left the family. "I love that stuff."

"You'll have to settle for chocolate cake," her mother informed him, walking toward Jason and pointing at something inside the fridge. "Hand me that tray. It's lasagna. I just made it a few hours ago."

"Thank goodness you didn't answer your phone," Jason said, handing the requested container to Kat's mother and elbowing the door shut. "Do you know how long it's been since I had home-cooked anything?"

"I'd have thought your mom would keep you well fed since you moved your folks to California," Kat's mother replied.

Kat digested that with a twist in her gut, her gaze dropping to the floor in an effort to hide her immediate reaction. How had she forgotten that Jason had moved his parents to L.A. a few years back? Sure, he'd bought a house here, a convenience and tax write-off, while filming this season's show, but he had one there as well. He was no more rooted here than he'd been before. Not really.

"My parents have minds of their own," Jason replied. "They hated L.A. and they hated being retired. They both took jobs teaching English in Thailand two years ago."

"They're in Thailand?" Kat asked, her eyes lifting, seeking Jason, and finding him propped against the counter, arms and legs crossed, his gaze on her.

"Yes," he said, the look on his face telling her that he knew what she'd been thinking. "They're in Thailand."

So he wasn't bound to L.A. by anything but the work he might choose to take, but hadn't.

She swallowed hard. "Aren't you worried about them?"

"I was until the first time I went to visit them and saw how happy they are," he said, "though I admit the visit was meant to beg, bargain and plead for their return."

"Oh!" Kat's mother exclaimed. "I would love to do something like that. I've been volunteering at the children's hospital and Hank has been helping out at a free legal service since selling his firm. We are both going nuts with nothing to do. I've been trying to talk him into travel." Her gaze settled on Jason. "Maybe I could talk to Isabel about it?"

"My mother would be thrilled to hear from you," Jason assured her. "Call her on Skype by using her first and last name. She's always online."

"Skype?" Kat's mother asked, looking confused. "Is that the same thing as Twitter? Because I don't want to tell the world my life story in ten words or less. I just want to talk to Isabel."

Kat and Jason exchanged a look and laughed. "Twitter is one hundred and forty characters or less," Kat informed her mother. "Skype is a private chat without long-distance fees, a lot like instant message. I'll show you how to do it."

"Is it forty characters or less? That seems very limiting."

"No limit," Kat assured her. "Just type as you like and you can even do video if you want."

"Perfect," her mom replied, putting the food in the oven and rubbing her hands together. "Dinner in about fifteen minutes."

"*That's* perfect," Jason agreed. "I have to admit the one thing I'd change about your daughter is her hatred of cooking."

Kat's mother laughed, but that forced and tense

quality to her demeanor had returned, and abruptly, at that. Even her tone was tight as she jokingly replied, "Kat prefers eating to cooking." She winked at Kat and turned away to the stainless steel stove, opening the door and checking the lasagna, as if she hadn't just put the tray inside.

Kat and Jason exchanged a concerned look. "Where's Dad?" Kat asked, determined to find out what the heck was going on.

"Yeah, where is ol' Hank?" Jason asked. "He and I haven't gotten in a good game of chess in years."

"Oh, he went out for a while," Sheila said, using a pot holder to adjust the foil on the tray before fiddling with the temperature only to change it right back to what it had been a second before.

Kat walked to her mother, resting her hand on her back. "Talk to me, Mom. What's wrong?"

Her mother inhaled heavily and stood up. "I don't know. I just…don't know."

"What does that mean, Sheila?" Jason asked, sounding as concerned as Kat felt.

"It means that Hank says that he's out drinking and that every man deserves to go drinking now and then. And when I told him I was calling Kat, he got mad, and now he won't answer his phone."

"Dad is out drinking?" Kat asked, glancing at Jason and confirming he was as baffled as she was.

"Since when does Hank drink?" Jason asked. "I could barely get the man to have a beer with me during the holiday football games."

"He started today, apparently," Sheila said. "Which is why I know something is wrong. He doesn't want me

to know about whatever it is." She shook her head. "I...
What if it's another woman?"

Kat gasped and grabbed her mother's hand. "Oh,
God, Mother. It's not another woman." She hoped.

"It's bad, whatever it is," she said. "And I'd rather
him be cheating than hiding some medical condition
from me. What other two things can you think of that
he would want to hide from me?"

"Hey, Hank," Jason said, and Kat and her mother
turned their gazes to find the phone to his ear as he
continued talking. "What's this about you having a
drink and not inviting me?" He listened a minute and
then added, "Yeah. I know the exact spot. I'll see you
in about half an hour." He hung up and dialed another
number. "Yeah, I need a cab." He quickly spouted off
Kat's parents' address and ended the call.

"Where is he?" Sheila asked. "And why did he answer your calls and not mine?"

"Or mine? And why did you call a cab?" Kat asked.

"In the order asked," Jason replied, "I'll try to answer. He's downtown at a casino. He answered because
I check in with him every now and then, and he knows
my number. And finally, I called a cab because sometimes a man has to dump back a few drinks to get another man whose already drinking to talk."

"I'm going with you," Kat said at the same time as
her mother .

Jason smiled. "No, you both are not."

"Yes—" Kat and her mother said again at the same
time.

"No," Jason finished for them. "If you want to know
what's going on with Hank, then give the man some

space to talk to me. I'll get us both back here alive. Maybe not sober, but alive."

Kat and her mother looked at each other and then reluctantly nodded. "Call us when you know what's going on though," Sheila insisted.

"I will," Jason said, and gestured to the door at Kat. "Wait for the cab with me outside?"

She nodded and they headed outside, with Jason calling over his shoulder, "Don't eat all the cake while I'm gone, Sheila. I'll be back."

Kat smiled at his comment, his natural way with people, that made him a great leader on a set. They stepped onto the porch, pulling the door shut behind them.

"Do you have any clue what's going on?" Kat asked.

Jason twined the fingers of one of his hands with hers, and pulled her close to him. "Only that he was quick to invite me to join him, and he told me to come alone. That tells me he needs to talk."

"It really could be either of those things my mom said, couldn't it?"

"Let's not jump to conclusions," he said, settling down on the top step of the porch and pulling her down beside him. He slid his hand over her knee, aligning their legs. "Maybe he's simply experiencing the same thing your mother is, lost in retirement."

The feel of Jason's hand possessively on her leg, his hip joined with hers, warmed her well beyond the physical desire he so easily stirred within her. She was worried about her parents, and he was here for her.

"Why not just tell her that?" Kat asked.

He faced her more fully. "Maybe he's afraid she'll

think this is something to do with her, when it's about him."

"What if they've grown apart? What if—"

He kissed her, his fingers curling on her cheek. "They haven't," he said. "There are a lucky few people in this world that have a special bond, Kat, like they do. Like we do. Space and time doesn't divide those people. It hasn't divided us."

Kat's lashes fluttered, the warmth of his breath teasing her lips. "Jason," she whispered, because there were no other words ample enough to explain what she felt. She didn't even know what she felt.

A horn honked and Kat jumped at the sound. The cab had parked in front of the house.

"My limo has arrived," Jason joked, brushing his thumb over the corner of her mouth. He stood and helped Kat to her feet. "I'll text you when I get to your father's side."

"That would be great," she said. She trusted Jason. He was very much a part of her life again. When she'd told him she didn't know what she felt, she was wrong. She felt scared of getting hurt, scared of what might be going on with her parents, but she could say that to Jason and he would listen, he'd care. And that made her feel lucky.

"Jason!" Kat yelled, running down the steps to catch him.

He paused, halfway inside the cab, and stood up, turning to her. Kat rushed up and leaned into him, pressing to her tip-toes to kiss him, and then whispered, "I missed you."

His arms closed around her, his tongue pressing past her lips, caressing hers. "I missed you, too. Later, I'll show you how much."

9

JASON WAS INSIDE the busy downtown Blue Moon Casino, searching the blackjack tables for Kat's father, Hank, within fifteen minutes of sliding into the cab. To say that he was eager to get back to Kat after that "I missed you" proclamation she'd made by the cab was an understatement. But because he loved Kat, he was also eager to find out what was going on with her parents, especially her father.

Jason easily spotted Hank at a busy table, with a drink in his hand and a sexy red-haired woman twenty years his junior batting her eyes at him. Jason grimaced, and moved in Hank's direction, cursing that Sean Connery appeal Hank had with women, hoping this wasn't a sign that he was cheating and this was his mistress.

He slid into the only seat across the table from Hank and dropped a hundred dollar bill on the table. "Hello, Hank."

"Jason, my boy," he said as the dealer swept away the chips that Hank had just lost.

"Oh my God," the woman said, blinking at Jason.

"You're... Oh my God. You're the judge from that dance show." The dealer and the three other people at the table immediately looked at Jason.

Jason grimaced quickly and said, "No. No, but I get that all the time. It's the name. He's older and shorter. I swear." He loved the judges' table, helping dreams come true and helping new stars develop. He didn't like being recognized, or becoming the star himself. It just wasn't him.

The woman smiled. "Well, you'll do just fine by me."

"Shuffle," the dealer said, and one of the people at the table got up.

Hank elbowed the redhead. "That's my son-in-law," he explained to her. "Would you mind if he switched places with you?"

"I'll share my chair," she purred.

"Son-in-law," Hank repeated. "As in married to *my daughter.* If he shares a chair with you, I'll be kicking him in his seat."

"Oh." She pouted and grabbed her chips. "In that case, I'll leave. All you married guys are no fun."

Relief washed over Jason. Hank wasn't flirting with the woman, that was clear. Jason grabbed his hundred since the dealer had yet to touch it, and moved to the stool next to Hank.

"*Was* married to your daughter," Jason said softly.

"I'm counting on you to fix that," Hank told him. "The power of positive thinking. She's happy when she's with you. Just stop running off and leaving her behind."

"I plan to," Jason said, feeling the reprimand like

a slap in the face and a reminder of the past he had to overcome with Kat.

The dealer called for bets and slid chips in front of Jason. Hank slid two twenty-five dollar chips to the table.

"Since when do you gamble?" Jason asked, sliding his own bet forward.

"Since today," Hank said, downing his drink and flagging the waitress to say, "Two shots of tequila."

No food and alcohol. Not a winning plan, Jason thought, catching the waitress to add, "And something to eat. Pretzels, nuts, whatever you can get me that's allowed in the gaming area." He turned back to the table as the dealer looked to Hank to make decisions on his cards. Hank hit sixteen when the dealer had a three. You never hit a sixteen when the dealer had a three, because you knew the dealer's best hand was thirteen while your chances of going out were high.

The dealer threw down a face card and Hank now had more than twenty-one. He was busted. He cursed. Jason had a three and a five. He took a hit and was dealt another three. He hit again. The dealer gave him a face card and a solid winning hand of twenty-one. Hank's screw-up worked out okay for him. The rest of the table—not so much. Everyone else lost their hand. Someone grumbled about bad players and got up. Jason didn't blame him. He might not make a habit of gambling, but he knew his game when he did and he didn't play with people who didn't.

Jason cocked his head at Hank. "Why are we here, Hank? You know Sheila and Kat are worried sick."

The waitress stopped beside them and Hank tossed

down a few gambling chips for a tip, then grabbed his shot off the tray, downed it, and gave the waitress the empty glass. "We're here because I'm trying to make back mine and Sheila's stock portfolio she has no idea I lost."

Jason sat there in stunned silence before emptying his shot glass as well, and giving it to the waitress. He ignored the bowl of nuts and his phone vibrating at his hip. "How much?"

"Two hundred and fifty thousand," Hank said, and then to the waitress. "Another round."

"Scratch that," Jason said to the woman. "We're going to the bar where they have larger glasses."

"I'm all for that," Hank agreed, and shoved his chips toward the dealer. "Cash me out."

"And me," Jason said, pushing his forward, but he suddenly realized the waitress was still standing there.

She thrust her empty tray at him with a pen and a napkin on top. "Can I have your autograph?"

"Why does everyone think you are that guy on that show?" Hank asked in an impressively convincing voice. "You're not near as good-looking even if you think you are." He eyed the waitress. "You want my autograph, too? I'll sign Sean Connery if you want. You can tell them all I have a lot more hair than you thought I did."

The girl was young, not more than twenty-one, and she blushed, her cheeks flushing a bright red. "I'm so sorry. I really thought you were him. You just look so much like him and I heard he was in Vegas for a show."

Her embarrassment sent a rush of guilt through Jason. His fame was a blessing, even if it didn't feel like it at times. He knew that. It let him do things for his family. It would let him help Kat's. He just couldn't get used to living under a microscope. He enjoyed creating stars, not being one himself.

Jason grabbed the he napkin and signed it, then snatched the hundred dollar chip the dealer had given him to cash out and tossed it on her tray. "Please make sure anyone you told I was here believes you were mistaken. At least, until I'm not here anymore."

"It *is* you," she whispered. "It is."

"Yes. It is."

She smiled brightly. "My lips are sealed. You are not *you*. Thank you so much." She rushed away.

Jason and Hank quickly headed for a dimly lit bar area with leather armchairs and round glowing blue tables. Hank flagged a waitress and ordered drinks while Jason quickly typed a message to Kat. Bad phone reception in casino. No other woman. No one sick or dying. Try to sleep. I know you won't but try.

She immediately replied, What is going on?

At least he knew she got the message. He typed, I'll explain later, and then knew Kat wouldn't take that answer, and quickly added, retirement jitters, now go to bed. Trust me, Kat. Everything is going to be fine.

"Must be hell to be famous," Hank said. "I mean, it has to be tough to have all them girls pawing all over you, and movie stars hanging on your arms."

Jason tensed, more than a little surprised by the accusation in Hank's words when he'd sensed nothing of this before now. They did say that alcohol made people say what was on their minds, and there was no missing the undertone. Nor did Jason doubt the fragility of it coming from a protective father with too much tequila and a really bad day under his belt.

Jason returned his phone to his belt without answering Kat's next message and focused on her father, looking Hank straight in the eye. "The life I want is with Kat."

"Now that you got the starlets out of your system?"

"Kat and I were split up," he said. "I tried to move on. It didn't work."

"It took you too long to figure that out."

That wasn't true, but that was a conversation for Jason and Kat. "Things between Kat and I have always been complicated."

"Then it won't work out now any more than in the past. You should walk away before you tear her apart right when I'm about to destroy her mother."

Destroy? Whoa. That was a strong word and Jason was officially concerned that there was more going on here than he'd first imagined. Jason leaned forward, resting his elbows on his knees. "Talk to me, Hank. What happened? What the hell is going on?"

A muscle in Hank's jaw clenched. "You hear about the Smith-Wright investment company?"

"Yeah," Jason said, seeing where this was headed. "It's been all over the news. All of the key executives were arrested for fraud."

"That's the one," he said. "They had our retirement portfolio for ten years, though Sheila never knew. I take care of our finances and I always have. Those guys gave me reports, showed I'd doubled our money and kept me investing. According to them I'd turned two hundred thousand dollars into five hundred thousand dollars

over that decade. Sheila and I were set for retirement."
He scrubbed his hand over his lightly stubbled jaw and
when the waitress appeared by his side he paid her and
downed his shot before handing Jason his.

"Don't make me drink alone, son," Hank said when
Jason went to set the glass on the table. "Not tonight."

Jason didn't enjoy being drunk or out of control, not
even a little bit. And even if he did, like it or not, he
was famous, and he had to guard his public behavior.
He also needed Hank to keep talking.

Jason braced himself for the bite of the liquor and
poured the shot into his mouth. "That's it for me until I
eat," he announced when the burn let him speak again.
"I'm done."

"It's gone now," Hank said, and he wasn't talking
about the tequila. "All of the money is gone. Every
dime Sheila and I had saved. Every dime Kat insisted
we take when I didn't want to take it. I figured I was
just investing it for her. I'd give it back with a little
extra in return."

"And you thought coming here was the way to get
the money back?" Jason asked, trying to ignore the
angry churn of his stomach and hating the slight buzz
in his head.

"Why the hell not?" Hank demanded defensively.
"I see people get lucky all the time, living on the edge
and doing things wrong. I've spent a lifetime doing everything right, planning and preparing, and where did
that get me? Sheila wants to travel. She's waited that
lifetime with me, and worked her backside off to see
the world. Now I have to tell her she waited with the
wrong man. I destroyed her dream."

Jason and Kat had spent years apart, chasing opportunities he'd naively called dreams that were supposed to make them happy. For him that idea had been a big failure. "You two have something special, Hank. Whatever goes right or wrong, you have each other, and that's what matters."

"I know that," he said. "I do. But Sheila has always dreamed and I swore I'd make those dreams come true."

"You still can," Jason said. "I'll give you the money you lost including the return you were promised."

Hank stared at him blankly, as if he didn't compute what he'd said. "You're telling me that you'd give me five hundred thousand dollars," he snapped his fingers, "just like that."

"Without a second of hesitation."

Hank blinked at him and then scrubbed his jaw. "Holy hell." He mumbled something to himself and then refocused on Jason. "I'm not taking your money, son, but the fact that you just offered it to me tells me that you love my daughter even more than I thought you did. You do what you have to do to make her see that. You win her back."

"I'm going to give it a try," Jason assured him. "Look, Hank, you and Sheila have always been family to me. Besides, the studio pays me an insane amount of money for sitting at the judging table. Millions of dollars which I invest and turn into more. I won't miss this money, but you will. You and Sheila go live your dreams together, the way Kat and I should have lived ours."

"If you were me, would *you* take the money?"

No, Jason thought. He'd have too much pride. "This will be our secret with no strings attached. If Kat kicks me to the curb, it changes nothing. This is my gift to you."

"I'm not taking your money, Jason."

There was such absoluteness to the tone that Jason knew he had to change strategies. "How much do you have left in your retirement fund?"

"Ten thousand."

Of the five *hundred thousand* he'd thought he had. Jason knew that had to sting. "You say you want to gamble tonight? To throw caution to the wind?"

"That was the idea."

"Then bet with me. Give me the ten thousand dollars to play, because let's be honest here, you don't know what you are doing at those tables. If I can turn that money into a hundred thousand, then you let me take it to my investment guy to work some magic. Your money turned into more money. No borrowing and no gift. No need to be prideful. You can forget any of this ever happened and book your first trip to wherever you want to go."

"How are you going to turn ten thousand into a hundred thousand?"

"I'm really good at craps," Jason said, pushing to his feet. "Which I'm going to play at the high stakes tables. You have to bet big to win big."

Hank stood up, his eyes clouded over, his pupils dilated. "And if you lose?"

Jason patted his back. "We'll be needing a lot more tequila."

The waitress approached but Jason waved her away before Hank saw her. The last thing Jason needed right now was more of a buzz going on in his own head.

They left the lounge area with Jason fully intending to get Hank to take his money one way or another. Jason was taking care of Kat's parents. The craps tables were confusing to newbies, and though Jason really was good at the game, Hank would never know if Jason won or lost. Not if he tipped the right people enough money, which he intended to do. He had this under control despite the tequila. *Everything was going to be fine.* And Jason believed that right up until the moment he and Hank walked around a corner and straight into the path of two men in suits. Hank and the two men stopped dead in their tracks.

Hank—calm, collected, normally reserved Hank— was apparently hanging by a thread that snapped. "These two buzzards work at Smith-Wright," Hank growled and shoved one of them.

Before Jason could even react, the cameras began to flash and people gathered around them. Trouble was here and it wasn't going to go away without dragging him and Hank into a whole lot of that spotlight Jason didn't enjoy. And he knew the press. They'd investigate Hank, and they'd figure out the connection. He and Kat were about to be outed as exes and if he didn't calm Hank down, that might be the best of the worst to come.

AN HOUR AFTER Jason's last text, Kat snuggled into the oversized blue chair in her parents' living room, with her mother resting on the matching couch, and flipped on the ten o'clock news.

"I wish they'd call," her mother murmured, clearly not watching the television. She leaned up on her elbow. "What if it's not retirement jitters? What if Hank is having a full-fledged midlife crisis and we're not as happy as I thought we were?"

"Stop doing this to yourself, Mom. I read you Jason's text. If there was something to worry about, he would have told me."

"You're sure?"

"Yes, I'm sure."

"What if Hank hadn't told Jason everything yet? And my God, what did he tell him?"

"Mom," Kat said softly, understanding how she must feel. How Kat herself would feel if this were Jason acting strangely. "Jason is with him. Dad knows he will tell me what is going on. If he didn't want you to know do you think he would have been that quick to invite Jason to join him?"

"…Jason Alright from *Stepping Up*…"

Kat's attention whipped to the television and her mother sat up and increased the volume.

"…was involved in a disturbance at the Blue Moon Casino…"

Kat and her mother were both standing now, both dialing their phones, trying to reach Jason and Hank.

"…a section of the casino was shut down but has now reopened. No more details are available."

"No answer," Kat said.

Sheila shook her head. "Let's get over there. I'll call the hotel while you drive."

"And the police station," Kat said grimly. "And let's hope they aren't there."

10

JASON AND HER father weren't answering their phones, but they weren't in jail, per her mother's call to the police station. That was the one good thing Kat had to cling to as she and her mother rushed to the front desk of the Blue Moon Casino.

"I need to locate Jason Alright," Kat said to the tall, thin twenty-something male attendant behind the counter.

"Jason Alright?" the man asked, looking down on her from beneath his dark rimmed glasses.

Her brows dipped. "I know you know who I'm talking about."

"No, ma'am," he said primly. "I'm afraid I do not."

"Listen up," her mother said, letting the tough E.R. nurse who took charge in the center of disaster shine through for the first time tonight. "You can't tell me you don't know the judge from *Stepping Up* when he was the center of attention right here in this hotel only a short while ago. Jason is her husband. Find him, find someone who knows how to find him or just plain go get him yourself."

The man stared at her for several terse seconds and then eyed Kat, inspecting her T-shirt and messy hair with a bit of disdain. Thank goodness her leggings were hidden below the counter. His lips tightened. "I'll return momentarily." He turned away and left them to wait.

Kat glanced around the crowded lobby, and it was clear that her mother's loudly spoken words had garnered unwanted attention as pointing and whispering had begun. Kat cringed as numerous cell phone pictures were taken. She was officially outed as Jason's wife, and she wasn't even his wife anymore. Nevertheless, they had a history, and the connection between them was bound to come out. She'd simply hoped to get a little farther into the show than the first week of rehearsals.

"Mom," Kat said. "Jason and I—"

"Love each other," she finished. "So don't let him go. This time is it, Kat. I feel it in my gut. He's going all the way or he's going away and it has to be that way. You both have to get on with life, one way or the other."

Kat sucked in a breath at the blunt reality etched so precisely into those words. Deep down Kat knew that if Jason exited her life again, he was gone for good, but hearing it from her mother was a blow. Her stomach knotted because history said he would leave again, and while part of her said this time together was something, they needed to be able to move on. Another part of her though could still feel his touch and smell him on her skin, could still hear his deep voice, see his smile, and that part of her hoped for a future with Jason.

"Ms. Moore?"

Kat turned to find a big burly giant who wore one of those concrete expressions that screamed "security" even more so than his black jacket and the ear piece.

"Yes?" her mother asked the man.

Kat raised her hand. "And yes. Same name."

"Your party is waiting for you, and I'd send you without an escort but it appears you've drawn a bit of attention." A camera flashed and he glanced at a group of three women, studying them. "We don't need any more excitement here tonight."

"I guess I shouldn't have told the world we were here to see Jason," her mother admitted with a sigh. "I forget he's a big star now."

"Not a problem," the man assured them. "I'll just get you out of the crush here and I'm sure everything will be fine." He motioned them forward and indicated a path, before falling into step behind them.

Kat replayed her mother's words in her head. Jason was a star—no—*big star,* she'd said. Boy, oh boy, was her mother throwing bombs tonight.

"Sorry I got a little loud and out of control," her mother said. "I didn't mean to get us an escort."

"Let's talk later," Kat told her, having some experience with this kind of thing after traveling with Marcus, whose fans were downright rabid. "There are cameras everywhere, and believe me, everything and anything could end up in the tabloids, especially given what happened earlier tonight."

"We don't know what happened," her mother exclaimed. "That's the point."

"We know it ended up on the news." And they knew that Jason was that big of a name now to draw that kind of attention, which drove home how much *Stepping Up* had changed his life. Yet he seemed like the same Jason she'd always known, virtually unchanged, and that was special, unique even.

She'd seen plenty of people changed by stardom. He'd helped her parents tonight without question, and not just because of her. He was just that kind of guy, and always had been. If anyone deserved fame, he did. Her stomach sunk at what that meant. To hold him back would be selfish and she loved him too much to do that. She had to get a grip.

Emotion tightened her chest, but she didn't have time to analyze her feelings as they had arrived at an elevator corridor. From there, the three of them—Kat, her mother, and the stone-faced guard—traveled to the twenty-seventh floor.

When the doors opened, their security escort placed his hand on the button to keep them from shutting again. "Room 2711," he instructed, evidently not joining them beyond this point.

"Thank you," Kat said, and she and her mother exited the car.

The instant the elevator shut behind them, her mother asked, "Do you think this is some kind of security screening room we're going to?"

"We're about to find out," Kat said, pointing in the direction they needed to go.

"I'm guessing the code isn't a good sign," her mother said as they passed several doors, and appeared to be heading to the far end of a long hallway.

"VIP floors are reserved for big money, government officials and celebrities," Kat explained. "Extra security isn't a sign of anything being wrong." She lifted her chin to indicate the final door. "This is us."

"Finally," her mother said, rushing forward and knocking three times.

Kat caught up to her right as the door flew open to reveal Jason standing there, looking so sexy that Kat could have sworn her legs wobbled. His hair was rumpled, his jaw shadowed, his body long and lean, and yes, hard. Every bit of this man was hard and made her soft and yet hot for him. She couldn't resist him. She was weak. She was selfish. So very selfish because she didn't want to let him go.

"Where's Hank, Jason?" her mother asked. "Is he okay?"

"He's fine considering he's hanging over the toilet with tequila fever," he said, stepping back to let her mother pass. "Other than that, everything is fine."

Kat knew Jason well enough to know that he wouldn't make any declaration lightly and relief washed over her.

Her mother didn't seem to agree, exclaiming, "Oh, God!" and hurried into the room.

Kat hesitated, also knowing herself. One touch from Jason and she'd forget why selfishly wanting him was wrong. Jason reached for her and tugged her inside the room, shutting the door behind them. His touch sizzled through Kat like an electric charge, the spicy male scent of him she knew and loved so much, tickling her nostrils. And when his eyes met hers, for the briefest, most intimate of moments, and he bent down to brush his lips over hers, she might as well have been chocolate melting in the hot sun.

"What happened?" Kat's mom asked, drawing their

attention to where she'd stopped at the edge of the room, her focus on Jason. "Why were you on the news? Why are you in this room?"

"He drank too much and almost got into a fight," Jason explained without an instant's hesitation. "Fortunately, the powers-that-be here want our show here next season. They eagerly comped us a room so we could hide until the media calms down and we can get out of here."

"Why didn't you call us?" Sheila demanded. "Why didn't Hank call me?"

"He's not capable of conversation right now," Jason said. "And we'd just made it to the room when I heard you two were up front."

Kat watched her mother curl her arms in front of her chest, the distress and tension rolling off of her as she asked, "Why was he here drinking, Jason? Why was he here at all?"

"He needs to explain that to you, Sheila," he said, trailing his hand down Kat's arm to rest his hand on the small of her back. "I doubt he's capable of that right now, but know this. He's not cheating, he's not dying and he's still very much in love with you. In fact, tonight was more about how much he wants to make you happy than anything else. Let him get the tequila out of his system though. He drank a lot for a man who doesn't drink. Hell, he drank a lot for a man who does drink."

Kat's mother studied him a moment and then turned away, disappearing down the hall.

Jason immediately pulled Kat into the box-like kitchen immediately to Kat's left, pressing her against the counter, his muscular thighs framing hers, the warmth of his body heating her skin. His gaze searched her expression. "What's wrong?"

"You were on the news. I was worried sick."

"That's not what's wrong."

"I just… I…" She drew a breath and let it out, her hand settling on his chest. "Yesterday I was telling myself 'I don't want to want him again' and already today it's changed to 'I don't want to lose him again.'"

His fingers slid around her neck, his eyes darkened. "I don't want to lose you again either." He kissed her, a deep, sexy kiss, and she could taste the tequila and desire on his mouth.

Kat moaned and wrapped her arms around his neck, unable to fight the sweet, hot, warmth of his tongue against her, the feel of his hands running over her back, molding her closer.

"God, I missed you," he murmured. "Your parents need time alone and so do we. Let's get out of here."

She swallowed hard, fighting through her need for Jason, to focus on her love for her parents. "What happened with my father?"

"He made a bad investment," he said grimly. "Really bad. Enough so that he's worried he can't take your mother traveling like they'd planned."

"Oh, no," Kat said. "He's so cautious. How did this happen?"

"Fraud by the investment firm," he said, "but it's handled, Kat. I'm getting my investment guy involved to make back the money they lost. In the meantime, I figure we can give them a trip for their wedding anniversary next month to start them off."

Kat leaned back to study him more closely. "We?"

"We," he repeated softly.

Kat studied him, her heart squeezing with the reference, with the "we" she wanted to be with him again. And while she might not have him forever, she knew one thing for certain, with all of her heart. She was so done fighting Jason. If this was truly their last hurrah, she didn't want to waste a moment of it.

"Let's get out of here, Jason," she said, and pressed her lips to his.

AN HOUR LATER, after they'd been discreetly ushered out of the hotel by security, Jason followed Kat up the stairs from his garage again, on the phone with Calvin Newport, his long-time agent.

"I wasn't drunk," Jason said grumpily. "I wasn't fighting."

"You have a moral clause," Calvin said.

Jason scrubbed a hand through his hair and stomped up the last step to his living room. "I know I have a moral clause. And like I said, I wasn't drinking and I wasn't fighting."

"They want to talk to us in the morning," Calvin said. "A conference call."

"This is ridiculous," Jason said, rubbing the ball of tension at his neck. He was concerned. He might not want another season with *Stepping Up,* but he did want this Vegas show to go well for him and Kat. "What time?"

"Nine," Calvin said. "I'll get them on the line and then dial your office."

"Fine," he said, his gaze lifting to find Kat watching him, her expression etched with more than a little worry.

"Fine what?" Calvin pressed.

Kat turned and walked toward the kitchen and he heard the balcony door open and Jason quickly tried to end the conversation. "I'll expect your call, Calvin."

"Try to get some rest so you won't be this foul."

"Goodnight, Calvin," he said, snapping his phone shut to follow Kat.

He found the door cracked open and Kat standing at the wooden railing with her back to him. He stepped outside but she didn't turn.

He walked up behind her, wrapped his arms around her, and held her close.

The stars were bright, the sky clear, the moon full and high in the night sky. It was warm, but there was a breeze off the mountains, lifting the silky blond strands of her hair off her slender shoulders. His gut, and his groin, tightened at the sight of her, and the soft feminine scent of her.

"Don't turn this into an excuse to push me away, Kat."

She turned in his arms to face him. "The studio's all over you, Jason. Do you have any idea how much I regret letting you go to that casino tonight?"

"You didn't *let me* do anything. You didn't even ask me. I did it because I wanted to and I'd do it again if I knew the outcome."

"The press is going to figure out our past, Jason, and then the studio will, too."

"The studio knows about our past, Kat."

"What?" Her eyes went wide. "How? When? Because of tonight? Jason, I'll leave before I let this affect your career. I'll—"

He kissed her, slanting his mouth over hers, his tongue stealing a quick, sweet taste of her. "Before you signed the contract. I had no intention of hiding our relationship past, present or future, for any reason but your request."

"Oh," she breathed out. "I'm pretty sure after tonight everyone is going to know anyway."

He stroked her hair. "How do you feel about that?"

"I would have liked to have it come out once I was more established, but honestly, Jason, all I care about right now is you. I don't want this to hurt you with the studio."

"Ah, my little KandyKat," he murmured. "How am I going to get you to understand that the only thing I care about is *you*. Hmm. I think I'll start with you in my bed again."

"I thought we were going to my place?"

"We were," he said. "But your clothes are never going to stay on that long." He bent down and picked her up, as he had done earlier.

Kat clung to his neck and laughed, a sexy, lilting sound that heated his limbs and stirred his emotions. If he heard that laugh every day of his life, it wouldn't be enough.

11

KAT WOKE UP in Jason's bed to him nuzzling her neck, and with the scent of him, the feel of him, all around her. "It's time to get up, KandyKat."

"Hmmm." She sank deeper under the blankets. "Hit snooze, please."

"You said that seven minutes ago."

"Just once more," she murmured, pressing her backside against his hips, and pulling his arm around her. Oh, how she missed waking up to this man.

He laughed, low and rough in her ear, nipping it gently. "You've said that twice now."

She groaned and rolled to her back, blinking into the dim light of the lamp he'd turned on. "What time is it?" she asked, running her hand over the sexy stubble on his jaw.

"Four-thirty."

Her eyes went wide and she sat up, the sheet falling down her naked body. She had to get to rehearsals. Jason's eyes raked her breasts and he reached for her. She darted off the bed, dodging him. "We can't do that right now. I have to shower." She rushed away from him, grabbing her bag on the way to his massive white tiled master bathroom.

"I'll guess this means you don't want me to join you?"

Kat peeked around the door frame. "I'll be late if you do that." She closed the door and headed to the shower. When done, she dressed in clean leggings and a light blue T-shirt she'd had in her bag. By the time she was blow drying her hair, she had officially begun to worry about the day before her.

She and Jason agreed that secrets fed gossip. They would tell their story before the press did it for them. They used to be married and they were seeing each other again. It had seemed like a good plan when they'd talked about it, but now, with it about to be put into play, she had doubts. What if the studio felt Kat was a bad influence on Jason? What if they wanted her fired and he didn't want to do it? What if...? There were so many what ifs.

Kat followed the blessed scent of coffee and found Jason leaning against the kitchen cabinet with a cup in his hand. His hair was damp and rumpled, his jaw clean shaven, his jeans low on his hips, and his Black Sabbath T-shirt pulled snug on his impressive chest.

"I'll quit the show before I let what happened last night hurt your job, Jason," she blurted. "I need you to know that."

He frowned and set his cup on the counter before reaching for her. "Come here," he murmured, wrapping her in his powerful arms, and stroking her hair. "If last night puts your job or mine on the line, then I have no desire to keep working for this studio."

"You—"

His lips brushed hers. "Want you very badly, so unless you want me to strip you naked and set you on this counter, I suggest you go now."

"Jason—"

He slanted his mouth over hers, his tongue stroking, hot with demand, and anything she might have said faded. Kat's arms slid around his neck, the spicy taste of him warming her, calming her. When they were together like this she felt like they could face anything and survive. They could even survive being late to work, but when he tore his mouth from hers, and warned, "Last chance," Kat took off for the door, laughing.

This was their last chance, she thought, sliding into her car. Right now, despite the media drama, it felt like their best chance, too.

NEAR NOON, KAT stood on the stage next to Ellie and watched a group of dancers perform. She'd spoken to her mother during a short break, just long enough to hear that her father was too sick to head home yet, and to tell them that Jason had taken care of the room for them for the day and even the rest of the night if they wanted. Both she and Kat had expected her father wouldn't want to move too quickly. Drinking tequila like a fish when you didn't regularly swim equaled drowning in pain.

She hadn't mentioned the investment loss that had brought on the drinking binge. She wanted to give them time to talk that out on their own and she wasn't sure her father would be up for that yet.

Kat's gaze slid to the distant doors of the auditorium, willing Jason to walk through them. She hadn't heard from him and no one had seen him all day, which only made people more curious about what was going on. The buzz about the night before was loud and steady, but the connection between Kat and Jason had yet to be made. It wouldn't take long. Kat had been around the tabloid mess more than a few times, most recently with Marcus, who was a total media magnet.

Another half hour passed, and another set of dancers were running through a routine when Kat's skin tingled with the awareness she always felt when Jason was watching her. Her gaze lifted to find him sauntering down the center aisle with a loose-legged sexy swagger that had her conjuring up images of the night before: of him naked, of her naked and in his arms. No man but Jason had ever affected her so easily, so completely, though she'd tried to find one. She'd tried to forget Jason and always failed.

He held a thumb up to Kat, silently telling her everything was okay, and relief washed over her. Whatever had tied him up today, the results were good, and ultimately that was all that mattered.

"Bossman sure stirred up trouble last night," Ellie commented quietly. "Any idea what happened?"

Kat wasn't a fool. Ellie had seen her thumbs-up exchange with Jason, and she was digging to find out just how close Kat and Jason really were.

"My father had a retirement crisis and dragged Jason along for the ride," Kat explained.

"What?" Ellie asked, shock hissing through her whisper. "Your father knows Jason?"

Kat glanced at her. "Well, he *was* at our wedding."

"What?" she asked again, facing Kat now, and ignoring the dancers. "Whose wedding?"

"Jason and I were married a very long time ago," Kat said. "It's not a secret."

"You said you were old friends. You didn't say you were *married*."

Kat shrugged. "Now I am."

"I knew something was up with you two," Ellie replied. "I knew it."

Kat's gaze veered over Ellie's shoulder, her attention caught on the opposite side of the stage. There, Carrie and Tabitha were clearly arguing. Kat could see Carrie's face pinched in anger before she turned away, exiting behind the curtain. Tabitha immediately followed her.

"Are you and Jason—"

"Hold that question," Kat said. "I think we have trouble with that situation I told you about this morning. Tabitha and Carrie just headed off stage in the midst of an argument. Call for lunch if I'm not back in fifteen minutes."

Kat darted behind the curtain and rushed toward the other side of the stage, arriving just in time to see Tabitha disappear out of a door leading to the dressing rooms.

Kat hurried after her, covering the distance in a near run. She really didn't need this turning nasty and she'd seen the way Tabitha and Carrie had interacted on the DVD the night before. It wasn't pretty. Right now, Kat and Jason had enough trouble brewing without a fight on set.

Kat shoved open the door Tabitha had used and quickly headed down a long, narrow hallway. She was almost to the end, where there was a section of twelve dressing rooms, when she heard Tabitha's raised voice.

"I put up with you in the contestant house," Tabitha said, "because I knew you weren't good enough to stay around long. If you think I'm going to tolerate you here, you'd better think again."

Kat stopped at the end of the hall, listening to get a true picture of what was happening.

"Are you threatening me?" Carrie asked, her voice soft but surprisingly confrontational for what Kat had observed of her personality.

"No," Tabitha said. "I'm making you a promise. If you interfere with my work, which includes how I handle my understudy, I'll make sure you get fired and we'll be better off as a show for it. You weren't good enough for the competition, you weren't good enough for Jensen and you aren't good enough for Vegas."

"She's not only good enough for me," came a male voice, "I feel lucky she thinks I'm good enough for her."

Kat checked around the corner to see a tall hunk of a guy with a military haircut and a broad chest wrap his arm around Carrie. He had to be her fiancé. Go, Carrie! And go, fiancé for coming to the rescue!

"Who are *you*?" Tabitha asked snidely but there was a crack in her voice, a chink in her armor.

"The new head of security here at the hotel and Carrie's very protective fiancé." He glanced at Carrie. "Are you out for lunch?"

"Yes she is," Kat said as she stepped into the large room. "Take her to eat. I need to have a word with

Tabitha alone anyway." Kat glanced at Carrie. "And I look forward to being properly introduced to your fiancé soon. After all, Carrie, we will be working on some choreography together."

Carrie beamed. "Thank you, Kat. I can't wait." She and her fiancé left the dressing room.

"So, Tabitha," Kat said, "let's find Ellie and have a chat." Kat knew having a witness to any reprimand was smart with someone like Tabitha. It kept details from being twisted.

"She started this," Tabitha blurted. "She involved herself in my work with my understudy. Why would you send Carrie to lunch and then talk to me?"

Kat sighed. "Okay, Tabitha. I'm going to make this quick. I've observed how you treat Marissa and it's simply not acceptable. I saw how you treated Carrie tonight, as well, when Carrie is simply trying to protect Marissa. Marissa is your understudy and you have to be nice to her. You make snide comments and sneer at her. This is not appropriate and it undermines our opportunity to be a team that succeeds together. I'm going to draw up a warning for you to sign. If you continue such actions then you simply won't be here any longer."

"I have a contract," Tabitha stated. "I can't be fired by the choreographer."

"Read the contract," Kat said. "It specifically requires your professional behavior on the set."

"I will not be threatened," Tabitha spat.

"It's not a threat," Kat said, repeating Tabitha's words. "It's a promise. Be respectful to the cast and crew or you won't be here."

"I'll go to my agent. He'll take care of this and you."

"I would, too, if I were you," Kat said. "Have your agent help you understand the terms of the contract."

"This is crazy. I'm going to talk to Jason."

"I'm right here." Jason stepped to Kat's side, his brand of cool confidence and casual authority expanding around them. "And I heard part of the conversation. Kat is far from just a choreographer. She has my permission to make any casting changes needed and I didn't sign on to this show with my hands tied. No one is here without an exit plan in place if needed. We have a small window to make this show perfect. Either you want to be a part of that or you don't."

"I do," Tabitha said, sounding sweeter than Kat had ever heard her sound. "That's why I don't want to be silent when someone isn't giving their all."

"Then don't," Jason said flatly. "Tell Kat. She's your boss. One of the reasons Kat does such a good job is that her dancers know she'll take the fall for a problem rather than place blame, but she deserves loyalty in return." He glanced at Kat, those wintery green eyes of his warm in a way that made her hot. "You got a few minutes?"

Yes. Yes. Yes. She desperately wanted to know how his meeting went with the studio. "We're about to call lunch so it's perfect timing." Kat's gaze returned to Tabitha's. "Let's skip that second meeting with Ellie, Tabitha. You're talented, and I look forward to helping you shine, but as one of the stars of the show, I need you to be a positive leader."

Tabitha crossed her arms in front of her. "I will be."

The statement was wrapped in barely contained resentment and Kat mentally sighed. No. She wouldn't. But with any luck Tabitha now hated her more than

Marissa, and would focus her anger Kat's way. At least then poor Marissa could catch a break.

"You should go eat, Tabitha," Kat said. "We have a long afternoon ahead."

Tabitha gave a little lift of her chin and headed back toward the stage entrance.

Jason let out a soft whistle the instant Tabitha was out of view. "You weren't joking about that one. She's a problem."

"She and Carrie had a spat on stage. It wasn't pretty but most importantly—" she lowered her voice though they were alone "—I've been worried sick all morning."

"Everything is fine, baby," he said gently. "I told you not to worry."

"What's your definition of 'fine'?"

He grinned. "I convinced them I'm not a lush."

"Oh, God, Jason, tell me they didn't actually call you that?"

"Might as well have," he said, "but in the end, surprise surprise, they're pleased to report that website hits for the *Stepping Up* site tripled last night. Free advertising at our expense. Which reminds me, we need to get your parents on a vacation and out of town before the bloodhounds find them."

Kat nodded. She wasn't eager for them to take off when she'd only just arrived, but she'd already figured out how much traveling meant to her mother. "I think that's a good idea."

"I was hoping you'd say that. I bought them tickets to visit my parents in Thailand this morning but I didn't want to send them over until you gave me the okay. I didn't think they'd take the gift if it wasn't framed as a job. Not with the pride thing your dad has going on right now."

Her lips parted with her surprise. "Jason, you didn't have to do that."

"Yes, I did. I made public the one time in your father's life he ever had a meltdown. I got together with my investment guy as well and he'll meet with them tomorrow, before they head to the airport."

Kat blinked at him, speechless for a moment. Without her father's craziness in that casino, Jason would never had ended up in the news, but he didn't blame her father. He blamed himself. "Fame hasn't changed you. I don't know why, but it hasn't."

"I'm still the same guy who can't stand this close to you without wanting to kiss you."

Her knees felt weak again. He had a way of doing that to her. "And I'm apparently the same ol' Kat who likes that about you." Her lips curved. "Except, of course, when I'm trying to resist you."

"And are you?" he asked. "Trying to resist me?"

"If I knew what was good for both of us, I would be," she said. "But no. I'm not. Whatever is going to be, is going to be."

The door burst open from the stage area and voices filled the hallway as the dancers rushed forward. Ellie had clearly called for a lunch break.

"Let's make a run for lunch before some other crisis stops us." He motioned toward the direction Carrie and her man had headed out.

"I'm all for that," Kat said, rushing down the hall with him.

They were in the hotel and almost at the diner when

they heard Ellie calling after them. "Kat! Jason! Wait. Wait. I need you two."

"So close to escaping," Jason whispered.

Kat laughed and turned with him to greet Ellie. "What's going on?"

Ellie jerked to a halt in front of them. "That tabloid website 'Truth' just posted a story about the two of you being married. The minute we broke for lunch and the cast and crew cranked up their smartphones, the news was out. We have to figure out what to say about it."

Jason glanced at Kat. "I don't know about you, but I'm starving. I say we go eat. I need to talk to both of you about a nightclub promotion the hotel wants us to do anyway."

"I'm all for lunch," Kat agreed. "How about you, Ellie?"

Ellie gaped at them. "That's it? You two want to eat lunch? Aren't you worried about this?"

Jason shrugged. "The studio knows we're exes. It's not a secret. And it's certainly not taboo. You married one of our producers. Darla married the host of *Stepping Up*."

"So, do nothing?" Ellie asked, looking distressed by that idea.

"Besides tell anyone who asks that it's true and to focus on a rapidly approaching opening night?" Jason said. "Yes. Nothing. This only has the wings we give it."

Ellie's gaze flickered between them. "You're positive?"

Kat glanced at Jason, who gave a firm, "Yes. Positive."

Kat couldn't help but hope he was right.

12

SEVERAL HOURS LATER, Jason was finally through with the studio heads and media damage control, and could get to work on his real job of directing. He sauntered into the theater and headed to the front row seating where a table was set up for staff. Kat and Ellie stood center stage, talking with the script manager, while dancers prepared to work through the opening scene of the show. Seeing Kat up there, doing what she loved, back in his life, felt right like nothing else had in a very long time.

He settled into the chair on the end of the row, next to his assistant director Ronnie Wilks, a young film school graduate that was quickly building an impressive resume.

"How's it going, Bossman?" Ronnie asked, turning his Texas Longhorns hat backward and running his hand down his jeans-clad leg.

"As fine as any day in the tabloids can go," Jason replied dryly.

"That's what you get for being famous," Ronnie joked.

Only it wasn't a joke to Jason. It was reality, and one he was ready to leave behind. "Let's make this show the star," Jason commented. "Not me." He motioned to the computer on the desk. "Do we have the schedule drafted for tomorrow? We need to be fully blocked and on to polishing by next week."

Jason and Ronnie talked through their plans briefly before the entire cast of more than a hundred filed into the theater and filled the seating across the aisle from Jason and his crew. The energy in the room changed almost immediately, the glances between Jason and Kat impossible to miss.

Ronnie called out a list of names to ensure everyone who was supposed to be on stage was, and then leaned in close to Jason. "You and Kat sure know how to shake things up. Talk about an armadillo in the room."

"An armadillo?" Jason asked, arching a brow.

"That's the Texas version of an elephant in the room."

"I get it," Jason said, and he knew Kat felt it. She was stiff on the stage, and tension radiated from her. "It'll pass."

Apparently Kat didn't think so. She grabbed a microphone. "I need everyone's attention, please. We have a show to get ready and everyone appears to be distracted. So let's just cut to the chase and get focused. The answer to all the whispered questions is that yes, Jason is my ex-husband, and yes, we're dating. And finally, yes, Jason was with my father last night when a group of reporters did some creative story building. Any questions?"

Jason saw his producer choke on a drink and silence zipped through the room as if she'd hit the mute on a remote control. Ah, his KandyKat. She had a way of making a point. Jason scrubbed his jaw and laughed— because really, what else could he do?—and then he leaned across the table and grabbed a microphone of his own. "I have a question…"

It was late that evening and Jason and Kat sat with her parents at their kitchen table. Dinner was darn good lasagna that Hank was finally well enough to enjoy, and the past twenty-four hours had given them plenty to laugh at.

"So we're standing at the diner and I told Ellie that we weren't going to make any announcement," Jason said, recounting the moment when they'd discovered the tabloids had found out he and Kat were exes. "And we all agreed and went to eat lunch. The next thing I know, I'm sitting in a theater with the entire cast and crew, with the whispers and gossip buzzing around the room. So what does Kat do? She finds a microphone and says, 'I need everyone's attention, please.'"

Hank laughed and Sheila went, "Uh-oh."

Jason laughed and speared a tomato. "Exactly what I said. Uh-oh."

"What was I supposed to do, Jason?" Kat asked. "The dancers kept whispering to themselves. Nothing was getting done. We needed focus."

"What'd you do, Kitten?" Hank asked Kat.

Kat motioned to Jason. "Oh, let him tell you. He started this story."

"Don't mind if I do," Jason agreed. "Kat proceeded

to make her version of a public service announcement that went something like this. 'Yes, Jason is my ex-husband, and yes, we're dating. And yes, he was with my father last night when a group of reporters did their creative story building. Any questions?'"

Sheila gasped and covered her mouth and Hank chuckled. "Were there any questions?"

"Surely no one had the nerve to ask a question," Sheila replied, dropping her hand from her mouth.

Kat's eyes flashed at Jason. "Oh, yes. Someone did." She pointed at Jason.

"Oh, God," Sheila murmured. "What did you ask?"

Jason shrugged. "I asked if anyone had an aspirin or maybe ten."

Hank and Sheila both laughed. "Then what?" Sheila asked, laughing now herself, and wiping tears from her eyes.

"Everyone laughed but me," Jason said. "I was serious. I had a damn tequila headache, no thanks to you, Hank."

"Did you get your aspirin?" Sheila asked.

"I didn't even get a Tic Tac," he complained. "But everyone seemed to get focused and do their job after that."

"Oh, good," Sheila said. "I hope that means last night is behind you two."

Kat's questioning eyes found Jason's, and he answered with a quick nod. She grabbed her purse and removed the plane tickets. "Jason and I were talking and we think the press is going to keep coming at us, and you."

"So I called my parents today," Jason added. "They

invited you both to come visit them and see what they do in Thailand."

Kat placed the tickets on the table, hopeful her father wouldn't let his pride over the bad investments get in the way of this trip. "You leave tomorrow and we bought a non-refundable package deal. The money is spent. You might as well enjoy the trip."

"We can't take those tickets," Hank said quickly. "No. We can't. It's too much money."

"The money is spent, Dad," Kat said. "So either you take the trip or the money goes to waste."

"I know why you're doing this," Hank said, his gaze meeting Jason's. "And no. I told Sheila everything. We'll meet your investment expert, but we won't take charity."

Jason slid his plate aside and leaned forward. "Nick— that's my investment expert—is expecting you at ten in the morning. Your flight is at two. The trip is a gift from myself and Kat, for all the love and support you showed us both while we worked to build our careers. A gift that pleases us both very much to give you."

Jason watched Sheila and Hank look at each other. He took Kat's hand under the table as they waited for a response. "You think we can get teaching jobs there?"

Jason hesitated and glanced at Kat. He knew she was excited to be back with her parents, but she gave a nod of her head, her approval. "I know you can."

Sheila glanced at Hank, who said, "You really want to do this, don't you?"

She nodded. "I do."

He hesitated, seeming to struggle with his pride before letting out a breath. "Okay then. We'll go."

Sheila clapped and hugged him before rushing to

Jason and Kat for hugs as well. "My parents want us to call them on Skype," Jason announced when things finally settled down.

A few minutes later, after dialing up his parents, Kat and Jason left Sheila and Hank in front of the computer, talking excitedly about their trip.

Jason followed Kat to the wooden deck off the back of her parents' house. "Our families have always gotten along as well as we did," Jason commented, sitting down on the wooden swing next to Kat. The sky was clear, the moon full, the stars bright, and the cool breeze off the mountain a perfect temperature on what could have been a hot night.

"They did," Kat said, glancing at him. "They do. I'm excited they're going on this trip." She angled her body toward him, lacing her fingers in his. "Thank you for making this happen for them."

"There's a lot of things we can do for them, Kat," he said. "For both of our families. It's what we always wanted. What we talked about."

She drew a deep breath, shadows dancing in her eyes. "We did. Yes."

He drew their joined hands to his mouth and kissed her knuckles. "We didn't get here the way we wanted to, but we're here, nonetheless."

"Yes," she said, shifting away from him, her gaze lifting to the sky. "We're here now."

His gut clenched. She didn't have to say more for him to read the subtext that said, "But for how long?", before she added, "I believed we'd really make all of those things happen, too."

"So did I."

She turned back to him, her soft fingers trailing over his jaw. "I know you did."

"We let distance exist where it shouldn't have."

"There wasn't a way around it," she said. "One of us would get a job offer when the other was already committed and we both would know it was too good to pass up. And if one of us missed an opportunity and never got another that good, or big, it would have fed resentment." She shook her head. "We couldn't have done anything but what we did."

Guilt twisted inside Jason because he knew he'd had opportunities to put Kat first, to turn down work that in hindsight hadn't moved his dreams along. Not only had they not been the best career moves, he'd lost the person he wanted to share his dreams with. He'd lost her.

"We did a lot of things wrong, Kat—I did a lot of things wrong—but they molded me, and us, into the people we are now. We can't change those things but we can use them to make a better future."

"I don't want to think about the future. When I do that, I think about a time limit, because we always have one. I want to think about right now. I just want to enjoy what time we have."

Jason fought the urge to argue, to demand she see his sincerity, his regret, his love. They had years of pain and separation, years of built-up emotions.

"Kat—" he started.

"Jason!" Sheila called. "Your mother wants to talk to you."

Jason silently cursed the bad timing, needing to tell Kat how much he loved her.

"They're all excited and that's because of you," Kat

said, and leaned in to kiss him. "Now is good, Jason. Now is what I want to live." She got to her feet and pulled him up with her, motioning to the door.

TWO HOURS LATER, Jason parked Kat's rental car in his garage and got out. He would have rounded the car to get Kat's door, but she was out before he could make it. He met her at the hood of the car.

"I should have gone to my place and picked up some clothes."

Jason kept his expression unchanged and said, "Why would you do that?"

"Well I…I thought I was staying here."

He shook his head and wrapped her in his arms. "I'm packing a bag to stay with you, if you'll have me."

"What? Why? We're here."

"Because I've made you believe my world is more important than yours and it's not."

"No," she said, her fingers curling in his shirt. "I don't think that."

"Well," he said, "I'm just going to make sure you don't feel that now and I know I can't expect to prove that to you overnight. So I'm going to make a deal with you, or I hope I am, if you'll agree." He brushed the hair from her eyes. "I'll stay with you until I leave for the auditions. We'll live in the present. Then, Kat, when I'm back next month, when you know I'm really back, I'm going to ask you to marry me again."

Shock slid over her face. "Jason—"

He kissed her, and her moment of resistance melted into a soft, sensual joining of tongues.

"Don't respond," he said. "I'll take the living in the 'now' if that's what you want. But know this. I hope the 'now' is still going on in fifty years."

13

WEEKS LATER, KAT stood inside a busy, oversized dressing room, where a group of twenty dancers, as well as makeup, hair and costume people, were preparing for a live television special inside the hotel's Blue Moon nightclub, with Jason and a list of special superstar guests hosting. Kat knew the guest list, but few of the others did, for security reasons.

Nicole Smith, a rising star who'd been an opening act for Marcus on Kat's last tour, would be there. The idea was to promote the stage show and the new season of *Stepping Up*. The TV show would begin auditions in a week, and Jason would leave with it.

Kat's fingers tightened on the clipboard she held. She told herself to stop thinking about "the end" when it came to her and Jason. Over and over, she had to remind herself to enjoy what time they had together, not to regret living outside the present.

"I need my female understudies now," Kat shouted into the room. Three excited dancers rushed forward.

Kat felt they'd earned their own special moment on stage, and choreographed a unique performance for them.

Kat frowned as her fourth dancer failed to appear. "Where's Marissa?"

The room turned to a murmur with shouts for Marissa randomly being heard, but Marissa simply wasn't present.

"She's been gone a good half an hour," one of the hairdressers commented. "She got a phone call and left."

"Kat!"

Kat turned at the sound of Ellie's voice behind her. "We have a problem," Ellie said, entering the room.

"What problem?" Aside from Marissa being nowhere to be found, Kat thought grimly.

"Marissa says she's too sick to dance," Ellie said, as if replying to Kat's unspoken concerns.

"I can fill in for her," Tabitha said, stepping into the room, dressed in sweats and a tee. "Kate taught me the routine."

Why would Tabitha have one of the understudies teach her this routine? Warning bells went off in Kat's head, and her gaze brushed Ellie's. The look on the other choreographer's face told her that Ellie heard those bells as well.

"Where's Marissa?" Kat asked Ellie, repeating her earlier question to someone who hopefully could give her an answer.

"In the bathroom right off the stage," Ellie said. "She says she can't come out without throwing up." She laughed without humor. "I asked her if she was pregnant." She held up a hand. "Don't worry. She said she isn't." Her gaze brushed the three dancers' skimpy outfits. "And a good thing in those outfits. Yowza, they're sexy." She sighed and rubbed her stomach. "I better cut back on the chocolate or I'll never be able to wear anything but a clown costume again."

Tabitha snorted. "That doesn't stop a few dancers I know from indulging."

Kat's gaze flicked to Tabitha, who'd just barely contained her nastiness to Marissa since their talk a month before. Kat had heard a few too loudly spoken remarks from Tabitha and her slender frame compared to Marissa's more Kim Kardashian-type figure, not to know who she was talking about. "How did you know to be here, Tabitha? You were off tonight."

"Marissa called me and told me she needed me to fill in for her."

"Marissa called you," Kat said flatly, her gaze boring into Tabitha's. She didn't believe her, not for a New York minute. She watched the young dancer, waiting for her to break under scrutiny, but quickly surmised that wasn't going to happen. Tabitha was an ice witch, after fame at all costs. Kat was pretty sure Marissa was the one paying, or she would be, if Kat let it happen. Kat glanced at Ellie. "Jason wants the featured dancers on stage to meet Nicole before we go live."

"Should I get into costume?" Tabitha called from behind Kat.

Kat turned at the door, grinding her teeth at that question because her gut said that Tabitha was up to no good. "Yes," she said, pausing. "As a precautionary measure."

Kat headed out of the dressing room and double-timed it down the narrow hallway, pausing to the shout of her name at least four times in a short distance. Finally, Kat managed to make it to a small private bathroom just off the stage door, and she knocked on the wooden door.

"Marissa?"

"Yes," she said immediately and Kat could hear the stuffy nose and gravely voice that could be from sickness, as easily as they could be a product of tears. "I'm here."

"Can you open the door?" Kat asked.

"No. No. I'm sick and I don't want to make you get sick. Opening night is coming."

Kat frowned. "Marissa, what's going on? You weren't sick an hour ago."

"I was," she said. "I was hiding it. I tried so hard to hide it."

Kat didn't believe her. She just didn't. "If you're sick then let's get you to your room. Open up, Marissa. I can't go deal with the show knowing you might pass out in there and be seriously ill."

"Kat, I'm fine. I am. Please go do the show."

"I can't do that, Marissa," Kat said, testing the theory bouncing around in her head. "I know Tabitha has something to do with this."

There was a telling silence before Marissa said, "I'm sick. I really am sick."

Oh, man, Kat thought. Marissa wasn't sick. Kat had been right. Tabitha was up to no good. "Let me in and let's talk."

"You have to go do the show."

"So do you," Kat said. "This is your dream, Marissa." Silence. "Open up, honey. We need to talk." More silence and then the lock on the door popped. Marissa appeared in the doorway with mascara dripping down her pale cheeks, her eyes red, her hair a dark, rumpled mess of curls.

Kat stepped into the bathroom and urged Marissa back inside. "Talk to me, Marissa."

Marissa hugged herself. "This just isn't for me, Kat," she said, bypassing the sick excuse.

"Funny," Kat said. "It sure looks like it's for you when you're dancing."

"I…" She hesitated, her lip quivering. "No. I…don't think so."

"You do know that Tabitha wouldn't waste her time taunting you if she wasn't intimidated, right?"

Marissa cut her gaze away.

"Marissa," Kat said softly. "Talk to me."

She looked at Kat. "I don't like the nastiness," she said. "It's not who I am or what I'm made of."

"You're talking about Tabitha," Kat said, and it wasn't a question.

"It's not just Tabitha," Marissa said. "It's a lot of people in this business."

"That's true," Kat said. "I've dealt with my share of egos, but I've met big stars who were humble, and who did good things for others with the rewards of their success, too. I focus on those people."

"I just want to dance, Kat," she said. "I don't want to play the popularity contest. I don't want to be threatened and bullied."

"Wait. Who threatened you?"

"It doesn't matter."

"It does matter. Who threatened you?"

"It wasn't really a threat. Not directly." She bent down and pulled something from a bag on the floor, a newspaper clipping, and held it out to Kat.

Kat took it and read the headline, about a robbery ten years before, and glanced up at Tabitha. "What does this have to do with you?"

"My father," she said. "My mother had a heart condition and we didn't have the money for her medical care. He tried to rob a bank. He's out now and rebuilding his life. It would destroy him to have this all over the paper and it would be a scandal for the show."

Kat's heart squeezed. "Your mother?"

"Died six months after he went to prison." Her voice cracked. "So you see why I can't go on."

"No," Kat said, knowing now why she liked Marissa, and even felt protective of her. Marissa was a sweet girl and a good person. "I see a reason for you to do this show and rise to the top. Tonight comes with a big paycheck and a whole lot of exposure."

"I know but—"

"Did you call Tabitha to take your spot?"

"Yes."

"Because she gave you this clipping, didn't she?" Kat asked, holding up the paper.

Marissa looked to the ground.

"That means yes," Kat said, furious now. "Are you willing to write a statement about what happened tonight?"

Her eyes went wide. "No. Kat, no. If I do that she'll call the tabloids and turn this into a nightmare."

"She's not dancing tonight in your place," Kat said, "so I suggest you get to hair and makeup and then meet me on stage in fifteen minutes. We'll head to the club from there."

"I can't do this, Kat."

"You can," she said. "And by doing so you'll make a better life for you and your father. There will always be a bully in everything you do. That's life. Face this down and fight for your dream. No one else can do it for you." Kat hugged her. "Fix your face so no one knows you were crying and head to the dressing room. I'll see you on stage for some last-minute instructions before we head to the club."

Kat didn't give her time to say no. She exited the bathroom, quickly heading out onto the stage. She was already walking toward the group standing in the center when she stopped dead in her tracks.

"Marcus," Kat croaked at the sight of the tall, dark and good-looking, incredibly famous pop singer—the ex she hadn't told Jason about.

"There's my tigress," Marcus said and then rolled his tongue. "Surprise, baby. Somebody had the flu so I'm filling in. I came to help give you a grand opening."

The old saying "you could hear a pin drop" had never been so true. The room had just learned what she'd failed to tell Jason and what Marcus clearly assumed everyone already knew—that she and Marcus had dated. Everyone but Marcus understood the implications of Jason and Marcus standing there side by side. Kat's gaze went to Jason's and she saw the hurt in his face.

Someone called his name from below the stage. "Jason! We need you at the club. We have a problem."

"Kat," Jason said, and there was no mistaking the tightness in his voice. "Marcus is going to perform for us tonight. He says you know the number and he only needs one dancer. *You.* I'll leave you all to talk this out." He turned away without another word.

Kat's gaze went to Marcus's dark brown stare, the rest of the room fading away. "That, Marcus, would be my ex-husband I told you about."

His eyes went wide. "Jason is your ex? Oh damn, Kat. You never told me his name. I'm sorry."

"I know," she said, already in motion to follow Jason. Marcus wasn't the type of person to start trouble. In fact, he hated people who were. This was her fault for not telling Jason. It was past history, and it just hadn't seemed important.

Kat caught up to him. "Jason, wait. Please."

"Now is not a good time for this, Kat," he said without looking at her.

"I love you, Jason."

"Just not enough," he said. "That's the part I never seem to get."

She grabbed his arm forcing him to stop walking. "That's not true."

He turned to her. "I get the math, Kat. You left Denver and went to him."

"No," she said, shaking her head. "I hadn't even met Marcus when we were in Denver."

"Jason," Kevin, one of the production assistants, shouted running down the hall toward them. "Camera one blew. I'm trying to move in another one but I'm having trouble with the club manager."

Desperation expanded inside of Kat, tightening her throat. "I know now isn't the time for this, but please tell me you'll give me a chance to explain."

He stared at her a hard two seconds and turned away without an answer. A vise tightened on her chest. Kat couldn't watch him leave. Taking action was the only way to fix this.

She made a beeline to the bathroom and knocked. "Marissa, if you're in there, open up now."

Marissa appeared almost instantly. "Come with me," Kat said. "You're going to dance with Marcus tonight and I need you to learn the routine."

"Marcus? As in the amazingly hot pop star Marcus?"

"I wouldn't say amazingly hot," came Marcus's voice from behind Kat and she would have laughed if not for the fact that she wanted to cry. Marcus wasn't conceited. In fact, he was as perfect a guy as anyone could want, minus one important detail. He wasn't Jason.

14

AFTER SENDING MARISSA to the costume department and getting Marcus to the right person to fit him with a microphone, Kat headed to the stage where Ellie, Tabitha and the three other featured dancers were still congregating.

"Tabitha," Kat said, already with a plan in mind. "You're dancing for Marissa." She glanced at Ellie. "Marissa will be dancing with Marcus, so I'm going to be working with them to get ready. Can you please make sure they have Marcus performing last?"

"Done," Ellie said, her eyes alight with interest at the announcement. "He's already set up to be the final guest so we can tease the audience with a surprise coming at the end of the show. So, you're not dancing with Marcus?"

"No," Kat confirmed. "I'm not dancing with Marcus."

"Why is Marissa dancing with Marcus?" Tabitha demanded, her hands on her hips. "I'm the one the audience already knows."

"Marcus is the one the audience already knows," Kat corrected, hoping she was teaching Tabitha a lesson about how doing things wrong wasn't going to get her to the top. "And why are you not in your costume yet?" Tabitha looked like she might argue, but decided against it and hightailed it off the stage.

Ellie motioned to the remaining dancers. "You three, go get on your Egyptian robes and make sure the others are lined up at the exit door." The robes fit into the theme of their first pop star's performance. It was the beginning of a big show with a grand entry. So big and intensive to put together that Kat was thankful Jason had given everyone the next day off. She glanced at her watch. "We have ten minutes until we do the dramatic walk across the hotel to the club in the west wing."

The dancers scurried away, whispering with nerves and excitement about being in throne-like chairs carried by other dancers.

"Try not to fall out of those chairs," Ellie yelled after them. "I'm too pregnant to catch you." They laughed and disappeared.

Kat and Ellie stepped closer to one another. "You're taking a risk with Marissa." Ellie sounded concerned. "All eyes will be on Marcus's performance. Are you sure she's ready for this?"

"All eyes will be on Marcus," Kat repeated, "not Marissa. And Marcus won't let her look bad. He's a nice guy. He'll take care of her."

"A nice guy, but not the *right* guy," Ellie said, reading between the lines.

"Exactly," Kat agreed, and in a rare moment of spilling her personal baggage, she added, "It's killing me that Jason thinks there's something going on with me and Marcus."

"It sure seemed that way," she pointed out grimly. "Marcus greeted you like his girlfriend. And let's face it, Marcus is one of the few men that could make someone as confident and sexy as Jason feel insecure. It's not a good combination."

"Thank you for the words of encouragement," Kat said, feeling as if a knife had just torn through her chest. Jason was confident, and jealousy had never been a problem for them, but this wasn't exactly a normal situation.

Ellie squeezed Kat's arm. "I'm just being honest. But honey, dancing with Marcus would have been the kiss of death with Jason if I'm reading him right. You're doing what you have to and not only does it show you love him, you sure as heck have my respect for this. Not many people would pass up the spotlight for a relationship."

She didn't want the spotlight. She never had. She wanted Jason. "I just hope it matters to Jason."

"It will," Ellie said with a firm nod. "I'm sure it will. How can it not?" The door to the stage burst open and dancers filed in. A rush of activity took over the room. Ellie's eyes lit up. "Here we go. The beginning of something grand, I hope."

Fifteen minutes later, the dancers were gone, and only Kat, Marcus and Marissa were left on the stage. Forty-five minutes after that, Kat was feeling pretty darn good about Marissa's performance and she knew Marcus well enough to know he approved as well.

"You learn fast," Marcus complimented Marissa.

"Consider yourself invited to join my next tour." Marcus winked at Kat. "That is, if I can steal you away from your boss here."

Marissa didn't jump up and down, and didn't scream with the excitement others would have. She paled instantly, as if she had just received bad news. "I hope you still feel that way after the show."

Marcus arched a brow in Kat's direction, seemingly surprised at the nervous gulp. She gave him a quick nod, her look meant to tell him that she thought a lot of Marissa. He returned the nod, and his gaze settled back on Marissa, his expression softening. Kat knew how Marcus struggled with the insincerity of the people around him, and how everyone wanted a piece of him. And she knew right then that he saw what she did in Marissa.

"I need to check on the rest of show," Kat said, wondering if Marissa might be just the woman Marcus needed. "You two keep working."

Kat exited the stage area and smiled at the romantic door she'd just opened, if not for the door Jason had shut on her tonight. She regretted not telling him about Marcus, but the truth was that it hadn't seemed important. Marcus had been more a friend than a lover. They'd both been riding the bumpy path of heartache, trying to fill a hole in their lives. She'd simply been a little more ready to admit it than he had been that their relationship hadn't filled the hole.

Jason's words replayed in her mind. *Not enough,* he'd said about her loving him. She'd said those exact words to herself about him before she'd left Denver for Marcus's tour. She knew what they meant, and she knew they came with great pain. Her stomach knotted with fear that he might have sealed the door shut forever.

Kat had just reached the cluster of empty dressing rooms when the door from the main hotel was shoved open. Tabitha hobbled inside with Joe, one of the production assistants, holding her up, one knee bent to keep her foot off the ground.

"What happened?" Kat asked, rushing toward them.

Tabitha sobbed, but there were no tears, which struck Kat as odd. "I fell off the podium."

"There's a doctor on the way," Joe said as the three of them made their way into the closest dressing room.

Tabitha sat down in a chair and buried her face in her hands. "I can't believe this is happening."

"Ellie said she has to have her replaced and quickly," Joe said. "The empty podium is obvious to the cameras."

Right, of course it was, and when Marcus performed, the four dancers would do a lead-in routine and then freeze frame, like mannequins. That would leave the podium obviously open if Marissa tried to do both dances.

Kat studied Tabitha, pretty darn certain that Tabitha was up to no good. "You're sure your ankle is too bad to dance on?"

Tabitha let her hands drop to her lap for a moment and her eyes met Kat's. "Positive." Kat saw an instant of hatred in the other woman's expression that was quickly replaced by a sob and crinkled-up expression. "Yessssss." A whimper followed and she buried her face in her hands again.

Kat ground her teeth and stood up. She had no doubt

Tabitha intended for Marissa to miss her moment in the spotlight with Marcus, and she was done trying. She'd have to proceed cautiously so Tabitha couldn't say she was being fired for getting hurt on the job, but nevertheless, Tabitha had just sealed her exit from the show. No one here had time for these kinds of manipulative games. Kat pushed to her feet, her mind racing with options, searching for an answer that didn't leave her dancing with Marcus again.

"HI, BOSS."

Jason heard Kat's voice in his earpiece through the mic system he used with his crew. Nearby, music blasted through the speakers as a pop singer named Stacey P performed. He stood by the stage, and despite the rowdy crowd that was more sardines in a can than an audience, he knew without looking the instant she was beside him. He could feel her there, as he always could feel her.

He cut her a sideways look, taking in the skimpy outfit she wore that matched that of the other three featured dancers, cursing the tightening of his body at the sight. He wasn't surprised at how hot she looked, but he was surprised she'd chosen an outfit to match the other dancers, rather than something special for Marcus's performance.

That thought had him grinding his teeth, and about breaking his jaw from the force. It was eating him alive to think about Kat rehearsing with Marcus, about her performing with Marcus, about her kissing him.

"I need Tabitha or Marissa on that podium at commercial," he said into his mic.

"You got me instead," she said, "and I'm on my way. I'll be where you need me to be."

"How are you going to cover your spot on the podium and be where Marcus needs you?"

"Marissa is dancing with Marcus," she said. "Not me, Jason." She cut around him, her hand discreetly brushing his back, until she was on the opposite side of him, and staring up at him to repeat. "Not me." Their eyes held a moment, and more than music thrummed through his body. Every emotion he'd ever felt for Kat was there, too, twisting him into knots.

"Thirty seconds to commercial," one of his people said into their ears.

Kat turned away immediately, darting through the crowd, and when the song ended, he wasn't watching the famous singer on stage. He was watching Kat, who had taken the podium in a skimpy outfit that was getting plenty of male attention. But not Marcus's.

She wasn't dancing with him now. It should have made Jason feel better. So why did he still feel as if he'd lost something valuable?

Jason didn't have time to analyze it. He had to be on stage himself, acting as if nothing bothered him. He didn't like the on-camera work, and he wasn't a host. This judging stuff had spun out of control, as had this night. But he'd agreed to all of this for a reason. To make this show work, and to create an opportunity where he and Kat could stay in one place together.

Jason headed to the stage, greeting the singer, and exchanging some banter with her for the audience and the cameras. And when he and Stacey P, a pretty blond singer most men would kill to be with, stepped off the stage to allow Marcus to claim it, she stayed by his side.

"So, Jason," she said, leaning in close, her hand settling on his arm. "I'm in town through tomorrow if you want to get together later tonight."

Jason knew just about every man watching this show would say yes to the offer, but he'd been there, done that, and didn't give a damn about the shirt. Nothing, and no one, replaced Kat. Jason politely declined and fortunately had directorial duties to attend that made escape easy. From Stacey that was. There was no escaping Kat, and after what he'd learned tonight, that was about as hard to swallow as it got. One way or the other, tonight, this was it for his relationship with Kat. He was in or he was out for good.

KAT HAD STOOD on the podium, after striking her mannequin-like pose, while Marcus and Marissa performed brilliantly. She felt like a proud mama watching Marissa coming out of her shell, showing her talent to the world.

When the number ended, Jason stepped onto the stage with Marcus and Kat felt her hopes fall and land hard. She knew how awkward this moment was for Jason, and she feared what Marcus, even with good intentions, might say.

But the moment came and went quickly. Jason said goodnight to television land and shook Marcus's hand. The crowd shouted and chanted for Marcus to sing another song and he agreed.

"Cut," Jason said into the microphone feed. "We are

off air. Dancers, hold your positions for Marcus's final number. Kat, Marissa is headed up there to replace you."

It wasn't long before Kat was giving Marissa a quick hug and stepping to the top level of the club, only to find Jason standing there waiting for her. He took her hand and pulled her down a hallway, around a corner and against a wall. His hand rested by her head.

"Do you have any idea how I'm feeling right now?"

Kat wanted to wrap her arms around him and tell him how sorry she was, but she knew Jason. She knew he needed words, he needed understanding. "He is a friend."

"Don't patronize me, Kat. I saw how he looked at you, and more so, I saw your face when you saw him."

"You saw dread," she said, her heart beating so fast it was making it hard to talk. "Not happiness."

"And why exactly would you feel dread if a friend was here to help, Kat? You went from my bed to his."

"It wasn't like that," Kat said. "I told you. I barely knew Marcus before I started the tour. And yes, I dated him. I was trying to get over you, Jason."

"I wasn't trying to get over you, Kat," he said. "I was trying to reach you. I was trying to get you back in my life."

"I dated him, Jason. It meant nothing. Come on. You dated that one Hollywood actress for months and there was talk of marriage. How do you think that made me feel?"

"I never once talked marriage with her," he said. "I never even thought about it. I didn't marry her. I married you."

"And I didn't marry Marcus," she said, knowing the statement had been a mistake before it even left her lips.

"He asked you to marry him?"

She'd never lied to Jason, never wanted to, until this moment, but she wouldn't. She couldn't. "I didn't marry him, Jason. I married you."

"Did he ask you to marry him?"

"Yes, but——"

He cursed and shoved off the wall, giving her his back.

"Jason, he wasn't you——"

He whirled around and leaned in close again, his hand back on the wall. "Let me guess. You convinced him to keep it all about sex."

"No——"

"We're done, Kat. I'm done. You've had a decade of my life in some way, shape or form. That's enough."

He left her standing there, gone before she could say a word, and it was all she could do to not chase him. Making a scene wouldn't help anything. Worse though, she didn't think anything would help. He'd never before said he was done with her.

Truthfully, they'd never had a fight like this. A spat, a disagreement, a little thing, yes. But nothing like this and that alone said everything.

He meant what he'd said. He was done.

15

MARCUS'S NEW SONG broke through the haze of Kat's shock and she came back to the present. Jason's words had devastated her. How long had she been paralyzed against the wall? She didn't know. She just knew it hurt, she hurt. Her heart raced wildly and she drew a deep breath and let it out slowly, forcing herself to calm down.

"Pull yourself together," she whispered. She had to be professional, and deal with the cast and crew. She was supposed to relieve Ellie fully so she could rest. Ellie, who was pushing herself too hard. Ellie. Right. She marched back into the main bar, and wove through the crowd. She focused on her purpose, on taking care of Ellie.

"Ellie," Kat said, tapping the button that would allow the crew to hear her through the microphone. "Can you meet me in the dressing rooms?"

"On my way," Ellie said immediately.

A few minutes later Kat and Ellie were in a private dressing room, while Kat changed back into her clothes.

Ellie rubbed her increasingly large stomach. "So how are things with you and Jason?" she asked before grimacing. "Oh, wow. Not feeling so good. I need to sit."

Kat pulled her T-shirt over her head and grabbed a chair for Ellie. "Are you okay?"

Ellie sunk into the seat the instant it was behind her. "I've been feeling sick all day. I think it was the pressure of the show. Tonight's ratings will be looked at hard by the studio, and not just as a feeler for how the stage show will be received. They'll see tonight as a preview of interest for the third season of *Stepping Up.* Jason should have gotten a call about the ratings by now. I really—" She stiffened and made a funny face.

"Ellie, honey, what are you feeling? Was that pain?"

"It's nothing," she said dismissively. "The doctor said it's from ligaments stretching. It's normal."

"All the same, let's get you up to your room so you can lie down."

"Really, I'm fine," Ellie insisted. "I want to find out about tonight's ratings before I go upstairs."

"We'll call Jason from your room," Kat suggested. "Will that work?"

"You don't need to walk with me," Ellie said. "You stay and close things down here."

"I'm coming with you," Kat said, not pleased with how pale Ellie looked. She was worried. "And you don't know me well enough yet to understand this, so let me save us both some time. I'm stubborn as a mule and proud of it. You're going upstairs to rest."

Ellie laughed and then grimaced again. "Maybe I do need to rest." She stood up and swayed. Kat grabbed her arm and Ellie laughed without humor. "When was the last time I ate?"

"Too long ago if you have to ask," Kat chided. "Room service it is."

"Room service for sure," Ellie agreed, as she and Kat stepped into the hallway and directly into the path of Jason, his assistant director Ronnie, and several of his crew members.

Kat's eyes met his and awareness rushed over her, along with a huge dose of emotion. She cut her gaze away before she could see the rejection, the anger, and maybe something worse, that might be in Jason's expression. She'd have to manage this quickly to be professional on the job, but not tonight, not when this change between them had just happened. The hurt was too raw.

"Oh, good," Ellie said at the sight of Jason. "Talk to us, Jason. What's the ratings news?"

"Fifteen million viewers," he said. "A couple million over expectations."

It was an announcement Kat would normally have celebrated with Jason, but instead, she turned to Ellie. "See? Now can you rest?"

Ellie let out a breath. "Now I can rest."

Kat flicked a fleeting look in Jason's direction. "She's feeling sick. I'm taking her to her room and feeding her."

"We can finish up here," Jason said. "Ellie, you should slow down. Consider taking off the entire weekend like I told you to."

"I'm fine," Ellie insisted. "I just need food and bed."

One of the cameramen shouted Jason's name from behind them, and Jason turned to address the man. Kat took that opportunity to hustle Ellie toward the stage. "Let's exit through the theater to avoid running into anyone who might convince you something is going on you need to be involved with."

She laughed. "I guess you know me pretty darn well."

It wasn't until they were alone in the elevator that Ellie studied Kat. "What happened?"

Kat didn't pretend she didn't know what she was talking about. "We fought."

"Everyone fights, Kat."

She shook her head. "Not us, not like this."

"You want to talk about it?"

"I can't," Kat said. "Not without really losing it and I don't cry often, but when I do, I do it right. I'll be swollen up like a blowfish and I'll never get out of here without everyone knowing."

"You can stay with me tonight," she said. "Or you can have your own room a few doors down."

"Thank you, Ellie, but I need to be home tonight more than ever." Home was a place she hadn't felt she'd had in a long time, a place where she could retreat and deal with this.

The elevator dinged open. "I understand," Ellie said.

It didn't take long for Kat to get Ellie settled onto her bed and order room service. Ellie still felt dizzy and Kat offered the kitchen staff a big tip if they rushed the food. By the time she hung up, Ellie's husband David called and Kat felt awkward listening to them talk.

"I have to chat with Kat," Ellie told him.

Kat shook her head. "No. No, it's—"

"I'm off tomorrow. I'll sleep all day. I'm fine. I'll call you when I'm done eating."

Kat sunk down onto the mattress with Ellie and did something she never did. She interfered in Ellie's personal life. "What if *Stepping Up* decided to film in Vegas every season?"

"I'm sure you and Jason would be happy."

"I'm not talking about me and Jason," Kat said. "I'm talking about you."

Her expression sobered. "We've talked about it," she said. "It's only a few months every year."

"And the audition travel."

"The baby can go with me," she said, "and by the time she's in school, it won't be likely that this show will still be around. We'll make it work. We both know this job is our chance to retire young and just be with our kids and each other."

"That's what Jason and I said every time a big job came up that separated us. And before you say, you're close, you won't fall apart like the rest of us, we did, too. Look. Ellie. I regret our choices. I regret saying there might not be another opportunity. What there might not be is another shot at each other. Just…think about it. Be cautious. None of this matters without the person you love with you to share it."

A knock sounded at the door. Kat quickly paid for the food and sat down with Ellie to eat. Kat rolled the tray to the bed so Ellie could stay and rest.

Ellie sat up and uncovered her sandwich, staring down at it as Kat pulled the desk chair opposite the cart. "It's all very confusing," Ellie finally said, her eyes lifting to Kat's. "I hate being pregnant without him here and I make plenty of money for him to quit. But how can I ask him to give up his career for me?"

What could Kat say? She knew this dilemma like she knew her own name. Far too well. "Find a solution," she said, and poured ketchup on her plate. She was starving, which surprised her considering how knotted up she was over Jason.

They ate in silence for a short while before Ellie asked, "What would you do?"

The answer was immediate for Kat. "I don't know. I just know what I did do before didn't work."

"That doesn't help me."

"I know," Kat said. "But it's the only answer I have."

"I need more than that," she said. "Because when I see how you and Jason look at each other, I know how much you love each other. Yet, still this business tore you apart."

"Not this business," Kat said. "We did. We made our choices and we have no one to blame but ourselves."

IT WAS NEARLY two in the morning when Kat left Ellie's room, having spent a solid hour with her. Ellie wasn't in pain and Kat had left her in her bed and talking to her husband. Kat, however, wasn't feeling better. Not at all. Talking about her fears of losing her relationship only drove home where she and Jason were, which was in no place good.

Kat tracked a path past the club. Everything was back to normal and Marcus was no longer around. She'd thanked him for his help tonight when they'd been rehearsing with Marissa, but she owed him another one.

She didn't want to hurt Marcus. He was, and she hoped he always would be, a friend.

She was almost back at the theater to check on things and grab her purse before she left, when she heard Marcus call her name. She turned to find him hurrying toward her and met him at the entry to the dressing rooms.

"I have to head out early tomorrow," he said. "I've got an interview."

She felt his departure like sandpaper roughing up an already raw wound, and she didn't know why. Her eyes prickled and she fought back tears.

"Hey," he said softly, lifting her chin to see her face. "What's wrong, baby?"

"I'm…okay."

"No," he said. "You're not. I really screwed this up for you, didn't I?"

"I did," she said, pressing two fingers to her forehead. "I didn't tell him about you and…it's a mess but you aren't to blame."

"You're shaking, Kat," he said, drawing her hand into his. "I've never seen you like this. I messed this up. I'll talk to him."

"No," Kat said, pressing her hand to his chest to still him. "Please. No. He will not respond well to that."

"Kat, I caused this," he said. "I'll fix it."

"You didn't cause this, Marcus. I did."

"Kat—"

"Please, Marcus. I'm fine. And you are a wonderful friend I don't intend to lose. You came here tonight because of that friendship and—"

"I came here tonight because I still love you," he said. "But I'm no fool. I see exactly what you told me now. You love Jason. And I care enough for you to want you to be happy."

"You don't love me, Marcus. You'll see that when you really fall in love."

"You keep saying that."

"Deep down you know it, too. You love me but you are not *in love* with me."

"Is there a difference?"

"Yes," Kat said. "And I love you enough to hope that you find that out very soon. You deserve it."

He kissed her hand. "You're sure I can't—"

"Positive," she said. "I'm good. You just take care of you, okay?"

"I'm going to get something to eat. You want to come with me?"

She shook her head. "I need to go home."

"I'll call you," he said and kissed her forehead.

"You better," she insisted as he walked away. She was about to head into the dressing rooms when she spotted Marissa waiting nearby. Marcus stopped by her side and she smiled as she caught a glimpse of his expression. Maybe, just maybe, Marcus was on his way to falling in love sooner than later.

That smile faded as she walked through the dark hallway and felt the emptiness. Everyone was gone. Jason was gone.

She made the walk to the parking area and the shaking started again. Or maybe it had never ended. She pulled out of the garage and rain pounded her window. She ignored a fleeting thought that it was dangerous to drive this tired, and this upset, in this bad of a storm.

She turned up her wipers to see through the fury of the storm, determined to get home before she fell apart.

JASON NEEDED TO ride, needed the wind and feel of the motorcycle humming beneath him, the escape it gave him. He pulled out into the storm, refusing to stay at the casino for the night. He had a helmet and he had proper riding gear to survive fairly damage free, at least from the rain. He'd seen Kat with her hand pressed to Marcus's chest and it had done a good job of shredding him to the core.

That Kat had walked to her car alone and departed only seconds before him should have eased some of his ache, but somehow it only made it worse. No, what made it worse was how much he wanted to ignore what Denver told him, what her actions said loud and clear. That she didn't want what he did or it would have happened long before now. He and Marcus were two of a kind, fools for the same woman.

He pulled onto the highway, the rain blinding him, but he didn't stop. He pressed onward, following Kat's taillights, his mind following the path of their relationship over the past few weeks. He wanted to see Kat not dancing with Marcus as a sign of her love, but he knew Kat. She wouldn't do anything to intentionally hurt anyone. She'd skip the dance to keep from hurting him. And it would have hurt.

Thunder roared and lightning blasted through the darkness, followed by a loud pop. Holy crap, Kat's tire had just blown. His heart stopped beating as he watched her struggle for control and skid toward the ditch. Jason came to a halt, ripping off his helmet and leaving his bike at the side of the road. He could barely breathe with the fear of Kat being injured as he took off running.

16

THE CAR SLID down a slope and stopped halfway into a ditch. Kat sat there, frozen in place, afraid it wasn't really over. She didn't breathe, didn't blink. Suddenly, she was years in the past, back in the day that she and Jason had decided to divorce.

"Of course you have to take the job," Kat said, her chest tight with emotion, her voice strained as she tried to hide her disappointment that he wasn't joining her on her movie set at the end of the week as planned. "It's a huge opportunity. You'll be directing one of the biggest stars in Hollywood."

"It's filming in Paris, KandyKat," he said. "We've wanted to go there. I'll arrange to have you flown out. Just tell me the exact day and I'll arrange everything."

"No," she said. "No. I can't. I have the Ms. America Pageant to choreograph in a week. You know that. I took it because you were going to be free by then and we could be together. By the time I'd get there I'd have to leave."

"Kat—"

"It's just how it is, Jason. It's how it always is. I think... I think it's time we face reality."

"What are you talking about?"

"We just can't make marriage and our careers work."

"That's crazy," he said. "Yes, we can. I won't take the job. I'm coming there."

"I'm leaving early," she said. "The movie I've been working on wrapped."

"Kat—"

"It's time, Jason," she said. "We've battled this for years and spent more time apart than together. I just can't stand the idea that I hold you back."

"You don't hold me back. Stop this. Please. I love you. None of this matters without you. We planned this out. We'll take the hits now and retire early. We'll travel, then have kids."

"I love you, too," she whispered. "Too much to hold on to you like this no matter how much I want to."

"I'm holding on," he said. "I'll hold on tight enough for us both if I have to."

The car door jerked open.

"Kat!" Jason shouted, bending down beside her. "Kat, are you okay?"

"Yes." Kat could barely pry her vise-like grip from the steering wheel. "Yes, I'm okay. Just shaken up."

She turned toward him, letting her legs slide over the seat. Jason pulled her to her feet and into the rain before wrapping his powerful arms around her.

He brushed her hair from her face, inspecting her carefully. "You're sure? You don't hurt anywhere?"

She stared up at him, not caring about the storm,

the car, or the deserted highway. "Yes," she said. "My heart," she said. "My heart hurts because you—"

The next thing she knew, Jason's mouth came down on hers. She moaned and clung to him, the taste of him pouring through her, the rain pouring over her. There was a desperateness to the kiss she recognized as hers, as his, a hunger for each other that washed over Kat, filled her and gave her hope. No two people who felt this passionately for each other belonged apart. They had to make it work, they could make it work.

He tore his mouth from hers. "Let's get out of here," he said, taking her hand to help her up the slope to the highway, and she was far from complaining. She wanted to be alone with him, to talk to him, to be in his arms.

They ran to the motorcycle, where he wrapped his jacket around her. When he started to put his helmet on her as well she stopped him. "Wait," she said. "To your house. I want to go to your house." The idea of being somewhere he could walk away again was too much right now. She couldn't deal with that tonight.

He stared at her, unaffected by what seemed like gallons of water pouring over him before he raised the helmet again. She let him put it on her this time, wishing he would have replied, wishing she could say more, but the blasted rain stifled the conversation.

Kat watched him climb onto the Harley, and then took her spot behind him. *Her spot.* The place she'd ridden many times before. She leaned into him and wrapped her arms around him, the warmth of his body seeping through his now wet shirt, and right through to her soul. She held on, not for safety, but on to him, to the years that had led them here, to the past few weeks that had brought them back together. She'd known when they'd begun this project together that this was it, a new beginning or the end of their path together. And those years, those weeks, had come down to now. Whatever happened tonight really was it. But he was here with her, and he'd kissed her.

She clung to those things, telling her they meant something, right up until the second when she realized that Jason wasn't taking her to his house. He was taking her to her own home, where he would leave her and go to his. He'd meant his words back in that bar, when he'd told her he was done. She knew him and he'd never said anything like that to her.

When the bike stopped in her driveway, Jason shouted over his shoulder, "Garage door opener?"

No, she realized, with yet another kick in the teeth when she'd had too many already tonight. In the midst of the mess created by her raging emotions, she'd left her purse in the car. That meant her keys and her phone were also on the side of the road.

Kat pushed off of the bike and shoved Jason's jacket at him, then tugged off the helmet. "Thanks for the ride," she shouted over the engine and another loud roll of thunder from directly above them. "I'm fine from here." She took off running.

The backyard was Kat's target destination, and she prayed she'd left the sliding glass door open. But she didn't leave things unlocked any more than she normally left them in places they didn't belong, like the side of the road, so the chances of getting inside were slim.

"Kat!" Jason shouted, but she didn't turn. She pulled open the gate and would have closed it behind her but it hung on mud and grass. She struggled with it, and seeing Jason running in her direction, she abandoned the door.

She was up the concrete stairs and under the covered patio that spanned most of the back of the house, when Jason shackled her hand. "Kat, damn it," he growled. "What are you doing?"

She whirled on him, pulling out of his loose hold. He'd left his jacket and his T-shirt was soaked, outlining his perfect torso. "I'll call the rental place. They'll take care of this from here."

Water ran over his face. "Let's go inside and talk."

"No," she said, hugging herself. "We have nothing to talk about."

"We have years of things to talk about."

"You said you were done," she said. "And I get that, Jason. I know you and I know you meant it. And I know why you brought me here. So you could leave when you were ready. Well, leave then. You're really good at leaving."

He stepped back as if she'd hit him and Kat couldn't believe she'd said those words. She'd never, ever thrown his past choices in his face, but she'd felt those choices with a whole heck of a lot of pain.

"I never wanted to leave you," he reminded her, "and I know you have to know that."

"But yet you excel at it," she said, unable to hold back. "I didn't leave you for Marcus, Jason. You left me in yet another hotel room, alone."

"I had no choice," he said. "The auditions were the next day. I was contracted. We talked about this before I left."

"We did, and like always, I knew you had to go. Denver was just a repeat of history, a look into the same future. You feel good when I'm with you but you feel really bad when I'm not. And when I sat there in that hotel room, I swore it was the last time."

"You had a tour you didn't even tell me about," he argued.

"I would have," she countered. "But you told me you were leaving long before I had the chance."

"And I foolishly didn't ask," he supplied.

"You didn't ask," she agreed. "That night, I swore you would never leave me in a damnable hotel room alone again. I swore that I was done. And still you haunted me, Jason. Still, I couldn't forget you. Marcus's one of the good guys fame hasn't corrupted. He was good to me, but he wasn't you, and I couldn't make him you no matter how I tried. But Jason, I did try. For the first time since we divorced, I really did try. And still, I failed. I couldn't get past you, and I wanted to."

Long seconds ticked by, the silence filled with nothing but a steady, slow tapping of rain on the ground.

"Let's go inside, Kat," he finally said, his voice softer now, his eyes as dark and turbulent as the weather.

"I don't have my keys," she admitted. "I left them in my purse in the car."

"Damn. I should have thought about your purse. I'll go get it, and then we have to talk, Kat. Really talk about all of this, not talk around it." He turned to leave.

Kat grabbed his arm. "No. I don't want you to help me. If you're done, you're done. Be done and go home."

Before she knew his intent, he pulled her close and

she wanted to push him away. Again, she failed. She couldn't push Jason away. She just didn't have it in her.

"I'm never done with you, Kat," his voice raspy with evident emotion. "Even when you hurt me like you did tonight with Marcus, I can't say it's over and mean it."

"I didn't know he was coming."

"And you didn't tell me about him, either."

"Because he changed nothing between us," she said. "Or so I thought."

He studied her intensely, then said, "Let me go get your purse and—"

"I can't stand here and wait for you to get back," she said. "I'll go crazy. I'll end up breaking the window to get off this porch."

"Then come with me."

She shook her head and backed away from him. "No. Then you'll take me to your place to prove something when it's too late. You brought me here. This is where you wanted me and where I belong. I don't have my phone either. Just please call me a cab and I'll take care of this."

"I can be there and back before the cab ever gets here," he said. "And I brought you here because I swore to you, and myself, that I wouldn't force you into my world."

"You never forced me into your world, Jason. You forced me out."

"I'm the one who pursued you, Kat," he said. "I tried to hold on to you. I tried to get you back." He ran his hand over his wet hair. "Look. There's plenty more I'd say right now, but your purse is important. I'm going to get it and I'll be back." He turned away again.

"Marcus didn't know who you were or he wouldn't have come."

He kept his back to her, his spine just a little stiffer. "So you never even told him about me either."

"I never told him your name. Our relationship was, and is, ours alone. I simply told him I had an ex-husband I was still in love with."

He was perfectly still, the sound of the rain pattering on the roof filling the silence, before he finally said, "Wait for me." And then he was gone. How many times had she said those words in her head? *And then he was gone.*

THE EX-HUSBAND *I was still in love with.* Kat's words replayed in Jason's mind as he rode through the rain, keeping his Harley on slow and easy. There was nothing slow and easy about his thoughts, that was for sure.

He loved Kat. He wanted Kat. He needed her. But she was tearing him apart. In his heart, he yearned to believe that Marcus meant nothing, to her or about them. *Leave. You're good at it.* Those had been her words, in various rephrased ways tonight. Marcus wasn't the problem. The past was the problem.

Jason pulled to a halt behind Kat's car when a police vehicle pulled up behind him. He headed toward the officer who was wearing a yellow rain jacket and met him halfway.

"Not a good night to be out," the officer shouted. "Anyone hurt here?"

"We're fine," he said. "My wife had a blowout, and we forgot her purse inside the vehicle." Wife. He'd said wife, just like Kat's father had in the casino. How easily that had come out of his mouth, too.

"You call for roadside assistance, I assume?" the cop asked.

"Not yet," he said. "The rain was pounding on us too hard. It's a rental."

"I'll call for you," the officer said. "Who's the agency?"

Jason told him, having seen the bumper sticker on Kat's car. "I'll stay here and make sure you get off all right," the officer offered.

Jason gave him a salute and took off down the muddy incline. He slid inside the vehicle, the water pouring off him.

"Glad it's a rental and not the BMW you've always wanted," he murmured. His hands tightened on the steering wheel with the thought. They were supposed to car shop tomorrow and he'd been looking forward to it. He wanted to buy that car with her, he wanted to be there for her, share her excitement at finally getting "the" car she'd always pined for.

He grabbed her purse and had a terrifying flash of the rental sliding off the road. Too easily, things could have ended up differently. She could have flipped. She could have died. He pounded the steering wheel. Life was too short for them to screw around like this, pussyfooting around issues. He could have lost her tonight forever. He grabbed her purse, shoved it under his jacket and ran up the hill. He and Kat were going to do something they should have done a long time ago. They were going to really clear the air, they were going to fight and yell, and get everything out in the open. And then, if he was lucky, they'd make love and they'd stay in love. He refused to consider any other option.

17

Jason pulled into Kat's driveway, putting the garage door opener he'd fished from Kat's purse, along with her keys, to good use. Finally, he was out of the downpour and off his bike and he had plenty he wanted to talk to Kat about. He shrugged out of his jacket and left his bag behind, making a beeline inside the house and to the sliding glass door off the kitchen. The instant he was outside, Kat rounded the wall to face him, her hair beginning to dry and forming wispy strands around her face.

"Jason—" she started, sounding surprised.

He didn't give her a chance to finish. He closed his arms around her and slanted his mouth over hers, the sweet taste of her like an addictive drug filling his senses. When he was certain he'd kissed her thoroughly, he said, "I love you, Kat. I want to marry you again. I want you to be my wife. Just remember that before, and when, we're fighting."

"I love you, too," she said breathlessly and leaned back. "Wait. What? Fighting?"

Jason led her inside and shut the door, then put the table between them. When he was touching her, he couldn't think. He just wanted to forget everything, to touch her and to love her.

"It's time we have it out, Kat. We need to say everything we have ever thought and see if we can survive it."

She sucked in a breath, and looked terrified at the idea. "I can't," she said, shaking her head. "If you say anything that hurts I...I can't take anymore, Jason."

"What hurts is goodbye, Kat," he argued. "I took jobs because you encouraged me to take them."

"What kind of selfish person would I have been to do anything but encourage you?"

"But yet you blame me for taking the jobs?"

"No," she said. "I don't blame you."

"But?"

"No but."

"Kat, damn it—"

"Don't curse at me, Jason."

"If that's what it takes to get you to be honest with me—"

"I knew your career was the most important thing to you."

"*You* were the most important thing to me."

She made a frustrated sound and took off toward the other room. Jason caught up with her quickly. "We talked about this, Kat. Build up our careers and retire young, raise a family, travel. Whatever we wanted to do."

"That's what Ellie and her husband are doing," she said. "And he's missing her pregnancy."

"We aren't them, Kat."

"No. They're still together."

A knot formed in his chest. "I'd turn back time if I could. I'd do it right because I clearly didn't do it right the first time. But I will this time if you give me the chance."

"Tonight, you said you were done with me. I let you back in and in a snap of your fingers, you broke me like a twig."

"I found out about you and Marcus in front of a group of people who knew we were in a relationship," he said. "Not only did it feel like a ten-ton boulder had been dropped on my chest, I had to pretend that boulder didn't exist. For the first time in my life, Kat, I wanted to walk out of the show and just say I'm done with everything. You have no idea how hard it was for me to get on national television and act like I was okay. Because I wasn't. I *wasn't* okay." Suddenly, he needed space. He left the kitchen, walking down a small flight of stairs that led to her living room.

"Jason," she said, catching his arm as he reached the landing. "I'm so very sorry that happened. I'd never, ever, put you in a position like that. I'd never intentionally hurt you, either."

"I know," he said. "But I don't think you know how important you are to me, or how important you always have been to me. We can't fix this, can we, Kat?"

"Don't say that," she whispered. "Don't say we can't fix things." She held his hands. "I want to and that's one of the reasons you saying you were done hurt so much. I'm really trying. I really want this time to work."

Jason picked her up and Kat laughed. "You're always picking me up. I don't remember you doing that in the past."

He sat down on her couch, with her back against the arm of the sofa, and her legs draped over his.

"I just realized that I am soaking wet and now your floor and your couch are, too."

"I don't care," she said. "You're here. That's all that matters." She leaned forward and pressed her lips to his, before whispering, "On second thought, I think you should take those wet clothes off."

He cupped the back of her head and kissed her, a quick, passionate kiss. "Do you know why I keep picking you up?"

"Why?"

"Because I'm always afraid you're going to run away again."

She shifted, climbing on top of him, straddling him, and then pulled his wet shirt off and tossed it behind him.

"I'm not going anywhere."

She tossed her shirt with his, but when she tried to remove her bra, he tugged her against him.

"Don't do that. I can't think when you're naked and we haven't solved anything yet."

"I'm not going anywhere, Jason," she promised.

"But you think I am."

"I don't want to hold you back, Jason. If you feel like you can never take another job that requires you to travel, that isn't any more healthy than me always feeling like you will. I don't want that for you or for us."

He let his head drop back, staring at the ceiling. He

felt defeated in a battle he'd given everything he was in order to win it. She kissed his throat.

"What did I say wrong? What is wrong with me wanting the best for you?"

"I'm not taking any more jobs that require I travel unless you can go with me," he said, bringing her back into view. "Not after I get past these auditions. If I don't do them, I break my contract, and the studio will either kill the stage show or replace me. I did this for us."

"I know," she said. "I know you did and that scares me. Jason, I feel the same fear I always did. What if you get bored with the show and resent me because you're tied to it?"

He rolled her to her back and came down on top of her. "I have traveled the world. I've worked with some of the biggest names in show business. I have more money than I can ever spend. And I'm not happy. You are what makes me happy. You, Kat."

"Until you have to miss something big because of me."

"I already missed the only thing that mattered, and that was us. I want you to believe that right here and now, but I know you won't. I know it's about time and actions and all I can say is, I'm up for the challenge. And by the way, about me bringing you here tonight. I already told you I was staying here. I'm not leaving unless you kick me out." His lips quirked. "Besides, I have a personal goal of making love to you in every room and then doing it all over again." He glanced around. "Starting with the living room."

She slid her arms around his neck. "We do have all day tomorrow."

"I like how you think." He reached underneath her and unhooked her bra before tossing it away and melding her chest to his. "And I love how you feel. I love you, Kat."

Jason took his time showing her—one lick, one kiss, one pleasurable moment after another. If he had the chance, he'd spend a lifetime showing her. But he wasn't there yet—to the place when she'd give him a lifetime. He knew that, no matter how much she told him she was. He felt it, sensed it. He knew his KandyKat. He was going to have to do just what he'd vowed: be patient and prove to her just how well he really could love her.

It was nearly dawn and Kat wasn't sure how long she and Jason had been talking, but she didn't want to stop. It felt like forever since she'd had her best friend to talk to.

"We should sleep," Jason said, absently stroking her shoulder. "We have to go find you a car tomorrow and then Sunday we're back in the whirlwind of preparation for next week's opening."

Kat propped herself up on her elbows. "You didn't comment on how well Marissa worked with Marcus last night."

"No, I didn't," he said. "That was risky, by the way."

"I had a feeling she and Marcus would hit it off," she replied with a smile.

He laughed. "I didn't even notice."

"I paired them up because I believe in Marissa," she said. "And because I thought throwing her into the spotlight with someone I knew would keep her from stumbling, both literally and proverbially."

"And you thought they'd make a good couple," he said, showing just how well he knew her.

"Yeah." She grinned. "I knew. And you should have seen how they were looking at each other."

"I saw you with him," he said, suddenly solemn. "He had you cornered by the door, and…"

"He was saying goodbye," she said, climbing on top of Jason, naked and determined to get him to focus on her, not Marcus. "And Marissa was waiting on him a few feet away." She reached behind her and stroked his cock. "I'm waiting for you, right here in bed."

He rolled her onto her back, spread her legs and settled between them.

"Always playing director, aren't you?" she teased.

"I'll let you direct later," he promised, lowering his head to kiss her.

"Oh. Wait. I forgot to tell you something I'm afraid you'll be upset about."

He stiffened. "What? Tell me."

"I have to fire Tabitha. She pulled something—"

He kissed her, a deep, passionate kiss that left her breathless for more. "It does nothing for my confidence," he half growled, "when you talk about Tabitha when I'm on top of you."

She laughed and held on to him tightly. "Well, you are my director. If you want me to be silent I'll be silent."

"Unless you're talking dirty to me, or telling me how much you love me, yes. Silence right about now would be ideal."

He pressed inside her, filled her, and Kat moaned rather loudly. "I'm not sure I can follow that direction."

"You never follow my direction," he said, "but somehow you always get it right."

"So do you—"

Jason drove slowly, deeply inside her.

She moaned again.

COME MORNING, OR rather mid-morning, Kat was in her favorite short Minnie Mouse robe, making coffee with a smile on her face. That smile grew when she heard Jason whistling his way down the stairs. It had been too long since she'd heard that whistle. He cursed as he passed the living room, and she knew why. She leaned on the counter and waited for him to enter.

Wearing nothing but a pair of blue-checkered pajama pants, he strolled into the kitchen. "Holy crap, Kat," he said. "We need to make a little deal."

She arched a brow. "Which would be what?"

"Don't go into the living room until I have time to get someone to clean your carpet and your couch." He glanced down at the muddy floor by the sliding glass door. "And to mop."

"I already looked," she said. "And I'm not freaked out. It'll clean."

"If it won't, we'll buy a new whatever we have to buy."

"I really am not worried about it." Material items weren't her thing.

He sauntered over to her. "You aren't. I know you aren't. You don't get all worked up over stuff and I've always loved that about you." He stopped in front of her and eyed the counter, grabbing the whipped cream. "You still use whipped cream in your coffee."

"Yes, I still do."

He picked her up and set her on the counter and she laughed, knowing where this was headed. "You are not putting whipped cream on me. I just took a shower."

"We'll take another together." He toyed with the can of whipped cream.

"No, Jason," she warned. "Don't you dare."

He tugged at her robe. The phone on the wall rang. Kat frowned. "Only my parents have that number. That can't be good. They'd call my cell, which is—"

"In the garage in my backpack, with mine," Jason said. "Make sure nothing is wrong and I'll go get them." He set her down on the ground and she rushed to the wall by the fridge and answered.

"Hello."

"Is everything okay?" her mother asked. "You aren't answering and I was worried."

"I'm fine, Mom. I had the day off and slept late. Are *you* fine?"

"I'm more than fine. I'm wonderful. Thailand is wonderful. We are loving life here."

"Good," Kat said, and nodded to Jason that everything was okay. He visibly relaxed and pointed to the garage before heading that way.

Her mother murmured something to someone else that ended with, "I'm going to ask. Just hold your horses." She spoke into the phone again. "So, Kat honey, big plans for your day off?"

"Isn't it the middle of the night there, Mom?"

"Well, yes. Yes, it is. We couldn't reach you, so we all just stayed up chatting. So…big plans or what?" She murmured something to someone else again.

Kat frowned. "Are you talking to Dad?"

"Yes," her mother confirmed. "And Jason's parents."

Jason walked back into the room and set his back-pack on the table, which he unzipped.

"Is Jason there with you?" her mother asked.

"Yes," Kat answered. "Do his parents want to talk to him?"

"He's there," her mother said, sounding excited. Laughter erupted before Kat heard Jason's mother say, "I told you so." Next, Kat specifically heard her father say "you owe me fifty bucks."

Kat gaped. "Mother! Are they betting on whether or not Jason and I would be together?"

Jason laughed, a deep, sexy sound that always did funny, wonderful things to Kat. He joined her by the fridge and kissed her on the nose. "Let me talk to my father."

"We bet because we all want you back together," her mother said indignantly.

"Jason wants to talk to his father," Kat informed her mother. She handed the receiver to Jason.

He covered the receiver with his palm. "Why shouldn't they bet on us? I am." He winked and kissed her. "I think our phones are beeping with messages. Can you check my voice mail and make sure there isn't anything urgent? Thanks."

Her gaze touched his with understanding. It was a small request but it meant a lot. He was offering her an invitation back into his life in every possible way and it was surprisingly scary. Why? Why was it scary?

"Yes," she said. "Of course." She tried to move away,

but he caught her, a question on his too-handsome face. She loved this man. Why was she scared?

She rose onto her toes and kissed him. "Talk to my father. That's an expensive call you're just sitting on."

He hesitated and let her go, but she could see and feel the reluctance in him. "What's this about a bet, *Father?*" he asked in a playfully authoritative voice, as if he was the father, not the son.

Kat gave Jason her back as she grappled with, and tried to identify, whatever this was that she was feeling. She removed her purse from the bag and grabbed her phone from where Jason had set it down. She knew Jason's calls were probably more urgent than hers but she wasn't sure she was ready to listen to his.

She had a number of text message alerts from different people. First was Ellie, who'd let her know that Tabitha had come to her early this morning, claiming her innocence for whatever Kat had accused her of. I suggested strongly that she smarten up and start respecting you. Kat snorted.

"Like that is going to happen," she murmured and went on to the next message, which was from Marissa.

Kat glanced up, giving in to the urge to look at Jason, bringing his profile into view. She could tell that he was now talking to her father about some big investment return they'd both gotten. He leaned on the counter, handsome and shirtless, with his hair rumpled and sexy. But it wasn't his looks that made her heart beat a little faster. It was the way he was chatting with their families. The way he was truly a son to her parents. He fit her so well.

Kat inhaled and forced her attention to her phone, and read Marissa's message.

Marcus is the most amazing humble, sexy person. I like him too much. It's kind of scary. Need girl talk, please? Oh, and Tabitha called to apologize. Please don't fire her, Kat. I don't want to ruin anyone's career.

Kat smiled at that final part of the message. Marissa was a special person and Tabitha had no idea how lucky she was she'd picked Marissa as her target. Kat would give Tabitha another shot because of Marissa. Hopefully, Tabitha would finally see the light, and value her second—correction—her third, chance. Kat checked her call log and found four attempts from her parents to reach her. She set her phone down and picked up Jason's, an unmistakable flutter in her stomach. His call log also showed four missed calls from his parents. She could just imagine the four of them all sitting together, talking, laughing, and betting that their children were together in the same house. Then urging each other to try the calls again. They hadn't been worried. They'd been curious and hopeful.

The final call on Jason's phone was a number that Kat didn't recognize and it had gone to voice mail. She punched the button and listened to a studio executive telling Jason how impressive the show's television ratings had been. The studio wanted to talk contract renewal with Jason.

"I'm working on that," Jason said behind her. "Yes.

I am. I promise. I'll let you know when I've properly convinced her."

She squeezed her eyes shut, certain she knew what he was talking about, because she knew him so very well. *Marriage*. She wanted to marry Jason again. She wanted it very badly, but it had taken them years to get here, to a place where they were together again.

She wasn't going to rush things now. She needed to know they could find a way to make their careers and love mix. No matter what he'd claimed about his career not being important, it was. It mattered and it had to matter to make this work. He'd worked hard and he'd earned a call like that from the studio. She wasn't going to take that away from him.

Suddenly, Jason was behind her, having ended the call much sooner than she expected, but then it was the middle of the night in Thailand. "You okay, baby?" he asked, his breath warm on her ear.

Kat turned around, letting her hands settle on his chest, knowing now what was bothering her. "I need you to know that I don't blame you for us breaking up. We were young. We made mistakes. I probably didn't deal with what bothered me the way I should have, and certainly not like I would now."

"It wasn't your fault either, Kat," he said. "I would have done a million things differently myself. And believe me, I've replayed far too many of those things over and over in my head."

"That's just it," she said. "The past is the past. And Jason, I'm proud of your accomplishments. I'm so very proud. You of all people deserve success. You're the same humble person you always have been when I've seen plenty of others in your type of role get carried away with arrogance and ego. If you get a great opportunity, you have to take it, and I'll be excited with you, I promise."

"Kat—"

She kissed him. "It won't destroy us. We're both at different places in our careers and our lives. If you turn down something wonderful to make me happy, you won't make me happy at all. We'll work this out. We will. I know we can."

He studied her, his gaze keen. "What was on my voice mail that brought this on?"

"It wasn't the voice mail," she said, and then reluctantly admitted, "Not entirely. You had a call from a studio executive named Sabrina something. She complimented you on the show's ratings last night and wants to talk about your contract renewal for the television show."

He wrapped his arm around her waist. "I'm done with television, Kat. I've meant that every time I've said it. I want out of the spotlight. But yes, I want to direct. It's my second passion and you're my first." He brushed the hair from her eyes, his expression turning grim. "I'm dreading the day I have to get on a plane for auditions. I have the gut-wrenching fear that it will be the end of us."

"It won't," she promised. "I won't lie to you and say I'm not nervous about it, but it's necessary for all kinds of reasons. I think...I think we both need to know we can survive a separation and be okay. I need to know you'll be back. You need to know I won't be gone when you get here."

It would be the ultimate test of their relationship.

LATE THAT EVENING, Jason was in the passenger seat when Kat pulled her shiny new black BMW into her garage. They'd been all over the city, and he'd found her many excuses to keep driving more than a little adorable. Ending the night at their favorite Chinese restaurant had been a walk down memory lane in a good way, but then, that wasn't unexpected. He and Kat had far more good memories than they did bad.

Kat killed the engine and ran her hands up and down the steering wheel. "I can't believe I finally bought this car. I think I might have to sleep out here."

"Oh, no," he said, shaking his head. "I'm not sleeping in here, and you're sleeping with me." He tried to open his door. She locked it.

"Oh, no, you don't," she said, grinning. "You're my captive and I want to celebrate."

Jason arched a brow. "What have we been doing the rest of the day?"

"Celebrating," she said. "But not enough." She pushed her seat back and then climbed onto his lap, straddling him.

Jason laughed, and by the time she had that sweet backside of hers nestled against him, he was hard and more than willing to participate in her celebration.

She tugged his shirt up and pressed soft, cool hands against him with a scorching effect. He reached for her and she leaned back, a teasing glint in her eyes before she moved her finger back and forth.

"I'm the director of my celebration," she said. "You get kissed when I want to kiss you." She sighed and laughed. "Which would be now."

Jason chuckled, wrapping his arms around her, and

welcoming her mouth against his, her tongue's soft caress. She tasted like honey and tea, and like forbidden fruit no longer forbidden. He twined his fingers in her hair, deepened the kiss, hungry for more of that taste and more of her.

His cell phone rang and dang it, he knew who it was, and that he had to take it. He broke their kiss. "I have to answer."

"No, you don't," she said breathlessly, trying to kiss him again.

"I do," he said, struggling to remember why. "It's important."

Her hands were on his face, her lips a hairsbreadth from his. "You do know that you taking a call during my celebration is far worse than me talking about Tabitha while we were making love, don't you?"

"Oh, no," he said. "Not even close." He punched the answer key.

"It's Daniel," the man on the other line announced. Daniel worked with Jason's investment guy, Nick, and specialized in real estate.

"What do you have for me, Daniel?" Jason asked, trying to focus while Kat nibbled at his neck.

"The house has a good hundred-thousand in equity that we can invest smartly and turn into a larger sum. But the housing market is in the ground right now. Selling it will take a good six months to a year."

"I'll buy it," Jason said. "Then I get the tax write-off from two properties while you're re-selling it."

Kat drew back and gaped at him. "You took an investment call." She tried to wiggle off his lap and he laughed and held her, mouthing "I'll explain."

"Sure," Daniel continued, "We can buy it right away. You want me to contact the owner?"

"No," he said, trying not to laugh again as Kat crossed her arms in front of her, and glared at him. "I know the owners," Jason continued, "I'll handle contact. You guys just need to deal with the bank while I'm gone. And I'll give you the hundred grand in advance to go ahead and start investing."

Daniel whistled. "Your wish is most definitely my command."

Jason ended the call and Kat immediately blasted him. "We were…celebrating, and you took an investment call. Seriously, Jason? Maybe I don't know you because you never would have done that before."

He laughed hard. She glared harder. "Ask me why that investment was important," he ordered.

"I don't care about the investment."

"Not even if it was to help your parents."

She deflated instantly and then blushed and buried her face in his shirt. "Oh, no. I'm sorry."

He ran his hand down her hair. "I'm not." He pressed her against his lap, showing her what he meant. "You're sexy when you're mad."

She lifted her head. "While I might, ah, appreciate your method of complimenting me," she said, "I still feel like a jerk."

"I talked to your dad about selling their house and investing the money."

She leaned all the way back. "What? Why? You think they're staying in Thailand? Jason, I grew up in that house. I love that house."

"I'd pay it off and just give it to them, but they

wouldn't go for that. I had to be a little more creative to make this happen. I told them we weren't going to need two houses, but I needed a tax write-off so I'd keep my house and just let it sit. I explained that if they take it over, it saves me from paying a property management company to look out for it."

"And they didn't ask why you'd need a property management company when you were here in town?"

"Of course they did," he said. "I told them my schedule was too crazy to think about a second house."

"You really want to give up your house?"

"I'm home with you, Kat. Right here is fine by me." He grinned. "I do mean the house, not the car. I like the car, but it's a bit cramped."

Her fingers curled in his shirt, her gaze fixing on his chest. "I don't want a house that's mine. If we do this, Jason." Her lashes lifted. "If we really get back together—"

"We're already back together."

"I want something that's ours."

She couldn't have said anything that would make him happier. "Then we'll call my guy back and start looking."

"Not yet," she said. "Not until after the auditions, when we have solid time together."

Translation: not until she was sure he was really coming back to stay. "Kat—"

She kissed him. "I know you're coming back." She tugged his shirt upward, and he helped her pull it over his head. Then he watched her remove hers. Next came her bra. She sat there, looking gorgeously naked, with her full, high breasts and her pretty pink nipples begging for his mouth. He wanted her.

When she leaned in and pressed his hands to her breasts and her mouth to his, he wanted her even more. But he couldn't celebrate. Not until he was home to stay. No. Not until she believed he was home. And somehow he had to make that not about a place, but about them, about their relationship, about being anywhere in the world, and being home because they were together.

Together. That was the key, and one he couldn't turn, at least not until he was home for good, with the auditions behind them. The next seven weeks were going to feel like a lifetime.

18

THE WEDNESDAY NIGHT opening came with a full house and huge success. Despite Jason's departure the next day, and to of all places, Denver, Kat was happy. She stood backstage in the midst of a flurry of excitement with champagne and roses everywhere, and was not one bit surprised to find Marcus beside Marissa.

"Aren't you two a cute pair," Kat teased.

"Cute is really not what a guy wants to hear," Marcus said with a grimace.

"It works for me," Marissa said playfully, laughing up at him, and Kat didn't miss how the rather timid Marissa didn't seem timid with Marcus at all.

Jason joined them, not one bit of hesitation over Marcus's presence showing in his demeanor. "It's over. I feel like I just gave birth instead of Ellie."

"Great show, man," Marcus said. "You and Kat make a hell of a team."

Jason glanced at Kat. "Damn, he really is a nice guy. I'm gonna have to like him, aren't I?"

"Funny," Marcus replied. "I said the same thing

when Marissa was telling me about the way you treat the cast and crew."

Kat watched the two men shake hands and if it was possible to fall more in love with Jason, she did in that instant. So few people could be as accepting as Jason was about Marcus.

"And by the way, Marcus," Jason added. "We appreciate you helping us out the other night."

"I think me being here was in the cards," Marcus joked, and slipped his arm around Marissa to be clear about what he meant. Marissa blushed and Kat grinned at her.

"Kat!" someone yelled.

"Jason!" someone else shouted.

"Someone call 911!" came another cry.

Kat and Jason took off running toward the voices, which led them to the hallway outside the stage. Kat gasped as she found Ellie slumped over on the ground, with Tabitha of all people, kneeling beside her.

"She was dizzy and stumbled, and God, Kat," Tabitha said urgently, "I tried to catch her but I couldn't. She fell hard."

"I'm okay," Ellie said as Kat and Jason bent down beside her.

"No," Kat said firmly. "You are not okay. You've been working too much and you won't listen when I tell you to go home."

"You won't listen when I say I'm fine," Ellie said, trying to smile and failing. "Nag, nag, nag."

"Apparently, nagging is a skill I need to perfect," Kat said. "Or you wouldn't be on the floor."

"Get the hotel medic!" Jason shouted, standing up.

"Someone go find the medic and make sure 911 is on the way."

"I'll go find someone myself," Tabitha said, hurrying away.

"My husband can give you lessons," Ellie said, and then gasped with pain.

"What was that?" Kat asked, officially terrified for Ellie. She should have forced her to slow down.

"Same pains as last week," she said. "They're normal but... David, my husband. I need to call my husband."

And that alone told Kat that Ellie didn't think she was okay.

Jason squatted back down beside Ellie. "I'll call him, Ellie. What's the number?" He punched it in and then rubbed her arm. "Try to relax."

Ellie laughed in the midst of a frown. "Nothing like the floor for a good rest."

Kat drew Ellie's hand in her own, reading her fear through the humor. "You're not alone. You're not. I'm here and Jason is here." But Kat knew there was only one person that could possibly comfort Ellie right now, and that was her husband, who was in another state, and couldn't possibly get here tonight.

KAT AND JASON sat in the hospital room with Ellie, who was dehydrated and exhausted. She was also very lucky that she and her unborn baby were fine.

"I guess I won't be joining you for auditions tomorrow," Ellie said, trying to laugh but sounding like she might cry instead.

"The auditions don't matter," Jason replied. "What matters is you and your baby. The studio knows that."

"The studio is about money," Ellie insisted. "They can replace me for the season and work me out of the show. My contract is up this year."

"You have a contract though," Jason said. "They can't do that to you this year and you'll be on the live shows which are the ones that really matter."

"Read the fine print in your contract," she said. "I've read mine. They can replace me. They still have to pay me but it will be my final check."

"If they replace you over this," Jason asserted, "I'll be clear that I'm walking out."

"What?" Ellie gasped. "No, you will not. Kat, tell him that no, he is not."

"I'm not going back next season anyway," he said. "I think now would be a good time to tell them that. It will encourage them to hang on to you. They won't want to shake anything up too dramatically."

"Or it could make them think they have to make changes and so they might as well get it over with," Ellie said. "So that will do you no good. You can't quit. Do you know how much they will pay us for next season?"

"I don't care," he said firmly. "I'm done, Ellie." He shifted his attention to Kat and back to Ellie. "Not only is the spotlight not for me, I'm ready for roots and family. I'm ready to have my wife back."

Ellie's expression softened. "I understand that. I can see that in you. I don't want to care, either. I don't. The pressure feels too much sometimes. I want to have this baby and enjoy every second."

"Then have the baby and enjoy every second," Jason insisted. "This baby, this pregnancy, is an experience you can't relive."

"Choreographers do not earn the kind of paycheck I'm earning," she argued. "After another couple of years with this show, ratings be with us, my child, and my child's child, and that child's children, will be taken care of forever. How do I not make that happen, if I can?"

"You're not just a choreographer," Jason countered without missing a beat. "This show has let you demonstrate that. You, unlike me, are a television personality."

Ellie shook her head, utterly baffled. "How do you not see yourself as the star you are?" She glanced at Kat. "How does he not see it? Because I know he really doesn't."

Kat noticed Jason and she knew exactly why. She even went so far as to let herself, for the first time, believe it was true. "He knows what he wants and it's not the show," she said. Jason's eyes warmed with her obvious understanding, and she added, "He wants to direct. He doesn't want the spotlight." She refocused on Ellie. "But if you want to host, or judge, or whatever it is you want to do, you'll get to do it. There's always an opportunity for someone great and you *are* great, Ellie. I've worked with you. Many big-name stars have worked with you. Everyone sings your praises. The studio knows you're worth waiting for."

Ellie swallowed hard, looking pale and strained. "David wants to quit his job to be with me. I don't want him to quit. His career is important, too. What if he blames me for losing opportunities that may never come up again?"

Jason's cell phone rang and he glanced at it. "That's our producer checking on Ellie. I'll take it outside."

He headed out of the room and when the door was

shut, Ellie asked, "What do I do, Kat? I don't know how to make this work. What did you do when it was you and Jason?"

Everything wrong, Kat thought. She'd done everything wrong, and so how could she dare offer advice to Ellie, when she herself had failed in the same circumstances? But how did she sit back and watch Ellie make the same mistakes?

Kat let out a breath. "You go with your heart, not your ambition, and only you know where that is. But more than anything, you take care of yourself and you take care of your baby."

"I don't want to lose my baby or my husband, and I've worked so hard for my career. I thought I could have it all. Maybe that was overly ambitious."

"You can have it all," Kat assured her. "Just don't let yourself get wrapped up in the fear factor this business creates. You and your husband sit down and think about how to make your dreams come true, but don't forget that dreams are to be shared with the person, and people, you love. Don't make rash decisions. Talk to David. Really talk to him about your actions and how they impact both you and your family. Then listen to his thoughts, his feelings, his needs. Both of you have to voice your fears. Don't hold them inside. Don't assume the other one knows what they are."

The phone rang and Ellie answered it, and Kat quickly realized it was David. Kat stood up and headed to the hallway, exhausted to the bone, and didn't see Jason anywhere. It was three in the morning and Jason would be leaving that afternoon. She sank down into a chair. In only a few hours, he would get on a plane and fly to Denver.

Kat rested her elbows on her knees and dropped her face to her hands. This situation with Ellie was like reliving her past with Jason. She couldn't help but let her thoughts travel to the biggest regret of their relationship, and the one moment that had changed everything. To a hotel room and a phone call that had led to "the end."

Suddenly, Jason was there, kneeling in front of her. "We aren't them," he said, one hand stroking over her hair and the other resting on her leg, strong and comforting in a way only his touch could be.

She lifted her head, trailing her fingers over his cheek, feeling the anguish of her memories. "I should have come to Europe. We *wanted* to go to Europe."

He covered her hand with his and brought it to his lap. "We still can. We have the rest of our lives."

"I should have gone then."

"And I should have been confident enough in myself as a director to ask for a few days to think about the Europe project. I could have flown to you and talked to you in person. I should have made sure we decided our next move together."

"I guess we both have a lot of regrets. Ellie is going to have them, too, and I don't know how to help her."

"Be there for her. Give her someone to talk to who understands her situation. Not everyone does but you do. I'm not sure there's much else you, or I, can do for her."

"I'm scared that I'll tell her the wrong things and I'll be to blame for something else that goes wrong."

"Tell her that," he said. "Tell her you can share your

experiences, but she has to make her own choices." He gently cupped her face. "Just please remember that we aren't them. We've been there, yes, but we're here now, together, and we can choose to be better and stronger than our past. I need you to promise me that when I get on that plane, you won't forget that. It's the only way I'm going to be able to get on that flight."

"I'm okay," she said. "I'll be okay with this, Jason. *We're* okay."

"Kat!" came Ellie's shout from the room.

Jason and Kat were both on their feet in an instant. They rushed into the room and Kat brought a smiling Ellie into focus. "I have an idea!" Ellie declared.

Kat and Jason both let out a breath and joined Ellie by her bed. "Good gosh, woman," Kat chided. "Don't yell like that and scare me or I might need a bed rolled in here for me."

Ellie grinned. "Sorry about that. I just got really excited. I was talking to David and I was fretting that the studio would have guest judges fill in for me, and they'd all be pining for my job."

"You mean my job," Jason corrected. "I'm leaving the show."

She waved that off. "We'll see about that. Anyway. I said there was only one person that I not only thought would be a great judge, but that I knew didn't want my job. And that person is Kat."

"Me?" Kat repeated, stunned by the announcement. "I'm not a television personality."

"Welcome to my world," Jason said. "Neither am I, but I've made it work. I love the idea."

"We could change roles until the local filming begins for *Stepping Up,* Kat," Ellie added eagerly, sounding more excited by the second. "David is going to try to arrange to be here for the next six weeks, so he can help out, too."

Kat didn't know what to say. "I…no. That won't work."

"Why not?" Ellie asked as Jason arched a brow in question.

"Because…it won't work." Because she needed to know that she and Jason could survive this. He needed to know that, too. She needed to overcome this one last fear to say "I do" a second time. Distance had destroyed them once before. If it could do it again, it was best they found out now.

JASON PULLED KAT'S BMW into her garage right at four in the morning. He was bone tired and his flight left at three that afternoon, but sleep was the last thing on his mind. He glanced at Kat, who was curled on the seat with her eyes shut, only he wasn't sure she was sleeping. Or if she was, he was pretty sure it was to avoid talking. She hadn't made eye contact with him since Ellie had suggested she become a guest judge.

On their walk to the garage to get Kat's car, he'd gotten a call. By the time he got off the phone, Kat had snuggled into the seat, and was sleeping with her hand curled under her cheek. Later, he hit the remote to Kat's garage, watching the door rise, and thinking about car shopping with her a few days before.

She'd been adorably excited while they'd shopped. Even more excited when she'd been able to drive the new car off the lot. He pulled into the garage, a smile tugging at his lips as he thought of their celebration, and of her climbing into his lap in this very parking spot.

He put the car in Park and hit the remote to shut the garage. The door ground its way to a close, and still Kat didn't move. He sat there, not moving, just thinking. He'd paid for her car in cash, though she didn't know it. She thought it was financed. And it was, for all of a few hours.

He'd planned to make it a surprise engagement gift, but knew he had to get her to agree to put a ring on her finger before he could get her to really accept the car. He'd thought that was just a matter of getting past these auditions, but her complete rejection of the idea that she should judge in Ellie's place baffled him. He wasn't sure what to make of it. He was pretty darn sure though that it was somehow directly connected to his ability to get said ring on her finger.

Jason opened his door and rounded the vehicle to Kat's side of the car. She didn't twitch a muscle when he reached for her. He carried her inside and thought about her comment. *You're always picking me up.* Then his reply. *So you can't run from me.* Was she running from him? Was he fooling himself into thinking everything was going to work out?

He set Kat on her bed and went so far as to remove her shoes and cover her. Still she slept. She was exhausted, he knew. She'd been tireless for weeks and it had clearly all just hit her now.

Jason didn't lie down. He walked to the bathroom, cracked the door only slightly in case Kat called for him, and turned on the hot water. He pressed his hands on the sink and stared in the mirror. Directing had taught him that he could only do his best, and then what followed was what followed. Once something was on film, it was done, and he couldn't change it. He'd applied that rule to his life and it had served him well. Except with Kat. He replayed the past far too often. She was right. He had regrets.

He stripped down and stepped under the water, letting it pour over him, trying to relax, when suddenly the curtain was pulled back and Kat, naked and beautiful, joined him. She wrapped her arms around him.

"I don't want to go with you because I need you to know you can leave and I'll still be here. And I need you to know that I'm not the same person I was when we divorced. I'll understand. I'll go to Europe this time, Jason, or wherever life leads us."

"But you won't take the judge's job?"

"It hasn't even been offered."

"I can make it happen," he said. "I think you know that. I *want* to make it happen."

"Then how will you know that I'll be okay the next time you have to leave?"

"Don't you mean, how will *you* know?"

"No. Yes. I don't know."

"You're making this an obstacle course it doesn't have to be. You're scared, baby. I'm scared, too. Let's be scared together. Say you'll take the job."

She scraped her bottom lip, a fretful look on her face, but she nodded her acceptance. "Yes. Yes, I'll take it."

Jason wasn't sure if Kat had ever made him as happy as she did with those words. He held her in his arms and kissed her, having absolutely no intentions of sleeping, or allowing her to sleep, before he got on the plane later that day.

19

KAT WOKE CURLED at Jason's side, her head on his shoulder. She inhaled, drawing in the rich male scent that was so him, so perfect, so… Suddenly, she realized a cell phone was ringing and she blinked into sunlight. Sunlight. She sat straight up, ignoring her nudity. "What time is it?"

Jason pressed to his elbows, his hair a rumpled, sexy mess, his eyes heavy with slumber. "What's wrong? What's happening?"

The phone kept buzzing. Kat scrambled over Jason, and grabbed it from the nightstand, and in the process, she launched her bare backside in the air. Jason smacked it.

"Hey!" she yelled over her shoulder, noting the clock with a cringe.

"I will happily wake up this way every day of my life," he said, leaning up to kiss one cheek of her backside.

Kat snatched her phone and answered it. "Ellie. Hold

on a second." Kat covered the receiver and slid off Jason. "It's noon. We have three hours until you leave."

"Oh, crap," he ground out. "Say it isn't so."

"I wish I could." She didn't even remember how they'd ended up asleep when they'd vowed not to. They'd made love. They'd made love again. They'd... fallen asleep talking.

"Are you okay, Ellie?" Kat asked, watching Jason scramble off the bed to pull on a pair of boxers.

"I'm fine," she said. "David's here and I'm busting out of this place any minute now."

"You're not going to the auditions?" Kat asked.

Jason tossed his bag on the bed. "Surely not?"

"No," Ellie said and Kat shook her head to Jason's question as Ellie continued, "I'm released to work but the doctor here doesn't want me traveling and my regular doctor agrees. I'm supposed to limit my hours."

"You can't push it, Ellie," Kat chided. "We just talked about this."

"David got approval this morning to work here in Vegas from the production location for the live shows until we start filming. He'll be around if Ronnie needs him, too. He says he's happy to help if it will get me to slow down."

"Your own personal bodyguard," Kat said with approval. "I can see you enjoying that."

"Don't you know it," Ellie agreed.

"This is all good," Kat said. "It really is."

"I know," she chimed quickly. "And I do get carried away. It's better that I'll have David here to tie me down if needed." She laughed and Kat heard her add,

"I didn't mean that literally, David," before she spoke into the phone again. "I've told David that even if you aren't here, now that the show is together, I won't need to work around the clock. David's still waiting for a call back about you and I switching places."

"Jason talked to one of the studio executives at eight this morning," Kat said. "He thinks it's going to happen."

After a few more seconds of chatter, Kat said goodbye to Ellie and ended the call. Jason gave her an inquiring look. "This is all starting to sound too good to be true," Kat told him.

Jason zipped his bag and settled onto the bed, taking her with him. "Don't you think we deserve 'too good to be true' after everything we've been through?"

"Yeah," she said, running her fingers through his hair. "I do."

"The way I see it," he continued, the playfulness in his voice barely masking the rasp of desire in its depths. "I have an hour and thirty minutes to try my best to get enough of you to last through my Denver trip." He brushed his mouth over hers, slid his tongue past her lips and teased her with a quick taste of masculine spice before he added, "It's never going to be enough."

His kiss was passionate, deep, dragging her into escape. The last thing she remembered beyond pure bliss for at least an hour and twenty-nine minutes was thinking how hard it was going to be to watch him get on that plane.

KAT'S FEELINGS WERE in knots when she and Jason walked hand in hand through the airport and stopped

in front of the security area. Thankfully though, due to
the private, studio-owned plane that Jason was flying
on, Kat was able to make it to this point in the airport.
She'd take every extra second she could get with him.
They had yet to receive studio approval for Kat to fill-
in for Ellie and travel with Jason.

Jason dropped his baseball hat and sunglasses in a
bin to be x-rayed. Both items were used as a disguise
and meant to prevent unwanted attention. He'd grumbled the explanation when she'd inquired, and made
his dislike of having to hide from the press evident. *I
don't mind fans,* he'd said. *It's the paparazzi that drive
me crazy.*

Kat watched Jason put his boots and belt back on,
and tuck his glasses and hat into the bag he carried.

"Jason," she said. Anything else she might have
added slid away, and they were lost in each other's
eyes. Neither one of them made any attempt to move,
and Kat felt like her chest was going to explode with
the swell of emotion.

"I don't want to go," he said, his voice low, rough
with his own dose of emotion. "I'm not going to go."

He meant it. She saw it in his face, heard it in his
voice. He was going to do something crazy, like ruin
his reputation with the studio. "I don't want you to go,
but you have to." She took her hand in his, and tugged
him along. "Let's go and get this over with so you can
come home." A large clock hanging from above a desk
at one of the gates caught Kat's attention. "You leave
in ten minutes. We are really pushing it."

"Kat," he repeated, stopping near his gate and pulling her to face him, his hands on her shoulders. "I—"

"Sir," the attendant said. "We're ready to get you on board and prepare for takeoff. We have another stop on the way to Denver."

"I'll be right there," Jason said.

"You have to go," Kat urged. "They're waiting on you and we both know this is necessary. I'm fine, Jason. It's a few weeks that will protect your career. And in case you start thinking too hard on that plane, I don't think you're choosing your career over me, and I regret ever saying that to you. You're doing this for us. I know that."

A muscle in his jaw flexed. "I'm going to leave but I'm coming back."

"I know," she said, lacing her words with confidence, determined to be strong right up until the second he was on that plane and out of sight. Afterward, she was fairly certain that she was going to have her second meltdown, like the one when Marcus had shown up.

Jason kissed her, and it wasn't some proper public peck, either. He kissed her Hollywood style, with everything he had, wrapped her in his arms, and tasted her like a starving man who hungered for her and only her.

"I love you," he growled near her ear, and started walking away, as if he was afraid he wouldn't if he didn't go right then. Too quickly, he went out to the tarmac, and didn't look back.

Kat ran to the window to watch him walk toward the plane. Her eyes prickled. She could feel the tears burning to escape and she fought them. Jason stopped at the stairs and turned to her, waving when she knew he couldn't see her. But he knew she was there. She inhaled and she thought she was okay, but when he stepped onto that plane and disappeared again, the tears spilled down her cheeks. She backed up and sat down in a chair, burying her face in her hands to try and pull herself together.

JASON SET HIS bag on the leather seat of the luxury plane, but he remained standing, his hand on the overhead bin. He had his phone out, dialing the studio again. He got voice mail again.

Leaving Kat was crazy. In fact, why was he leaving her? Ellie would be here to look after things. Why the heck hadn't he thought of this several hours ago? There was no reason Kat couldn't come with him. They didn't need anyone's permission to be together. He hesitated, thinking of Kat's complicated obstacle course that required him to leave and come back, as if that proved they were going to make it.

He dialed his boss Sabrina again and left a message. "I'm chartering a plane to Denver," he said. "Don't worry, I'll make auditions. I'm taking Kat with me though, so whether you put her at the audition table or not, she's coming along for the trip. Ellie, her husband and Ronnie are covering the show." He hung up and grabbed his bag.

"Do you need me to put that somewhere for you?" a stewardess asked.

"No," Jason said. "I'm not staying. Feel free to depart without me." Jason was out of the plane and running toward the airport door in a flash.

He burst through the door, praying that Kat wasn't already gone. "Kat!"

"Jason!"

He spotted her in a seat with tears streaming down her face. "Baby," he said hurrying to her, tossing his bag on the ground, and dropping down on one knee in front of her. He wiped dampness from her cheeks. "Why are you crying? Don't cry. I don't ever want to make you cry like this."

"Because you're leaving," she said. "It's just hard. I… why aren't you on that plane?" She grabbed his arm, her eyes wide. "Go get on that plane." She tried to stand up.

Jason kept her in the seat. "I left, just like you said I had to. I didn't like it and you didn't seem to either. So, I came back. That exercise is done and over. We passed the test."

"Jason, you have to get on that plane. The studio—"

"I'm chartering a later flight," he said. "I'll make tomorrow's audition. And you're going to be on that plane with me if I have any influence at all. Ellie is here. There's no reason you can't come with me."

"But—"

He kissed her. "No 'buts' allowed. I want to show you something." He unzipped his bag and pulled out a velvet box, but kept it out of her sight. "I carried this with me to remind me of what waited on me at home, Kat. I planned to do this when the auditions were over, but I can't wait." He lifted the box and opened the lid to display a platinum ring that he'd had designed for her. It was shaped like a lily, the flower theme they'd had at their first wedding. "I need my wife back to share my life with. Marry me, Kat. You are, and have always been, the woman I love. Marry me in Europe. Marry me in the Elvis Chapel, or heck, let's find someone here in this airport who has the power vested in them, and let's get married now."

Kat hugged him tight.

"Please tell me that's a yes," he said, holding on to her, holding his breath at the same time as he waited for her reply.

"Yes, yes, yes," she quickly said, and leaned back, cupping his face and kissing him. "Of course, it's yes." She stared down at the ring and started crying again. "It's gorgeous. It's perfect. It's our flower."

Jason slipped the ring onto her finger. "I only have one other request," he said.

"Don't lose the ring?" she asked.

"That, too," he agreed. "But I was thinking more along the lines of don't divorce me again."

She laughed. "You're stuck with me this time. In fact, why don't we go find that airport preacher right now?"

He laughed and kissed her and they really did go look, but they had no luck. Instead, they spent the flight to Denver planning a wedding in Thailand, where they and their parents could bet on forever.

THREE MONTHS LATER, Kat stood in the empty house they'd purchased, having just returned from Thailand newlyweds yet again. Jason walked in the front door and set down a box. They were only a few miles from her old place, and close to his house that was now her parents'. Not that she thought they'd ever use it. They were in love with Thailand.

"The moving guys said they'd be here in half an hour," Jason announced.

Kat spun around in the center of the hardwood living room floor. "I love this place."

Jason laughed and wiggled an eyebrow. "You do know we'll have to test out every room in our own very special way?"

"Hmmm," she said. "I do like your way of breaking in a new house."

A car pulled into the driveway. "Is that the movers?" Kat asked, walking to the window, and then looking over her shoulder at Jason. "It's your agent, Jason. Oh. Wait. It's both our agents." With the ratings for season three of *Stepping Up* at an all-time high, the studio had been after both Jason, and unbelievably, Kat, to sign on as judges for the new season.

Jason joined her. "They're trying that ol' double team thing, I guess. This is Ellie's fault for leaving the show."

"She got her own reality show," Kat said. "I can't say I blame her for moving on."

"They're going to offer us ridiculous money," Jason said.

"Yeah," Kat agreed, glancing at him. "What do you want to do?"

"I want to make that independent film that I told you about. And I want you to try your hand at producing."

She wound her arms around his neck. "Then I say, let's make that movie."

Footsteps sounded on the porch and Jason grinned. "Want to teach them a lesson about surprising us like this?"

She shook her head. "Oh, yeah. What did you have in mind?"

He kissed her, a hot wild kiss that was sure to

make even a grown man blush, or in this case, two grown men.

Life really was too good to be true, Kat thought.

* * * * *

LONE STAR SURRENDER

To Janice for the insight and support that make me so much better. To Diego for being the light that lifts me up. To my Mom and kids for always believing in me.

And to my Red Hot Readers—you guys are wonderful!

1

HEAT. DESIRE. ATTRACTION.

He watched her from across the ritzy Hyatt Regency Hotel bar, his attention riveted by her every move. Her every nuance. The sultry beat of a slow song filtered through the smoke-filled bar, echoing the thrum of awareness dancing through his body. She shifted in her chair, her baby-blue skirt riding high…exposing long, sexy legs.

Legs he'd love to have wrapped around his waist, her body pressed close.

His reaction to his target, the woman he'd been following for two days now, came as a surprise. He didn't normally find his work distracting. But a woman like this one could make a man forget that business and pleasure didn't mix. She could make a man debate the merits of crossing the line to do things he might later regret. A line he had no intention of crossing.

Nicole Ward sat among a group of people, all there to congratulate her sister, Brenda, for passing the bar exam. His target's sleek blond hair still in the prim-and-proper knot she wore at work. He wondered what it took to get her to set it free, to let the woman run wild.

The idea of finding out appealed to him far too much.

He suspected she allowed the world to see only certain parts of her life. To see the uptight federal-prosecutor persona who lived for her job.

Even there, amongst a crowd, with a celebration underway, she remained reserved and well in check. There had to be another side to her…one she kept concealed. Perhaps too carefully. Perhaps hiding something she didn't want explored.

Which was why he was here.

He intended to find out what was beneath her exterior.

Constantine Vega knew everything that a file could tell him about Nicole Ward, down to her shoe size. Seven. Narrow. She took two creamers in her coffee and drank at least three cups each morning, in place of breakfast, but not until she completed an hour in the gym.

She'd come straight out of the University of Texas here in Austin to work for her father's law firm—a firm where decisions were made based on money, not justice. A job she'd excelled at.

Shortly after joining the law firm, she'd married her father's young protégé, Mike Parker. Divorced a year later, she took back her maiden name, and left the firm to join the U.S. Attorney's office, and now fought for people rather than power and wealth. From his observations, thus far, he thought that was true, but he had to know for sure.

After all, this blonde beauty could very well hold his life in her hands. In just a few days, she'd know what few did—that he wasn't the drug lord Alvarez's right-hand man. What he was, was an undercover FBI agent who'd spent the past few years with Alvarez, preparing to take him down.

Alvarez could control people in high places; the mighty dollar, his weapon. Ironic, considering it was also the weapon of choice that Nicole's father and ex-husband had chosen. When money didn't work, Alvarez could find other ways to be persuasive. Constantine had to be sure Nicole couldn't be influenced by money, as she once had been.

Tomorrow his team would arrest another big player in the cartel, and with that takedown, Constantine's cover would be blown. Not a minute too soon, either. Just in time for him to testify against Alvarez. Although the cartel would see him dead before that happened… if given the chance.

Constantine chugged his beer with that thought, images of some of the things he'd seen, some of the things he'd done, twisting his gut. Hating himself for the blind eye he'd turned to so many wrongs.

But it was all for the greater good, he reminded himself, setting his bottle down and swallowing the bile forming in his throat. He'd made choices he wasn't proud of in order to save thousands. A few sacrificed to save many. The problem was, he wasn't so sure he believed that what he did made a difference anymore.

He'd lost too much. Gambled too much. There was just…too much.

The final cards would be played soon.

Glancing at Nicole Ward, he took in her innocent looks. Ah, but he'd seen devils who looked like angels. He had a way of getting people to share their secrets, of getting them to talk. A little sweet talk and a smile, and he'd either confirm her honesty or expose her nasty side.

He watched as she sipped from her second Tequila Sunrise. The "ice princess"—as she'd been nicknamed by the federal investigators who couldn't score with her—had broken her own one-drink rule. Did this mean she was feeling good?

Ah…but he didn't believe she was cold, this one. Not at all. Constantine had seen her ex-husband's file. The man had a thing for kinky sex clubs and a variety of women. A habit that dated back to his married days.

Either a naughty side lurked beneath Nicole Ward's conservative exterior, or she'd been burned badly when she'd learned of her ex's habits and gone into withdrawal. Constantine's gut said she had a well-concealed kinky side. And his gut had never steered him wrong before.

If ever he'd seen a woman in need of some loving, it was this one. She was wound tight and ready for release. He could tell by the way she crossed those gorgeous legs and let her shoe dangle from her foot. He bet that her toenails were painted red, not some soft pink-and-cream color. Red for seductress. A seductress who hadn't come out to play in a very long time.

An innocent game of flirtation would get him past

her defenses. Too bad he'd have to stop at a bit of word-play. Even at that, if Nicole was, indeed, innocent of wrongdoing, she'd be mad as hell when she met him again—as her new witness. When she calmed down, she'd understand. She had to. He'd acted out of ne-cessity, faced with what might be a decision of life or death... His.

Constantine shoved off his bar stool, and started walking toward his target. A long time ago, he'd learned to never look back.

Tonight, he would play the game, consequences be damned.

"I SHOULDN'T BE HERE," Nicole said, raising her voice to be heard over the familiar pop tune the DJ played. "I have a trial starting in less than a week."

Brenda sipped from her straw. "This night is big for me, so you will just have to deal with it. Besides," she added, "it's about time you had fun." She waved two fingers at an all-American-looking, football type across the bar. "Ooh, he's cute."

"Enjoy him, now," Nicole said, wishing Brenda would take a different path. She'd been trying to con-vince her to rethink her plans for months. "Going to work for Daddy means you have no life."

Brenda snorted. "Unlike you, I'm not giving up sex. I don't need a relationship, but, honey, I need a good man and I need one often."

"Right," Nicole said with disbelief. Brenda really didn't get how their father's world would consume her. How it could destroy her individuality and steal her life.

"You'll be so buried in work, you won't remember what goes where. Sex will be a distant memory."

"You and Mike seemed to find time for sex. I seem to remember a laundry list of places you 'did it.' The storage room, the elevat—"

"Enough!" Nicole said, hating that subject. Even after three years, thinking about what she'd allowed herself to become still bothered her. "Don't remind me about Mike."

"Don't avoid the subject," Brenda retorted. "You and Mike might not have talked, but you had lots of sex, despite working at Daddy's firm. You found time and so will I. Admit it. You know it's true."

Nicole took another long sip from her straw, suddenly needing a drink. Yes, she'd had lots of sex with her ex. Too much. It had controlled her, just as money had. "Life is not about sex. That's my point." Silently she added, *Or money, as Daddy would have you believe.*

"Aha," Brenda said, crossing her arms in front of her chest and nodding as though in mock cross-examination of a witness. Her baby-blue eyes sparkled with mischief. "So you were having lots of sex."

"That's all I had with Mike," Nicole replied dryly.

"I see." Brenda pursed her lips as she reached for her Tequila Sunrise. "He was one of those. I figured as much."

Nicole's brows inched upward. "One of those?"

"You know," Brenda said. "The 'fuck you and roll over' types."

Running a finger over the rim of her glass, Nicole pondered her response, seeing no reason to hold back at that point. "Actually, he was the 'fuck me three times and roll over' kind of guy."

They shared a laugh and suddenly, having spoken the painfully true words out loud, Nicole felt better.

With a new, more relaxed mood, Nicole enjoyed a playful conversation with Brenda, even finding humor in her sister's ongoing flirtation with the jock guy.

Finally, when Brenda had teased the man enough, he sauntered over to the table. When the jock asked Brenda to dance, she accepted, and then cut Nicole a look. "I'll be back." She pinched the straw in Nicole's Tequila Sunrise and leaned close to her ear. "S-e-x. I need it and so do you. Find yourself some, honey."

Nicole cast a wry glance at the ceiling as Brenda scurried off to the dance floor, her hand in the jock's. A second later, as if he'd been beckoned by Brenda's naughty intentions on her sister's behalf, a stranger appeared.

And what a stranger he was. The man could heat an iceberg.

Shoulder-length raven hair, with a slight wave, framed a square jaw and high cheekbones. Chocolate-brown skin and a dark goatee spoke of a Hispanic heritage; the indentation in his chin and the small scar above his full top lip, of a renegade.

"Hello," he said, his voice hard to make out over the music.

But she didn't need to hear him. Her gaze locked with his, and the impact was nothing short of explosive. Awareness sent a rush of heat straight between her legs. Awareness that spoke of the kind of instant attraction rarely shared between strangers. Potent. Electric.

She swallowed hard, looking into deep, dark eyes. Dim light hid their exact color but, again, it didn't matter. They were soulful. Rich with mystery and seduction, perhaps a hint of danger.

Before she knew his intentions, he closed the distance between them, kneeling down beside her. With her legs crossed, her knee was angled toward him. His gaze dropped to the sandal dangling from her toes, and then did a slow glide up her calf, leaving goose bumps in its wake.

When his eyes lifted, his lips hinted at a smile and one right dimple. "Nice color," he said, glancing at her ruby-red toenail polish.

She uncrossed her legs, feeling amazingly aroused by something as silly as a man noticing her toenail polish. If he was this detailed in his observations out of bed, well, she couldn't help but wonder what detail he'd manage in bed.

Tugging on her slim blue dress, she pushed her knees together, despite an incredible yearning to simply spread them for this stranger. Compliments of the intense scrutiny she'd just endured from those seductive eyes of his, she could distinctly feel the gathering of wetness on her panties.

The man got her that ready, that fast.

It's what she called talent, because no one had done that to her in a very, very long time. So long she'd started to wonder if her sexuality switch had been flipped to a permanent off.

He inched forward, still kneeling, now so close he could lean in and be touching her. She wanted him, too. Almost as much as she wanted to reach out and feel the silky strands of his hair.

He offered her his palm, but the invitation of more sizzled in the air. "Dance?"

Her gaze dropped to his hand. A strong hand with long fingers. A hand that could be gentle and forceful. A hand that could deliver both pleasure and pain. And for the briefest of moments, she wondered what his hands would feel like on her body. *Relax,* she told herself. *Enjoy this brief interlude. Enjoy.*

"No name?" she asked, a playful note in her voice matching how she was feeling. "No introduction? Just straight to the dance floor?"

His hand settled on his leg and her gaze followed, a quick summation of his appearance in progress. Black boots, black slacks. Her eyes traveled, heart racing as her attention skimmed his midsection, his zipper. She swallowed hard and jerked her attention upward, away from the temptation, to his matching V-neck sweater that stretched snugly over a nice, broad chest. He was nothing like the men in her world in their conservative suits and ties, and she liked it. She liked it a lot.

Suddenly, his cheek was next to hers, the warmth of his body surrounding her. "The name is Constantine," he whispered seductively, drawing her attention back to his face. To the dimple in his chin and his dark, mesmerizing eyes. He offered his hand again. "Now we dance?"

She should say no. She didn't have time for sex games

and drama. She'd seen what they did to her ex and had almost done to her. How they distorted perceptions, shifted priorities. But then, this was nothing more than a simple dance, a fun diversion that meant nothing. It was crazy to think she couldn't have a little enjoyment without losing touch with reality.

Nicole slid her palm against Constantine's, suppressing a shiver as he closed long, sensual fingers around hers. "Now we dance," she declared.

2

NICOLE WARD made him hot. Plain and simple. Far more than he'd expected at a distance.

And with her soft curves pressed against his body, swaying to the rhythmic beat of a slow song, dangerously hot possibilities played in his mind. To say he was aroused would be an understatement. He was aroused all right, cock stiff, hands burning for exploration.

She was a petite little thing, and his chin easily rested on her head; he inhaled the floral scent of her hair. Jasmine, he decided, with just a hint of vanilla. Would her skin smell like that, too?

Suddenly, the dance floor was far too crowded. Bending at the knees, he nuzzled her neck and ear, and then whispered, "Let's go to the lobby bar where we can...talk."

She flexed her fingers on his chest and then tilted her chin up to look at him, her eyes probing, intent. Finally, she eyed the table she'd been sharing with her sister. Following her lead, he eased her around for a better view, still working with the flow of the music.

Table confirmed empty, Brenda nowhere to be found, Nicole pushed to her toes, whispering in his ear, as he had hers. "Just talk, right?" she asked, easing back onto the balls of her feet to look into his face, her eyes probing his. Hesitation fanned her delicate features.

He'd asked her to the bar, not to bed, though he'd prefer the latter. A warning went off in his head—the bold attorney who charged at a drug lord was hiding from him. Why? Suspicion flared. What was she afraid of? Her own secrets? Someone else's?

Concerned he might spook her if he pushed, he winked, and held up two fingers. He needed to get past her walls, to reassure himself of her innocence. "Just talk. Scout's honor."

She let her brow inch upward as if she didn't trust his vow. He laughed. "Okay, so I was never a Scout," Constantine admitted. "I thought about it, though. Does that count?"

"Not really," she said, her expression serious. Then, she smiled, the tension from moments before fading. "But I'll accept it anyway."

She had a beautiful smile, he realized. One he'd seen rarely in the past few days of watching her. Why was that? He found himself determined to find out. Protectiveness flared in him. He told himself it was duty, honor. Nothing more. Taking her hand, he led her through the crowd. They cleared the exit and stepped into the modern-looking lobby. Abstract paintings filled the walls with splashes of red to accent the matching chairs.

Constantine turned to face Nicole, startled by what he found. Light illuminated Nicole's ivory skin and deep blue eyes. A cute pointed chin and heartshaped face spoke more of an angel than the tough-edged prosecutor she showed the world.

His gaze dropped to her red-stained lips. Red that said, kiss me. He wanted to kiss her. No. He wanted to take her to his room and lick every inch of her body. Which wasn't an option. That would be going way over the line, and he knew it.

"You didn't tell me your name," he said, hating the charade he had to play. He lied in his world all the time, as part of his job, his cover. But Nicole wasn't like the criminals he locked away. He'd have to face that later... along with his lies. Though what options did he have? He had to evaluate her, to do his best to know she wasn't compromised by Alvarez's influence before he revealed his identity. His life depended on it.

"I guess I didn't tell you my name," she said, smiling again. "But then I don't remember you asking."

"I'm asking now," Constantine said, his brow inching upward when she didn't immediately answer. "Is it a secret?"

"Nicole! There you are!" Constantine turned to see Brenda rushing forward, an athletic-looking guy by her side. Constantine eyed Nicole. "It's not a secret anymore," he said, flashing her a grin. "Nicole."

She laughed and focused on her sister. "I was just getting some air."

Brenda detached herself from her man and went to Nicole's side, giving Constantine a blatant once-over. "I see why." Still inspecting Constantine, she said to Nicole, "I'm headed out." She dragged her gaze back to her sister's. "Looks like you don't need me."

Constantine couldn't believe his luck. With Brenda out of the picture, he would have Nicole all to himself.

Unfortunately, Nicole didn't seem to share his opinion. She snagged her sister's arm and eyed Constantine. "This is my sister, Brenda, and we need to talk." She held up a finger. "Be right back."

Constantine exchanged a quick glance with Brenda's date for the night, a guy who looked barely old enough to be inside the bar. They both shrugged and turned their attention to the ladies.

Constantine noted the stern look on Nicole's face and knew what she was saying to Brenda. She was warning her to be careful about strangers. Constantine agreed, and couldn't help but think well of Nicole for being so caring.

Nicole's expression turned softer, and Constantine saw her transform from tough older sister to a nurturing one, reaching out and brushing hair from Brenda's eyes before planting a kiss on her forehead.

His chest tightened at the display, an old emotion he'd thought buried flaring inside him—the pain of losing his younger brother a year before. He had died in the line of duty, killed by a perp who'd gotten off on a technicality. Constantine had been undercover with Alvarez then or he'd have seen justice done.

Facing his loss and the failure of the system, Constantine had wondered at his own career choices, and the price they demanded. He shoved away the thought as Nicole and Brenda approached, clearly done with their talk.

A few mumbled goodbyes later, Constantine and Nicole stood alone again, except that Nicole's mood had shifted to one of retreat, not surrender, her arms crossed protectively in front of her body.

"I, ah, better go, too," she said. "I have to work tomorrow."

Constantine narrowed his gaze on her, knowing he couldn't allow her to leave, not until he knew more about her. But there was a deeper reason, one he felt on a personal level.

He glanced at his watch. "Tomorrow's Saturday."

"I still have to work."

"Have one drink with me," he offered. "I'm only here for the night. We won't get another chance."

The words lingered between them, true in more ways than she could possibly know, heavy with the implications they held. Her lashes fluttered, shielding her eyes from his view. He could almost feel her internal struggle. Almost taste her desire.

"One drink," she finally agreed, fixing him with a smoldering hot stare. A stare that told him he could have more than a drink.

And Lord help him, he wanted more. This night could end only one of two ways. If she were on Alvarez's payroll, he'd have her naked in all of two heartbeats. But if she weren't working with Alvarez, which he strongly suspected to be the case, he'd be taking one hell of a long, cold shower.

SLIDING INTO THE corner booth of the deserted lounge area, Nicole felt the flutter of anticipation in her stomach as Constantine settled in beside her.

"Tequila Sunrise?" he asked, flagging the waitress, who quickly found her way to the table.

Nicole nodded, surprised he'd noticed her drink, but pleased. Pleased to the point of feeling…aroused. Actually, everything about the man did that to her.

He ordered the drinks, and Nicole studied him. He had a strong profile, a straight nose, a solid set to his jaw that spoke of confidence, full lips meant for kissing. Her gaze slid to his hands. What was it about his hands? Strong with long fingers.

It had been forever since she'd had this kind of reaction to a man, and she wondered, why now? Why this man? Not that he wasn't hot. He was. In fact, his body, his good looks, all but screamed "sex." Still, she'd met plenty of good-looking guys. Until this man, though, she'd felt pretty darn cold. Really, truthfully, work had ruled her world, and she liked it that way. It was safe, free of emotional baggage, free of distractions.

Nicole let a slow trickle of air slide past her lips as her eyes settled on the candle flickering in the center of the table. She didn't know the answers. What she did know was that when a man could make a woman burn without even trying, she'd be in trouble when he turned up the heat. Maybe it was the setting. Or maybe her body was rebelling against the complete lack of male attention she'd imposed on it ever since her divorce.

She'd left her past behind, and sex had been a part of it. A part of the greed that had led her into a dark place she didn't want to go back to. Her stomach clenched as she thought of the case that had changed her life. Of the murderer she'd gotten off only to see him kill again. It had been a wake-up call beyond her years—a crime in and of itself.

Only recently—after putting away as many criminals as she had—had she begun to look at herself in the mirror again. To accept the past and allow herself to live again. Even so, it didn't stop her shame. Her total hatred of what she'd allowed herself to become. But it was long ago.

She was drawn to him in a way difficult to ignore. Maybe it was time to stop running and face the final part of letting go of the past. Maybe it was time to enjoy a little sexual exploration without fear.

"Finally alone," Constantine said as the waitress departed, turning a mind-melting smile on Nicole.

Dark and deserted, the lounge certainly qualified as offering privacy. Apparently, the louder bar they'd left was the popular spot for the night.

Nicole commented, quick to busy herself in conversation rather than naughty fantasies about an upstairs hotel room. "What brings you into town?"

"Business," he said. He paused, reaching for her hand and enclosing it in his.

The waitress set the drinks on the table. "What kind of business are you in?" Nicole asked, telling herself she cared about the answer, knowing she should. But she really didn't want to talk at all. She wanted to kiss him. Or just go to his room. The thought, unbidden, confirmed what her body already knew. She had to have this man.

"I'm in imports and exports." He paused, and his voice lowered, lifting her hand to his mouth, and fixing her in a sultry stare. "Unfortunately, I rarely find my way to Austin."

She swallowed, staring into those sultry eyes and feeling lost, sinking deep into the haze of attraction. In the far corners of her mind, his words still registered. Hearing that she'd probably never see this man again delivered a tiny jab of disappointment, but it also offered freedom. Freedom to explore without fear of being connected to the U.S. Attorney's office, prosecuting one of the biggest drug lords in existence. It was a rare chance to test the sexual waters again without a tomorrow to face.

"So you're staying in the hotel?" she asked, her gaze never leaving his.

His eyes darkened ever so slightly, a reaction to the implication of her question. "I am. You?"

"No. I came for a celebration," she said. He still held her hand and his thumb stroked her wrist, sending darts of heat up her arm. "My sister passed the bar exam."

His brow inched upward. "Impressive. An attorney. Does it run in the family?"

"I guess you could say that. I'm an attorney. My sister is going to work at my father's firm."

"You don't work there?"

"Ah, no." Too late—she realized how sharp the answer came out.

Judging from the look of interest on Constantine's handsome face, he hadn't missed her tone. A couple, arms around each other, walked by and Nicole was darn glad for the diversion. This was a sexy fling, not a place for dirty laundry.

Constantine let go of her hand to reach for his drink, and Nicole felt the loss of his touch instantly. She busied herself by reaching for her drink and taking a long swallow, a bit taken aback by her reaction to this man.

Constantine took a swallow from his longneck beer. "What kind of law do you practice?" he asked.

"Criminal."

"Which side?"

She tilted her head at the odd question. "What do you mean—which side?"

Just a hint of a smile played on his lips before he lifted his beer and took another drink, apparently not in a hurry to respond. When he set the bottle down, he scooted closer to her, molding their legs together, and resting his arm on the booth behind her.

He enclosed her with his body, in the intimate way a lover encloses his woman, framed her, hiding her from the rest of the room. "Do you get the bad guys off or put them behind bars?"

"I'm a federal prosecutor," she said, certain the simple declaration would end the strange direction of the conversation.

His free hand settled beneath the hem of her skirt, resting on her knee. Tipping his head downward, Constantine's lips lingered just above her ear, his warm breath caressing her neck and sending a shiver down her spine.

"Do you like making the rules...or breaking them?" he asked.

The sexual undertone of his question became quite clear. Nicole eased back enough to look into his eyes, her body heavy with desire, her nipples tightening with arousal. "I most definitely make the rules," she whispered.

His expression held a challenge, a look that said...she was wrong. A look that said he made the rules. "Breaking the rules," he said, in a voice so sultry, it stroked her nerve endings and further drew her under his spell, "can be quite...enjoyable."

As if to prove his point, his hand inched up her thigh, beneath the red tablecloth, to touch her lap. He caressed and teased her sensitive flesh, so close to her core. So close... She sucked in a breath as his fingers brushed the damp silk between her thighs.

"I don't break the rules," Nicole managed to respond, her hand sliding beneath the table to still his, their eyes locked in a smoldering standoff. "I make people who do, pay for their bad behavior."

"Really?" Constantine asked, with clear interest in his tone. "A real good girl, are you?" He nudged her legs a bit farther apart and then maneuvered their hands so that hers settled on top of her core. His forehead settled against hers and he said softly, "You aren't acting like such a good girl right now, Nicole."

The way he said her name—with a roll of the L—

made her hot. She couldn't answer him, biting her lip to hold back a moan, as their combined fingers brushed along the tiny silk barrier of her panties. His lips brushed her ear as he murmured something in Spanish that she didn't understand. Then he said, "I like a woman who knows when to take charge," and his fingers worked with hers to shove aside the panties and brush her swollen clit. "A woman who knows how to get results."

Her lashes fluttered, her mind lost in her body's demands. Her fingers worked with his, sliding along the slick folds of her core, gently caressing. Teasing. When Constantine inserted one long finger inside her body, she could barely breathe for the pleasure. He cupped her mound with both their hands, massaging even as he stroked her inner wall.

"Come for me, baby. You're so wet. I know you want to come."

He got that right. She was barely containing her desire to rock with the motion of his hand, or rather their hands. "I…I…oh…"

She fought a moan that would surely draw unwanted attention. But it just felt so…good. She couldn't hold back. She needed this, needed release so badly.

As if Constantine knew what she struggled with, his mouth covered hers, swallowing the sound of gratification before it filled the room. It was a kiss that branded her with sensual heat, his tongue delivering such perfection it seemed to stroke her clit just as his thumb did.

Nicole quivered with the impact, her body tensing with the onset of release—a release that became so intense, she hurt with the pleasure of it. He worked her through the orgasm, his fingers, tongue and hand taking her higher and higher...then bringing her to slow, sweet bliss.

When eventually Nicole stilled, Constantine's fingers remained between her legs, and she knew she should be embarrassed. Instead, she stared up at him, dumbfounded by how lost she'd become in this man, this stranger. How easily he'd made her forget her surroundings. Forget her life. Forget the past and even the present.

Nicole had delved into some fairly kinky, and quite agreeable, places with her ex. But never, ever had she felt removed from the world. Never had she just experienced the pleasure as an escape. Always before, she'd felt...detached—like a spectator who watched from outside the scene.

This was new territory, and Nicole didn't even know how to react.

Constantine eased her clothes back into place and then smoothed her hair down, his touch gentle, his expression unreadable. Maybe even a bit dark. He drew a deep breath, and then squeezed his eyes shut. One second. Two.

His lashes lifted. "I'm sorry."

"For what?" she asked, confused.

"I have to go," he said, and without another word, he popped out of the seat and left.

Nicole stared after him, stunned.

Had he really just gotten up and left? Simply given her an orgasm and then said goodbye?

CONSTANTINE STRADDLED HIS motorcycle and kick-started the engine, beyond ready to feel the bike's speed beneath him. He'd been a fool to take things so far with Nicole, not walking away the minute he'd ruled out foul play from her agenda. But no. He'd stayed. Drawn into her presence, into his attraction to the woman, he'd stayed.

For some crazy reason, he couldn't help himself. Seeing her so hot for him, so eager to be pleased, had driven him to the edge.

"Chingado," he cursed, and added a few other Spanish adjectives under his breath.

He'd done what he had to, Constantine told himself, trying to feel better about his actions. Survival demanded desperate moves. Surely, she'd understand. Nicole had studied the Alvarez case. She knew how vicious, even poisonous, the man could be.

Shaking his head, Constantine laughed, but without humor. Who was he fooling? He'd stayed because he'd wanted Nicole. Wanted her damn bad.

Even now, he could halfway convince himself to go back inside that hotel, get a room and fuck her all night long. Why not? The damage was done. She'd hate him when she found out he was her new star witness against Alvarez.

He muttered again, and revved his engine, forcing himself to drive away. Hating what this job had turned him into, and vowing to walk away when this was over.

Nobody could gamble as much as he had without it catching up with him and he knew it.

3

"You have to use his testimony. This man, this agent, has spent three years of his life undercover for this. He gave up everything to see Alvarez fall."

"I don't have to do anything," Nicole insisted, flattening her palms on her desk, and leveling Agent Flores with a stare. "It's two days before the trial, and you're telling me I can't even meet this witness before he goes on the stand. That's insane." She leaned back in her well-worn chair, the overused metal base squeaking. "I'm a lot of things, Agent Flores, but crazy isn't one of them." *Unless you count how I acted in that bar over the past weekend,* she added silently.

He eased to the edge of his chair, where he sat directly across from her. They'd been arguing a good fifteen minutes. He'd been on his feet and back down again more times than a pogo stick.

"I told you," he said, through gritted teeth, "it has been a delicate operation and though I am the lead on this, everyone on the task force agreed we should wait until the last minute. The longer Agent Vega is inside, the less time he's a target, and the more time we have to gather evidence."

His explanation didn't please her and sarcasm laced her reply. "Glad you and your task force are in agreement. Might have been nice if you'd included our office."

His cell phone rang, and he reached into his suit jacket and withdrew it. "I need to take this."

Nicole nodded in understanding, glad for a momentary reprieve. Agent Flores seemed determined, pressing her hard on this witness. A tiny spot of concern flared at his absolute insistence. She'd been given second chair on this case, but her boss, Dean, the U.S. Attorney over Western Texas, had a wife with cancer, and he had all but handed her the first-chair duty. He was counting on her not to screw up, and she didn't want to let him down. And though she knew dismissing a material witness with critical information was a bad idea, she couldn't feel good about blindly trusting a person's credibility.

Easing back in her chair, used by numerous others before her time, she glanced around the room, taking in the corkboard bulletin board and steel file cabinets.

Her office wasn't fancy. Her job wasn't, either. Lousy pay. Long hours. Lots of yelling when things went wrong. Nicole wouldn't change a thing. She'd seen the other side of things, the money and power. And she'd paid the price.

Agent Flores, thankfully, put away his phone. Nicole was ready to end this conversation. "You can't bring a witness in from nowhere and expect me to be okay with it." She held up a staying finger to stop the argument she knew he'd offer. "We are talking about putting the biggest drug lord in the known world behind bars. I'm not going to do anything to jeopardize that. I haven't even met your witness."

"The agent is your ticket to conviction. If you can't see that, maybe the U.S. Attorney can."

That flared her temper. She didn't want Dean bothered with this. He had enough to deal with right now. "Don't even go there, because I promise, you won't like the results. Dean doesn't like it when his people are crossed. He'll back me and shut you down. The bottom line is this—we won't put a witness on the stand who we can't meet before the trial. Either give me a meeting with your agent or this discussion is over."

"It's too dangerous," he said, his lips tight, his words terse.

"Dangerous is going into court blind," she said, pushing to her feet, a strand of blond hair slipping from her neat bun to fall into her eyes. Swiping at it, she started gathering her things for court and shoving them into her briefcase. She wasn't foolish enough to walk away from a witness that could help her case; she just needed to validate his worth, which meant playing hardball. "I have to go."

He stared at her, silent a little too long. "You need him, Nicole." His voice was low. Intense.

She knew Agent Flores quite well. He rarely used her first name, and she didn't miss the plea being issued. Nicole felt torn about her decision, questioning her own judgment when she normally would not. She imagined she had her weekend adventure in that bar to thank for that.

She hadn't used her head then. And she didn't want to let Alvarez slip away by refusing a witness. Still, gambling on an erotic encounter with a stranger was one thing. This case was too important to roll the dice and take unnecessary risks. Her resolve thickened. Putting a witness on the stand under these circumstances would be reckless, and she had no doubt that her boss would agree.

"I can't give in on this," she repeated. "There's simply too much at stake."

"Fine," he said, drawing a deep breath and letting it out. "You can meet him."

She rearranged some of the things on her desk. "I'm listening."

"I have to talk to Vega, but he won't come here, I know that much. You'll have to go to him."

That didn't sound good, but neither did missing out on a chance to ensure a conviction. "Where?"

"I'll call you with the details," he said. "But tonight. I'll make it happen. For you alone, though. No one else. Vega is going to be pissed as it is."

"You won't be able to reach me. I won't be out of court until around six."

He nodded. "Call me when you're leaving. I'll have everything arranged by then. And don't tell anyone else about this. It's too dangerous. Any leak could get him killed."

"I know the way it works," she said, but a feeling of

unease danced along her nerve endings. Nicole grabbed her briefcase and purse and headed for the door, but not before fixing him with a hard stare. "Don't make me regret this."

NICOLE SAT IN the passenger's side of a government-issued, unmarked Buick sedan with an unfriendly U.S. Marshal driving. She stared out of the window, noting the sun shrinking beyond the horizon as a rainbow of color filled the sky. She'd been required to stop at three pay phones and then leave her own vehicle behind. Why she had allowed herself to be talked into coming out to the middle of nowhere, she didn't know. As soon as she asked the question, though, she knew the answer.

Alvarez.

He was as bad as they came, linked directly and indirectly to getting a lot of kids hooked on drugs. To Nicole, the kids mattered in a big way. She'd grown up in Padre, ten minutes from Brownsville, a city on the border of Mexico. A city that sucked teens into drugs, both using and dealing. She'd seen them destroy too many people.

She was about to ask how much farther they had to go, when she spotted a small house tucked away in a cluster of trees, nearly invisible but for the moonlight.

As they drew nearer, she could see it was more a cabin than a house. Vehicles parked in front were further confirmation she was at the right place. Rather old, the cabin had a rusty tin roof and boards hanging off the porch.

The marshal pulled up next to a truck and killed the

ignition. She started to reach for her briefcase, but before she could turn, the door was jerked open.

Shocked, she whirled toward the door to find a stranger there, another marshal she assumed. "What—" Her words were cut off by the harsh look on the man's face.

"Get out."

One glance at the driver's seat told of the other marshal's exit. She eyed the gruff man at her door. "I just need to gather my things." Nicole paused. "My briefcase and purse." Something made her hesitate, waiting for a reply.

Perhaps his size. The man was a monster. Bigger than big, with linebacker-wide shoulders, he had a menacing edge to his presence. A jagged-edged scar decorated his right cheek, making him seem even more sinister. She couldn't help but wonder how he got it.

"First, you meet Vega." It was an order. "If he trusts you, then I'll get your stuff."

If he trusted her? Hello? She was the one here to decide if she trusted him. She opened her mouth to say so, but then quickly shut it. Something about this guy said, don't argue.

"Let's go," he said, sounding like a guard talking to his prisoner. He reached for her as if he might grab her arm.

Appalled, she jerked her shoulder away and glared. "Don't you dare touch me."

Defiance flashed in his eyes, but for only a mere second, before it disappeared behind an indecipherable mask. Taking a step backward, he gave her a gallant wave forward. "Ladies first."

Mumbling a few, barely audible, choice words, she stepped out of the car. Tossing her hair over her shoulder with an angry flip of the wrist, she marched ahead, wishing she'd left it pulled back. Her nerves were frazzled and her professional armor, which included her normal hairdo, would be welcome right about now.

Two men stood outside the door of the cabin, guarding the entryway, and blocking her passage forward. She glanced at the man on the left, noting his sunbaked skin and short brown hair. His counterpart to the right was his exact opposite in appearance. Fair hair and skin, and shoulder-length, tangled hair, which gave him a wild look. Neither looked friendly.

They both seemed as cranky as the man on her heels. "Great," she mumbled, as she started up the porch steps. "They come in threes."

As she stepped toward the men, neither moved. She'd changed into sensible dress pants and boots, but she still sported heels. Man, would she like to dig one of them into a foot to get a reaction. She'd never been treated this way before, and she planned to vocalize as much later.

Apparently, she had the green light to enter the house by herself. She looked from one man to the other. "You mean I don't need my hand held?"

The sunbaked guard dog answered. "He knows you're here."

She didn't ask how. Didn't want to know. She just wanted to get this entire affair over with.

Without another word, Nicole reached for the doorknob. The hinges creaked as she pushed it open, almost as if it were issuing a warning to the occupant of the house.

"Hello?" she called out as she continued through a narrow entranceway.

No answer.

Inside, she found herself in what appeared to be a living room. She took in her surroundings quickly, noting the rustic, sparse furnishings. A couch, a chair and one table were the extent of the decor. There were no pictures, no knickknacks that people collect and display as they go through life. Nothing.

Either no one actually lived in the house, or the inhabitants cared little for life, in general. Probably, no one lived here. After all, it was some sort of safe house.

As her inspection continued, her gaze moved to a huge rock fireplace, the centerpiece of the room. A weird feeling made her stomach flutter. Her gaze shifted, as if instinctively, to a corner window.

That's when she saw him. This man called Vega. She could hardly believe she hadn't noticed him before. It wasn't as if the room were huge or the man small. Somehow, he blended or hid or something, whatever it was, to make himself invisible. He was so still, so utterly unmoving, that it was as if he were a part of the room.

His back was to her, but she knew with complete certainty that he was one hundred percent aware of her every move. He faced the window, seeming to survey the view beyond the glass.

Her stomach flip-flopped as the feeling that had drawn her gaze seemed to intensify. A carnal awareness slid through her body, her skin heating, her heart thumping like a drum in her chest.

She knew him.

No.

It couldn't be.

She swallowed, finding it hard to process mentally what her physical self was telling her. How could the stranger from the bar be here?

But it was him. She knew it with every fiber of her being.

If he were here now, and he had also been at the bar... A sick flutter went through her stomach as the possibilities flew through her mind. A combination of anger and embarrassment began to churn in her gut, and she shoved the worthless emotions aside as premature. Maybe it wasn't him, the man from the bar. Maybe her mind was playing tricks on her. She studied the man from behind, hoping it wasn't Constantine. Praying she'd not been betrayed, sucked into a trap by someone using her desire as a weapon. The very thing that had destroyed her life once before.

Then, as if answering her silent question, he turned, giving her a view of the true man. Their eyes locked and held. Recognition came to her mind, confirming what her body and senses already knew. This was the man from the bar.

Images of Friday night, of how he'd touched her, played in her mind. She saw it in his eyes, too. The memories. Maybe a flash of guilt. The knowledge that he'd taken from her without being honest.

He gave her a quick nod. "Hello, Nicole."

The way he said her name, with that sexy Spanish accent, sent a shiver down her spine. And she hated him for having that impact on her. No. She hated herself for allowing this stranger to deceive her. For being weak enough to become prey to a man with an agenda.

"That's my name," she said, stiffening. "What's yours? Constantine? Vega? Where do the lies start and stop?"

He leaned against the wall, crossing one booted foot over the other. Soft denim hugged his muscular thighs, drawing her gaze and making her remember touching him.

Being touched by him.

Though he made no effort to close the distance between them on a physical level, his eyes seemed to touch her more intimately.

Her fists balled at her sides as she fought the urge to launch herself at him and smack his face, to make him pay for what he'd taken from her—her control, her self-respect.

She drew in a slow breath, cautiously concealing her discomfort behind an unreadable mask reserved for prosecuting in a courtroom. This man had only gotten where he had with her because she'd let him. He wouldn't get past her guard again.

"Well?" she demanded.

He studied her for several seconds, his gaze far too probing for Nicole's comfort. She felt as if he knew her secrets, and she wondered if he did. Just how much of her life had he investigated before he'd seduced her?

"Constantine," he then said, confirming his name. At

least one thing about that night had been true. "Agent Constantine Vega." He paused as if giving her time to digest his words. "I can give you the conviction you seek, Ms. Ward."

A conviction and an orgasm, she thought bitterly. How perfectly efficient of him. And devious. He'd been after something. What? Her eyes narrowed on him, suspicion replacing her anger. Agent Flores had given no indication that he knew she'd met Agent Vega before today. If he didn't know, then Vega had been acting on his own. Agent Flores trusted this man, which lent some support to his credibility. Still…could either or both of them be working for Alvarez? Had she been seduced by the enemy?

"You know what," Nicole said, starting to back away. "This was a bad idea." She turned and headed for the door. She managed all of three steps when she found herself whirled around, pulled tight against a long, hard body. Her breath lodged in her throat, fear and arousal merging together, radiating through her limbs. Her hands pressed against his chest, her legs and hips aligned with his.

"Let me go," she whispered hoarsely, wishing like hell she didn't still want him, wondering why she did when he'd used her in such a way, and when she knew she couldn't believe whatever he said.

"Not until you hear me out," he countered in a low, dangerous voice. "I'm no angel, but I'm not the enemy. I had no option but to check you out before I came forward. I trust my instincts, not a file folder with your name and stats inside. Until I knew I had a sense of who you are, I wasn't going to come forward." That pissed her off and some of her fear slid away.

"How exactly did sticking your hand up my skirt convince you I could be trusted?" An icy tone chilled her words.

"What happened between us wasn't supposed to. I didn't plan to want you, nor did I plan for you to want me. Am I sorry? I should be, but I'm not. My only regret is walking away before we'd finished what we started. But this moment was destined to come anyway."

Call him on his boldness, Nicole told herself, and demand an apology. That is what she should do. Just as she should be indignant, appalled. Instead, Nicole found herself savoring his seductive claim of a shared secret, remembering the bliss of his hands caressing her skin, seducing her until she was ready to melt. Upset at herself over the way he'd tricked her, she reached for that ripe anger, still burning inside her, and let it expand in her chest. The man was leading her down a passion-filled path to trouble, awakening a dangerously erotic part of her that had once ruled her life. She should walk away. But she couldn't. Not with so much on the line. Not when Constantine might really be the key to Alvarez's conviction.

"I'll hear what you have to say," she said, because it was her only option. "On one condition." Constantine arched a brow in silent question. She shoved at his chest. "Let go of me and do not touch me again."

Her body might still remember the pleasure he'd delivered, but she wasn't a fool. This man was trouble. And now he'd had the audacity to use that big body of his to force her to listen. She didn't like it. It was time he learned he wasn't in charge anymore. No seductive prowess was going to change that, either, she vowed.

4

NICOLE GOT TO HIM in a big way—a way no woman had done in far too long to remember. So much so, that her anger challenged him, made him want to kiss her into submission.

Let her go or kiss her? A tough call. Her lips were full and red—tempting lips that he already knew tasted sinfully sweet. Yes, kissing her would be a delicious distraction from the hell he called his life right now. But then, it wouldn't work toward earning her trust, nor would it aid his efforts to put Alvarez into permanent retirement.

Constantine ground his teeth together, accepting the inevitable conclusion that he must behave. He gave her lips one last wistful look before forcing himself to release her and step backward.

Nicole immediately crossed her arms in front of her body in a guarded stance. The act thrust her breasts high, giving his eyes yet another delicious distraction. Damn, the woman was killing him.

He sat down on the arm of the couch, which served dual purposes. It put Nicole out of reach and brought the two of them closer to eye level, so he wouldn't tower over her. The goal was trust, not intimidation.

Their gazes connected, silent tension filling the air. She was angry and probably embarrassed, though he doubted she would admit that part. "I think you should know," he said, attempting a path to a truce, "no one knew I was following you, nor do they know about what happened between us."

"How long, exactly, were you following me?" she asked, her boot doing a slow tap on the floor, telling of her agitation as much as the steely look in her beautiful eyes.

Inwardly, he cringed before he answered. "Two days." He left out how much he'd enjoyed watching her those two days, how many ways he'd fantasized about making love to her. He figured it wouldn't help his situation any.

She made a frustrated sound; her hands dropped to her sides—perfectly manicured hands with pink nails curling into her palms. "Two days." The words were flat, her cheeks flushed. Her gaze dropped to the floor as she mumbled, "Two days and I never suspected a thing." It wasn't a question. It was more a statement of disbelief directed at herself. Her chin lifted, eyes latching on to his with accusation. "You expect me to believe the feds let you disappear for two days without any idea where you were?"

"I wasn't supposed to pull out of Alvarez's operation until the last minute. It left me less risk of exposure.

But three years of my life were on the line, and I know how easily Alvarez corrupts people. I didn't care what your file said. I needed to get a sense of who you were myself. Alvarez is going to find someone in the middle of this to corrupt, I promise you, if he hasn't already."

"I know Alvarez's type," she quickly asserted.

"Sweetheart, you only think you know his type." Constantine had seen things—hell, done things himself during these past few years—that would bring grown men to their knees. "Murder is worthy of popcorn and a soda to Alvarez. As for corrupting someone inside this case, he'll do whatever it takes to get out of that jail cell. Even threaten the lives of their families." His voice softened. "I approached you that night as a means of survival. What happened from there was pure chemistry."

Her lips thinned. She opened her mouth to speak and then closed it again. "I need my briefcase from the car. There are questions—" A slight sound on the roof sent her gaze upward and Constantine to his feet. "You heard that, too, right?" she asked, worry etching in her lovely face.

He had heard all right. Which was why his hand now rested on his side, ready to draw his Glock. "Most likely the wind," he stated, but it wasn't. He'd grown up here and he knew every sound, every nuance.

Two knocks sounded on the front door, a code for his men before entry. A marshal known as Smith entered, his big body tense, his expression grim. Constantine cursed under his breath, knowing the news was bad before it was even spoken. "We have company," Smith stated, confirming Constantine's assumption.

"What does that mean?" Nicole asked.

Drawing his gun from the holster on his shoulder, Constantine ignored her question, focusing on getting the facts. "How many?"

"I wish I knew," Smith said, no longer hiding his weapon. It was in his hand, ready to be put to use. "We have movement on the roof. Two spotted coming up the west side of the property by foot. Probably more we have yet to identify."

"Oh, my God," Nicole whispered. "I did everything Agent Flores told me to do."

And Flores had tailed her to make sure she wasn't followed. Someone had betrayed him, not that Constantine found this surprising. That's why he had an escape plan plotted. And even that was only partially shared with Agent Flores, who he trusted as well as he trusted anyone. Truth was, he trusted no one completely. Not after everything he'd seen these past three years. If he got her to the woods, he could get her to safety.

He turned to Nicole, hands going to her shoulders; he fixed her in a steady stare. "How they found us doesn't matter. What matters is our safety. And as you've already seen, I don't take chances. I plan in advance. I can get us out of here."

She seemed to be weighing his words, then said, "I know how to fire a gun."

"Why doesn't that surprise me?" he said, thinking that not much about this woman did. He bent down, removing a lightweight Wesson 35 from a holster around his ankle and handing it to her. "Six rounds, one in the chamber. Got it?"

She nodded. "Yeah. I got it. I wish I didn't have to, but I do."

Constantine wished the same thing, but he had to admire her courage. No tears for this one.

He turned to Smith and told him, "Cover the east side of the cabin so we make it the woods." He grabbed Nicole's hand and pulled her toward the kitchen window.

"What if they're right outside?" Nicole demanded as he opened the glass.

"Smith and his men will cover us," he assured her.

"The same ones that made sure no one found us?"

He hiked himself up on the counter. She had a point, but he didn't say that. "I'll go first so I can make sure it's safe." His fingers brushed her cheek. "Don't fret. No one knows these woods like I do. I grew up here." He let his hand drop. "And I put up with three years of Alvarez's shit. I have no intention of either of us dying before we make that sorry bastard feel some pain." Then, he lowered his voice, his words full of promise. "Trust me."

ON THE RUN, the very man who had betrayed her the week before now held her hand, leading her through the wilderness—her lifeline from those who hunted them. And on the run they were. For hours it seemed. They'd run and run some more.

Long ago, Constantine had broken off the heels on her boots, but not before painful blisters had formed on her toes. Still, she wasn't complaining. They'd had a close call with a couple of Alvarez's men near the cabin, barely ducking out of sight. That was enough to make Nicole thankful to be alive—blisters be damned.

Right now, she had only one thing on her mind, and that was staying alive.

Constantine drew abruptly to a halt, pulling her to a squatting position behind a cluster of bushes. Nicole obliged, struggling to catch her breath, the humidity making the air thick and hard to inhale. Her hair clung to her neck, sticky and uncomfortable. There was no wind, so the heat was a stifling wall of discomfort. Thunder rolled in the distance, warning of rain, and right now, she welcomed the relief it would bring.

With a silent look, Constantine let her know his intentions—he was going to scout ahead as he had several times before. She barely inclined her head and he was gone, moving with a silent, stealthlike agility that a man his size shouldn't possess. But then, he'd stayed alive inside Alvarez's gang. No doubt, that had to have taken some fancy footwork. Three years of living that life was a long time. That he had a backup plan, a hideout no one knew about, shouldn't surprise her. She imagined those three years had made him resourceful.

Alone now behind the cluster of bushes, she peered into the darkness, searching for trouble, her ears straining for any sound that might signal danger. Nicole sucked in a surprised breath as Constantine was suddenly behind her, no sound warning of his approach. Every time he touched her, awareness teased her nerve endings, taunting her with her inability to control its presence. She rotated around to face him, her thigh aligned with his, pressed close. Their eyes locked, the connection hitting her with lightning force, attraction sizzling around them despite the danger they faced.

But there was more than attraction that lured Nicole to Constantine at present. Crazy as it was, this stranger, a man who'd lied to her only a week before, offered comfort and security that she desperately needed right now.

"Not much farther," he murmured, his voice a low whisper.

"Shouldn't we call someone?" she asked, matching his low tone, wishing she hadn't left her cell phone back at the cabin.

"No need. A rendezvous is set up with Flores in the event I run into trouble. A time and location not far from here. We just need to get underground and safe until then. Besides, we don't know who we can trust, and any call could be monitored."

"If I don't show up tomorrow, they might do something crazy to delay the trial. I know you don't want that."

"What I want is to stay alive." He pushed to his feet, staring down at her as he offered her his hand.

Nicole took a moment to stare up at the foreboding, but oh-so-sexy male, before slipping her palm into his. His cheeks were chiseled, his jaw strong, something in those dark eyes wary and lonely. He was a stranger who'd snuck past her guard in far too many ways, an undercover agent who oozed danger and sex, with no telling what kind of sordid past. Yet in just a week's time, she'd put both her life, and her libido, in his hands.

Hands she hoped were as experienced at surviving in the wild as they were at giving pleasure.

5

RAIN FELL SLOWLY, steadily, and seeped into Nicole's clothes and cooled her skin as she followed Constantine through a heavily wooded area. Tree branches and bushes had to be shoved aside and dodged. For a stormy night, the sky was remarkably bright, the way a sky was lit before a tornado. Nicole didn't want to think about that now. She focused on keeping pace with Constantine, pushing herself as hard as she could. That was until her foot hit a rock that bit through a sore spot on her sole. Pain rocketed up her shin, and to her complete dismay, her ankle twisted to the side.

Constantine grabbed her arm to steady her. Suddenly the deadly sound of a rattlesnake filled the air. "Don't move, *cariña,*" he warned, his voice low, tight. "Don't move."

"Oh, God," she whispered hoarsely, fear shooting adrenaline through her body and telling her to run. Somehow she stayed still. "Where is it?"

But he didn't respond with words. With agility and

speed, Constantine somehow pulled his gun and fired. Her body stiffened, ready for the snake's strike if he missed.

Instead, she found herself engulfed in his strong arms, his hand sliding down the back of her head. "It's over. It's dead."

Nicole blinked up at him as the words sank in, and then she abruptly whirled around to see the proof. Constantine shined his penlight so she could see the snake. She breathed calmly at the sight of the dead rattler, but it didn't last, as his arms dropped away and he grabbed her hand, and told her, "We need to move. That gunshot just announced our location." He had no sooner spoken the words than he tugged her into motion.

Her heart pounded in her ears; her adrenaline, still high from her snake encounter, now shot beyond her control. Constantine was relentless in the path before him, half dragging her, clearly compelled to get distance between them and where the gunshot had sounded.

Several branches snapped to their right, and Constantine stilled instantly, pulling Nicole down into the bushes. Nicole's stomach churned. Oh, no. They'd been found.

Constantine motioned to other bushes that formed a circle and pulled her into its center. There was barely room for the two of them. Next, he retrieved the Wesson revolver again from his boot holster, where it had been secured while they were on the run. He pressed it into her palm and then slid his cheek against hers, his lips to her ear. "This is about staying alive. Don't talk yourself out of pulling the trigger." Leaning back, he searched her face, showing his in the process. A chill raced down her spine. Those warm, chocolate-brown eyes of his held fiery determination and strength; she could see he was willing to demand the same of her but he didn't have to. She'd do anything to protect herself. She drew a breath and nodded her understanding. Satisfaction filled his gaze.

He leaned close again, the warmth of his body penetrating her wet skin, the stubble of his chin brushing her cheek with an intimate touch. "Don't come out until I say to."

The contact disappeared as quickly as it had come, leaving Nicole with a fluttering heart. Constantine shifted his weight, poised to dart away, then male voices sounded nearby—one she recognized.

Nicole grabbed his arm, relief flooding her. She whispered, "That's David Wright. He's an FBI agent. A good one." They were saved. She started to move, ready to get the heck out of the woods.

About to stand, she quickly found herself yanked downward. Suddenly, her back was molded to Constantine's chest, his chin on her shoulder, lips next to her ear. "Trust no one," he warned. "No one."

Irritated at being manhandled, she half hissed her low reply. "I know him. He's honest."

"You can't know that. Not with Alvarez involved."

"I do," she insisted. Her instincts were rarely wrong, and they'd served her well in her job.

"And if his family is threatened, then what? Would he protect you over them?" He didn't give her time to respond. "Choose now. Trust me or trust David. But if you go to David, go with your gun drawn because you're going to need it."

He let go of her with such abruptness, she barely steadied herself from tumbling over. She maneuvered around to face him, and the look he fixed on her was hard with steely anger.

Time seemed to stand still, just as it often did in the courtroom when she found herself under fire, when she was forced to make an educated gamble. She had to roll the dice here, and her money was on Constantine.

Her chest was tight with conflicting emotion, but her decision was made. She settled back down on her heels, planting herself, silently telling him she was staying. The voices were coming closer. Out of her peripheral vision, she realized Constantine had drawn his weapon and was aiming it through the cover of the bushes. She followed his lead and did the same.

"Damn it. Where the hell are they?" It was David. He was close enough that Nicole could see his face through the branches.

"Relax," the other man said. "The gunshot puts them within reach. If they aren't already dead, we'll make sure they get that way."

"Relax?" David's voice was filled with disbelief. "My wife, my children...everyone I care about has been threatened."

"Alvarez gets what he wants no matter what it takes. You should have taken the money he offered you and ran. I did."

Nicole felt as if she'd been punched in the stomach. It wasn't news that someone like Alvarez would stoop so low, but the magnitude of his reach was downright chilling. If she wanted to stay on this case—and all this experience did was make her more determined to put the brakes on Alvarez—she would have to go underground until the trial. And she would have to do so with Constantine. The one person she knew she could trust to help her stay alive. She slowly inhaled. A man who was dangerous to her for reasons that had nothing to do with this case.

David and the other man exchanged a few more words before splitting up. For long minutes, neither she nor Constantine moved. He was like a statue— completely, utterly still, yet somehow alert, ready.

Abruptly, he pushed to his feet and stared down at her, his expression hard, his anger toward her obvious. "Let's move." And he took off walking. This time there was no offer of his hand. He was pissed.

Nicole watched in disbelief as he pushed through the bushes and walked away. How could he be pissed? She had every right to doubt him, every reason. He turned back to her, and glowered. "Now." His voice was low, but, oh-so-lethal.

She glowered at him and then did what she had to do—marched forward. What choice did she have? Right now, he had the upper hand. She needed his ability to survive against Alvarez and his thugs. She'd gain back some control though—somehow. This was about more than surviving this night.

She didn't want to die, but then, she didn't want to lose Alvarez, or even the careful confines of structure she'd put around her world. Not now, not ever. And cer-

tainly not because of some hot Latino man with attitude
who thought he could steal her orgasm under false pre-
tenses as if he had every right as long as he cloaked it
in work-related precautions. Well, he hadn't the right.
And they hadn't fully explored that topic yet, but they
would. Oh, yes, they would.

HEAVY RAIN TORTURED them for a good hour until minutes before they arrived at their destination. He turned
to Nicole then, the first time he had even considered
speaking to her since their clash over trust. His acute
irritation was irrational but no less real. So real it had
driven him to be a coldhearted ass, pushing Nicole
harder than he should have, ignoring the pain he knew
those damn boots were causing her, communicating
nothing. But the simple truth was, he wanted her to give
him her trust without question. Hell, he wanted more
than her trust—he wanted her.

"This is it," Constantine informed Nicole, inspecting the cave entrance a few feet away, a cave he had
explored with his father as a young boy.

The minute he'd registered the way her wet clothes
clung to her curves, he ground his teeth. He wasn't a
man without control, and he'd certainly known his share
of pleasure, his share of women—some so beautiful,
they could bring a man to his knees. They hadn't gotten to him though, that was the thing. But Nicole just
might have that power, and he wasn't sure he liked it.

He found himself lost in an inspection of Nicole, trying to decide why she drove him so insane with desire.
Water clung to her lashes, to her lips, her hair soaked to

the sides of her face, emphasizing her high cheekbones and full mouth. He followed the path of rain as it dotted her face, her neck, her blouse outlining her full breasts and erect nipples. His cock twitched, and he bit back a growl. He needed to focus on business, not desire. He should bed this woman and get her out of his system. Starting something he hadn't finished was where he'd gone wrong. That was it. That was what was killing him. Get her naked and beneath him so he could stop fantasizing about it.

The decision made, he savored those plump, pert breasts a moment longer, before his gaze lifted. Their eyes locked, collided actually, in a fiery contact that took his twitch to a full hard-on. Damn it, distraction was dangerous. She was that and more at this point.

"When we go inside the cave, it'll be pitch-black. Just hang by the wall while I open the door to the hideout. There is light, food and supplies there. We have a few hours before our rendezvous with Flores."

Her face went instantly pale. "Are we talking about hiding in that cave?"

His brows dipped. "Right. There's a hidden cavern beneath the surface. Even if they search the cave, they won't find us."

"That's, ah…" She hesitated. "I guess I didn't mention I'm claustrophobic?"

Once he managed to maneuver her inside the cave, he kept her near enough to the entrance that darkness didn't completely consume her, giving her time to adjust to the small space.

He pressed her against the wall. "Don't move. I'll be right back."

She grabbed his wrist, and tightly wrapped one leg around his calf. "Where are you going?" Her voice held panic.

Crap. The woman was killing him. He wanted nothing more than to have those long legs wrapped tight around him, but now wasn't the time. He was about to say as much when he realized she was shaking. The tough-as-nails prosecutor, who'd barely blinked when faced with guns and a snake, was quaking in her boots over a phobia. Her fear was as irrational as his anger over her mistrust, but that didn't matter. In fact, somehow it made her seem more human, more vulnerable. The tough courtroom persona that she often showed had fled completely.

Everything inside him went soft in a way he didn't know he was still capable of. The past few years had made him hard, not easily enticed into sympathy. Just another bit of proof this woman had bewitched him in a big way.

"Easy, *cariña,*" he whispered, his thumbs stroking her cheeks. Her face was in shadow, but he didn't have to see it to know the fear it held. He could feel it in the way she clung to him, in the ragged way she was breathing. "I haven't let anything happen to you thus far, and I'm not now."

She seemed to struggle with words, her expression tormented. "When I was a kid, I went exploring in a vacant apartment complex near my house. I fell through a floor and was trapped for hours under some boards.

I've…never been able to kick the trapped thing. It's stupid, but—"

His thumb brushed her lips, silencing the words. "It's not stupid," he said, sensing this wasn't a confession she delivered with ease. His chest tightened with that knowledge, with unexplainable emotion that he didn't want to feel. "You could have died. But you didn't and you're not going to now. I used to come here when I was a kid, actually. With my father. I've spent lots of time in this cave."

Her hands went to his wrists as if she were afraid he was about to leave. "You're sure it's safe?"

"Very. And we'll only be here a few hours before we make our connection with Flores. Give it a try." He paused intentionally, careful not to push too hard. "Yes?"

She hesitated again, and then said, "Okay." The one word quivered with discernible apprehension. He was proud of her for the bravery it took to speak it. Phobias were like criminals lurking in the mind waiting to attack, and were hard, often impossible, to defeat. He was lucky that some of the things he'd seen hadn't done the same to him. Some of his fellow agents hadn't been as fortunate.

"Good," he said of her agreement, reaching behind him to ease her leg from his with gentle insistence. "Stay here. I'll be right back." He settled her foot back on the ground and worked her fingers from his wrists.

He realized then that he'd gotten the trust he wanted. But now that he had it, that trust felt like a hot potato he should toss back. All the women he'd been with these past three years were of Alvarez's world. They were criminals, no better than the man they served, because of their choices. He'd tried to group Nicole into that category—just part of his assignment, gratifying his own needs. But Nicole wasn't one of those other women; she wasn't anything like them.

At the same time, he himself wasn't the type of man who walked in her world. He barely remembered his real name half the time. He didn't even have a home right now. Everything was in storage. His life was danger, sex, poison, in all different flavors. Nicole's world was a direct contrast to his: full of order and the pursuit of justice, by way of perfect appearances and rules.

Yet…he still wanted her. Not only did he want her, he had to have her. Just one time, he told himself. He'd make sure she enjoyed every last minute of it, too.

6

NICOLE HATED DEFEAT, and defeat created by one's own self was the worst kind. For all the structure and control in her life, claustrophobia had been her nemesis. She'd learned relaxation techniques to deal with it. She had even managed to get on a plane, albeit slightly sedated, but still, she'd managed to fly and not panic. She could do the same with this damn cave, and doing it without drugs would be a sign of real progress.

Easier said than done, she thought, as she stared at the black hole Constantine had disappeared into, and waited impatiently for the light he'd promised. All sorts of horrid fates that could befall him raced through her mind. Maybe a wild animal? Another snake?

Her eyes went to the giant rock Constantine had removed from blocking the hole that seemed barely big enough for him to slide down into. Retrieving a rope hidden somewhere inside the cave, he'd tied it around the rock, which she assumed was to pull it back in place when ready. She couldn't see how else the rock would get there once they were belowground. Quite ingenious.

Suddenly, a warm glow filled the cavern, and Nicole let out a breath she hadn't even realized she'd been holding. That was the signal to follow him. She steadied herself, pressing one balled hand to the center of her chest and her racing heart. She could do this, and she would not hyperventilate. Inhale, exhale. Okay. Maybe this was just what she needed. To face her fear.

Thunder crashed overhead, almost directly on top of her, and Nicole jumped at the ferocious sound. The violence of the storm somehow reminded her of the violence hunting them. This stupid phobia was not going to get her killed.

She didn't give herself time to think any further; she quickly narrowed her gaze on the makeshift stairs Constantine had told her about. Clear on where to step, she went into action, and started down the wall, the steel stakes, thankfully, as sturdy as Constantine had promised. She passed an electric lantern—the kind that campers use—hanging to her left a few steps down. It was a comforting sight as these lanterns weren't likely to burn out.

She focused on each step, refusing to look down, except that she ran out of metal stakes too quickly, with nowhere to go, and the ground still a long ways off. Nicole twisted around, placing her back to the wall, to find Constantine standing directly below her. She scanned the area, surprised to find it the size of a small bedroom.

Constantine held his hands out. "Jump," he said, pulling her attention to him. "I'll catch you."

If she tried, Nicole knew she could think of a million reasons not to jump. But then, she didn't want to try. She was frustrated with herself—for her fear, her blisters, for letting herself expose a weakness to a mere stranger. She jumped, her heart all but stopping with the act.

A second later, Constantine's hands settled on her hips, the fingers of one hand spread on her backside, seemingly holding her without effort. The heart that had stuttered was now back to pounding a rapid drumroll.

Constantine slid her body down his rock-hard perfect one with delicious slowness, their hips melting together. Somehow they froze like that, her feet not yet on the ground. The instant her gaze found the heat in his, her body reacted, nipples tightening, thighs aching with the burn of desire. He certainly knew how to take her mind off the small space.

"Glad I could help," he murmured, the hard line of his sexy mouth lifting ever-so-slightly as he gently eased her to her sore feet.

"Tell me I didn't say that out loud," she said, stunned that she would speak before thinking. That wasn't how she operated.

His eyes twinkled with mischief. "I'm glad to be of service. Let me seal the opening so we can't be found and I'll get right on it." His expression turned serious, his strong hands rubbing her arms, giving her goose bumps and making her realize how cool the cavern was despite the Texas heat. "Will you be all right for a minute?"

No. Don't leave me down here. Don't seal us in this tiny hole. Suddenly, the cave felt more like a phone booth than a small bedroom. She swallowed hard, fighting the urge to beg to be taken back above. "Yes," she lied, trying to smile and failing. "I'm fine now. I'm okay."

He didn't look convinced and reluctantly stepped away from her. "I'm fine," she repeated, responding to the doubt lingering in his eyes, hating that he apparently thought she needed coddling. Her voice turned stern. "And stop looking at me like I'm some needy child. What happened to the cold-shouldered jerk who led me here? Bring him back."

He stared at her, his gaze probing, seeing far too much, she was sure. "He'll be back when you're feeling better and can keep up with him."

"I'm fine!" she admonished in a whispered voice, because noise wasn't such a hot idea considering this was a hideout. "I can keep up just fine."

With an agility most didn't possess, Constantine sidestepped Nicole and jumped in the air, grabbing a steel stake with one hand. He hung there a moment, rotating around to face her. He winked. "We'll find out if you really can, soon."

No doubt of his meaning, her body purred in response. He gave her no chance to reply to the bold statement, presenting her with his back as he climbed the wall. Muscles flexed under his wet T-shirt, denim hugging his nice tight ass. She bit her bottom lip. He was so much trouble, but he might just be worth it. And it wasn't as if he was out of line.

Her little comment had given him an open invitation to come seduce her into calmness, which hadn't been her intention. Not really, anyway. Or maybe it was. Her subconscious was working at getting her what she really wanted—Constantine. She'd wanted that man since meeting him in the bar, despite knowing he didn't fit her perfectly painted world of vanilla sex and strict rules—correction, lately it had been no sex and strict rules.

Nevertheless, her current way of living had firmly placed her wild past behind her. And she felt her work helped her make amends—or try to, at least—for what she'd done back then, for getting that damn killer off and watching him take another life. She still had nightmares about the victim.

Her mind's stroll down memory lane landed her smack-dab in reality. In the small cave. In her present state of discomfort. An easier discomfort than the past held, at least. Her hand went to her throat as she watched Constantine disappear through the same opening she'd just climbed through, leaving her alone. In a hole. A small one. Okay. Maybe this wasn't better than revisiting the past.

Nicole drew a long breath simply because she wanted to make sure there was plenty of air. Then, with supreme effort, she forced herself to stop staring at the exit.

Scrutinizing her surroundings, it appeared she was in a well-planned hideout, not just some cave Constantine knew as a kid. All the basics were present: a small mattress, a small fridge, battery-operated fans and even a few books. Her attention went to each wall as she circled around, feeling as if those walls might close in on her. Her head started spinning, and she knew she was about to hyperventilate. Not something she wanted to do with Constantine nearby. Time to put her relaxation techniques to use.

She quickly sat down on the hard ground, before she fell down, her legs stretched before her. She was too wet, and didn't want to risk damaging the mattress. Resting her head against the wall behind her, her gaze went to the ceiling. Could it collapse? Fall on top of her like the apartment floor had done so many years before? No. This wasn't the way to calm down.

Nicole squeezed her eyes shut and tried to focus on something soothing. Birds. Flowers. Sunrises. Instead, her brain took her to an image of Constantine's sweet ass in those dark jeans. Then to the way he'd caught her when she'd jumped, and that sensual slide down that steely body. Her imagination went wild as she fantasized stripping off his wet shirt, exploring those defined biceps and hard abs she'd felt through his clothes. He'd be wild, demanding, incredible in bed. She knew this, felt it in every inch of her being.

Yes, she missed wild, wonderful sex. But if she opened the door to a dangerous form of sensual pleasure, would she open the door to that person she'd once been? The one who'd put power and money, even pleasure, above all else? In her tormented moments, when the past had twisted her in knots, she had blamed her ex for influencing her behavior, which was a joke. Her choices were her own. No matter how much she had tried, she couldn't deny she possessed a dark, wild persona that she had tried to smash into retreat. So surrounding herself with people like Constantine, who could free her of her inhibitions—that was a dangerous proposition. Dangerous. Yes. That was Constantine. Dangerously tempting. Dangerously hot.

Vague noises indicating Constantine was moving around at the entrance drew Nicole's attention. Her lashes lifted the instant he jumped down to the cavern floor again. He tossed the rope in a corner, leaving no evidence above of their presence. He stood at full height. This space really wasn't so tiny, she thought, comforting herself with the fact.

Constantine brushed his hands together. "All secure."

She wondered about that. "If you grew up on this land, don't you think that made it easy for them to find you?"

He walked to the fridge and knelt down, pulling open the door. "The title is buried too well for that." He removed a bottle of water and offered it to her. "My grandmother registered the land in her maiden name, and since then it looks as if it's passed through several owners' hands. Now it's registered under an alias. So, no. The land isn't how they found us."

She accepted the water, surprised it was cold. "How did you manage electricity?"

He patted the top of the fridge. "Special order. Industrial battery-powered. Cost a nice penny, but it's worth it."

Nicole had to agree. She unscrewed the bottle and gulped half the contents while Constantine, squatting down near her, did the same with his own water.

Discarding the bottle on the ground, she said, "I better stop. I'll need to go to the bathroom."

He inclined his chin toward a blanket dangling in front of an opening in the left wall. "Camper toilet."

"You really thought of everything," she said, grimacing at the humble facility. "Still. I think I'll try to avoid using it."

Switching back to safety issues, Nicole considered what he'd said about the property, and vocalized what was running through her mind. "If the title wasn't traceable, then someone on the inside gave away your location."

Constantine finished off his water and discarded the container. Still in a squatting position, he faced her. "Has to be."

"What about Agent Flores?"

Something serious flashed across his face, subtle but distinct, wiped away with the speed and discipline of a man who knew how to live behind an emotional mask. But not fast enough to escape Nicole's notice. She made her living reading people.

"It's not Flores," he said dismissively. "It could have been any of the marshals involved in my protection."

His tone was short, clipped, insistent—even a bit defensive. Her brows dipped, her eyes narrowing on his face. Deep down, did he suspect Flores? Perhaps he didn't want to admit it, or just didn't want it to be true.

"Does he know where we are now?" she asked, treading on the thin waters of a bad subject, but also concerned for their safety.

"No one knows where we are but us," he assured her, his voice holding a confidence that soothed her concerns a bit—but not much.

She frowned. "I thought he was meeting us?"

"At a nearby location."

She nodded, relieved.

Their eyes locked and sexual tension spiked as if it had been shot into the room with a cannon. Silence fell between them, heavy with the sudden charge. Constantine was studying her with such intensity she felt as if he could see her soul, unveil what secrets her file hadn't already revealed. Wordlessly, he inched closer.

Instantly, Nicole's heart began to race, anticipating his touch, his nearness. He reached for one of her boots as if he meant to take it off. But that set off one of her phobia alarms, dousing the sexual heat of seconds before. How did he expect her to get out of this place without her boots? Nicole jerked her feet toward her, pulling her knees to her chest and hugging them. "What are you doing?"

"Getting you some comfort. You know your feet are killing you."

"I can't run in bare feet." Running in boots with the heels cut off was bad enough.

"You won't be running anytime soon," he informed her. "We have six hours until we leave. You might as well get some rest and dry off."

Her throat went dry. "Six hours? Several hours is now six? In this cave? Is there oxygen?"

"Yes. Plenty of ventilation points throughout the caverns."

She shook her head. All her efforts at relaxing flew to the wayside. "Still. No. I can't. I…I can't be in this hole that long." Constantine's expression softened.

"Don't look at me like that. I am fine. I just can't stay here that long."

He reached out and cupped her cheek with his hand. "You can." Somehow he was closer now. His knees touched hers, a small gesture in a small space. "I'll help you."

"I don't need your help. Just give me some room to process all of this." Crowding her would only make things worse.

But he didn't back off. His fingers slid around one of her calves and inched her pant leg upward; his callused fingers brushed below her knee. Tiny darts of anticipation shot straight to her core. And considering her current state of anxiety, that shouldn't be possible, but yet, he was proving it was. Maybe she didn't need space. Maybe she needed him. She focused on the sizzling sensations he was creating in her, focused on his face so she wouldn't look at the enclosure of the walls. His gaze swept her mouth. "I'm not sure I'm capable of giving you room right now," he said. "I want you too badly, Nicole."

She swallowed at the directness of his words, finding herself mesmerized, lost in those chocolate-colored eyes of his. Desire pooled in her limbs, driving away the fear once again.

Slowly Constantine began to inch the zipper on her boot downward, his fingers trailing her bare skin in its wake. Nicole suppressed a shiver, not willing to let him see how easily he affected her. The man even made removing a boot sexy.

"I didn't want to leave you that first night," he murmured.

The unexpected comment drew a hint of anger from her. Instinctively, she reached forward and covered his hand with hers, stilling his action. In the process, their lips drew close. After hours in the woods, he shouldn't smell good but he did. Spicy and male.

"But you did leave, didn't you?" she questioned, thinking of how he'd snuck under her guard and then left her sitting at that table, feeling a fool. It stung and the memory stiffened her spine.

"If I had stayed, I would have taken you up to a hotel room and made love to you in as many ways as you would have let me." His fingers slid around her other calf, and she couldn't find the will to stop him. "But then, morning would have come, and you would have hated me."

"I should hate you," she whispered, torn between her desire to embrace her attraction to this man and her fear of what doing so might mean. The fear that he might wake a part of her that needed to stay dormant. "What you did was wrong."

His gaze lifted from her mouth. "Do you?" he asked, staring at her. "Do you hate me, Nicole?"

She raised her chin slightly. If he thought lust and admiration, or even like, were the same, he was wrong. Her ex had taught her well—sex could be just sex. "I haven't decided yet."

His mouth quirked ever so slightly. "Good. Then I still have a chance to affect the decision."

Leaning into her, Constantine brushed his lips over

hers in a seductive caress that left her wanting more. "Anger can be a powerful aphrodisiac," he murmured softly. "Perhaps you can think of some ways to even the score."

And so the challenge was issued. Play or fold?

Should she hover in this cave and let her phobia get the best of her or show Agent Constantine Vega just how out of his league sexually he really was?

She gave him a sly, sensual smile a second before she nipped his bottom lip with her teeth. "Let's get started, shall we?"

She quickly slid out of his reach and rested against the wall. "Stand up and take off your clothes."

7

"STAND UP AND take off your clothes." Nicole repeated her words, letting them linger in the air, a challenge issued. She knew Constantine wasn't a man who easily gave away control, the exact reason why convincing him to do so now held so much excitement. "If you dare," she added, her words meant to provoke a reaction.

But Constantine wasn't one to be lured into an emotional response. He appeared frozen, no discernible expression on his handsome face. Ah, but she could sense the calculation in him, the struggle within his soul.

Finally he spoke, his voice low, taut. "Once we're even, we're even. The game starts all over again."

"This isn't a negotiation," she said with defiance.

Constantine merely crossed his arms in front of his big, brawny chest and cocked an eyebrow. Without words, he was demanding she concede.

Stubborn man. She had to find a way to steal some of the power. "Fine," she replied. "But I say when we're even."

And yet his expression said he wasn't biting. She made a frustrated sound. "What do you suggest then?"

The corners of his full mouth hinted at a smile, the look on his face now crystal clear. It was hungry, aroused, downright full of sexual heat.

His voice vibrated with that heat as he responded. "We'll both know when we're even." Confidence was clear in more than his words, it showed in his actions as he reached behind him and tugged his shirt over his head, tossing it aside.

Oh, mama, did Nicole get an eyeful of perfection. Constantine's light brown, sun-kissed coloring somehow emphasized the rippling, absolutely drool-worthy abs he possessed. Six-pack be damned. The man had an eight-pack. And nice pecs, too, with just the right amount of hair sprinkled around dark, flat nipples.

But the most arousing feature Constantine possessed thus far was the perfect line of hair seductively trailing downward and breaking at the depth of his inverted navel. It then continued lower until it disappeared into his jeans, a road map to sin and sensation she couldn't wait to explore.

Heat pooled between her legs, arousal radiating through every nerve ending in her body. She was wet and not from the rain. Wet from wanting. A want that had started a week ago when she'd met Constantine, but which had never been fully realized, or fulfilled.

Her gaze slowly slid back up that delicious path of hair. "Finish," she ordered, her voice far more affected than she would have liked it to have been.

"Whatever you want," he said, reaching for the top of his jeans.

"Remember that," she commented, thinking the list of wants was likely to be a long one at this rate. She wanted and wanted. Then, wanted some more. On top. On the bottom. Sitting. Standing. But not yet. Not until she'd tortured him as he had her. Not until that scoreboard was nice and even.

The zipper of his jeans slid down as she impatiently waited for all to be revealed. Unfortunately, he took a short detour, bending down and taking off his boots and socks. That had to be done, she reluctantly admitted, feeling impatient for her prize—a good look at Constantine in the raw.

When finally the denim slid away from his long limbs, so did the boxers. They came off in a swish of movement, leaving nothing but sinfully naked skin and amazing male perfection. Constantine stood before her, his cock jutting forward and all six foot plus inches of taut, mouthwatering muscle—the kind that came from dedicated hours in a gym.

Biting her bottom lip, Nicole debated. Crawl right on over and give him a lick or stand up and do a nice, visual walk around, check out that tight, now naked, ass of his. He deserved to wait for her mouth. Too bad that meant she had to wait, too.

She stood up and quickly made her way behind him. He started to turn. Nicole grabbed his hips. "Don't even think about it. This is my show right now."

"We'd both enjoy this more if you were naked, too."

"I'm enjoying myself just fine," she murmured, one

palm gliding over the contour of one firm butt cheek. Damn, it was nice. Tight. Muscular. Her brain went wild with more images: him on top, a mirror overhead, an exquisite view of his body as he pumped into her. Her sex clenched, her body needy for satisfaction. She settled for more exploration, palming the other cheek of that fine ass and then sliding her hands over the back of his upper thighs.

"You are enjoying yourself, Constantine," she purred, scooting closer to him, her fingers skimming his waist, teasing low on his stomach, taunting him with how near her hands were to his erection. "Aren't you?" Her teeth scraped his shoulder.

"You're killing me and you know it," he responded, his voice raspy with need.

"Am I?" Nicole questioned in mock innocence, moving her hands from his stomach and walking around to face him. Her eyes locked with his as she refused to look at his cock. "What can I do to make you feel better?"

"Take your clothes off." It was a command.

"No." She smiled seductively. "I'm sure I can soothe your needs some other way, though."

Taking a step forward, she brought his hard length to her immediate left, careful not to touch it with any part of her body. She slid one hand through that dark sprinkle of hair on his chest.

He reached for her and she smacked him away. "No. Don't make me tie you up. I'm sure you have the tools here in your well-stocked hideout."

She scraped his nipple with her fingernail. Constantine sucked in a soft breath, staring at her through heavy-lidded, passion-filled eyes as he vowed revenge. "I'm going to make you pay for this later."

Something told her she'd enjoy paying the price for her behavior, but she kept that as her secret. "That wouldn't be very gentlemanly of you, considering you brought this on yourself."

"I never claimed to be a gentleman, now did I?"

Her lips pursed. "True enough," she agreed, her fingers exploring the muscular contours of his chest before caressing their way to his stomach and brushing the dark hair of his pelvis area. "But then, I'm not exactly the girl next door, either."

"More ice princess," he accused.

Her brows dipped at the accusation, her hand moving swiftly, issuing punishment as it tightly wrapped around his cock. "Does this feel like ice?" she demanded, exploring his length and teasing the head, spreading the drop of dampness there around the smooth tip.

A low sound of pleasure slid from his parted lips, but he still managed a rebuttal. "You're coldhearted, darlin', and we both know it. Otherwise you'd let me touch you."

She pushed to her toes, her fingers still working his cock, her lips lingering a breath from his. "Making you pay for your bad behavior doesn't make me cold. Giving me the control simply makes you feel vulnerable, and you don't like it."

"I don't feel vulnerable at all," he replied quickly, a glib edge to his voice. "Perhaps it's you who does. Perhaps that's why you're afraid to let me touch you."

Nicole jerked back to glare at him, his words striking an unexpectedly raw nerve that she didn't like one bit. He quirked a brow as if he knew he were right, his expression a silent taunt. Her desire to wipe that sexy, smart-ass look off his too-handsome face sent her to her knees. She'd show him control.

She settled back on her heels, her fingers wrapping around the base of Constantine's erection. Bringing the soft tip of his cock near her mouth so that her breath teased, her chin tipped upward, her eyes found his. "Who has the control?"

His lips were thin, his body tense with anticipation. "You do, *cariña,*" he said gently, his voice hoarse. "I never said otherwise."

Not directly, but he'd inferred his own control. She lapped at his erection and then denied him further satisfaction. "Yes." The first word held a bite; the rest were an explanation for her actions. "You did."

"If you didn't have control," he spoke through clenched teeth, "I would have my hands in your hair right now, pushing your mouth back to my cock. But be warned." He paused, obviously to let the meaning of his words sink in. "If you tease me too much, I might take more than control."

His words both infuriated and scintillated. He was impossible, this man. Most men would beg at this point. He ordered, demanded, threatened to take her. And despite his attitude and his resistance to her command, he made her hot. She could feel her thighs trembling, her sex aching. Damn, the man. He would not win. He would beg before this was over.

Nicole ran her tongue down his length, licking him with long, teasing caresses, watching him watch her, aroused by the hunger in his gaze. She worked him with her tongue, stroking over and over, doing everything but taking him fully into her mouth. Still, Constantine used restraint; he didn't touch her, didn't ask for what she knew he wanted…what she wanted—for her to take all of him.

Eventually, she gave in to her own desire and drew him into her mouth, pleased when she heard his intake of breath. And while she wanted to see the desire in his features, she found herself absorbed in tasting him. Her lashes settled on her cheeks as she began to suckle him deeply, intent on the pleasure of giving pleasure. Her nipples ached, her clit throbbed. She wanted him to touch her. Still, he did not. His ability to refrain irritated her.

Fully determined to push him over the edge, she took him deeper into her mouth, her tongue stroking the underside of his shaft. Nicole's hand pumped even as her mouth slid back and forth. His hips began to work against her hand. She palmed his ass, using it to anchor her body as he thrust harder, faster. She could taste the salty proof of how near release he was. So close. Satisfaction filled her, driving her to push him further into his pleasure zone. She slid her fingers along the crevice of his ass, exploring all she could, everywhere she could.

Success came to Nicole when Constantine's hands slid into her hair, as if he feared she would stop working him, stop tasting him. She didn't push his hands away as she might have minutes before. She wanted him to come. Wanted to know she'd taken this powerful male over the edge. She suckled him completely. He was hers now, lost to passion, lost to what she'd taken from him—control. Oh, how she loved it. She'd won the minute he'd touched her head, the minute he'd begun to cling to release.

But just when she thought she'd won, Constantine surprised her, totally taking her off guard. In a movement both fast and hard, he pulled himself free of her. Before she knew it, he'd bent down and picked her up as if she weighed nothing. She either had to let her legs dangle or wrap them around his body, which is what she did. His hands tangled in her half-dry hair, his lips claiming hers, his tongue blasting her with wild fire, stealing her objections with its bittersweet perfection. Everything in her world seemed to melt into that moment, into Constantine's kiss, his body.

Long moments later, he tore his lips from hers. "We're even now. You've thoroughly tormented me."

"I'd only gotten started," she hissed, her voice filled with passion. She wanted to kiss him again.

"I am going to make you come so many times you won't remember your name. Just mine."

His mouth claimed hers in a dominating, hot kiss that left Nicole no room to resist—not that she wanted to. This man's kisses had the unique ability to arouse her entire body. Pure unadulterated lust licked at her limbs, his promises playing in her mind and delivering an extra thrill. Constantine had claimed control, which belonged to her, and she should care. She would care. Right after this kiss.

He seemed to read her mind, tearing his lips from

hers. "Nicole," he whispered, his jaw sliding along hers, lips by her ear. "Since we're even now. No more hiding behind that control of yours. It's mine now. You're mine now."

8

CONSTANTINE WANTED Nicole's surrender, and he planned to have it this night. He swallowed her objections with another hot kiss, savoring the sweet taste of her. His fingers sprawled on her back, caressing their way over her side, and upward, until he cupped her breast. His thumb slid over her nipple, back and forth, and she rewarded his actions with a soft moan. A moan that spurred his hunger for another one. Yet, he had one thing to attend to first. One absolute must.

Reluctantly, he set Nicole down, driven by the incentive to strip her naked. The barriers had to go, both in the form of her clothing and her games. He'd studied her file. He knew she'd hit the sex clubs with her ex, but he also knew she'd left all that behind years ago. Had covered herself in a prim-and-proper facade—the untouchable ice princess. The idea of making her melt thickened his shaft, arousing him with the sweetness of her submission.

He reached for the buttons of her blouse, impatience

making him forgo the effort. "Take it off before I rip it off." He leveled her in a steady look. "And don't think I won't do it. You successfully achieved your goal." Constantine stroked his shaft. "I'm on edge. I want you in a bad way."

She took a step back from him and knelt down, removing her boots, her gaze going to his hand as he stroked himself, her teeth sinking into her bottom lip. "I could have taken care of that for you."

"You will," he said with certainty. "My way."

She stood up, boots and socks discarded, her toes painted a light, delicate pink. Everything about her body was feminine and perfect, soft in all the right spots. But then there was that hard exterior she hid her emotions behind. That had to go. He wanted her in full submission, which meant the walls had to come down.

"What if I don't want to do it your way?"

He quirked a brow at that. "You have something against pleasure? Because, that's what I intend for both of us."

Surprise flickered in her eyes, his response obviously taking her a bit off guard. She hesitated, and then brought her fingers to the silk buttons of her blouse, working them with speed and agility. Her actions, whether she knew it or not, offered her first bit of submission. She'd agreed to allow him his way. They were already making progress.

Without preamble, Nicole finished her task. She slid the blouse off her shoulders, leaving her in a damp, sheer pink bra that clung to her breasts, the red pert nipples beneath the material exposed for his hungry eyes.

Thankfully, she didn't stop there. In less than a minute, her slacks were gone, giving him a delicious view of her long legs and creamy white skin. Next came the panties, the tangle of blond curls drawing his gaze to the V of her body, and he wondered if she was wet—no, he knew she was. He wondered how she would taste, how she would feel wrapped around his cock.

That thought skidded to a temporary halt as that sheer bra flew to the ground, allowing him to worship those full, high breasts with a more thorough examination.

"I'm all yours, Agent Vega." Her hands went in the air, to her sides, a come-and-get-me invitation. "What are you going to do with me?"

A smile touched his lips with that challenge. Somehow, she'd given in to his demands but still managed to make her own. Damn, this woman got to him.

"On the mattress," he ordered.

Her eyes didn't leave his face. One second, two—she seemed to consider this path of submission that she was treading down. Then, as if she'd decided it, she said, "All right," and settled on the mattress. She sat with her hands behind her, breasts thrust forward, legs slightly parted in a tease of a pose.

Constantine wasn't in the mood to be teased. Not anymore. He found the edge of the mattress with his knees. Before she knew his intentions, she was on her stomach.

His hands braced on either side of her head, his face buried in her neck, cock brushing that lush backside. "My way," he murmured, his nostrils flaring with the sweet scent of her arousal. "You'll like my way, just wait and see."

Slowly, he eased back to his knees, one hand on her lower back in case she decided to turn, the other giving her backside a tiny little slap. Not hard. Just enough to let her know who was in charge.

She pushed up on her hands. "Hey——" The objection became a soft moan as his one palm slid under her stomach, lifting and holding her hips even as he slid a finger across the slick wet heat between her legs, parting her swollen lips. He stroked her sensitive skin, preparing her a moment before sliding his finger inside her.

Her arms went limp, fingers curling in the blanket covering the mattress. A soft moan came purring from that full mouth that had been on his cock only minutes before. He moved the hand he held on her stomach, sliding it to her clit, tweaking and flicking, the action encouraging her hips to arch upward.

Her ass tilted up, giving him better access, inviting him to explore more. He palmed her cheeks, taking a moment to admire that stellar ass in the air before he rotated to lie on his back. He scooted beneath her hips until he found his target. He lapped at her clit and then suckled it. She bucked against him, moving with his actions.

While some women might have stayed on their stomachs, Nicole wasn't one of them. Nor had he expected her to be. She pushed to her hands and knees, but not to escape. She wanted more, spreading her legs, and rocking with the thrust of his tongue. Constantine licked and teased. Her clit was swollen, the delicious honey of her body proof of her nearing orgasm. But just when he thought she'd surely go over the edge, she moved.

Suddenly, Nicole was straddling him. A second later, she took him inside her, surprising and pleasing him all in one action. In unison, they moaned with the impact of her taking his shaft deep inside her body, warm, wet heat consuming him.

She braced her hands on his chest, her voice raspy. "We're trying to get to 'even,' right? You didn't come without me. I didn't want to come without you."

She had wrapped her actions in a sexual taunt, but there was more to it than that. The give-and-take, the status of "even" rather than of one defeating the other— something about that touched him on an emotional level and shifted the mood.

As if she sensed that and it scared her, she quickly whispered, "That doesn't mean I don't hate you," as her hips worked his cock in a slow, circular tease of a motion. He watched her, enjoying the way her breasts bounced ever-so-slightly with the gentle movement, a visual pleasure, like the rest of her lush body.

"You don't hate me," he said, her actions proving just the opposite.

"I might," she whispered again, but her eyes locked with his, full of intimacy that reached deeper than their connected bodies.

"Don't," he told her firmly. "Don't hate me."

His words altered the mood further, and with the suddenness of a lightning strike in a summer storm, all their power plays, all their games, simply evaporated. Their bodies stilled. There was only this—only the two of them. Perhaps, the uneasiness of their futures, of the way this race for their lives would end, contributed to their feelings. Their connection deepened beyond the physical.

They moved as one. She leaned down as he reached for her. Their lips met in a kiss that was tender, passionate, their tongues stroking, caressing, tasting. Their bodies began a slow dance that matched the rhythm of their tongues. He murmured her name. She murmured his. Their hands explored. He felt her every breath, tasted her every moan. And reveled in the gasp that came a second before her orgasm.

She tensed, burying her face in his neck, her sex spasming around his cock, wet heat begging him to pump harder, deeper. He gave her what she wanted, what he, too, wanted. One hand on her back, he pressed her tight against his body even as he lifted his hips. Suddenly, he exploded, pleasure inching through his groin with an intensity that shook him from head to toe.

Later, they lay there, sated for the time being. She was soft and delicate in his arms. He still wanted her, he realized, arousal forming yet again—his desire to take her was nowhere near depleted. His idea that having her would satisfy his need for her hadn't worked. But even more concerning was what he felt. There was more in the air than good sex. The air crackled with an emotional awareness that he suspected had taken her by surprise as much as it had him. He wasn't a man that did relationships. His career simply didn't allow it. So why wasn't he moving? Why did he want to hold her, to make love to her again?

Before he could give his reaction to Nicole any real consideration, she lifted her head and stared at him, blond hair now dry, wild and sexy around her face and creamy white shoulders. Seconds passed, her attention fixed on his face, probing, intense. Then, without a word, she slid off him and onto her back, arm draped over her face as if she didn't want to be seen. Or perhaps she didn't want to see the ceiling of the cave. Her claustrophobia was still very real; he'd simply distracted her thoughts, her mind, her fears.

It pleased him he could do that for her, that she'd wanted him enough to forget a phobia that clearly controlled her on many levels. An odd desire to pull her close again overwhelmed him. Which was exactly why he didn't reach for her. His life allowed them nowhere to go but to bed. Period. The end.

The dampness on his stomach needed attending, which gave him a "holy shit" reality check. They hadn't used birth control. He always used a condom. Always. Even had one in his wallet, which he'd intended to use. Nicole had overwhelmed him, straddling him like she did, and he'd forgotten himself. Scrubbing his jaw, he resolved himself to the conversation that had to take place.

He reached inside a box that sat beside the mattress, grabbed a small towel and wiped his stomach before moving to Nicole's side. He settled the towel between her legs and held it there, silently asking for her attention.

Her arm lifted from her face, her expression holding a question. "We didn't use a condom," he stated.

She didn't so much as blink. "I take a Depo shot for birth control every three months. Have for years. We're safe. Of course, being responsible adults, we should have used protection for other reasons. Still..." Worry flashed in her eyes. "If Alvarez has his way, we won't see another day, anyway."

The relief he'd felt when she said she used birth control faded with the rest of her words. Constantine recognized the subtle confession she'd offered of being scared over their situation. He was a hard man, not often one to offer comfort, but Nicole touched a softer spot in him, an effect that he wasn't sure he liked. That hardness in his soul had kept him alive a good many times. But somehow it didn't matter where she was concerned, and he didn't know why.

Pulling Nicole into his arms, her back to his chest, a little sound of surprise slid from her lips—surprise that mimicked what he felt inside by his own actions. She didn't resist being held, and that pleased him on a level he preferred not to analyze.

Soon, they were spooning, and inevitably, her soft curves had his body responding to her nearness. He was hard again and he didn't try to hide it. Instead, he tucked himself between her legs and simply held her. She relaxed against him, again showing him a sign of that trust he'd wanted so badly. Her hard shell had melted away for him. Maybe it would be back tomorrow, probably would, in fact. Probably should. But right now, he wanted to deserve what she'd offered. Resolve formed. Constantine had seen Alvarez destroy too many lives. Nicole wasn't going to be one of them. He'd brought this situation on her; he wouldn't leave her high and dry. And he wasn't about to allow the past three years to mean nothing.

He tucked his chin by her shoulder, her hair tickling his cheek. "Everything will work out. I promise."

9

NICOLE SNUGGLED into the warmth around her, a feeling she clung to, a shelter in a storm. "Nicole. Wake up."

A caress touched her hair, her shoulder. "We have to go soon." The voice came near her ear. Male. Sexy… It jerked her awake. Nicole sat up, looked around her, sucking in a breath that felt a bit out of reach. "Cave," she gasped. "We're in a cave."

"Easy, *cariña*." Constantine was sitting beside her now, pulling her back into those warm, safe arms, against that hard chest she'd explored not so long ago. His hands stroked her hair, her arm. She melted into him as the confinement of the small space worked a number on her nerves. She wasn't weak. She overcame her fear earlier. She could do it now.

Inhaling again, she tried to pull some air into her lungs; she reached for calmness. "I hate this so much."

"I know. We're leaving in about an hour from now."

"I didn't mean this place, but the way I respond to it. I hate it." Why had she just admitted that? Nicole

gently pushed out of his arms. "I'm okay." She scooted
to the edge of the bed, telling herself the exposed feeling was her nudity when she knew it was her emotions.
Something was happening with Constantine. She'd gone
to him in lovemaking, and now she'd opened up about
her inner fears.

He slid a sheet over her shoulders, as if offering her
shelter. His hands stayed on her shoulders. "We all have
things we wish we could change about ourselves."

She shifted her position to face him. "Yeah?" She
didn't wait for an answer. "What would you change?"

"Being too weak to kill Alvarez when I had the
chance." Constantine scooted to the edge of the mattress.

"That wasn't weakness," she assured him. "Doing
what is right is harder than doing what you desire." She
knew this firsthand. Knew it because she'd lived a life
where money and excitement, even sex, drove her actions. Where winning wasn't about what was right. It
was about what it could do for her.

He didn't comment, and for some reason, she thought
he regretted his admission as much as she had hers. She
opened her mouth to ask why and shut it again—the
sight of Constantine pushing to his feet, his jeans in his
hand, stealing her words. He was naked and, with the
flex of all that muscle, breathtakingly male.

As if he wanted to tempt her into an outright erotic
fantasy, he gave her a show, pulling on his underwear
and pants, his long legs, and tight ass, too spectacular
to ignore. Amazingly, she managed to reach for her bra

and slip it on, thankful it was almost dry. Somehow, she even pulled on her wrinkled mess of a blouse.

Her gaze swept the broad expanse of his chest, the bulge of his arms. She had slept like a baby in those arms, despite the cave. How long had it been since she'd slept in a man's arms? Two years? Three? It didn't mean anything. Nor did the desire she had for this man. He wasn't pulling her back into her old life, her old world. She was stronger now. She could separate her sexual needs and wants from her other choices. In fact, wasn't Constantine helping her to see that?

Constantine grabbed his shirt and pulled it on, covering up the chest and arms she'd been inspecting. Nicole finished dressing, easing her pants over her hips. She had justified her actions by her need for a distraction. Who would have known a hot man could put an end to her claustrophobia, or at least put it in check?

Nicole was about to put her boots on when Constantine kneeled beside her and stilled her actions with his hand on her leg. He indicated a box beside the mattress. "There are bandages and ointment in there. It will help ease the pain."

His touch sent a barely concealed shiver down her spine. "Thanks," she said, cutting her gaze away from his too-attentive eyes.

While Nicole bandaged her foot, Constantine filled a backpack with supplies and then sat down next to her.

"Hungry?" he asked, offering her a granola bar.

Her stomach rumbled loudly and they both laughed. A smile touched his lips. He was handsome when he smiled, and the awkwardness of their confessions faded away.

"I guess that answers your question," Nicole responded, pressing her hand to her abdomen and accepting the food.

He grabbed a couple bottles of water from the fridge and they ate in silence. Nicole could barely wait to leave. She thought back to how understanding Constantine had been of her phobia. Her ex rarely crossed her mind these days, but he did now. He'd been impatient over her claustrophobia, irritated because their sexual escapades never included her being tied up, and embarrassed when she panicked on business flights. She hated those memories, but considering their current life-and-death circumstances, Constantine's patience had been a surprise. He was a contradiction, demanding and hard, yet gentle and understanding. It made her curious about him.

"You must have spent a lot of time out here to know the land so well," she commented, hoping for a look inside his past.

"I moved in with my grandmother when I was twelve. My grandfather died in Vietnam and she never remarried." He cut her a sideways look. "My mother died of breast cancer and my father threw himself into his work after her death. He died a year later on an undercover assignment."

"FBI?"

"Yes."

"You must have been proud of him to follow in his footsteps." She and her father hadn't agreed on a lot of things these past few years, but he'd been her idol growing up. Seemed Constantine had felt the same about his father. She continued, "I went into law because of my father. Of course, I ended up choosing a different direction for my career. I'm sure you read all of that in my file."

"I did," he admitted, not appearing uncomfortable with her private details. "Must be awkward to have your ex still working with him."

Nicole shrugged. "I've learned to accept being the outsider." She fiddled with the paper wrapper around her granola bar. Even her mother acted as if she'd betrayed the family.

"Your sister is going to work with them now, isn't she?"

"My file has a little of everything, doesn't it?" She didn't wait for an answer. "I don't want her to but she won't listen. She wants to be the defense attorney no one can beat and have a paycheck that proves it." She shifted the conversation back to him. "Do you have any siblings?"

"No," he said, his tone clipped, as if she'd asked something offensive. Perhaps a sign he was done with the personal talk.

Either way, all this chatter about the darkness hidden in his past, in her past, took her mind back to something he had said right before falling asleep. "Everything doesn't always work out no matter how hard we try."

A shadow flashed across his face. "This will," he said, his gaze locking with hers, that edge of danger she'd seen in him on other occasions igniting like a sudden flame. "I walked away from too many chances to kill that man for us to fail now. I'm getting you to that trial, and you're going to convict him. I won't let him walk away."

Nicole's eyes went wide. Something about his last words, his promise that Alvarez wouldn't walk away, bit into her nerve endings. What exactly did that mean? Was he saying he'd kill Alvarez if she failed to convict him?

Before she could reply, a beeper on Constantine's watch went off and he pushed to his feet. "Time to go."

She stood, feeling lighter with the prospect of escape from the cave, but no less concerned about his comment. "I'm all for that."

"Stay here," he ordered, as he had so many times in the woods. "I need to check the surface for unwanted visitors." He didn't wait for an answer; he started up the wall. All the warmth of before had fled. He was cold, calculating, a soldier on a mission.

Constantine was willing to do whatever it took to take down Alvarez—even become a murderer himself. She'd walked the line between right and wrong, and it was a dangerous place to balance. A place that would steal your soul if you let it and she almost had. Nicole realized why Constantine scared her so much. He was walking that line just as she had. He was walking it and she was afraid he'd pull her along with him.

AN HOUR AFTER traveling in the pitch-black night, Nicole found herself, once again, hiding in the bushes, Constantine by her side. The rain was gone, but a starless, moonless sky spoke of more to come. Eerie silence thickened in the humid night air, heavy and ominous.

With an incline of his head, Constantine directed her attention to what appeared to be a small trailer park only a hill beyond the cover of the woods.

"We're meeting Agent Flores there?" she whispered.

He pointed, indicating lights bobbing and weaving down the old dirt road leading to the trailers. She swallowed hard, her stomach fluttering with worry. He thought something was wrong. She could tell by the stiffness of his body, and by the uneasy vibe he gave off since departing the cave.

He didn't look at her when he spoke. "Stay low and let's move." And then he was gone. Nicole scrambled forward as he disappeared beneath the waist-deep grass, making fast tracks down the hill. She bent down, following his lead. The possibility of another snake crossed her mind, but she shoved the worry aside. She had to keep up with Constantine. He was moving so fast that she had to push to catch up. And then, as if slamming into a wall, he stopped. Chest heaving, Nicole skidded to a halt and kneeled beside him.

She watched in silence as a nearby car's lights went off, and the passenger's door opened, inviting them inside. A safe haven was only a few feet away.

Nicole grabbed Constantine's arm, silently asking for confirmation that this was their ride. He gave her a quick nod. Before she could fully embrace the glory of being saved, he took her hand and pulled her forward, making a beeline toward the car. And that was when all hell broke loose.

Out of the silence, the sound of motorcycle engines blasted the air, and Nicole knew without being told, they were in trouble, about to be found. Their ride was so close. Nicole clung to the hope of shelter, but to her horror, Constantine tugged her in the opposite direction, detouring from the nearby safety that merely taunted her.

Moments later, Constantine maneuvered her behind a trailer, completely out of Agent Flores's view. "Why aren't we with Flores?" she whispered urgently, watching as Constantine bent down and yanked a piece of underpinning from the trailer.

"They didn't find us on their own." He motioned her forward, into the darkness beneath the trailer. "Go."

She would have argued but gunfire filled the air, followed by the sound of a motorcycle engine growing closer. Without further hesitation, she scrambled beneath the house, Constantine at her heels. Cobwebs skimmed her face and she bit back a yelp. Constantine quickly put the siding in place not a second too soon, as a motorcycle sped directly by their location. Any fear of what was in the darkness disappeared as Nicole realized how close they'd come to being discovered.

Her heart pounded furiously in her chest, her mind racing just as wildly. Sooner or later they would be found. What would happen to them? What about the innocent people in this trailer park? Did Constantine think Flores had led the attackers to them on purpose? Surely not. That had to be his gun firing at the bikers. Someone in the trailer park might have called the police, but they were so far off the beaten path. Would it be soon enough to save them?

A penlight came on, barely illuminating Constantine's face. He motioned her forward. "This way," Constantine whispered, leading her to the front end of the trailer, weaving through the darkness as if it were daylight.

The sound of a motorcycle neared again...no, two—two motorcycles. Constantine waited until they passed and then eased a small patch of siding away to scan the situation beyond it. Nicole scooted forward and did the same. Unbelievably, they were right beside a pickup truck.

"Bingo," he murmured, glancing at her. "The minute you see the passenger's door open, start running and don't stop until you are inside."

As usual, he didn't wait for a reply. He was already on the move, slipping through the opening that seemed too small for him. She tried to get her mind around everything that was happening, trying to make it some nightmare, not her life. But it was her life.

She watched Constantine stealing the truck. Pressing her fist against her chest, she thought her heart might explode. She let out a sigh of relief as the car door opened. She sucked in another breath before wiggling through the hole, not giving herself time to think about what might happen if this went bad.

Nicole cleared the trailer and crawled toward the truck. A motorcycle sounded again, then another gunshot. Her heart lurched. Digging her knees into the ground, she pushed forward. Finally, she was there, climbing into the truck. She pulled the door shut, ducking below the window, and not a moment too soon. A motorcycle sped by, but this time it stopped. Male voices sounded, pieces of the sentences reaching her ears. They were going to start a search on foot.

Constantine worked the wires beneath the dash, his head low. "Good," he said of the conversation they'd overheard. "We want them on foot so we get ahead of them." He motioned with his chin. "There's a gun inside the bag on the seat. Get it out. You're going to need it."

She did as he said, removing the hefty handgun that was sure to fire with a kick that would jolt her from here to Mexico.

The truck's engine roared to life. Yes! Nicole screamed in her mind.

Constantine floored the accelerator, the tires on the truck screeching against dirt and rock as he made a rapid turn to the left.

A motorcycle appeared by her window; the driver pointed a gun at her. Her hand tightened on her gun. Constantine swerved at the rider and the bike crashed. One danger gone. More to come.

Nicole slid open the rear window of the cab; a pair of bikers were on their tail. Aiming, she shot at the tires of the nearest motorcycle. She hit her target, but the backfire of the weapon sent a jolt of pain up her arm, through her shoulder and into her chest. Worth the pain though. The biker skidded across the terrain and crashed as the other one had.

She steeled herself to fire again, but was thankful when the second pursuer dropped back before she had to. Sinking into her seat, she let out a breath. "I think they're gone."

"They'll be back."

She glanced over at him. "I figured, but let me revel in momentary success."

"Those were Carlos Menchaca's men," he announced. "I'm sure you've seen his name in the file."

"Menchaca," she said, ready to focus. "Right. He runs drugs along the border for Alvarez."

They'd cleared the woods now; a highway was within sight. "Carlos will see what I did as a personal betrayal. He considered me a friend. I fooled him when no one has. He'll come after me for that reason alone. Pleasing Alvarez will be nothing but bonus points."

"I thought he was part of the Alvarez takedown?"

"He was supposed to be. Somehow he slipped away the night of the bust. I'd hoped he'd be found before he became a problem. But since that little fantasy hasn't come true, I have only one option."

Nicole swallowed. She knew what he meant. He was talking about going after Carlos.

Life as she knew it seemed to get more complicated every second she was with Constantine. Every time she turned around, he was walking that thin line she tried to avoid, stepping in the gray instead of living with black and white, right and wrong.

It was easy to decipher Constantine's reasoning without even hearing him speak. The world would be a better place without men like Alvarez and Carlos, and she didn't disagree. But she also knew the law existed for a reason. To protect people's rights. When you let it fade away, the system, and its foundation for existing, did as well. Which left her with the question of how to handle Constantine. She glanced at his ruggedly handsome profile, not sure of her answer.

Should she support him? Try to convert him to the straight and narrow? But then, a man like Constantine could make a woman forget herself. Maybe she should run like hell before she was the one to get converted.

10

CONSTANTINE CLUTCHED the steering wheel of the Mustang Coupe he'd nabbed about twenty minutes outside of the trailer park. Had Flores—one of the few people he trusted—betrayed him? He didn't want to believe that. Flores had been like a brother, a close friend, one of the few he'd ever called a friend in fact. But then, his world was corrupt; his life, riddled with enemies.

"No answer," Nicole said, dialing one of the disposable cell phones they'd bought at a twenty-four-hour, touristy-type store. They had both gotten T-shirts and cleaned up. Nicole had even bought a pair of tennis shoes. "Not from my boss or my sister. I can understand my boss. He's probably at the hospital with his wife, but I'll feel better when I hear he's keeping me on this case. I'm more prepared than anyone to put Alvarez away. Even with a slight delay of the trial from all of this I can be back in Austin and started in a week. If it goes well, we can keep the jury already selected."

"I'm sure your boss will see that," Constantine said,

his reply weak, distracted. Nicole's concern for her family proved how different their lives were. Back at the cave he'd almost convinced himself they were alike, that maybe he was ready for the kind of connection they shared. He was already leaving the agency, after all. But that wasn't the case. His enemies would always be in the shadows, a threat to him and anyone near him. Hell. Carlos would kill Nicole just to prove Constantine couldn't protect her. If he knew Constantine had feelings for her, that would only give him more satisfaction.

"I hope so," she said of her boss's understanding, drawing him back into the conversation he'd all but forgotten. "I mean, what's the point in putting another D.A. in danger. I'm already a part of this, and I've accepted being in hiding until the trial."

Nicole had asked him a million questions about where they would hide, and how they would pull off getting back for the trial. She tried to control things when she felt uneasy, he'd figured that out, both in and out of bed. It didn't bother him. In fact, he rather liked knowing he'd broken the barrier in bed. But why the idea of doing so outside of it appealed to him, he didn't know. Not that it mattered anymore. He had no business getting close to her. At this point, he had to stop the bond that was only beginning to take form between them before it was too late. He was a one-night stand and nothing more. She needed to know that. Hate him if she had to, but do so alive.

He cast her a sideways look; her hand was shaking ever-so-slightly as she punched the cell numbers again.

With a jerky movement, she shoved hair behind her ear. "My sister—"

"Is in Hawaii celebrating the results of her bar exam," he told her, his voice full of a calm certainty. "She's safe."

A frustrated sound slid from her lips. "I'd feel better if I heard her voice. I told you my father would refuse security. It figures he's the only one I've been able to reach."

Constantine tried to comfort her. "At least he agreed to send your mother away, and he's trying to reach your sister, too. Even though Alvarez is standing trial, his reach is far and deep. And his crew know what's expected of them." He switched gears. "Dial Flores again, will you?"

She thumbed through the list of numbers and did as he asked, handing him the phone. After several rings, Constantine gave up, grinding his teeth to keep from cursing.

"You're worried," she said, and he could feel her looking at him.

He focused on the white lines of the highway rather than her, not sure what she wanted him to say. He was worried and he didn't want to lie to her. Before morning he planned to be a long ways from here. He'd already told her he had a boat at Padre Island that was well-stocked with supplies, and even plenty of cash.

When he didn't answer, she probed. "Can't you call someone else?"

"I could," he agreed reluctantly, "but I'd rather not

until I figure out where the leak is. Carlos found us somehow."

"Could they have followed Flores?"

"Maybe." Of course, he'd considered that option, but Flores was careful—too careful for stupid mistakes. Constantine didn't say anything more, didn't want to add to her concerns.

"Try to get some rest," he suggested. "We have a few hours before we stop."

He needed to think. If Flores had betrayed him, where did that leave him? There were higher-ups he could go to, but again, who did he trust?

She let the seat ease backward and turned on her side, facing him, her hands under her cheek. As she watched him, she asked, "This won't end at the trial, will it?"

His gut twisted with that question. She didn't understand how true her assumption was. He'd learned the hard way. He'd lost a brother when the legal system failed. "Even if we put away Alvarez, Carlos will keep coming. For me. For you. For anyone he can bleed for vengeance. So in answer to your question, no, it won't end with this trial."

She was silent for several seconds. "Capture him and I promise to convict him."

He glanced at her. She couldn't promise that. She knew it as well as he did.

Darkness slid through him. He was angry. At himself for failing his brother. At the system for failing his brother. And at Nicole for working both sides of that system.

"You and I know that attorneys can get criminals off. You've done it yourself." The air chilled with his words but he pressed onward. "I get that you think you're cleaning your soul by doing things by the book. But frankly, sometimes that book does more harm than good."

"So murder is okay if you do it for the right reason?"

Who was she to judge him? "I'm not after a big salary or even recognition. I simply want Alvarez and Carlos stopped."

"You bastard," she hissed at him. "That was a horrible thing to say to me."

"I'm just speaking the truth, sweetheart, and I didn't say you. I meant in general. Tell me. How does the possibility of letting someone like Alvarez or Carlos walk on a damn technicality make you feel? It's okay to let them go and damage more people's lives? You can live with that?"

"No one says they will walk. But what would you have me do? Fabricate evidence to ensure convictions?"

"If you know that person is guilty, and you know they will kill innocent people, how can you let them get away with it?"

Her voice was a bit breathless. "I don't know what happened to you while you were with Alvarez, but whatever it was, it's destroyed your perspective." Her tone grew stronger, more forceful. "You can't work within a system you don't support. You can't convict criminals when you are willing to become one."

"Don't you get it?" he asked, laughing bitterly. "The system asked me to become one. That was the only way to take down Alvarez. You use all the wrongs done by people like me to make your cases and yourself feel safe and honorable. I am what I am because of the system. Hate me if you will, but if you fail to convict Alvarez or even Carlos, I'll finish the job for you."

He focused on the road, knew he was right about what he'd said, yet he could feel the heat of her angry stare, feel her judgment, her disapproval. And it bothered him. He tightened his grip on the steering wheel. Why? Why did this woman get to him so damn badly? Why did he care what she thought?

She said nothing more, turning away from him, offering him her back. He'd succeeded in pushing her away. Good. So why did he feel like absolute shit?

NICOLE JERKED AWAKE, her sleep restless, her conflict with Constantine—along with worry for her family— tormenting her thoughts.

She sat up as they pulled into a hotel parking garage. "Why are we stopping?"

"I need rest and to eat a real meal." He didn't look at her as he pushed the car door open and stepped outside.

She sat there a minute, debating how to handle him, noting his wording—"I" not "we." The tension from their argument remained as thick as the Texas heat, oppressive and ready to suffocate any cordiality left between them. And it bothered her. It bothered her in a big way.

She'd spent considerable time during the drive pretending to sleep, fretting over their argument. Trying to figure out why their conflict mattered so much. He'd been a complete jerk, saying things intentionally to hurt her. Painful things that hit a nerve because they were the same words she said to herself deep in the night when sleep refused to come.

Constantine pushed the limits of every rule he came in contact with. He was wild, living dangerously close to the edge of trouble, justifying his actions in the name of honor. He represented everything she'd been running from in her life. Running being the operative word. But it seemed she couldn't run from her past anymore. Inviting a renegade FBI agent into her bed proved that. What that meant exactly she hadn't decided. All she knew was she would not be intimidated or crushed by a few harsh words spoken by Constantine or anyone else.

And no matter what his claim, he'd rather defeat Alvarez and Carlos in a courtroom than outside the law. Otherwise, he would have taken one of the chances he claimed he possessed while undercover to kill them. He did want to do what was right. He was simply feeling the effects of three years in a hellhole.

One thing was for sure, Nicole thought, reaching for the door—they had to make this work. She couldn't run from him now. Nor he from her. They were stuck together for at least a week, maybe more. Constantine had to include her in the decisions being made. She wouldn't be shut out.

She walked to the rear of the vehicle and stopped in front of him. His hands were on his hips, the look on his face impatient. He wanted food and rest; she wanted answers. "Where are we exactly?"

His eyes glinted with steel. "An hour from the boat."

"Then why stop? I thought you wanted—"

"To eat and get some rest."

Her lips thinned, her eyes probing, searching the hard expression in those eyes for some vestige of peace. But she found none. No emotion, no sensuality, no comfort. He'd shut her out. "Constantine—"

He reached in his pocket and handed her a black wallet. She looked at it, confused. "Not Constantine," he said. "Michael Rodriquez."

She opened the black leather cover and stared at her own picture next to the unfamiliar name. "Sarah Rodriquez?"

"Right," he said. "You're my wife." With that said, he motioned toward the elevator. "Let's move."

She lagged several steps behind him, about to reach for his arm and demand they clear the air. But one look around the garage, cars lined up one after another, and she took off after him. Anyone could hide behind, underneath or even inside one of the vehicles.

She caught up with him in a half run. "We have no bags. Don't you think that looks funny? Even our clothes—"

"Looks like we've been rolling around on the beach. Two lovebirds who can't get enough of each other." He kept walking. "Don't overcomplicate matters."

She made a frustrated sound. "I'm just trying to survive here."

He stopped in front of the elevator and punched the arrow button. "Then do as I say."

He stepped into the elevator, faced forward and pushed the button to hold the door. She didn't move;

her blood boiled at the bossy arrogance of his attitude. He had made the act of entering that elevator some sort of submission on her part.

A car sounded behind her. His gaze went beyond her shoulder and then back to her face. His voice was low, but as intense as if he had shouted. "Get into the elevator."

Her heart skipped a beat just thinking about someone approaching. She moved forward. When she turned and could see the garage again, she was relieved to notice only a woman and a small child getting out of a car. She let out a breath, thankful she was safe.

Constantine let go of the elevator button, and stepped backward. "You relax far too easily. Everyone—man, woman and child—is a potential enemy. Don't forget it."

If everyone was a potential enemy, was he? He'd lied to her and done a split-personality routine. She was confused, tired. She didn't know what to believe at this point.

The elevator doors opened to display a busy, though very average-looking lobby. People seemed to be everywhere. Nicole stared into the hustle and bustle with concern. "Shouldn't we be secluded somewhere?"

His arm wrapped around her, pulling her close to his side. The warmth of his touch seared her straight through her clothes. Anger apparently did nothing to lessen his impact on her senses.

"Safety in numbers," he said, leaning down so that his breath tickled her neck, warm and inviting. The sensation brought back memories of intimate moments, of forbidden touches.

She tried to act like everything was fine. Like a woman would act with her husband. That almost drew a laugh from her. Marriage often came with tension. If her marriage had been any indicator, strain between her and Constantine would seem quite the norm.

Nicole clenched her teeth. Being this bitter wasn't what she wanted. And she really thought she had those old feelings beaten. She forced her demons away and smiled at the desk clerk.

Minutes later, she stood next to Constantine as he slid a room key into a door handle. Awareness charged the air and defied the coldness of his demeanor. They both knew they might disagree on the justice system, but there was one area they agreed on completely— sex. Something their one-bed suite was going to make hard to ignore.

11

CONSTANTINE SHOVED open the door to the hotel room, as aware of Nicole's nearness as he was of his next breath. More aware actually. Breathing came without thought. Every second he was near Nicole, he desired her. Hell. He could feel her body next to his even when he wasn't touching her. When he wasn't lusting after her, daydreaming over how he'd take her if he ever got her naked again, guilt nipped at his gut over what a complete, total ass he'd been to her, bringing up her past as he had.

She'd slapped him down for walking outside the circle of acceptable that she'd drawn around herself—making him the bad guy, good enough to fuck and nothing more—and it pissed him off. Actually, he'd welcomed a reason to be angry, darn near desperate to put some distance between himself and Nicole. To stop whatever connection was forming between them before it clouded his judgment and he forgot how dangerous he was to her. People wanted him dead. Alvarez. Carlos.

Plenty of others he'd taken down, too. She'd attacked his beliefs and given him the fuel to shove her away— and he'd pounced on it, holding back nothing. Living in Alvarez's world had taught him how to be a coldhearted bastard, if it had taught him nothing else.

He stepped aside, allowing her entrance into the room and motioning her forward. She hesitated, her gaze flickering over his face for a quick moment, as if she, too, knew the implications of the two of them alone, in a hotel room. Her chest lifted with a breath and she entered the room.

His gaze drifted to the sexy sway of her hips and the pert lift to that lush backside. There was no escaping the attraction between them, and his groin tightened with the proof. He wanted her. His body didn't care if they were from different worlds.

This crazy attraction he felt for her wreaked havoc on his mind and body, had him rationalizing her resolve to follow the system as easily as he did for working around it. He was, after all, aware of the pain hidden behind that facade of prim and proper—he'd used it against her in their argument. Only she wasn't prim and proper, and their lovemaking, like her past, proved as much.

Following her into the room, he shoved the door closed and locked it. She'd positioned herself at the window, her back to him. The room shrank—if that were possible—as he eased toward the bed, sexual tension charging the air, damn near combustible in its presence. Staying in a hotel room with Nicole, and keeping his hands to himself, was going to be a real task. No. Worse. His own little piece of hell.

"Don't get too comfortable," he said, not that she appeared to be trying. She felt what he did. The room was small. Too damn small. "We need to go grab some clothes and food."

The curtain she'd been holding fell back into place as she turned to face him, her eyes going to his, avoiding the bed. "Is it safe to go out?"

Her nipples pebbled beneath the cheap T-shirt and his gaze went where hers had not—to a king-size invitation to rip her clothes off and have his way with her. Was it safe to go out? Hell. Was it safe to stay in? His cock thickened, pressing painfully against his jeans. No woman drove him to this kind of insanity. He'd be dead a hundred times over if he let his damn dick control his decisions.

He ground his teeth as his gaze inadvertently flickered across those tight little nipples again. His cock throbbed. With a verbal backlash, he took out his growing frustration on her. "I don't plan to question your legal abilities. It's my job to get us out of this alive. We're safe. We'll stay safe. And we will get to the right people to get the trial under way. How about you let me do it without questioning my every move?"

He didn't expect her to cower at his attack, nor did she. For an instant, the gentle curve of her brows dipped, and then her expression transformed to an outright scowl, her petite hands jabbing at her curvy hips. "You didn't question my abilities?" she asked incredulously. "Do my job, you said, or you'll take matters into your own hands." Her tone mocked him. "In other words, you manipulated me into feeling I was responsible for either outcome. If that's not an inference of you questioning my abilities, I don't know what is."

"It wasn't about questioning you," he countered. "It's about reality. Alvarez cannot walk free."

She opened her mouth to speak and then tightened her lips into a thin line. An inhaled breath followed as she appeared to consider her words. "I'm going to detour from a subject we obviously can't agree on and say this. My life is on the line. Don't expect me to blindly follow your lead. I have a right to be informed about my own safety. Would you expect any less if you were in my position?"

They weren't talking about him and he almost said as much. Instead, he forced himself to consider her words. He wanted her to trust him, and, yes, do so blindly, because he was good at his job. But regardless she'd be foolish to operate without caution. Their history together had been a short, intense one, full of adversity.

He softened toward her. What was it about this woman that could take the hardness inside him and tear it down?

"Try," he said, his voice gentle, the edge gone. What else could he say? "All I ask is that you try."

Her expression slowly eased. Anger and accusation disappeared as she crossed her arms in front of her chest. She was still on guard, but not on attack. "I will. I promise."

That was something, he guessed. They'd both compromised. Now he needed some space before softness turned into something else…maybe comfort, more likely sex, exactly what he was avoiding. Sex with Nicole was as big a distraction as a man could conceive.

A quick glance at the clock told him it was only eight in the morning. "Let's make this supply run fast. If we step it up, we can make those phone calls, eat and sleep, all by sunset."

"And then?" she asked, and laughed, realizing she was already questioning him again. "Sorry. I can't help myself."

"I know you can't," he said, a smile tempting his lips, but he was too damn tired to see it through. But not too tired to admire Nicole's smile. Disheveled and without makeup, she still glowed. "But I don't have an answer for you. Not yet."

"Not until we know when the trial is." It wasn't a question.

"Exactly," he agreed. "For now, let's take care of ourselves and get some food." *Before I forget myself and feed my hunger with you.*

NICOLE STOOD IN the tiny store watching as Constantine threw chips, candy and all kinds of junk into a small basket. "I thought we needed supplies?"

"This is the critical stuff," he said with complete seriousness in his tone, grabbing a bag of Doritos. He appeared to be a man on a mission—to achieve a heart attack. "We should pick out some clothes."

She blinked at that. "From here?"

"Right," he said, pointing toward several racks of souvenir-type clothing. Holiday garb at best. "Grab some T-shirts and shorts for us both. A couple of pairs. And shoes. No sandals. I'm a size twelve."

She reluctantly headed to the clothing racks, wishing for something more substantial, but thankful for anything at this point. A bath and clean clothes of any type sounded like heaven.

Beside the racks, several tables held shirts and shorts. Nicole began inspecting the contents, selecting a few items. Two extra-large shirts for Constantine, two mediums for her, two pairs of print shorts for her. She picked dark blue parachute shorts for Constantine. His options were limited. It was either the dark blue kind or orange floral ones, which she couldn't imagine him wearing.

But then he deserved the bright neon flowers for taking those personal jabs at her. Smiling, she put the blue shorts back and grabbed two pairs of the orange.

She was reaching for a pair of tennis shoes, when a voice beside her asked, "Souvenir shopping?"

Nicole looked up to find herself staring into the interested eyes of a gorgeous, beach-blond god of a guy, not more than twenty-two. He towered over her at a good six foot plus and offered a charming smile. He was dressed in shorts and a tank top that showed off his picture-perfect body. Most women would be drooling—but not Nicole. She'd found a rather consuming interest in a certain tall, dark renegade, sporting a bad attitude and a hot temper.

Still, a friendly face was welcome about now. Nicole returned his smile and answered his question. "Something like that."

"Yeah, me, too." He reached for a T-shirt. "Gotta

take gifts back to the family." He studied her for a long, thoughtful, flirtatious minute…which was insane considering she looked like absolute hell. "I'm Rick."

"Nice to meet you, Rick." His comment about family had her thinking of her sister. She so needed to hear her voice.

"My mom is the hardest," he commented. "I never know what to take her."

She thought of her own mother—another bad subject. Nicole barely knew her anymore. Leaving the family business had ruffled a lot of feathers. Nicole hadn't even done family Christmas the year before, using work as an excuse. Her attention returned to Rick. "What's so hard about buying for your mother?"

"For one thing," he commented, hand waving over the table, "she doesn't wear T-shirts."

"No T-shirts?" Nicole teased, mustering a half smile. "Well, that only leaves you one option."

His brow lifted. "Which is?"

"A coffee cup, of course. Everyone knows they get a T-shirt or coffee mug from a vacationer."

They laughed together. "You won't convince my sister of that. She thinks shoes are the perfect gift, no matter what the occasion. If it can't be worn on the feet, it isn't worth having."

"Smart girl," Nicole said, offering her approval. "A personal favorite of mine as well."

"Of course." His expression said that was a given, a moment before he changed the subject. "How long you here for?"

The question took a second to register, her mind still

on her sister. "Um," she said, trying to think how to answer, "I haven't decided."

A disbelieving laugh filled the air. "You're at the beach and don't know how long you're staying? That's kind of unique. Most people come with a plan."

A hand touched Nicole from behind, sliding to the small of her back, branding her with possessive heat. Constantine stepped to her side, but she didn't glance at him. Shock, and a hint of panic, rolled across Rick's face. A look that only deepened as Constantine said, "She does have a plan." His voice was hard, deep, sexy. "Being with me."

Rick gulped. "Oh," he said. "I'm sorry, man. I wasn't... I mean..."

Nicole opened her mouth to say something, anything, that might save the poor kid some embarrassment. But Constantine put his arm around her shoulder and pulled her under the nook of his chin. That contact stole more than her breath; it stole her attention from saving Rick. Constantine's long legs pressed close to hers, electricity shooting through every inch of her body. It was a simple gesture commonly shared by couples but there was nothing simple about her reaction.

"Sorry if I interrupted," Rick said, his voice nervous as he started to back away, dropping the shirt to the table. Clearly he was ready for a fast departure.

Why did Constantine find it necessary to intimidate such an innocent young kid? It made no sense. She didn't take him as the kind of guy to throw around his strength in such a way. Anger began to build inside her.

"We should be going," Constantine said, his tone hinting at demand.

"Me, too," Rick agreed quickly, and he was gone, rocketing through the store as if he'd been set on fire.

Nicole whirled on Constantine and would have stepped out of his reach but he grabbed her waist, holding her so close their legs were entwined, hips aligned. The heated words she'd been ready to spurt a few seconds earlier took extra effort to crawl past her lips.

"What's your problem?" she whispered.

His tone was low, lethal. The look in his eyes full of impatience. "You don't seem to get the message. Anyone and everyone is a potential threat."

"He was a kid," she argued. "One you just about scared the hell out of."

"You've been in the system long enough to know what criminals are capable of. Alvarez isn't above anything. He'll do whatever it takes. Even pay an innocent kid to ID you."

"That kid was not with Alvarez."

A woman with dark hair and glasses walked past them. Constantine's eyes followed her, suspicious, his expression cautiously assessing. Did he know something she didn't? Tension slid through her body as the taste of fear thickened in her mouth.

Nicole watched Constantine watch the woman. And then watched his gaze slip back to her. Their eyes locked. Desperately, she searched his face, looking for a hint of what might come next. And what she found turned her fear to boiling hot anger.

He was messing with her head, trying to prove a

point. "Don't do that." She glared at him. "I despise stupid head games."

Leaning a bit closer, he said, "I assure you, this is not a game. Alvarez leaves a trail of bodies wherever he goes." Seconds passed, the mood shifting in some indescribable way, still tense, still charged. And then, unexpectedly, Constantine's attitude softened, much like it had in the hotel room. "I don't want you to be one of them."

She gave him a dubious look, her throat suddenly parched. Was that tenderness in his eyes? Worry? Surely not. And why did the idea of such things warm her inside? They'd had sex. The smoldering tension between them said they wanted to have sex again. It meant nothing. Or did it? When she delved into the depths of Constantine's eyes, she felt something more than attraction, a vague sense of kindred spirits that betrayed their exterior differences. Something that scared her as much as Alvarez did, simply in a different way.

Pressing past her emotional questions, Nicole had to admit Constantine delivered a persuasive argument. She couldn't be selective about her caution. She had to start thinking with the kind of ultraconservative mindset she used in the courtroom.

"You're right," she admitted. "I'll be more careful."

A look of surprise flashed across his face before he gave her a quick nod. "Good. Let's finish shopping and get out of here." He turned away from her then, but not before Nicole noted the confusion in his eyes.

At least she wasn't alone in her emotional turmoil. It appeared Constantine didn't know any more what to think about her than she did about him. They were trapped together for the time being, running from Alvarez. They could escape from Alvarez, she had confidence in that. But escaping whatever was happening between the two of them…she wasn't sure they could.

12

ON THEIR WAY back to the car, Nicole felt Constantine's hand on her arm, gentle, protective. She appreciated it more than the heat he fired within her. Nicole appreciated his presence, his strength, his willingness to risk his life to save her. They were in this together, and she needed to act that way.

Once they were settled, Constantine locked the doors. Silence filled the air, unspoken words between them thick with the need to be voiced. Nicole took the lead. "I guess I don't want this to be real. Intermittent denial."

"You don't seem to have that issue where your sister is concerned." It wasn't a question.

Looking after her sister had always been a priority. Their parents had pushed them both so hard. He had no idea how much truth rested in those words, or maybe he did. The man survived undercover by reading people.

She laughed, nervous about how easily he saw

through her, saw things no one else did. "I know. It's crazy. I blame it on the need for food and sleep."

Quickly he turned the engine over. "I can fix that."

She wasn't ready to end this conversation. Not yet. Her hand went back to his arm, drawing his gaze to hers. He went still, utterly still, his scrutiny so intense she found that the attention stole her breath.

Somehow, she forced herself to speak. "Thank you for what you've done to help me. For what you're doing to protect me and my family."

Silence followed, thick, potent. Finally, he said, "You know how you can thank me?"

Why did this seem like a trick question? "By convicting Alvarez?"

"Like this." He moved then, pulling her close, those strong arms embracing her, that firm, perfect mouth slanting over hers. That possessive, sensual tongue sliding against hers. One hand slid to the side of her face, his fingers entwined wildly in her hair. Nicole decided that agreeing with Constantine, as she just had, came with perks. He might be bad for her in theory, but he was oh-so-good in many other ways. And right now, with all that was going on, all that they faced, she wasn't sure she had it in her to deny herself this man. She wanted to kiss him, touch him, trust him. The future be damned—for all she knew, she wouldn't even have one.

Seconds passed as they kissed, sultry seconds where his mouth seduced her into surrender. And, damn, surrender felt uniquely sweet, a pleasure no other had ever given her. When he tore his mouth from hers, he leveled her in a sizzling stare.

"There are a hundred reasons why we shouldn't be doing this," he said.

In a barely audible voice, she agreed, "At least that many."

"You're a control freak."

"So are you."

"We can't both run the show."

That made her smile, her mind going to the cave, to their power struggle. "It was fun trying the first time."

A hint of a smile touched his lips. "Which brings me to my point." His mouth brushed hers, as if he couldn't resist one more taste, one more touch. "We'd be better off leaving what happened in that cave, in that cave."

"Right." She squeezed her legs shut, those memories sending an ache straight to her core. "Better off."

Neither of them pulled away despite their declarations that they should resist one another. Their lips lingered a breath from touching, electricity darting around them, through them.

"But the truth is," he admitted, "I've got too many other fires to put out to fight this one. I want you, Nicole. How do you feel about that?"

Wet. She felt wet. And ready. Like they were on the same path of satisfaction, both in mind and body. "I feel…ready to go back to the hotel."

Approval glinted in his eyes, and he scooped in for one last brush of her lips before reluctantly releasing her. He shifted gears and turned on the radio.

"Hurricane Ed appears to be headed straight for the Gulf of Mexico and speculation puts Texas in the line of fire."

Constantine cursed under his breath and Nicole knew why. It appeared passion wasn't the only stormy weather they had to ride out. Even Mother Nature seemed to be aiding Alvarez, stealing their safe zone. Because now there was no way they could hide on Constantine's boat, their ultimate destination, in the middle of a hurricane.

Nicole couldn't help but wonder how big this storm was going to be before it was over.

BACK AT THE HOTEL, Constantine curbed his more primal instincts, at least for a short time. He had business to get done, critical issues, like a shower so he wouldn't stink to high heaven. Most importantly, there were phone calls and plans to be made—when to return to Austin, how to do it safely. The best steps to take to ensure Alvarez was convicted, not freed. Not that any of that made him forget that long, hot kiss in the car. How could he? Nicole was on the bed next to him, and despite the room-service cart in front of them, a bed was a bed, suggestive as ever. And her shorts allowed him to admire those long, sexy legs more readily.

He glanced down at his tropical shorts and grimaced. She'd gotten quite the laugh when he'd appeared wearing them, so much so, he'd had the feeling something was up. When he'd said as much, she'd admitted buying them to spite him. Her amusement had been, well, amusing. He didn't get amused. But then there was nothing normal about what he felt for Nicole.

He had to have her again.

Nicole had somehow managed to eat her strawberry waffle in between calls to her father, her sister and now her boss. Constantine finished off a biscuit loaded with butter and honey right about the time she ended the conversation.

"That sounded encouraging," he commented before licking a drop of honey off his thumb, erotic images of licking honey off Nicole's body sending his pulse racing.

She tossed the cell phone on the bed, oblivious to how hot she made him without any effort, which somehow only made him hotter. "It was," she agreed. "Dean not only said I should remain on the case, he promised to fight to make it happen. He's calling the judge personally with a promise that he will take over if I can't make the trial—which is, of course, almost unheard-of. It will speak volumes to the court about how important Dean feels I am to this case. But it also means a delay of two weeks because of his wife's cancer treatments."

Constantine brushed crumbs from his hands, pleased with the announcement. "And my testimony?" he asked.

"He was sold before I brought it up. A guy named Nelson called Dean this morning. Told him if you were alive, you were needed."

Constantine paused, a glass of orange juice halfway to his mouth. He set the glass back down. "Why would Nelson be calling instead of Flores? If this Nelson is who I think he is, he has been working a drug task force in the Houston area, only helping with aiding the Alvarez takedown. No direct involvement."

Nicole continued to recount her conversation. "Dean mentioned something about how that came about. Flores took a bullet in his shoulder and spent the night in the hospital. That's why you couldn't reach him. So Nelson transferred into the Austin office and assumed his duties."

The food in his stomach downright rolled. "Wait one damn minute. Filling in for Flores or replacing him?"

She hesitated. "Dean used the word replace. I admit that seems a bit odd."

"You can say that again." Constantine rubbed the back of his neck, a weight exploding onto his shoulders. He'd met Nelson once when he'd been arrested along with a bunch of the Alvarez gang. He'd known Constantine's identity and he'd maintained the necessary secrecy throughout the process. But he couldn't trust him. Not when someone on the inside was dirty.

Nicole pushed the breakfast cart out of the way to face him, one knee on the bed, one foot on the ground. "I know you trust Flores, but is this an indication someone else doesn't? That they think he's the leak?"

He wanted to say no, but that would be a lie. "Either that or they want a fall guy in case things turn sour. You know how the story plays. This is high profile with lots of press. Someone has to go down if the operation fails."

She didn't immediately respond, the scrutinizing look she leveled his way a little too probing for his comfort. He scooted back against the headboard and kicked his legs onto the mattress. He let his head drift backward, lowering his lashes, withdrawing into a shell so he could deal with what he'd learned. His mind raced wildly with the implications of her news.

Suddenly, Nicole was there, refusing to be dismissed. She straddled him, sitting across his lap. His head shot up as her hands settled on his chest. Despite his state of mind, instantly he was hard, the thin shorts they each wore offering no barrier between their bodies. He could almost feel the damp heat of her body. Was she wearing panties?

Nicole hugged herself, covering her breasts and successfully drawing his attention to her face. "Are we okay?" she demanded. "Should we leave? What did she say?"

Hands by his sides, he resisted touching her, resisted reaching for her on all levels. Life had taught him to remain guarded. Caring meant pain. Loss. But she'd offered him insight into her life that a file folder couldn't give him and he wanted to know more. And right now, he didn't care that he'd have to share his own feelings to get to hers.

"Who betrayed you?"

"Does it matter?" she asked.

Yes. "It matters."

Shadows floated in her eyes, seconds passing, and he began to think she wasn't going to answer. Then she said, "My ex. It was my ex. Only not in the way you might think. It wasn't about other women. I let him pull me into his world and convince me it was mine. In the end, it was his, and what I wanted didn't matter. I was a tool to get to my father. Ironically, he never needed me for that. He's still my father's protégé." Pain flashed in her expression before she refocused on him, her hand brushing his jaw. "So you see. I hope Flores didn't betray you. It's clear you don't offer trust easily."

He didn't deny the truth. Nor did he point out their

similarities in that way. Instead, he found himself taking her hand, bringing her knuckles to his lips and then peering up at her from where his lips prepared for another taste. "Did you love him?" He didn't know what in the hell made him ask the question, nor did he know why her answer felt so important. But it did.

A hint of tension betrayed her body. He kissed her knuckles again, then her wrist. Slowly, her muscles softened, her expression softer now, too. "I guess it depends on how you define love. I said the words. I thought I meant them. Now...now I don't know. The only love I know for sure is for my family, my sister especially. We're very close. My parents don't approve of my life so it's strained." The tone of her voice said she regretted that last admission and she quickly fired a question at him. "Have you ever been married? In love?"

Constantine searched her face, saw the loneliness in her eyes. He knew then, that part of their connection was that solitude they both had lived. He pressed her palm to his, thinking how petite and somehow fragile she was, yet how brave in actions and spirit.

And when he would have dodged this question from another, he found himself answering honestly. "No, to both." Guilt twisted in his gut over the lie he'd told in the cave. Lying to her in that bar had been survival. Lying in that cave had been cowardly, his way of hiding from what he didn't want to face. He tried to shove it aside, and focused on telling her what she wanted to know. "I'm thirty-five and have spent my entire adult life in the FBI. My job doesn't exactly make me Prince Charming." He hesitated, recognizing some internal need to clear the air. "I lied to you." She gave him a startled look and he blasted forward, continuing before he could talk himself out of it. "I have a brother." He had spoken in the present tense before he could stop himself. But talking about Antonio as if he were gone bothered him.

"What? You said—"

"I know what I said. It's an automatic answer I give. It's easier than saying he's dead."

She sucked in a breath, understanding filtering into her expression. "How?" She whispered the question.

"He arrested a guy named Martini, not as heavy an operator as Alvarez, but still a big fish. Based mostly in San Antonio."

He hesitated and she commented, "I remember hearing about that case."

He continued, eager to get this off his chest. "Martini was released on a technicality and…" His voice trailed off. "You can guess the rest."

Her eyes went wide. "Oh, God." Her voice shook. "He killed your brother."

Constantine's gut twisted in knots. Years had passed and this still tore him apart. He couldn't speak, so he nodded.

She leaned forward, hands gently cupping his cheeks, the tenderness in the act squeezing his heart. It had been forever since he'd told anyone about his brother, years since he had felt a touch like this one, so caring, so understanding.

"That's why you threatened to kill Alvarez and Carlos," she said, her gaze searching his, pouring into his, reaching into his soul.

Somehow he found his voice, and confessed the sin that devoured his sanity every day of his life. "I was in deep with Alvarez when my brother died. I couldn't go to the funeral." To his horror his voice cracked. "I should have been there." He squeezed his eyes shut. "He was my kid brother. I should have saved him."

"Oh, Constantine." She brushed her lips across his. "Don't do that to yourself. I know it's torture, but you can't carry that blame all your life. It'll tear you apart."

He was surprised to see tears in her lovely blue eyes. "Easier said than done. We both know you blame yourself for getting a man off who killed again. I've seen how you turned your life around because of that case."

"That's different." Her lashes fluttered, her eyes lowering to his chest, gaze averted. "You had nothing to do with your brother's death. I got a high off being the best at my job, at being the most successful defense attorney in Texas." Her lashes lifted, tears tumbling over her cheeks. "I was self-centered and greedy, and someone died because of it."

She swiped at her tears. "I'm sorry," she said. "I'm tired and emotional."

Regret filled Constantine. He should never have brought this up. He didn't blame Nicole for being a defense attorney, nor did he blame her for being good at it. The system was the system and he was frustrated with it. Perhaps, had he met her before, he would have felt differently about her. But they were the same in what they ultimately wanted—justice for the victims of Alvarez, and those like him. Nicole's regret over the past was eating her insides out and he knew this. Just as his past had left a hole in his gut. "I'm sorry," he said. "I didn't realize how raw this was for you."

She inhaled a shaky breath. "Don't apologize. It's hard to get past the blame, Constantine, but you won't do it by pretending it doesn't exist. I know from experience that if you don't deal with what you feel, it gets worse."

Noting the stronger tone of her voice, he recognized her effort to pull her emotional armor into place. He didn't want it in place. They had a lot in common, the two of them. They were both alone, both torn up inside. Right now, he wanted only one thing. To get lost in her. To forget everything but this woman.

His hands went up her back, molding her close, easing her mouth to his. "I'm going to make love to you, now, Nicole." His mouth slanted over hers in what he meant to be a gentle kiss…but they were both wound tight, both in need of a release, a place to put the pain and loneliness. Outside a storm threatened their hiding place. Inside, passion thundered, threatening to take him to a place he'd never traveled before. A place he didn't dare name. A place he didn't dare go. A place he burned to make his own.

13

CONSTANTINE KISSED Nicole with a fiery passion borne of pent-up emotions. Why they'd surfaced now, why with this woman, he didn't know, nor did he care. Because he felt her giving herself to him, felt he was her escape as much as she was his.

For every stroke of his tongue, every touch of his hand, she gifted him with some unique response: a sigh, a caress of her tongue, a nip of her teeth. Yes, he was hers for sure.

He barely remembered removing his shirt, though he remembered every caress of her hands on his bare skin. She sat back, facing him, her lush backside framing his cock, teasing him with delicate pressure. Silky blond hair fell around her face in sexy, wild array. She wore no makeup, her ivory skin flawless.

Eyes the color of a perfect sky stared at him, eyes brimming with a message—with freely offered passion, with tenderness he'd never accepted from another, yet he wanted it from her. There would be no games, no battle for control this time.

Her fingers latched on to the hem of her shirt, and she tugged it over her head, tossing it to the floor. She wore no bra, her high, full breasts displayed for his viewing. Her nipples swelled and tightened under his inspection. But when he would have reached for her, he held back, willing himself to refrain from making demands, to enjoy every moment of her, every way possible. For now, he was savoring the view she made, which was tightening his groin.

A soft sound escaped her lips as she took his hands, pressing them to her breasts. Her mouth lingered near his. "I need you to touch me," she whispered, her teeth scraping his bottom lip, arching into his palms as he kneaded.

The boldness of her actions shot fire through his veins, but it was her words, and the passionate way she stared at him, that ran over him like a firestorm. Need. She needed him. Who was he to deny her?

He pressed her breasts together, using his thumbs to tease the erect rosy-red peaks of her plump breasts. She rewarded him with a moan, the response rocketing to his cock, thickening it with demand.

Burning to hear another, to pleasure her, his head lowered, his tongue lapping at one pert nipple and then suckling. Her hands went to his head, fingers sliding into his hair. She covered her other breast with her hand, aiding his efforts. He pulled it away, his mouth finding the unattended nipple, lavishing it with attention.

She whispered his name, and he lifted his mouth to

hers, somehow knowing a kiss to be her demand. Her lips were sweet, her tongue caressing his with careful strokes. He traced the gentle curve of her jaw with his fingers, before traveling the sensual line of her neck.

For a moment, he stared into her heavy-lidded eyes, touched by what he felt for this woman. As hot as he was, as much as he wanted inside her, the tenderness between them consumed him—it was unexplainably perfect. Their passion was both erotic and innocent, simple and complex. The emptiness inside him cried out, twisted in his gut, reaching for her.

Constantine kissed Nicole again, desire pulsing in his blood, warning that a kiss would soon not be enough. Nevertheless, he found himself lingering, savoring these moments. The taste of her, the feel of her skin against his, her breasts pressed to his chest.

Slowly, Nicole lifted her lips from his, depriving him of her kiss. She searched his face, emotion brimming from beneath her dark lashes, emotion that made words unnecessary. She was looking for confirmation that they felt the same way; he could see it in her eyes. There was something about her in that instant, a vulnerability that spoke to him with such completeness that he thought he might be looking in a mirror, seeing himself. A likeness that drove past the sexual desire they shared—a likeness that wrapped around them and made them one. He wanted to be one with her, buried to the hilt, the warmth of her surrounding him.

As if she read his mind, she inched away from him, reaching for her shorts. He did the same, working to shove the material down his hips. But his eyes remained riveted on Nicole. She wasn't shy about her body, as sunlight spilled through the window, and she showed no hesitation at being exposed. By the time he'd discarded his clothing, she was crawling toward him, her breasts swaying seductively with the action.

She bit her bottom lip as her gaze swept his erection. Her tongue darted over her lips, and he groaned, the action reminding him how sweet it would be on his cock. She settled at his right hip, again on her knees. Her left hand brushed his shaft and his heart jackhammered, his eyes shutting for a second before opening. He watched her hand travel over his length, the view of the exploration stimulating him as much as the touch did.

Delicate fingers swept up and down his shaft, trailing the ridge around his engorged head and then spreading the dampness gathering there, the proof he wanted inside her. But he held himself in check, aware that the wait would only make the bliss all the more powerful.

There were a million erotic things he wanted to do with this woman, but right now, right now, he simply wanted to be a part of her. He wanted to be lost inside the wet, perfect heat of her body.

"I need to be inside you." The words were guttural, hungry, and he hesitated no more. He pulled her across his lap, holding her weight as her hand wrapped around his shaft, guiding it to her core.

She acted swiftly, as if she, too, felt the urgency, slipping the head of his shaft inside her, and then starting the seductive slide downward. Adrenaline sizzled through his nervous system, stealing his breath. By the time they were one, pelvis against pelvis, a whisper from kissing, he was on fire—blazing red-hot and emotionally charged. In a far corner of his mind, he recognized this was sex—where the hell had the emotion come in to play?

His nervous system was in overdrive. Every breath he managed came with a sensation, a charge. And from the heavy rise and fall of her chest, she felt the same. But for some reason, he wanted to know for certain.

Intentionally, he kept his body still, fighting the urge to pull her hard against his cock and thrust into her. Instead, he brushed the mass of shiny blond locks from her creamy shoulders and caressed his way down her arms. She shivered and leaned into him, her arms wrapping around his neck, nipples brushing his chest. "What are you doing to me?"

And so he had his answer. She was as lost in him as he was in her, equally uncertain about why or how. He'd bedded his share of women. Hard and fast, slow and easy. Though never, ever, had he lost himself by merely having a woman take him inside her. But he was lost now.

His fingers brushed her nipples and then tugged lightly. A gasp escaped her lips, and the muscles of her body tightened around his cock. He tugged a bit harder and she moaned, her muscles squeezing harder this time. Suddenly, her mouth was on his, her tongue delving past his lips, her hips beginning to rock against him.

Pleasure shot through his groin and exploded throughout his limbs, threatening to consume him. But he wanted her pleasure more than he wanted his own.

He continued to tease her nipples, applying pressure, twisting and tugging. She gasped against his mouth.

Constantine started to pull back, afraid he'd hurt her, but her hands closed over his, her tongue stroking him with a hungry kiss. There was no pain in the kiss, only pleasure. She rocked forcefully now, and he pumped his hips to match her movements. When he had the position perfect, he used his mouth to suckle one nipple, then the other.

Her gaze fixed on his mouth as his lips worked against her breasts, her heavy-lidded gaze saying she was aroused by watching. The harder he suckled, the faster she jerked her hips, adding to the pressure on her nipple. He caressed and tweaked the other nipple, pleasuring her again and again, but also needing more.

He continued to suckle her nipple, but his hands went to her hips, wanting leverage. He thrust upward, and pulled her down at the same time. She cried out and grabbed his arms, using them to push herself down on him. Thrust, push, thrust, push. The room filled with noisy heavy breathing. They were wild with passion, fulfilling their need. To be closer, to move faster and harder. Nicole screamed with pleasure, softly pleading for him not to stop.

Tongues tangled as they devoured each other, hands everywhere, bodies bucking, primal animals in heat. Abruptly, he felt Nicole stiffen, heard her gasp a second before her nails dug into his shoulders. Spasms closed down on his cock, pulling at him, taking him. She shook with the force of her release. He took control then, grinding her hips down against his, pumped once, twice, three times—and then he exploded. The power of his release ripped through him from deep in his groin, and he, too, was shaking.

When eventually they stilled, their heads buried in each other's shoulders, surreal silence surrounded them. They inched apart enough to stare at one another, searching each other's faces. What had happened between them? That was the unspoken question in the air. Whatever it was had Constantine's insides quivering in an indescribable way.

Nicole reached up and softly traced his brow, tenderness sweeping across her face, and then she rested her head back on his shoulder. His heart squeezed; his chest was tight. He could barely breathe. This connection, this bond, had to be a facade, the result of the adrenaline rush of being on the run. Didn't it? But deep down, he knew it was more. He couldn't fall for Nicole. He was nothing but trouble. Hell. He didn't want to be worried about someone. He didn't want someone else to fear for. That part of his life was behind him.

"What are you doing to me, woman?" he whispered, repeating the question she had asked of him earlier.

Nicole didn't respond, but she tightened her arms around him. Seconds passed and they relaxed into each other, their breathing the only sound in the room. Holding her in those moments came with a sense of peace and serenity, an experience unique, never to be reproduced. There might be other special times, other amazing moments. Or perhaps there would be none. That possibility clenched his gut. He didn't move, nor did she. Perhaps they were both afraid of ending something that might never be repeated.

Constantine contemplated sleeping with her in his arms, recognizing his desire to keep her close. He had even started to ease them both to the mattress when a sudden pounding on the door brought him back to reality. He tensed, preparing to defend Nicole. Her fingers pressed into his shoulders, and she leaned back to search his face, anxiety shining in the depths of her eyes.

"Housekeeping," someone called through the door, the female voice carrying a heavy Hispanic accent.

Nicole expelled a breath, her body going limp with relief. Constantine felt nothing of the sort. They'd only checked in a few hours before. Housekeeping should know this. Besides, pretending to be "housekeeping" would be an easy trick to get the door open. With regret, he motioned for Nicole to climb off him; her expression quickly filled with worry again as she scrambled for her clothes.

Constantine snatched his shorts from the floor about the time the knocking started again. "Housekeeping!" A key was being jiggled in the lock. Thankfully, he'd flipped the inner latch so it would catch before the door fully opened.

"Ahora no," Constantine shouted out, telling the woman in Spanish "not now," dropping his shorts in exchange for the Glock on the nightstand.

He bolted across the room, arriving at the door as it came open, hitting the barrier of the steel latch. Constantine peered through the opening, the housekeeper looking at him through the crack. He repeated his prior words and went on to demand why she was even present when they'd only checked in hours ago.

The woman responded to his demands with an onslaught of Spanish, which concluded with an apology. Constantine relaxed marginally and sent the woman away. He slammed the door shut and slid the lock into place. Then he turned to stare at Nicole. Still on the mattress, she was on her knees, her shirt in place but nothing else, nipples peaking beneath the thin material, and clearly showing the dark triangle between her legs. His gaze devoured the sight, his body stirring.

Nicole hugged herself. "Are we okay?" she demanded. "Should we leave? What did she say?"

"We're fine," he answered, starting toward the bed. "I was being safe. Better safe than sorry."

"You're sure?" she asked, as he set the gun back on the table. Her eyes scanned his body, widening ever-so-slightly as she noticed the growing girth of his erection.

His knees hit the mattress. "As sure as I can be under the circumstances."

"On a scale of one to ten—"

Constantine cut her off with a disbelieving laugh and reached for her. She frowned, her hands pressing on his chest a bit defensively. "What's so funny?"

"You trying to find control someplace that it can't be found." He tugged at her shirt and pulled it over her head, finding no resistance on her part. His palms framed her breasts and then slid to her cheeks. "I said, we're fine."

She didn't look convinced, and he shook his head at her stubbornness. Grabbing the blankets, he motioned for her to join him underneath. They crawled under, lying down, heads on their pillows, facing each other.

"I know it's hard to be calm, but try."

She nibbled her bottom lip a minute, and he could see by her expression that her mind was racing. Another worry-laden question followed. "Shouldn't we flip on the news and find out about the hurricane?"

Remarkable, he thought, and found himself wanting to smile again. "Later." The mattress was starting to call him to slumber. "Come here." He urged her to turn around, her back to his chest.

She snuggled against him without argument, a surprised sound sliding from her mouth as he settled his erection against her backside. "You're hard again." She said the statement as if she'd just noticed, which they both knew wasn't the case.

"Hmm," he murmured. "I seem to have an unlimited appetite for you, even when I'm exhausted. In fact, I was thinking of some delicious ways of using the rest of the honey that room service brought with my biscuits."

"Were you now?" she purred seductively.

"Oh, yeah," he whispered near her ear, as he nuzzled her neck. "It'll taste much better on you. I'm sure of it."

A soft, sensual laugh slid from her lips, and she snuggled against him, her hips doing a sexy little wiggle. Then she sighed and seemed to melt, as if she were giving herself to the bed, to the need to sleep. Maybe to him. Yes. To him. Another time he would analyze why that idea appealed to him so much.

A full minute passed in which he assumed she was

falling asleep until her tentative voice filled the air. "What was his name?"

His gut clenched. He hated talking about his brother. "Antonio."

"Younger or older?"

"Younger by five years. He was twenty-seven when he died two years ago."

One second, two. "You felt protective like I do about my sister."

"Yes," he whispered. "Kind of ironic considering he was tough as nails and made his living protecting others."

She maneuvered to her back and touched his cheek before settling on her side to face him. "The horrendous crimes we see give us a reality no one else has. We know how easily life can be stripped away, without reason. How can we not? I eat breakfast, lunch and dinner reading case files telling gruesome stories with graphic pictures. You see those things firsthand. I can't imagine what that is like."

"It's part of our job," he said, realizing he'd had this conversation once before. With his brother.

"The job doesn't come without consequences. We have to deal with what we see, and it's not always easy."

But it was easy for him. He felt nothing. Hadn't since about a month after his brother's death. It was how he'd survived Alvarez. "Somewhere along the line I found a way to switch it off. I feel...nothing. Not really. Not often."

She made a disbelieving sound. "Yes, you do. I've seen the intensity in your eyes when you talk about Alvarez and Carlos. You found a way to tuck your emotions into some corner of your mind, but the feelings are still there."

"Is that how you deal with your past?"

"Yes," she replied, a hint of pain lacing her tone. "I'll be glad when I get as good at it as you, though. Being responsible, even indirectly, for a murder makes for a lot of sleepless nights. I keep thinking if I win enough cases, put enough criminals behind bars, I'll forgive myself, but so far it hasn't happened. Maybe it never will."

Guilt stabbed at his gut yet again. "I shouldn't have brought that up in the car. You were right. I acted like a jerk."

A smile touched her lips. "Yes. You did."

"Does it help to know I regret it?"

"Not much, but some." Her fingers slid into his chest hair, her eyes dropping to her hand.

He pulled her close, hand on her firm backside. "You're cutting me no slack, I see."

"It was mean," she said, her gaze lifting.

"I know. I'm sorry."

"Are you? Or do you deep down despise me for what I was?"

Pulling her leg over his, he slid his now throbbing erection back between her legs. "Does that feel like I despise you?"

"Wanting to fuck me is no indicator."

Her words, cold and bitter, caught him off guard. Before he could stop himself, he admitted what was better kept unspoken—since there could be no future for them. "There is more to what is going on with us than simply sex. And we both made assumptions about one another that weren't exactly true." His knuckles caressed her cheek, his voice tender. "You're brave, sexy and, I am beginning to learn, way too hard on yourself." He framed her face with his hand and gently met her lips with his. When he pulled back to look into her eyes, he saw that same vulnerability he'd seen while they were making love. If he didn't get her to sleep soon, he was going to find his way back inside her again. "We should rest."

She nodded. "Yes."

He eased onto his back and took her with him, settling her head on his chest. She wrapped her leg around his, and the act warmed him inside out. Yes, this woman did things to him. He ran his hand down her back— this moment in time too perfect to explain. He stilled, savoring the feeling.

Far too soon, they'd have to face the hell of running for their lives again. So, for a short window of time, at least, he wanted to pretend his world wasn't one big hole of darkness. And somehow, Nicole made that possible.

14

ON THE THIRD DAY of basically living in the same hotel room from sunup to sundown, Nicole blinked awake, giving the bedside clock a blurry-eyed glance. Eight in the morning. Only ten more days until they headed back to Austin for the postponed trial. Only. Right.

Weeks of her life would be lost before this ordeal was over. Not that she minded being with Constantine. He'd become quite a delicious distraction.

And speaking of her distraction… Beside her, Constantine stirred, pulling her into his arms. They rested, side by side, facing each other, heads on pillows. Feigning sleep, he kept his eyes shut, as if he had reached for her in slumber. But she knew better. She could feel his attentiveness.

Having spent every waking moment with him for these few days had taught her a lot about him. You could learn a lot about a person in those circumstances. Hours of doing nothing but making love and talking. Even watching the entire first season of *24* had unveiled little pieces of his life, telling her more than he probably even realized.

Thunder rumbled outside, reminding her of the hurricane, drawing her back into the present. She started to move, intending to find the remote and turn on the television, but she was stopped by Constantine, who shackled her legs and held her in place.

"Where are you going?" he asked, his voice rough from sleep, but his reflexes alert, telling her she was right about his feigning sleep. He was wide-awake and had been for a while. Of course, he was always on edge, ready for trouble. She took comfort in that. Then again, she hated it for him, and was coming to realize he had less peace in his life than she did, and she didn't have much.

Recognizing this sent a wave of tenderness through her, and Nicole placed a quick kiss on Constantine's forehead. "I'm trying to find the remote. There should be a solid storm path now." He hesitated and then released her legs. Nicole smiled and climbed over him to reach for the remote on the bedside table, the covers falling away from her naked backside. As he caressed her ass with his palm, she laughed and eyed him over her shoulder. "You are such as ass man, I swear."

"I worship all parts equally. I think I've proven that."

"Nope," she said, scratching the remote and then sitting back down. She cast him a teasing sideways look. "You're an ass man and I challenge you to prove otherwise." Scooting up against the headboard, she took the sheet with her and pulled it to her neck. Her teeth chattered as she flipped through the channels. "You turned the heat down again."

"You weren't complaining last night," he pointed out, sitting up on the side of the bed. He was referring to the marathon sex they'd shared mere hours ago.

True enough. She wasn't complaining one bit. Well, except for the honey. It had been great until after the orgasm—okay, two orgasms. Then, it had been sticky.

"Will you turn it up now?" she asked, a little plea in her voice.

He stood up, displaying all his taut muscle and naked glory. Would she ever be tired of seeing that man without clothes? "You didn't have to ask," he commented. "I was headed there now."

Inwardly, she smiled at that. "Thank you."

He winked at her and a thrill raced up her spine. Such a minor thing. It would have zero impact coming from someone else, but it set her on fire coming from Constantine. She couldn't seem to sate the desire. Somehow, it simply burned hotter.

She watched him cross the room, feeling surprised at how caring he could be, despite the darkness he carried inside him. No male in her life had ever given her a secure feeling. That Constantine could do so under such extreme circumstances said something. She wasn't sure what. Maybe she'd been hungry for a human connection, maybe they both had, and the situation had made it possible.

She refocused on the television and flipped through the stations, stopping on the weather and turning up the volume.

"There is no dodging this bullet for the Texas coast, as had been hoped. The good news is the storm has weakened to a category two with winds of one hundred and twenty miles per hour, expected landfall late tomorrow afternoon. Evacuation—"

Nicole muted the sound, more interested in what Constantine had to say at that point. The threat of the storm had left them in limbo or they'd already be at his boat.

"You said anything over a category one would put us on the road again," she reminded him. "So this means we're leaving, right?" He'd told her he wanted to make just one final stop, claiming the more they moved around, the more chance of making a critical mistake that gave away their location.

"Right," he agreed, messing with the thermostat before giving her his full attention. "As soon as we take care of some critical business." Offering nothing more, he headed toward the bathroom.

She gaped at his back. "What does that mean?" But she was talking to air. He'd disappeared around the corner, and a second later, the shower came on.

Nicole shoved aside the blanket and shivered. Hugging herself against the cold, she stomped into the bathroom, finding Constantine already behind the curtain. "What critical business?" she demanded. "There's a hurricane coming. A big one. We have to leave."

The curtain moved and he peeked out at her, water clinging to his long, dark lashes. Then he disappeared without a word. She flung her hands out to the side. Unbelievable! She climbed into the shower and faced him, instantly finding herself pulled into his arms, one of her legs lifted to his hip, his body fitted to hers. He was aroused, and suddenly she was, too.

She gave him a frustrated look, pretending to be unaffected by their naked bodies pressed together. "Why didn't you answer me?"

Mischief danced in his eyes. "Because I knew you'd get in the shower if I didn't."

Secretly, she was thrilled at his response. "Answer now."

"First and foremost, we have to make fast tracks down to the boat and pick up the money and supplies, before we can't get to it at all. Then, we do some fishing, prior to disappearing until the trial." His hand slid around her backside, fingers trailing the crease low enough to make her moan.

She reached behind her and covered his hand, struggling for coherent thought. "Stop. I can't think. What the heck are you talking about? Fishing?" Surely, he was joking.

He grinned, apparently pleased with that answer. "Then don't think."

That wasn't an option and he damn well knew as much. "Explain!"

A low, sexy chuckle slid from his lips. "We're going to catch us a bad guy," he said, derailing any further questions by kissing her, a fiery kiss that carried her into oblivion.

For only a moment, he raised his head, giving her a sizzling look before saying, "This is one of those times you have to let me do my job." The words had barely left his mouth, when he penetrated her, sliding his long, hard erection inside her and stealing her breath. Suddenly, the meaning of his words wasn't clear.

Did he mean, trust him to do his job, to get them out of here safely? Or trust him to give her an orgasm? Because as he began thrusting in and out of her, she was quite certain, the orgasm part was a sure thing.

AN HOUR LATER, Nicole sat next to Constantine, in the little Mazda he'd produced from who-knew-where, eating burritos from Taco Bell. The wind whipped furiously around the car; the clouds were dark and ominous, but no rain fell. According to Constantine, they were about ten minutes from the boat, having stopped to eat, and then they would begin the business of "fishing" for the truth. Translation: setting up Flores. She finished off a bite of food, listening to his plan to lure Carlos into the open and prove Flores to be innocent or guilty.

"It sounds dangerous," she stated, wiping sauce off her hand.

Crumbling a burrito wrapper, Constantine tossed it in the bag. "Less dangerous than going public at the trial without dealing with this."

Reluctantly, she agreed, wishing their fantasy hotel stay could have lasted a bit longer. There were no easy answers to any of this. No putting off reality.

She inhaled and exhaled. "Okay then. What do I do?"

"I shipped Flores a prepaid phone—"

"You're kidding! When? Won't they track the address you mailed it from?"

He gave her a reprimanding look. "You'll never learn

to trust me, will you? I bought the phone on the road the first night. I tossed a few bills at the clerk, and he mailed it for me."

Tension rushed from her shoulders. "You really thought ahead."

"You learn to do that when you live fighting for your life. I know Flores has the phone because I called him."

"When?" she asked, surprised by this news.

He patted the car's dash. "While I was nabbing our ride. He thinks things between the two of us are cool."

"But that's not the case." As much as he wanted to defend Flores, she'd seen the darkness in his eyes when the man's name came up, seen the doubt.

A muscle in his jaw jumped, his teeth clenched. "We'll know soon enough." He seemed to take stock of his emotions and, adopting a more businesslike, rather than bitter, tone, he said, "Here's how this will play out. I'll call Flores and tell him I need cash, that I can't get to my funds, but that I'll get back to him with the drop location. As soon as I hang up, you call him. Tell him I'm in a convenience store and you grabbed the phone. You're scared. Tell him I'm on a vengeance trip, hunting Carlos, planning to kill him. Tell him you need help, and then give him the boat's location."

She considered the plan. "You think he'll send Carlos?"

"If he's on their side, yes."

"And then we bust Flores and arrest Carlos."

"Right." He closed his eyes and took a deep breath before slowly letting it push past his lips. He was avoiding eye contact. What else was he avoiding? The truth? She didn't want to believe that.

True, they'd only spent a short while together, but she liked to think they'd come to an understanding. They'd talked about personal things, done personal things. Heck, she'd told him details she never would have told the man she'd called her husband. About her father, her mother, even her self-hatred over the past.

She touched his arm. "You are going to arrest him, right? Or is there more truth than fiction to the story I'm feeding Flores?"

Still, he didn't look at her. His lips thinned and tension crackled in the air. Finally, his lashes lifted and he fixed her in a level stare. "I'll try, Nicole, but if it comes down to him escaping…he won't be escaping. I won't let him walk away."

Nicole felt as if she'd been punched in the stomach. She'd asked for the truth, and he'd given it to her. Now she wasn't so sure that was a good thing. She didn't want to be faced with answering questions later and having to choose Constantine over the truth.

When she said nothing, he opened the compartment between the seats and pulled out a phone. He dialed Flores's number to set up Flores for Nicole's call. When the call ended, Constantine offered the phone to Nicole.

She reached for it, but he didn't let it go. "Carlos will hunt us down and kill us, Nicole. He can't go free or we'll never be free." He released his grip on the phone.

Didn't he see? If she had any more blood on her hands, she wouldn't be free, either.

But she didn't say that. She turned away from him and faced forward. "What's the number?"

He didn't immediately respond, the heaviness of his stare bearing down on her with leaden intensity. "Nicole—"

Shoving her hair behind her ears, she cast him a sideways look. "What's the number?" If he dared tell her what to say again, she'd quit the whole scheme.

He gave her the number and zipped his lips. Smart man. She dialed and did her best job of acting panicked.

Flores questioned her, a hint of suspicion in his voice. "How did you get this number?"

"I heard him call you. He went into a quick stop and left the phone. I thumbed through the numbers." She hesitated. "Oh, he's coming back. Pier thirty-nine. A boat called *Adiós*. We're only about an hour away." She disconnected and let out a breath before handing the phone to Constantine. "Now what?"

He gave her a steady look. "You did good."

She bit back an urge to ask why he would think she would do otherwise. "Now what?"

He shifted in his seat and started the engine. "Now we go get those supplies, find a place to wait, and see who shows up."

15

IN THE SHORT DRIVE to the pier, they didn't speak. Constantine didn't know why he'd tried to explain himself to Nicole. She didn't like lies, and it wasn't his problem if she couldn't deal with the truth. So why did it feel like his problem? He quickly whipped the car into a parking spot that offered a view of the boat. It also left them exposed. Not that he had options.

The parking garage across from the pier had been closed because of the approaching storm, and he didn't have time to waste finding another space. Carlos would be close by; he operated out of Padre. Exactly why they'd come here in the first place. Carlos would never expect him on his home turf.

Constantine debated. Leave Nicole in the car or bring her with him? A debate that ended when he admitted he couldn't risk her being in danger without him by her side.

He reached over Nicole, grinding his teeth against the sweetness of those barely parted thighs. Opening the glove compartment, he pulled out a gun, slammed the compartment shut and handed the weapon to Nicole.

"Where am I supposed to hide this?" she asked, referring to her thin shorts and T-shirt.

Good point. When all else fails, improvise. He grabbed the Taco Bell bag and dumped the contents. "Use this."

Her eyes widened in disbelief, but she took the bag. "A purse would be so much better." Her gaze skimmed his shorts. "What about you?"

"Bag in the back," he commented. "I want in and out of the boat in no more than ten minutes."

She nodded. "Got it. I was thinking. How are you so certain that Carlos himself will be here today? Couldn't Flores send someone else? Maybe Carlos isn't near enough to get here in time?"

The question he'd expected her to ask before now. She wouldn't like the answer. "I'm a gambler, remember?"

"And I'm not a dope, remember?"

Inwardly, he smiled. Damn, she was tough. "He'll be in the area."

A frown on her face, she turned to him. "How would you know that for certain?"

"I spent three years in his world. I know how to bait Carlos."

He cut off further conversation, reaching for his door. "We're wasting valuable time that could get us killed. Let's get this done and over with. Stay close to me." He hesitated. "I don't want you in the open any longer than needed. Count to ten once my door shuts. That'll give me time to grab my bag."

Without waiting for her answer, he stepped out of the car, the wind gusting at him with the intensity that would throw Nicole around like a feather. Damn it. He hated exposing her to danger of any type, but the idea of letting her out of his sight twisted his gut in knots. Not a feeling he cared to analyze right now, either. Instead, he focused on the horizon, where a dark wall of clouds was looming.

He squatted down beside the seat, eyes level with Nicole's. "Forget counting. Wait on me. I'll come get you. And forget the gun. The wind is too strong for you to try to hold on to it, let alone fire."

A grim expression on her face told of her understanding, so he pushed to his feet, slammed the door shut and scanned. By the time he retrieved the bag from the backseat, he'd inventoried the area. A total of five cars in the parking lot. To his right, a patrolman, a Padre Island police officer, talked in animated fashion to a young couple taking pictures, obviously trying to run them off. On the dock, two men worked to secure a boat, and Constantine frowned. The storm was ready to swallow them whole as it was.

He rounded the rear of the vehicle to help Nicole. Obviously aware of his location, she shoved open her door a second before he would have reached for it.

The minute she stood up, her hair blew in wild array around her face, and Constantine wished she had it pulled back as he did. She needed a clear view of what might be coming at her from both Mother Nature and man.

"We need to get out of here!" she hollered.

"Not without those supplies," he said, offering her his arm.

She slipped her arm under his elbow, not bothering to argue further. "You mean not before we get Carlos."

He planned to ignore her comment. She seemed to read his mind, refusing to be dismissed. She squeezed his arm and shouted into the howl of the wind. "I want him, too!"

Acceptance of his agenda shouldn't have been important, but somehow it was. Somehow, she'd known he needed to hear those words.

His hand closed over hers, silent appreciation of what she'd said, but he had to stay focused. Time was critical and so were the instructions he had given her. They needed to move. He pulled her forward, and they managed all of one step before a wind gust slammed into them. Constantine muscled up against the impact, and Nicole clung to him to keep from stumbling, yelling something he couldn't understand. He pulled her forward, fighting through the weather to get those supplies before Carlos arrived. He had a safe on the boat with enough cash to last a month. He figured it wouldn't be necessary. A month from now, she would be home, the trial complete. Or so he hoped.

Watching for trouble, holding on to Nicole and fighting the weather, Constantine charged toward the boat. As they walked down the dock ramps, water splashed and it didn't take long for them to be drenched.

Constantine climbed onto the wildly rocking deck of the *Adiós* and deposited his bag on the floor, before grabbing Nicole and pulling her to safety. Once he was certain she had a grip and steady footing, he retrieved his bag and guided her down a small staircase into the cabin.

Now, he had to fetch the money and supplies and get the heck out of Dodge. Easy. Fast. Yeah, right. Every nerve ending in his body tingled.

This juiced-up, edgy feeling was more than readiness; it was his inner alarm for trouble—the one that had kept him alive many a time. And he didn't plan to make this time any different.

THE BOAT CREAKED from side to side, forcing Nicole to cling to the wall. Constantine moved aside a picture and opened a safe, removing a smaller safe, which he shoved into his bag.

The inside of the boat was small and Nicole didn't like it. But she didn't have time to panic. Not now. Nicole inhaled; the cabin smelled warm and masculine like Constantine. The scent comforted and she focused on that feeling. He'd spent time here. This was his boat. "Is this your home?"

"Buying a boat had advantages. Mobility for one. And for a few bucks a year, I pay someone to do general maintenance."

If Constantine had been anyone else, Nicole would have asked if the person maintaining the boat could betray him. But she knew very well that Constantine would never let that person know his real identity. Not when she suspected this boat was his escape route in times of trouble.

He opened a cabinet and pulled out a couple of telephones and various other items that went into the bag. Ammunition, she thought. "The boat allows me to disappear if I need to," he commented, confirming what she'd been thinking. More times than not, he did that—finished her thought, answered a silent question. After a few days, she almost expected as much. He continued, "And it would have been the perfect escape if not for this storm." Moving to a closet, he pulled a rain slicker off a hanger. "Catch." He tossed it to her.

She snagged the shiny black jacket, noting the puddle of water around her feet. The ocean had drenched them far worse than the rain in the woods. At this rate, she would end up permanently shivering.

While she slid the oversize jacket into place, and rolled the sleeves up so they were manageable, Constantine strapped a shoulder holster around his body and shoved a Glock inside. He covered the weapon with a rain slicker matching the one she now wore.

Next thing she knew he was by her side, crisscrossing a small satchel over her chest and shoulder. He patted the bag. "Now you need a gun. Don't try to fire in this wind unless you absolutely have to."

"Like I would fire otherwise."

Displeasure flitted across his features. "I know how big you are on justice and doing the right thing. But out here in the field, a willingness to use your weapon can save your life."

She would have been irritated about being lectured

to on other occasions, but this time, the warning settled hard in her stomach. She could do this, she reminded herself. She was tough.

Resolve taking root, Nicole drew herself upright despite the roughness of the boat's movement. "I know. I'm no fool. I'll shoot if I have to. I think I've proven that."

"I know you aren't a fool," he said, his taut voice taking a gentler note. "But shooting tires and shooting a person aren't the same. It can be hard for the most experienced people to pull the trigger. You can't hesitate."

Right again, of course, and she knew it. "I'll shoot if I have to."

He studied her a moment longer and inclined his head, apparently satisfied with her reply and already back in action mode. Grabbing his bag, he pointed to the stairs. "Let's roll. I'll go first to be sure we're clear."

A few seconds later, they were back outside, and the weather had worsened. The rain had started, and the wind was even stronger than before. Constantine jumped to the docks and offered Nicole his hand, which she tried to accept, but with the wobble beneath her feet she couldn't quite connect with his palm.

Suddenly a scream ripped through the air, and Constantine retracted his hand, reaching for his gun. Nicole grabbed the boat railing with a solid grip.

More screams, this time more intelligible. "Help! Help!"

Nicole's adrenaline spiked into overdrive, her eyes searching in desperation for the source of the cries. Her gaze scanned the area, spotting a woman on the deck of a boat, several spots down from the *Adiós*. The woman was at the railing, struggling with a life preserver, steadying herself a second before she shoved it over the edge.

Hair blew in Nicole's eyes, slapping at her cheeks and brow, as she tried to see the reason for the woman's fear. She leaned down, looking beneath a sail and honed in on the water, where she saw a man struggling against the rough waves.

Oh, God. He was going to drown. She turned to Constantine and screamed his name, pointing out what she'd seen. He maneuvered closer, ducking down for a visual. A curse followed. Obviously he had managed to see what she did, his expression grim. He seemed to weigh his options, before turning to Nicole and reaching for her. "Come on."

Before Nicole could catch her breath, he had a hold of her and she was lifted from the boat onto the dock. The instant her feet hit the ground, he had her hand, and they were running, water and wind smacking them hard.

Seconds later, Nicole and Constantine climbed onto the woman's boat. She ran at them, frantically pleading, "Save him! Please save my husband."

Constantine handed Nicole his gun, dropping his bag on the ground.

Fear squeezed her heart. The water was insanely dangerous, the wrath of Mother Nature much worse than Carlos and Alvarez put together. "You stay alive, damn it!" she shouted, her gut churning much like the ocean.

He didn't answer. She wasn't even sure he heard her. Already, he was diving over the side of the boat. She faced the sobbing woman and asked, "Do you have a phone? Have you called 911?"

"No, yes, I...have a phone."

"Use it! Call! Call now! And go get help." Nicole ran to the ledge to check for a ladder. Thankfully, the woman had, indeed, extended a rope ladder over the side.

Preparing to help if needed, she dropped Constantine's gun and holster next to the bag that he'd left on the deck. She returned to the railing, gulping water as rain slammed into her face. Coughing, she swiped at her eyes, desperately searching for Constantine. The minute she spotted him swimming through the salty turbulence, she breathed a bit easier. He was moving; he was visible. And yes! He had the drowning man in his grasp. She watched as he swam toward them, pulling the man with him through the powerful waves.

How long Nicole stood there, terrified for Constantine, watching him struggle, she didn't know, but it felt like a lifetime before he finally arrived at the edge of the boat, the man still in his grip. Thankfully, the woman showed up with help. Nicole turned to find two men wearing uniforms of some sort—beach patrol, she thought.

The two men started to lift the drowning man from the water, which meant Constantine could follow. With the woman's husband safely on board, stretched out and unconscious, one of the patrolmen dropped to his knees and appeared ready to start CPR. The other cop was leaning over the side of the boat trying to help Constantine.

Nicole ran to the edge, fearful, wondering why Constantine hadn't shown himself. Her heart felt as if it would explode at what she saw. Somehow, Constantine had been swept away from the boat by the rough waters. She watched as he grabbed the life preserver, and she let out a sigh of relief.

She turned to check on everyone else, only to find an order barked in her direction. "Go flag the ambulance!" The shout came from the man doing CPR. Nicole blinked. Was he talking to her? She glanced at the wife, who was crumpled to the ground next to her unmoving husband. Nicole's gaze flickered to the victim; his face appeared somewhat bluish and she understood why the woman was crying. Her husband was dying. Nicole had to do something.

She started running, or rather stumbling, across the deck toward the dock. Her heart jackknifed in her chest. Constantine would not like what she was doing. She didn't like it herself. Carlos was coming. She jumped off the boat to the wooden walkway, landing on her feet, and then darted toward the parking lot. Her mind went back to the silent threat. Carlos. Coming soon. How much time had passed? Thirty minutes? Forty?

It didn't matter, she told herself. She had to do this. But fear gripped her as she had the thought; she realized she was creating more danger for these people. Everyone on that boat was in danger—they'd be in danger because they were near her and Constantine.

She should turn back. A dim eeriness had claimed what was daylight only an hour before, which added to the growing unease rattling her nerves. By the time she'd made it to the parking lot, she was nervous, and had convinced herself she'd made the wrong move. About to abandon her efforts, she was waylaid by flashing red lights that blasted through the haze of the storm.

Charging toward the ambulance, determined to get their attention and get back to the boat, Nicole felt hope form that all of this would work out. After all, the ambulance was here. That was something. She clung to that little bit of good news.

The emergency crew, which consisted of two men, pulled to a stop beside her and she directed them where to go. And then she took off running toward the boat, not allowing them time to respond, ignoring their shouts behind her.

Hope filled her. She'd pulled off helping that man without getting herself killed. Hope that quickly faded as she found a man standing in front of the walkway that led to the docks. Stocky, with an air of menace clinging to him. Nicole had no doubt who she faced. Carlos.

16

NICOLE'S SURVIVAL INSTINCTS kicked in at the sight of Carlos in her path. She turned and cut a sharp left off the path she was on, and started running toward the car from another angle—leading Carlos away from the unsuspecting emergency crew, fearful for their safety. A gunshot sounded behind her, a blast that cut through the fierceness of the wind with a vicious roar. Nicole nearly jumped out of her skin, cringing in preparation for pain that never came. Somehow she kept running. Another shot was fired. No, two. Two shots.

She took a sharp left, toward their parked car. Carlos would follow her, then no one else had to die. She reminded herself she had a gun in the car. Now she had to focus on running, on getting to shelter so she could use it.

The car came into view and she pushed through the sting in her legs, against the power of the wind, running faster, harder. She could use the car for a shield, and then she'd pull her gun. Constantine was wrong to doubt her willingness to shoot. She'd shoot and she'd survive.

She approached the car and to her amazement, and relief, Constantine was right behind her. He charged at her, grabbed her arm and dragged her to a squat out of sight, beside the driver's door.

He held her shoulders, inspecting her for injuries. "You're okay?"

She blinked at him, rain rolling over her hair and lashes. They were both completely, utterly soaked.

"Nicole! Are you okay?"

"Yes." The one word was barely audible. Her teeth were chattering, but she wasn't cold. Reality slipped back into her mind. "It was Carlos! Where did he go?" She grabbed his forearms where he held her. "Where? Where is he?"

"Close. Too damn close. I got a shot off at him, but I missed. He slipped out of sight. But he's here."

"And so are a lot of innocent people."

His jaw flexed. "I know that all too well." He fixed her in a reprimanding look. "You shouldn't have left. You could have been killed."

"I—"

He cut her off. "Now isn't the time. Stay down."

Constantine started to stand, but stilled when one of the police officers from the boat appeared, his firearm drawn.

"Drop your weapon!" the man ordered.

"Easy now, kid," Constantine said. "I'm FBI. Call it in on—"

"Shut up! My partner is dead. I don't give a damn if you're the Lone Ranger."

Nicole's heart sank. Oh, God. "He didn't kill your partner. He's FBI. It was—"

"Shut up!" the kid yelled again and focused on Constantine. "Drop the gun."

Constantine held his gun by his side, showing no signs of throwing it away. "That man who killed your partner is after us. Throwing down my weapon would be a death sentence."

"Please," Nicole added, "let him do his job. Before it's too late."

The patrolman shifted his gaze between them and then fixed on Constantine again. "I'll do it when the gun is on the ground."

The muffled sound of a motorcycle broke through the noise of the storm, and Constantine stiffened beside her. "That would be the man who killed your partner, and now he plans to kill us." The sound grew louder. "Look, kid," Constantine said, his tone like hard steel, "I'm losing my patience with you. You're impeding an FBI operation." He raised his voice. "If you don't stop aiming your weapon at me in about two seconds—"

Abruptly, he stopped talking. The sound of a motorcycle was fast approaching. "Get down!"

Nicole hit the ground. The patrolman didn't. Constantine launched himself at the kid and took him to the pavement, smack in the center of a puddle that splashed mud all over. And not a second before a spray of bullets hit the car. Nicole covered her head, her heart thundering along with the motorcycle engine as it sped by.

The minute the sound of the bike faded, Constantine shoved off the patrolman and stood up. Nicole followed his lead and did the same, moving to Constantine's side, the place he'd once again proven to be the safest.

The patrolman scrambled to his feet, his expression flustered and confused. Constantine looked at the man, his face full of disgust. "Call for backup," he ordered as he returned his weapon to the holster. Carlos had to have gone. How he knew this, Nicole wasn't sure, but she was learning not to doubt him. Not when it came to his job.

Constantine wasn't done with the patrolman. Not by a long shot. "When you call for that backup, tell them you just let Carlos Menchaca get away." He bent down and retrieved the kid's weapon from the puddle and let it dangle from his finger. The kid grabbed it.

Constantine motioned toward the car, and she didn't argue. She wanted out of there. Her life had become hell.

Once they were in the car, she was relieved to see the bag of supplies in the backseat. Constantine must have remembered to bring them. He started the engine and squealed out of the driveway. A second later, he grabbed the phone that was stuffed in the compartment between the seats and dialed. "Give me Agent Nelson. Tell him Agent Vega is on the phone."

Nicole gaped at that, shocked he trusted anyone at this point, especially Nelson after the way he'd reacted to his involvement. "Vega here," he said to the receiver, she assumed to Nelson. "Menchaca is in Padre, near pier thirty-nine. He killed a cop, tried to take us out, too." He listened a minute as they pulled up behind a line of traffic at a standstill. "Local police have their hands full with the storm."

Constantine did some more listening, and offered a few short, clipped words in reply. Then, he dropped his bomb on Nelson. "Flores is dirty." He went on to describe the way they had set him up and ended with, "I suggest you deal with him before I get back." Silence, listening, then he said, "And, Nelson. This doesn't mean I trust you. It simply means you're all I got right now. I'll be in contact soon."

He hung up. Neither Nicole nor Constantine spoke, the tension in the car as thick as the storm surrounding them. Nicole wanted to lie back and think, to calm the chaos going on in her brain. But that would have been too easy. She should have known there would have been complications to come. Without warning, Constantine whipped the car into a hotel parking lot, drove to the rear and shut off the ignition.

"Carlos knows this car. We have to switch vehicles. Wait here." Right. No keys to leave since it was hot-wired. His exit came with obvious effort, as he fought a gust of wind and lots of water.

So Nicole waited. Waited while he stole another car. And though she knew the government would cover the expense, it was still stealing. She tried not to think of a family in need, reminding herself they could rent a car. That she and Constantine would be dead without escape. They had no help. Worse, she wanted another car. She wanted to feel safe. If she kept at this a few more days, lived in Constantine's world, would she justify vigilante acts to save lives, too?

As she'd feared, the right circumstances, the right person—aka Constantine—and she was back to her old self. Or getting there. Suddenly, she didn't want to claim her darker side. She wanted to blame someone. Anger and frustration over all of that twisted inside her.

The back door opened, more wind, more rain. Constantine grabbed the supplies. "We're a go."

Steeling herself for the weather, Nicole reached for the door and pushed it open. Seconds later, she was inside a four-door sedan, a Mercury maybe, basically a perfect match for the car they'd left behind—wet and stolen.

"Where are we going?"

"Houston. They'll expect us to go farther. We won't."

She didn't comment. Houston. Dallas. Canada. All that mattered was that she got back to Austin, alive and ready for trial. Which would be delayed at this point, but she hoped not too long. Too many things could go wrong with a long delay.

In a matter of minutes, Constantine maneuvered them onto the highway, and into a traffic jam. Great. Trapped in a car, feeling edgy, in a traffic jam. In a storm. If that didn't trigger her claustrophobia, she didn't know what would.

She inhaled and let out a breath, focusing on anything but the small space, her gaze sliding to his profile. A strong profile, a grim set to his jaw. A stubborn, hard-ass man. Her anger hadn't faded. "You shouldn't have been so rough on that kid."

He glanced at her, his brows set in a straight line. "I saved his life." Constantine's voice was low, unaffected by her attack.

"Today," she countered. "What about how it affects him? How it will impact his ability to do his job?"

A sound of disbelief slid from his lips. "I can't believe you're comparing him to either of us. And don't deny you are because I know better. The impact of my words on that kid doesn't even begin to compare to what you and I have been through to get where we are now. In fact, what happened to him today might well save his life, and other lives, many times over. He won't ever be as careless as he was today."

"He lost his partner. That's the part you seem to be forgetting."

"And he acted irrationally and emotionally, ignoring his training. A good way to get others killed. We could have helped him get the man who killed his partner. Instead, Carlos is free, and he's going to keep coming. For me. For you. For anyone we care about. So did you think I was going to give him a lollipop and thank him for screwing us?"

She took those harsh words with a stunned blast and fell back in her seat, not even aware she had been sitting up in confrontation mode. Realization dawning, she said, "I thought this was about justice and helping people. Why does it feel like I'm hurting more than I'm helping right now?" Her lashes shut, blocking out nothing, when she wanted to block out everything—at least for a few minutes.

Silence followed before he replied, "You are helping,

Nicole. But there is no such thing as that easy black-and-white line that you want to believe exists. Fighting to find that safe middle wears on a person."

She turned to him, her lashes lifted. "Wears on you?"

"Hell, yes. That's why I'm getting out. I'm done and gone after this, and never looking back."

A hint of pain tinged his voice. She'd almost forgotten. "I'm sorry about Flores."

He shrugged, but he didn't look at her. "It's done. He's done. That's what counts."

"Do you want to know why he did it?"

"Nope," he said, glancing at her. "He was part of an attempt on our lives. He couldn't give me a reason that would matter. They'll suspend him and hold him for questioning until we get back and then I'll give them what they need to lock him away for good."

She drew a long, hard breath. This had hurt him. Betrayal hurt. If he wasn't ready to leave his job before this, she imagined that Flores had sealed the deal. Still… "You really think you can simply shut off this world? Forget this part of your life?"

He answered quickly, as if he'd given the question a lot of consideration before she'd asked it. "For a while. Then, I'll see where to go from there. I haven't had time to spend my money so I invested it. I have time to decide. Private hire work is an option. It would be nice to choose my own battles."

She turned away from him, lost in her own thoughts. Choose my own battles. She figured she'd done that by joining the U.S. Attorney's office. Now, she wasn't so sure. The battles sure seemed to be picking her these

days. The internal emotional battle to find her place—
the reason she'd made a career change—still existed,
never letting her find peace.

Nicole had opened this conversation with Constantine looking to blame him for how out of control she
felt. But the truth was, he not only wasn't to blame, his
words, his actions, made sense to her. He made sense
to her. He'd saved lives today, acted bravely. He was a
hero. A hero who didn't always play by the rules, but
he always had good intentions.

She admired him. She desired him. She felt safer
with him near. And she feared him. Or maybe she feared
herself and simply hated him for making her look deep
enough to know it.

Once again, she came to the conclusion he always led
her to—Constantine was dangerous. And that danger,
she feared, was becoming an addiction she wondered
if she would ever recover from.

17

CONSTANTINE HAD BARELY spoken to Nicole during the grueling hours in traffic, making the short trip to Houston progress far too slowly. But then, that was the idea. He wanted to get lost in the midst of the evacuation chaos. But along the way, he got lost in his own internal struggles. Now, walking down the hall of the high-end, high-security, downtown hotel toward their room, Nicole by his side, Constantine warned himself to dump the emotional garbage. It was dangerous, deadly, distracting.

The truth was, being betrayed by Flores had bitten him pretty hard, but it was nothing in comparison to when he'd climbed up to the deck of that boat and discovered Nicole was missing. That moment had pierced him with sheer terror. A feeling he'd had only once before—when he got the call about his brother.

Nicole had gotten under his skin, and apparently past an emotional barrier that he didn't know could be penetrated. He was pissed at her for running off, at himself for becoming susceptible to Nicole. People around him had short life spans. It was the curse of his world.

For the second time in an hour, Constantine shoved open the door to their room. "You're sure you have everything?" he asked, dropping a handful of bags on the floor and then locking up. They'd checked in under an alias, surveyed the room and then left to stock up heavily on items they might need for their extended stay. "We can't leave for anything. And I can't stress that enough. It's dangerous. We slid in here as part of the background to the craziness of the storm. Once that calms, we'll get more attention. We're here to stay."

Nicole sat down on the bed, settling several large Macy's bags on the mattress beside her. She'd been tentative with him the entire shopping spree, no doubt because of his foul mood, or perhaps she was still angry over how he'd treated that patrolman back in Padre.

"I have everything I need," she confirmed. "And thank you." She hesitated and repeated a question she'd asked several times before. "You're sure the department will reimburse you, right?"

If he answered truthfully, no. The department only covered basics, but he'd be damned if he'd admit that. Convincing her to shop from his wallet had taken heavy prodding. He expected the claustrophobia would kick in after two days of staying in the room, so having some of her personal comforts would help. Even people without a phobia got restless fast.

"I'm sure," he said, walking to the midsize fridge in the corner to unload a few items. He could feel her watching him, feel the heaviness of her stare.

They might be tense, but they were alone in a hotel room, two people who had more than their share of desire for one another. A sizzle of sexual energy crackled in the air. But then, their chemistry was a given at that point.

Nicole's soft laugh laced the air, a hint of nervousness in the sound, as if she were responding to the mixed array of emotional baggage between them and was as confused by it as he was.

"Thanks to the storm," she commented, toeing off her stained tennis shoes, "today was probably the only time in my life I could get away with walking into Macy's looking like a female mud wrestler."

Constantine deposited several cans of Diet Sprite in the fridge—Nicole's favorite drink. "For all the trouble that storm caused us, it certainly helped us in other ways."

He looked up to find Nicole unpacking their purchases, his gaze lingering on her graceful movements, her delicate hands reminding him of how amazing her touch felt. He didn't understand—when had looking at a woman's hands turned him on?

Inwardly, he shook himself, and went back to packing the fridge, but his mind played with the experience of watching her shop, which had been rather enlightening. All her products, her choices, had told a lot about Nicole. She had a thing for a perfume called "Passion" and apparently anything else sold at the Estée Lauder cosmetic counter. She liked red and pink silk pajamas, which he looked forward to seeing her in…and out of. At his prodding, she'd picked out a couple of work suits for the first few days of the trial; they were preparing to stay in hiding as long as possible. Her contrasting choices of sexy sleepwear and conservative work attire had intrigued him. She was the perfect woman. He paused in the act of putting orange juice away, wondering where that thought had come from.

Before he could venture further, Nicole drew him into conversation. "I really don't know how you stand always being undercover. I need my safe haven, my space that I escape to."

Which was why he'd made sure she'd purchased items she would use at home, hoping to give her a sense of control. "When you're deep undercover, you take on a persona that feels like it's you. If you don't, you won't survive."

She stopped what she was doing and stared at him. "Sounds like a hard way to live."

"After a while, the act becomes second nature. We can train ourselves to step out of our comfort zones." Just as she had. The writing was on the wall. She wanted to be the staunch federal prosecutor, but there were parts of that role she struggled to embrace. "But I suspect you know that." He didn't give her time to respond, not wanting to make her defensive, regretting he'd even spoken the words. They'd had enough tension during the long ride. He pushed to his feet. "You can have the shower first."

"That sounds good." She glanced at the clock. "I am supposed to call Dean in an hour regarding that motion to suppress your testimony by the defense."

"Which you're sure they won't get."

She scoffed, pushing off the bed with a bag in hand. "About as good a chance as snow in mid-July."

Her words held spunk; her mood seemed to lift as her zeal for victory appeared to take hold. Clearly, she enjoyed the battle, and enjoyed winning her cases. But then, it was clear that the lines they had drawn in order to reach success were the same lines that were creating all her conflict. They both lived the conflicting messages their legal system elicited, both struggled with them. But each of them had taken a different path to deal with the obstacles they faced from that system. She'd gone to one side of the line, he to the other. Ironically, neither of them liked the result.

Could there be two people so similar and so different in this world?

He watched her sashay past him, heading to the bathroom. His gaze dropped, lingered, riveted on her perfect ass, his groin tightening as he thought of all the things he was going to do to her there, in that room. They'd better enjoy what time they had.

Because when they left that room, there would be a tough trial and tough decisions. Like twenty-four-hour security for Nicole. Not something he planned to bring up until he had to.

Meanwhile, he'd protect her and then get the hell out of her life, so she could avoid the danger that always affected those around him. Which meant they should now burn out the chemistry they shared. And something told him that was going to require a lot of time in bed.

HEAVEN. HER BATH had been heaven.

Nicole slipped into the pink velour sweatpants and

matching T-shirt she'd bought, and inhaled the scent of her favorite bubble bath still floating in the air. She'd bought a few bras, but she didn't bother putting one on, nor did she bother with panties—panty lines were something she could do without.

Spraying on some perfume, Nicole felt nearly herself again. She didn't consider herself spoiled, by any means, but her little habits gave her a sense of pleasure she now realized should never be taken for granted. Next up, drying her hair, applying a little makeup. The idea of Constantine seeing her as a woman, not a mess, appealed far more than she cared to admit. Especially since they'd been anything but friendly the past few hours. Still, the attraction between them lingered, waiting for exploration as readily as a new day. No one resisted such an attraction in close quarters. Sex was a basic need, a need she'd long denied herself. Of all the things Constantine had awakened in her, her sexual appetite was top of the list.

She sighed and leaned on the sink, staring at her image. More than her sexuality had been reinvented since meeting Constantine. But then, she'd sensed he would do this to her. Sensed he was the catalyst that would create inevitable change in her life. Remembering the night she'd met him, she recalled the air of dangerous excitement he'd sparked in her. The way she'd known he would somehow make her look inside herself, force her to examine realities she wasn't sure she was willing to face. Deep down, she had known she'd been hiding from herself. Constantine had led her to a crossroads. When this experience ended, she would have to choose a direction for her life.

Would she fight to walk that narrow, perfect line or would she detour? More and more that line felt constraining, and hearing Constantine's opinions on things made her realize how not black-and-white life could be. But if she detoured from this path, where did that leave her? So what was she? Who was she? Unhappy, she thought. Miserable. Tired of being something she wasn't. That left her where? She had no idea. She wanted Alvarez behind bars and so did Constantine. That mutual desire and their shared attraction had melted away their black-and-white viewpoints. But had she lost herself to him? Lost everything she'd fought to achieve? Lost the moral fiber on which she'd based her past few years of living?

Her mind went back to seeing Carlos, to running for her life. Yes, she had hoped for Carlos's demise, for Constantine to kill him. Oh, God. She knew why she was drawn to Constantine. He was so like her that it was scary.

She squeezed her eyes shut. Her problem these past few years had been with the system. She'd changed sides but the battlefield was the same. Grabbing the hairbrush, she roughly pulled it through her hair. She couldn't do this now, couldn't think about this now. She had to be at her best during this trial, to put Alvarez away for life.

But later, she had to face some life-changing decisions, and she had Constantine to thank for that. Part of her hated him for it, while the other part felt grateful.

She'd funnel those emotions into the only outlet she had…sex.

NICOLE ENTERED THE bedroom to find Constantine lying on the bed watching the news, his head propped up against the headboard, long legs stretched out in front of him, shirt off. Her mouth went dry. She didn't hide her inspection.

He looked every bit the sexy stranger she had seen in that bar that first night and then some. Knowing he was a dangerous temptation had only served to enhance her desire for him, to solidify the dark danger of his allure. She stood, unmoving, staring at him, him staring at her. Awareness built like warmth turning to heat... ready to burst into flames.

"Feel better?" he asked, his dark eyes mesmerizing in their directness. His voice had that lusty, provocative tone he used when they were intimate.

"Oh, yes. I feel much better," she said, walking toward the bed and sitting down on the end of the mattress. "I need to call Dean."

He grabbed the phone off the nightstand and handed it to her. "I like the outfit."

She took the phone, realizing his gaze had settled below her chin. Her nipples tightened and peaked, the heaviness of his attention creating equal heaviness in her breasts. The effect was a rush of sensation in her core, between her thighs.

She put a finger under his chin and lifted his gaze to her eyes. "Go take a shower. I have to call Dean, and I can't do it with you looking at me like that."

A slow, mischievous smile slid onto his lips, lighting those dark eyes. Damn, he was hot when he smiled. He didn't do it enough. "You can join me when you finish."

"I already took a bath and you didn't join me," she reminded him.

"You didn't invite me."

"We were barely speaking. I didn't think you wanted to be invited."

"You thought wrong and the last time I checked, bathing doesn't require speaking."

She laughed. He kissed her, his tongue swooping past her lips with a soft caress she felt in every inch of her body. Too soon, his mouth was gone, his thumb lingering, sliding over her bottom lip. "It's an open invitation, talking optional." He left her wanting and wet, and headed to the bathroom. She wanted to follow, but she really had to call Dean.

The bathroom door shut and she climbed across the bed to lean against the headboard, dialing Dean's number. He picked up in one ring, obviously waiting for her call, and offered her good news—Constantine's testimony was a go.

"Excellent. He's a strong witness. His brother and father were both in law enforcement."

"I know," Dean said. "I had him investigated."

"That was fast," she said, pleased to hear there were no skeletons in Constantine's closet, but not surprised. He was pretty straightforward about who he was, the good and the bad.

"The FBI expected we'd want the information," Dean commented. "They handed his file over on a silver platter. He not only looks good on paper, he has the defense shaking in their shoes."

She frowned. "Exactly why Alvarez wants him dead."

"And you, too," he grimly added, his voice muffled by static on the line, probably from the storm. "Anything to delay the trial and come up with a loophole. Which brings me to some not-so-good news."

"Which would be?"

"I talked to your—" More static.

"What? Talked to who?"

"I talked to your sister today. Your father wants her home and at work. She wanted to know how sure I was she should stay gone."

Nicole sat up, her heart pounding like a drum against her chest. "You told her to stay away, right?"

"I did, but she is feeling pressured. Your father wants her at work. He assured her he has private security and that those security people have seen absolutely no signs of a threat. He says—"

"He has money to make. I know. Believe me, I know my father. Damn it!" She ran a hand through her hair. "Why is she so manipulated by him? Why does she want to be like him so badly? And why doesn't he see how dangerous this is?" She had practically forgotten Dean. "Is she still in Hawaii?"

The phone cut in and out. "Did you hear me?" Dean asked. "She's taking a flight home first thing in the morning."

"I have to go." She'd call him back later, to check on his wife. She dialed her sister's cell. The call dropped, no signal.

Pushing to her feet, Nicole moved to the window and

dialed again. Still no signal. Why did her father do these things? Did he love and care about anyone? Sometimes his wallet seemed his only love. Truthfully, he wasn't a nice person. He was about control. About career. There was a reason she didn't include him in her life. But she knew her sister wanted him there. Just as she once had. He had a way of manipulating you and stealing your self-worth—making it exist based on his approval.

Giving up on getting a signal for the cell phone, she headed to the door. Maybe near the elevator she could get a signal. She hesitated and rushed into the bathroom, calling to Constantine through the shower curtain. "I'll be right back. There's an emergency at home and I can't get cell reception."

He yanked the shower curtain back. "No. Wait on me."

"I can't. I'll be right back."

She heard him curse, but she didn't care. Her sister was all that mattered right then. She'd deal with his anger, if and when—she didn't care. It wasn't as if she were leaving the floor, or leaving without communicating. He'd understand when he heard it was about her sister. He had to understand.

THE HOTEL-ROOM DOOR closed about the time Constantine wrapped the tiny towel around his waist. Was she begging to get killed or what? It took him all of twenty seconds to find his gun and head for the door, having no qualms about leaving in a towel. The one second he hesitated could be the difference between life or death. But this was a hell of a way to stay under the radar.

After confirming the hall to be vacant, a small miracle considering how busy the hotel was, he flipped the lock around to keep the door from closing all the way. With long strides, he headed for the elevator, heart thundering in his chest, fear for her safety far more controlling than his professional standards should allow.

Rounding the corner, he found relief. Nicole was pacing, talking on the phone, a deep frown on her face. The minute she saw him, her eyes went wide, her gaze sweeping his half-naked body, spotting the gun in his hand. Her face went pale.

Her expression said she knew she'd pushed him too far, given him one too many scares that day. She knew she'd done this to him, pushed him over the edge. His patience officially snapped; his emotions were unrecognizable. He didn't like what he was feeling—hated it, in fact.

He charged at her and grabbed her hand. "Come with me now or I swear to God I will throw you over my shoulder and carry you."

A stunned look filled her face and she mumbled into the phone, "I'll call you back, but don't get on that plane until I talk to you again." Constantine gave her a warning look and she quickly said, "I'll call back," and hit End. "Constantine—" The elevator dinged, and panic registered on her face.

"Yeah, I'm in a towel about to give a peep show." He started pulling her down the hall and mumbled under his breath, "Which I have you to thank for."

"Ouch," she complained behind him. "You're hurting me."

He knew damn well he wasn't hurting anything but her pride. And that was lucky for her, but then, he wasn't through yet. Using one foot, he kicked open the door, and then reached up and flipped the latch, pulling Nicole inside the room. He used his foot again to make sure the door shut behind him.

Nicole tugged on her arm, leaning away from him as if to leverage herself. "Let. Me. Go."

He did the opposite. He yanked her to him, anchoring her against his body, palm against her lower back. Her body, soft and curvy, pressed into his. He prayed for patience. *"Por, Dios, da me paciencia."*

Palms flat on his chest, she glared at him. "Stop cussing at me in Spanish! If you have something to say, then you can say it in English."

"I didn't curse you. I simply asked God to give me the patience to deal with you."

"What?" she roared back. "I'm the one who needs patience. You're being a complete jerk. My sister is leaving Hawaii in the morning. I have to stop her from boarding that plane."

"I asked you to wait long enough for me to get out of the shower. I've risked my life for you over and over, and you can't wait for me to get out of the shower before you make that phone call? A few seconds was too much to ask?" His chest lifted with a hard inhalation that he quickly expelled. "You're driving me to insanity, woman."

"And you're such a joy, let me tell you!"

He knew he was overreacting, but somehow, quite out of character, he couldn't stop himself from doing so. He started toward the bed, but she dug her heels in. He pulled her tight against his body again, more than a bit irritated, and completely out of patience, hands cupping her round ass as he lifted her from the ground.

The act put her flat against his body, and his cock flared to life, the towel barely clinging to his hips. Her breasts pressed into his bare chest. She wore no bra, and he could feel her nipples as surely as he could her ass in his hands. Inwardly he cursed his lack of control. The heat of anger began to merge with the raging call of desire.

"Put me down," she admonished near his ear. A plea slipped into her voice. "Stop acting like this. Stop being—"

Her sentence was cut short by her back hitting the mattress. Constantine straddled her hips, his hands going to her wrists, holding them above her head. She struggled for a good minute before stilling. There was no chance she could get free and she knew it. He was bigger and stronger, and just as determined to hold her down as she was to get up.

His face was close to hers, his gaze latching on to hers with purpose, letting her see deep into the depths of his stare, letting her see how far she'd pushed him.

Take a deep, hard look, sweetheart. See what you've unleashed in me. See the stranger I don't even know as myself.

"Constantine," she whispered, soft desperation in her voice. But he was still too damn mad to back down, and she deserved to feel the brunt of it. But damn it, his gaze dropped to her mouth, to those full, perfect lips as they quivered. The desire to kiss her, hold her and touch her rose within him like a caged beast demanding freedom. He wanted to take her right now, to find his way inside her, to dispel all the emotion he felt, inside the warm, wet heat of her body.

But he also knew he needed space, needed to clear his head. Needed to stay mad and deal with the real safety issues. His towel slid from his hips; the will to get off Nicole and walk away slid with it.

_18_

CONSTANTINE WAS DESPERATE to resist claiming Nicole. But he kissed her, capturing her mouth with his, branding her lips with fiery need. Instantly, she submitted to him, and he silently reveled in the victory of her response.

But her submission was short-lived. Nicole tore her mouth from his, her hands pressing on his bare chest, her touch teasing him with the possibility of all the places they might travel. "No," she whispered, her words desperate, laden with desire. "I want you, but not like this. Not when you're angry for no reason."

He rested on his elbows, one on either side of her, and stared into her eyes. "You scared the hell out of me." His voice was husky, with a gravelly tone he barely recognized as his own.

Confusion flashed across her features. "I thought your job didn't allow for emotional responses. That sounds emotional to me. You told that patrolman—"

He'd come that far, he might as well go all the way.

"You're not simply a part of my job, Nicole. Not anymore." His fingers brushed her cheek, tenderness welling inside him…tenderness driving him insane with unfamiliar feelings. He didn't want to care about her, but there seemed no way to hide, nowhere to run.

Sliding her small wrists above her head, he easily enclosed them in one of his larger hands. Her chest rose and fell, drawing his eyes to her deliciously peaked nipples, his cock throbbing, demanding satisfaction. He searched her face for a reaction.

Heat and defiance glinted in her eyes. "Holding on to someone like this, who is claustrophobic, is a good way to see the claws come out," she warned.

He considered her words, his free hand sliding over her arms, her neck, her breasts. She sucked in a breath as he lightly tweaked her nipple through the thin material of her T-shirt. "I know you explored the kinky side of sex with your ex. You mean to tell me you were never tied up?"

"Never."

"You didn't trust him."

"What's that got to do with anything?"

"Handing over complete control requires trust." He molded her breast more fully to his palm, bringing his lips to hers.

"I trust you," she murmured against his mouth, opening to allow his tongue to delve in for a quick sensual stroke.

"You trust me to some degree, but not fully." He released her arms to make a point.

A flare of fire in her eyes turned to confusion and

then disappeared behind a mask of seductive play. "And if I wanted to tie you up? Would you let me?"

"Trust is a two-way street, sweetheart. If you don't give it freely, you don't get it freely." His hand slid up her shirt. "Take this off."

"I trust you," she argued, pulling her shirt over her head.

He worked her pants down her hips and tossed them aside. He spread her legs, running his palms up her toned calves, over her knees, and then settled his hands on her thighs. He inched her legs farther apart, and she willingly opened to him.

Yes. There was some trust—trust within limits. She no longer demanded complete control, no longer needed the edge of power to enjoy his pleasuring her.

He slid his finger along the center of her core, and she whimpered softly. "You're wet for me."

"Yes," came the barely there reply, her voice growing stronger as she added, "And I shouldn't be. Not after you acted like a caveman dragging me into the room like you did."

Ah, and there it was, a hint of vulnerability he'd seen in her during their lovemaking. The fear that she was giving him too much, not holding back enough. He settled his erection in the sweet heat of her core, determined to kiss away whatever emotion drove her to throw up a shield.

His hands slid to her face; the feel of her soft curves pressed into his body was heaven in the middle of all the hell. "It's okay to want me, you know."

Her bottom lip trembled. She started to speak.

Stopped. Started again. "You were right." The confession came in a shaky voice, a rarity for her, he was certain. She continued, "You do scare me. You scare the hell out of me. You make me question all the things I thought I knew and understood. You make me want things I shouldn't want."

"And you," he proclaimed, offering his own confession, "make me question everything I thought I wanted."

Silence—intense, full of sexual energy and emotion—fell between them then, their eyes locked in a soul-deep stare. On some gut level, he knew meeting Nicole was life-changing. She had touched him on a level he'd never fully recover from.

They moved then, together—at the same moment. They were kissing, crazy hot kissing, lost in the passion, consumed by the complete utter need for one another. Nothing mattered but here and now. He had tried to sate his desire to touch her soft skin, inhale that soft feminine scent, but nothing worked. He simply couldn't get enough of her, and he wondered if he ever would. Doubted that he ever could. She moved with equal, frenzied need, pressing close, arching into him. She felt what he did. Felt the burn he couldn't escape.

He realized then that all the obstacles between them had disappeared. What was left sent him over the edge, outside of reality. There were a million reasons why anything real between them couldn't work. His life and her life conflicted in far too many ways. He couldn't have her. But he could have her tonight, these few weeks—a stolen piece of time.

He took her then, finding his way inside her body,

thrusting his cock deep inside the wet heat of her core. She gasped and clung to him, her lips and teeth nipping at his shoulder with delicious results he felt from head to foot.

Driven to see the passion in her face as he made love to her, he leaned back, staring down at her. Her eyes were heavy-lidded, her mouth swollen from his kisses. Slowly, he teased them both as he pulled out all but the head of his erection. "Constantine," she pleaded.

A plea that reached deep inside him, demanding a response. He lunged into her then, burying himself to the hilt, pulling back and repeating the action. Her breasts bounced and she covered them with her hands, kneading.

He craved her taste, reveled in her beauty, her touch. Her hands slid from her breasts to his shoulders, his neck. He was pumping and rocking, her legs wrapped around his, her hips cradling his.

"More," she cried out. "More." But he wasn't sure how to fulfill her need, his need. Never in his life had he felt so lost in a woman, so impossibly in need of complete possession. That possession, however, that completeness, somehow lingered out of reach.

Long moments they pumped, together, then stilled, staring at one another, and he saw in her what he felt in himself. They were both confused by the array of emotions, of pleasures rushing through them.

Her hair was wild around her heart-shaped face, her lips parted, waiting for him. "Damn, you're beautiful," he murmured, his mouth lowering to claim hers, his hands reaching beneath her backside, pulling her tighter against him. He angled her hips as he pumped some more, and she took more...begged for more. Until finally, too soon, not soon enough, she shattered—tense for seconds before her body jerked into release.

He still rode her, watching her, enthralled by the sight of her coming. Holding himself back, he waited until he knew she was completely satisfied. When her body began to ease, then, and only then, did he begin to allow his own final pleasure to consume him. He shattered much as she had, shaking with the intensity, stars before his eyes.

When finally his muscles eased, his release complete, they collapsed together, his head buried in her neck. He was still semi-hard, the massive orgasm he'd spilled inside her nowhere near enough to satisfy him. He didn't want to let go of her; he thought maybe he'd roll her on top and do that all over again.

The tempting idea was ended by Nicole's panicky voice. "Oh, my sister. I have to stop her from getting on that plane."

He leaned up on his elbows. "We'll stop her." Reluctantly, he rolled off her and hunted down his towel before handing it to her. "Tell me what's going on."

Nicole explained the situation, and Constantine shook his head. "I know he's your father, Nicole, but—"

Lifting a staying hand, she cut him off. "I know. He doesn't act as if he is. The man had the nerve to tell Brenda I'm a coward for hiding, and that she shouldn't be one, too. Criminal law involves criminals, he told her. If she can't deal with those people without hiding, she doesn't belong in criminal law."

He didn't know what to say to such a blatant insult aimed at Nicole, and from her father to boot. "Your mother? What does she think of all of this? Isn't she worried?"

"My mother doesn't put a sentence together my father doesn't form. My father will convince her this is all melodrama. That he has security if my sister needs it. I just want her away, safe. At least until some of this heat calms."

He watched as Nicole climbed under the sheet and pulled it to her neck as if she sought the safety of a shield—beyond her mental barriers this time. Her parents' attitude blew him away. Death might have claimed his family, but they'd all loved him, and he, them. She had no one but her sister, it seemed. Which offered yet another explanation—why she'd run out into that hall without waiting for him.

"I'll handle this," he told her, determined to make this go away for her. He reached for the phone and punched Redial, hoping for a signal, and finding one.

"Who are you calling?"

"Your sister," he said.

Her eyes went wide, but before she could object, Brenda answered. "Nicole! Is that you? Are you okay?"

"Nicole is fine," he replied. "She's right here beside me. Brenda, this is Agent Constantine Vega."

"What's wrong?" Brenda demanded. "Are you sure Nicole is safe?"

"Yes, she's safe." He didn't look at Nicole because he was about to share some harsh words with her sister. "Your safety is the concern, and I'm not going to mince words here. The man hunting your sister means to kill her. He'll use anyone he can to get to her, but he prefers pretty women as targets. He'll do his homework. Probably already has. He knows how important you are to Nicole. If he gets his hands on you, he'll be brutal because he enjoys pain. He'll enjoy your pain. Stay where you are."

Silence. "I don't know what to do. My father says—"

"We aren't dealing with your basic criminal type here. Believe me, far worse. Does your father want the death of both his daughters on his conscience?"

More silence. "How is Nicole?"

Constantine glanced at Nicole for the first time since the call started. Her knees were drawn to her chest, sheet clutched in her fist, apprehension etching her features.

"She's beyond worried for you. If you go home, I'll have to tie her down to keep her here." Nicole's eyes went huge and he winked.

"I know who you are. She told me. You're the man from the bar."

He didn't like that statement. "Stay where you are, Brenda."

She hesitated. "I'm going to catch all kinds of heck for this, but I'll stay. Can I talk to Nicole?"

"Yes." He hesitated, though, eventually handing the phone to Nicole.

Nicole talked to her sister for a minute and hung up. "Thank you," she said. "Thank you so very much."

He tugged the sheet away from her and pulled her into his arms. "Thank me in that shower I never finished. After that, I am fairly confident I'll need to make love to you again."

He scooped her up. Standing with her in his arms, he carried her to the bathroom, a heated image playing in his head of what he planned to do to her once he got her there.

HOURS LATER, NICOLE woke, lying on her stomach. The room was dark, night having fallen during their sleep. She smiled to herself. Constantine's hand was on her bare butt. Definitely a butt man.

She sighed softly, thinking of the hours of lovemaking they'd shared. Lovemaking. His word, not hers. But what had happened between them had been far more fulfilling, far more potent than any sex she'd experienced before him. Indeed, lovemaking. What she'd had with her ex had been pure sex. This…this experience with Constantine ran deeper than simple pleasures of the body. It drew her into a mind-set where the rest of the world faded into a place she shared with only one other—with Constantine.

Her mind traveled to his comments about trust. She did trust him. What he had done with her sister blew her away. He'd come through for her, protected Brenda and done so for her. Yes. She trusted him. Mostly. With her life. But with her heart? That thought brought her back to her fears.

He scared her. No. Her reaction to him scared her. He reached inside her and saw everything she would hide from another. She didn't want to be hurt. Letting him get too close would only make saying goodbye harder. He was wrong for her, but he felt so right. The questions he made her ask of herself were difficult, but somehow necessary.

Here in Constantine's arms, she had found a different sort of comfort. Yet something inside her screamed to run from this feeling, to push him away. He'd leave soon, this would all be over. Back to her life, back to alone.

As if he read her thoughts, he pulled her into his arms, her back to his chest, into the shelter and out of the storm.

19

Silence fell between Nicole and Constantine as they prepared to leave the hotel room they'd called a safe zone for two weeks. The storm had long ago passed, danger had calmed as the hotel remained a secure hideaway. Knowing Flores was the leak had allowed communication to flow between her and her boss. Meanwhile, she and Constantine didn't speak as they packed what few things they had to take with them. There was so much to say, yet they said nothing at all.

They'd made love the night before. It had been passionate, heartfelt, perfect. She'd never felt this kind of connection to another person in her life. It was invigorating, exciting, scary as hell. She'd truthfully seen herself as a loner for the rest of her life, and perhaps she'd seen that in Constantine when she'd met him. What happened when two loners came together?

She didn't know. Maybe she needed to go home and find out if this was real. But there was no denying the idea that leaving this room and never feeling this way again burned a hole in her gut.

This was the first time she'd felt she belonged with a man. A man who, only weeks ago, she would have claimed was everything she didn't want. It was insane, yes, but she was done running from her feelings. She'd come to a conclusion: living to prove what she wasn't wasn't living at all.

In fact, over the past few weeks, she'd done a world of soul-searching, but clarity had come only the night before, as she stared at the ceiling, unable to sleep. She'd been living a lie her entire life, trying to be something she wasn't all to prove something to herself, and to the people she knew. She had to make changes. Which meant, she had to go home, convict Alvarez and then decide where that left her. What she didn't know was where Constantine fit in to those changes.

Done with her packing, Nicole sat down on the bed. She wore a blouse, jeans and tennis shoes, but soon she would be back to business attire. Today, she had awakened next to Constantine; tomorrow, they would be prosecutor and FBI agent, pretending to be strangers, on their best behavior for the jury. This was the end of the line. Their worlds would separate, perhaps forever.

Constantine zipped up a leather bag he'd bought from the hotel boutique and set it by the door. "Ready?"

The truth was that she wasn't sure she was ready at all, but she had no choice. She managed a nod, her gaze doing a quick sweep of his body in the process, lingering on his muscular thighs beneath the tight jeans he wore. The man was the caviar of denim. He made it sexy. But then, everything about him was sexy to her.

She drew a breath, knowing there was something she owed him—a confession of sorts. Her wish to pretend she was something she wasn't had made her blame him for things he had nothing to do with.

Not giving herself time to back out, she exhaled and blurted her declaration. "Back at the docks, I wanted Carlos dead."

Constantine didn't move, didn't appear to quite know what to say. "And you blamed me for making you feel that way."

"Yes," she whispered, her chest constricted. "How did you know?"

"The way you looked at me and then the way you couldn't look at me."

"I'm sorry," she said, feeling the odd pinch of tears in the back of her eyes. She never cried and she didn't want to now.

"It was human, Nicole. An instinct to survive."

He was so close, only a foot away, but right now so very distant emotionally. "I know. I've spent a lot of time trying to make up for the past, afraid of becoming what I was back then."

"And I scared you. I walk a line you don't want to walk. You think I'll change that. Make you like me." His jaw flexed. "I get that." The words held bitterness, a bite that hurt.

Nicole surged to her feet. "No. It's not like that."

"It is, Nicole." He hesitated, his jaw flexing. "We both know the limits between us. We simply stopped talking about them. Regardless of what you think, I'm not a cold-blooded killer, or Alvarez wouldn't be awaiting trial. But will I kill to save lives? Will I make a decision you might not feel fits your moral fiber? Yes."

How had this conversation gone so wrong? "I don't think you're a killer!" She took a step toward him, desperate to right this.

He held up a staying hand and she stopped. "You're going back to your perfectly planned life," he said, "free of bad influences like myself. I brought you into this thing with Carlos, and I will see you through it. I'll get you your life back. You have my word."

He grabbed the bags and reached for the door, pulling it open without giving her the chance to respond and tell him that what she really wanted was…him.

CONSTANTINE SPENT MOST of the ride to Austin in a foul mood, aware of her every move, her every sound. She drove him crazy with desire, with anger, with frustration. With…something more. Something he didn't want to think about. But he couldn't deny he had feelings for Nicole, nor could he deny how wrong he was for her.

He wasn't a man who lived within a structured set of rules. Nicole survived by creating control, which meant rules. He didn't think she was happy in that world, not for a minute, but it didn't matter. He wouldn't live as the man who made her question herself. His life had been danger and darkness, and regardless of his decision to leave the agency, he wasn't likely to change. He'd find trouble; he always did.

Nicole was upset now, but she'd get over it when she

settled into her life. He knew all the psych workups. People fell hard for those who protected them, who they depended on. Right now, she would find a way to justify the things about him that were not quite right for her world, but later…later she would see more clearly. There was no reason to make this hard for either of them. He had to take this back to business, back to the place where this started, and ended. It was the right thing to do. Right. So why did his gut have knots the size of Texas?

He glanced at a street sign, estimating they were about a mile from their destination. Breaking the silence, he cast her a sideways look. "A team of agents will be waiting for our arrival," he explained matter-of-factly. "They have the entire top floor of the Four Seasons Hotel blocked off with special security. They still have nothing on Carlos. He's vanished."

"You'll be there, right? Not just this FBI team?"

The hopeful quality in her voice tightened those knots in his gut a bit more. "I told you I'd get you through this, and I meant it."

She drew a heavy breath and exhaled, her response cold. "I have the utmost confidence in your ability, Agent Vega."

Damn, he hated this. He shouldn't reach out to her but found himself softly saying, "Nicole. I'll still be near, still be by your side. I'm not going anywhere."

She didn't look at him. "Okay."

Son of a bitch. He didn't know what to do here. He wanted to comfort her. Hell, he wanted her in his bed.

But he also knew what was best, knew she'd thank him later for this. So why wasn't this easy?

He grabbed the phone and called in, directing the car to the side entrance of the hotel. In a matter of minutes, they were being shuffled to a private elevator. Constantine grabbed Nicole's arm, wishing he could pull her close, but settling for keeping her within his grasp. They had appearances to keep up now, a jury to satisfy. He also had her safety to consider, and he trusted no one but himself to protect her. He was keeping her close, period.

Standing beside him, staring up at the blinking display of passing floors, she didn't look at him, but he felt her relax, felt her relief at his nearness. If he did nothing else for Nicole, he made her feel safe. That was something, at least.

His hand never left her arm as they stepped into the hall and traveled to the end of a long corridor. He let her go only when an agent opened the suite they would call home during the trial. He entered directly behind her.

In the center of the small living area, Agent-in-Charge Nelson waited. An ex-military man, he wore his hair buzzed; his suit, pressed perfectly.

He nodded at Constantine, a look of respect in his eyes. "Good to see you arrived safely." His attention turned to Nicole, and he offered her his hand. "Agent Nelson."

Nicole took his hand for a brief moment. "Thanks for your help while we were out there," she said. "How does this all work?"

"There are three bedrooms here. I put you in the one

to the left. It's bigger and nicer. Your boss dropped off some papers for your review. You'll find them on the dresser."

"Okay," she said. "Thanks."

Nelson continued, "We'll want you in a controlled environment as much as possible, so only your direct family and people related to the case can visit on a limited basis. I need a list of anyone who might be allowed in, so we can check them out. If they aren't on that list, they don't get in. You'll have two agents, in addition to Agent Vega, at all times." His gaze flickered to Constantine. "After what happened with Flores, I don't blame him for not trusting anyone." He spoke directly to Constantine then. "We arrested him last night. He's been asking to talk to you."

"The day hell freezes over would be too soon."

"Did he say why he did it?" Nicole asked.

"Threatened his family," Nelson said, giving her a quick look. "But we have procedures in place to handle those things. I suspect we'll discover it was more about money."

"Money is a powerful drug," she murmured softly, and Constantine knew she was thinking about her past. She'd told him how her father's firm wanted the big billing cases, no worry about what lowlifes they defended. "Can I go to my apartment to get some things?"

"I'm afraid I can't allow that. I can have a female agent pick up some things for you."

"Thank you." She hesitated. "Now, I'd better get on those papers that Dean left."

"Let me know if you need anything," Nelson said.

She inclined her head but didn't comment, nor did she look at Constantine. It took every ounce of willpower he had not to follow her with his eyes as she left the room.

He focused on Nelson. "Why don't we have Carlos yet?"

"We're trying."

"Not good enough. She'll never be safe if we don't get him. He'll hunt her down to prove a point. That he can get to someone I've been protecting."

"That he can get to you, and anyone near you, like you did him," Nelson returned accurately.

A muscle in his jaw jumped. "Yes. He won't kill me. He'll kill anyone near me. That means she's in real danger. I'm protecting her, so he'll want to prove he can kill her."

"And if you walk away from her?"

"It's too late," he said grimly. "He's got her in his sights."

"I'll start the relocation process. You want to talk to her or shall I?"

"Neither, damn it," Constantine said. "Get Carlos."

Nelson paused, then said, "I know you don't trust me—"

"I don't trust anyone at this point. It's not personal, man. This is the end of the road for me. I'm done after this. I plan to leave alive."

"You sure that's what you want? We need you."

He was sure. Damn sure. When the time came, he

was ready to walk away from the Bureau without ever looking back. Why did he think walking away from Nicole wouldn't be that easy?

20

Nicole entered the Austin hotel suite after a long day in court, ever aware of Constantine behind her, beside her, near her—there, but not there. Watchful, but distant.

She walked straight to her room, edgy, ready to turn and demand they clear the air. But they weren't alone. They were never alone. Besides, he'd made his position clear. Their relationship was over. They were fire and ice. He wanted fire and apparently thought she wanted ice.

She found the door to her room and quickly shut herself inside, letting her briefcase slide to the floor. She leaned back against the closed door, her head resting on the wooden surface, eyes closed.

Constantine had been right about her perfectly planned life. She'd built a glass house. So perfect there was nothing real inside. There was laughter—no happiness. Just her own need to prove she wasn't defined by the past.

But back in Houston with Constantine, she had found

what was missing. She'd gotten a taste of what it meant to share her life with someone else and she greedily wanted more. And more meant Constantine.

She inhaled, recognizing her emotions were turbulent at best and not all because of her relationship with Constantine. Her father's presence in the courtroom that day had messed with her head. He'd sat there, a judgmental look on his face. But no matter how flawed he might want to find her performance, he wouldn't be able to, and he only wanted to because she was doing work he didn't approve of. She was at the top of her game, performing her best. She wanted Alvarez put away, and she was going to make it happen. Her one regret was that she couldn't truly share the progress with Constantine, that they had to act as strangers for the sake of appearance. But they'd come too far to allow an affair to destroy credibility. They couldn't risk that getting out to the press, and maybe, inadvertently, the jury.

However, she wasn't going to be a wilting wallflower hiding in her room. She'd go out there, claim the desk and start working. Let Constantine hide in his room. She was done hiding. From herself. From her life. From him. Time to forgive herself. Time to stop wallowing in guilt. *Choose my own battles.* That idea had been working a number on her mind. Maybe she'd open her own law firm. She wasn't sure yet, but change was in the air for her. She was brave in the courtroom. Now she wanted to be brave beyond it.

No more hiding.

Constantine sat in his bedroom with the door open, listening to Nicole talk to one of the agents in the living area of the suite. Her voice trickled along his nerve endings, taunting him with what he wanted, what he couldn't have—her.

Staying away from her was killing him. Many times he'd considered saying to hell with putting some distance between them. No, he didn't fit into her prim-and-proper life, but he was convinced she didn't fit into that life, either. In fact, he'd convinced himself that throwing her over his shoulder and carrying her away from all of this would be best for her. He also knew Nicole had to see for herself, had to decide what was right for herself. Except now, she didn't have choices. Not after the news he'd gotten today. He scrubbed his jaw, dreading the conversation they had to have.

He shoved off the bed and walked to the doorway, leaning on the edge of the door frame. She stood behind the bar, pouring herself a Diet Sprite over ice, her gaze lifting to his as if she sensed his presence.

"We need to talk," he said. He motioned with his head, indicating his room. "In private."

Surprise flashed in her face. Not once since their return had they been alone. Her room was on the opposite side of the suite, their relationship strictly business to all those around them. Oh, but he could imagine being in bed with her, the sheets gone, his body all that covered her.

"Of course," she said, setting down her soda can and crossing the room, closing the distance. He watched her walk, her hips swaying in the velour sweats she'd bought back in Houston. Damn, how he wanted to lose himself in her. His zipper area expanded painfully, his body taut with the day's worth of desire that had gone unattended.

He backed up, letting her enter the room, shutting the door behind her. She walked to the bed and sat down. The bed. The place he wanted her. He leaned against the wall, crossing his arms over his chest. "We picked up one of Carlos's men today."

She gave him a cautious look. "I assume that's good, but you aren't acting like it is."

"He had some information. A message for me." He hesitated, hating this so damn much. "About you."

Her chin tilted downward. "And?"

"Anyone I get close to, he'll kill. Starting with you."

"No one knows about us."

"You're under my protection and have been. That's enough for him."

She blinked, swallowed and turned away. "And my family?"

"Alvarez wants this trial to end, so anything done to anyone that might cause a mistrial is still a risk. If something happened to your family, no doubt you'd have trouble going on. After this is over, Carlos will focus on me. That means he'll come for you."

She looked at him then. "But you can't be certain he won't go after my family."

"Not one hundred percent." He wished he could tell her otherwise. "You have no option but to go into a re-location program until Carlos is captured."

Her eyes went wide. "Oh, no," she said, rock-hard determination in her voice. "Not a chance." She pushed to her feet. "If there is one thing I have learned from all of this, it's that I'm tired of running. I ran to where I am now, to hide from what I was in the past. And I can't ask my family to give up their lives. Not that they will. They could die while I'm off hiding."

Uncrossing his arms, he pushed off the wall, going to stand in front of her, barely containing the urge to reach for her. "This is about staying alive, Nicole. I know it's hard but—"

"Would you run?"

What could he say to that? "My job is to hunt down criminals and capture them."

"Then do it now. Capture him. You said you'd make this go away."

He had promised. "I'm stuck in here or I would. I will." His hands went to her arms. "Nicole, baby—"

She shoved his arms away, a fierce frown on her face. "Don't 'Nicole baby' me, now. You haven't touched me in days. Don't use our fling as a form of manipulation."

"It's not like that. I wouldn't do that."

"Not like that. Then how is it? We've hardly said two words to each other since we returned, and now that you want me to do something your way, you pull out the 'baby' stuff?"

"Everything I've done, I've done to protect you."

She made a disbelieving sound. "This doesn't feel like protection. It feels like…" Her words trailed off, her lashes lowered, a few seconds ticked by. Her lashes lifted again and she gazed directly into his eyes. "The bottom line here is this. I'm not running anymore. Not from my past, not from Carlos. Catch him. Use me as bait. Do whatever. But I'm not going into hiding."

"I won't use you as bait."

"I want this over, Constantine. Even if I agree to hide, my family won't. My father has some 'man of steel' complex—I can't let them walk around with a bull's-eye on their backs because of me. If you won't use me to put an end to this, someone at the Bureau will." She narrowed her eyes on him, throwing out her dare. "So you decide. Will you use me or let someone else?" She tried to walk past him, and he maneuvered in front of her.

"No," he said. "I won't allow it. No one is using you as bait. I got you into this and I'll get you out."

They stared at one another, her lips parted, the world somehow separating them, when only a few days before it had pulled them together.

"I got me into this by taking this case," she finally said. "I'll get me out of it."

She sidestepped him and this time he let her go, turning around to watch her leave. "Nicole," he said, as she reached for the door. Looking back over her shoulder, her gaze sought his, a question in her eyes.

"This isn't over," Constantine stated.

Tension charged the air, seconds passing by before she turned and left, the door shutting behind her.

Constantine sat down on the bed and pounded the mattress. Time and time again, those he cared about ended up hurt. He had to make this go away. Had to protect Nicole. The idea of something happening to her destroyed him. Damn it, he didn't want to care about her. But he did. And no matter how hard he tried to run from that fact, he couldn't. He was in love with Nicole.

THE NEXT AFTERNOON, Nicole finished up a long day in court. Nasty details that should have been revealed to the jury had been suppressed and then manipulated by the defense; Nicole's frustration over the judge's decision was high.

She walked toward the exit, Constantine waiting for her, leaning against the back wall, watchful. He wore black slacks, a black dress shirt and tie, his hair pulled back. He even made dress clothes look dangerous and sexy, and right now she hated him for it. To say she was intensely aware of him would be an understatement. Every inch of her body screamed with arousal when she looked at him. Anger and hurt did nothing to dispel the feeling. She was all for fighting battles, all for standing up and making a difference, but for once, she'd thought she wouldn't be doing it alone. She'd been wrong. And she wished she'd never felt that "together" feeling— how do you miss what you don't know?

Constantine grabbed the door for her, and for an instant their eyes met. Her stomach fluttered, and she quickly averted her gaze. By the time she slid into the back of an unmarked car with him, their knees brushing together, Nicole was ready to come unglued. She shivered despite herself—with want, with emotion.

Another agent started to slide in on the opposite side of the backseat, and Constantine held up a hand. In other words, "go away." The agent nodded and did as ordered, shutting them into the backseat. Alone. A tinted glass window gave them privacy from the driver. She turned to him, surprised at his actions, not sure what to expect. The drive was short, a mere two blocks. But she didn't have to guess his intentions for long.

Suddenly, she was in those big, strong arms, warmth surrounding her, his lips slanting over hers, tongue delving into her mouth with possessive heat. Passion and emotion washed over her, taking control, stealing her breath.

When the kiss ended all too soon, Nicole stared up at him, searching his dark eyes, eyes she could lose herself in for a lifetime. Eyes telling her he cared. A knock sounded on the window and she jumped. The short ride was over. No. They needed more time.

"One minute," Constantine called, his attention never leaving Nicole. "I have to know you're okay."

She didn't ask why. The kiss, the look in his eyes, the way she felt in his arms, told her everything. He cared. He hadn't shut her out. "Then stay with me."

His eyes softened a second before another knock sounded. They had to get out and pretend to be strangers again, at least until the trial was over.

Constantine brushed his cheek against hers and whispered her name. Nothing more. The next thing she knew, the door was opening, and with regret, she followed Constantine out of the backseat. Distant, but not nearly as distant as before.

She entered the hotel room a few minutes later filled with the warmth of knowing she and Constantine were finding their way back to each other. Their shared glances, as they decided to order a pizza instead of room service, were so hot, she didn't know how the other agents could miss the sizzle. But she didn't care.

The trial was almost over, and these guys hated Alvarez. They wouldn't work against her. They'd been rooting for her in court.

Waiting for the pizza, she sat down on the couch and wrote down notes for her closing statements to review with her team. The two agents on duty played poker on the desk. Constantine took a call from someone, went to his room a few minutes to talk, then to her surprise, returned, no longer avoiding her. He took over a nearby chair and studied a security report that Agent Nelson sent him each evening.

When a knock came at the door, her stomach grumbled hungrily. "Yes!" she said, setting down her papers, preparing to get a soda.

But the agent didn't return with pizza. Instead, he returned with an awkward look on his face. He glanced at Constantine and then Nicole. "You have a visitor," he informed her. "Mike Parker. He's on the list. Says he's, ah, your husband."

"Ex-husband," she corrected, eyeing Constantine. He was already on his feet, his jaw set tight, eyes averted from hers. This was so not good. Her heart felt as if it had slipped to her stomach.

"Let him in?" the agent queried.

Reconciled to her situation, she nodded at the agent. "Let him in."

A few seconds later, Mike entered, dressed in designer dress slacks and a starched button-down shirt. Blond hair, blue eyes and a million-dollar, prep-school, fake smile were a few of the traits he used to manipulate people, both in and out of the courtroom.

He flashed her one of those smiles. "Good to see you, Nicole." The words held the hint of flirtation that he couldn't seem to speak to a woman without using.

She didn't invite him to sit down. "What can I do for you, Mike?" she asked, her cold tone reserved for him. Coldness meant to repulse his advances. He'd never stopped looking at her as his possession and tried to assert his claim every chance he could. Keeping him at a distance was her best defense.

Mike's gaze traveled to the table where the two agents played cards and then settled over her shoulder—to where Constantine stood, a flash of discomfort showing on his face; most people wouldn't notice, but she knew Mike better than she wanted to. Inwardly, she smiled, enjoying his discomfiture.

With a slow slide, Mike returned his attention to Nicole, acting unaffected by Constantine. A lie. He was good at those. "Watched you in court today," he said. "You looked good." He winked and glanced at her wrist. "See you still wear the bracelet I gave you for good luck."

The air crackled with tension. Willpower, pure and simple, was all that kept her from turning and explaining. She wore the bracelet as a reminder of what she never wanted to be again—either as an attorney or as a person. But Constantine would think otherwise. He would think she still cared for Mike—or worse, for her old life.

She swallowed hard, desperate to be rid of Mike and explain to Constantine. "Cut to the chase, Mike. What do you want?"

His lips twisted a bit. "Your father asked me to talk to you."

Figured. "So talk."

He glanced over her shoulder again and then back to her. "Can we do this alone?"

She considered declining but decided she'd better hear Mike out. "Fine," she said, pushing to her feet and heading to the bedroom, her gaze seeking Constantine, who was entering his own room.

Mike followed her into her room and tried to shut the door. She pointed to it. "Oh, no. It stays open." He grimaced, but left it open.

Nicole crossed her arms and turned to face him. "Now talk."

He was close, too close, but backing away more would make him feel powerful, as if he had intimidated her. And since he got off on intimidation, that would only drag this out further.

"Your father didn't send me," he announced. "I simply thought it past time we talked. You ran off over some outbreak of conscience. I get it that you felt you had to, but it's time to end this little emotional relay you're running. Now you've gone and put your family in danger." He took a step toward her and she countered with a step backward.

An evil smile formed on his lips at her actions as he continued, "You're going to win this case, and it's a masterpiece of a win. You'll pay back whatever debt you feel you owe society by putting Alvarez away. It's done. You can come home again."

"We're divorced! And, my God, you must think I am

stupid," she said. "You and Daddy planned this, didn't you? An effort to put the firm in the spotlight by way of the press I'm getting."

He moved quickly then, grabbing her before she knew his intentions. "You took the perfect life and threw it in the trash," he said, pulling her against his body. "I work for your father. I am supposed to be married to you. Have your affairs, have a separate life, but stop tearing apart the core of this family."

"You and I are not the core of anything!" She shoved at his chest. "Get off me or I swear I will get all three of those agents to make you leave."

"It'll only take one." Nicole looked up at the sound of Constantine's voice, thick with danger, his attention fixed on Mike, as he added, "You have no idea how badly I want to hurt you right now, so I suggest you let go of her."

Mike didn't let go, possessiveness in his rebuttal. "Touch me and I'll sue."

"If you live."

Mike let go. He stepped back as if burned. And Nicole didn't blame him. Something in Constantine's words, his presence, oozed downright menace. "Leave," Constantine said.

Mike headed toward the door. Constantine eased back enough for Mike to pass...barely.

Constantine faced Nicole. "You also have no idea," he said, his words taut, "how much I hate the idea of that pencil-neck, preppy lowlife touching you. But you know what I hate even more? I hate that you wear his bracelet."

And then he was gone, leaving her to gape after him. She couldn't lose Constantine over Mike. Couldn't. Wouldn't. Mike was nothing. Constantine was everything. Constantine was... She loved him. She loved him so very much.

She didn't think anymore; instead Nicole stormed out of her room—unconcerned about the other agents' noticing her—with one destination in her sights. Constantine's bedroom.

21

NICOLE DIDN'T BOTHER to knock before charging into Constantine's room. She slammed the door shut and leaned against it, hands flat on the wooden surface behind her, her chest heaving with anxiety.

Constantine sat on the bed, face buried in his hands. He looked up at her. "Go away, Nicole. We have nothing to talk about."

His words cut through her with the sharpness of a blade. "Mike means nothing to me."

He ran his hand over his thigh. "I don't want to hear this." Pain dripped from his words, although he tried to appear cold, as cold as she had been to Mike.

She didn't want Constantine to hurt, but at least she knew he cared. She darted toward him then, falling to her knees in front of him, and put her hands on his muscular thighs. Touching him. Touching him felt right. "I wear the bracelet to remind me of what I never want to become again. To remind me that no matter how bad it gets in court, I am not like him."

In response, he distanced himself from her—no sign of him reaching for her. His eyes were black ice. "That you need that reminder says everything," he whispered. "Your past defines who you are."

She ripped the bracelet from her arm. "I don't need the bracelet. I'm done running from the past. I'm done letting it define me. I'm resigning from my job. I'm going to start fresh. I need to start fresh. And I want to do it with you."

Surprise flashed in his face. A hint of hope. Then it was gone; the coldness, back. "Until I do something that makes you question yourself, or maybe my intentions. Something that has you painting me as a bad influence."

"No." How could she get through to him? At this point, proclaiming her love would fall on deaf ears. He believed she had a negative opinion of him and, on some level, didn't trust him. She recalled a conversation they'd had back in Houston—she knew what to do.

Her eyes traveled the room, looking for the tool she sought before pushing to her feet. At the window, she tugged away the sashes holding the curtains and returned to her prior position, on her knees, in front of him.

Nicole stared up at him, hoping he saw the truth in her eyes as she spoke. "I believe in you. I trust you." She held out the sashes. "Tie me up, Constantine. You know I wouldn't let you if I didn't completely trust you. Be the first. Be the last. Be the only one."

A look of disbelief crossed his face. "What?"

She repeated her words, eager to make them take root in his mind. "You said I wouldn't let you tie me up

until I trusted you completely. I do. I... Constantine."
She drew a deep breath for courage. "I have no idea
how you feel about me, but I—"

And then she was in his arms. He lay back on the
mattress, pulling her with him. A second later, she
was the one on her back, Constantine's big body on
top of her, kissing her, devouring her with passion and
warmth.

Long moments later, he tore his lips from hers. "You
want to know how I feel about you?" he asked, staring
down at her. "I love you, Nicole. I love you with all of
my heart."

Her arms wrapped around his neck, her heart swell-
ing with joy. "I love you, too. I love you so much."

Tenderness filled his face. "Then do run away. Run
away with me, Nicole. Take a year off from work, and
travel the world. With me. We'll be careful. Carlos won't
be able to follow us."

Her mind was still reeling from the "take a year off
and travel the world" statement, when he spoke again.

"It'll work, *cariña.* If we're lucky, he'll be in custody
by the time you and I hit our first destination. Nelson
is waiting for a yes, and then he'll coordinate everything. So say yes."

Everything was falling into place. "I... Yes. Okay."
Her fingers brushed a strand of hair out of his eyes.
"But I can't just run off for a year, as wonderful as that
sounds. I have to figure out what is next for me. Maybe
my own firm. I have some money, but—"

He grabbed her hand tenderly and kissed it. When
they were intimate, he did that often, and she loved it.

"Forget money," he said. "I told you, I have money. For travel, for whatever you need."

"I can't forget money." Working as a public servant didn't allow her much saving, and taking money from her father meant working for him, which would never happen again.

"If money weren't an issue, would you take the year and enjoy it?"

"Yes, but—"

He kissed her. And kissed her some more. By the time his lips left hers, she ached with need, and couldn't remember what they had been talking about. But he did. "Money isn't an issue," he declared. "We'll leave the day the trial ends."

She didn't consider arguing. She loved him and he, her, and she believed in that for the first time in her life. "All right, then," Nicole whispered. Somehow she still held the sashes in her hands. She smiled. "Want to tie me up to seal the deal?"

"Later," he murmured huskily. "Now I just want to make love to you, Nicole. Nice and slow." And he kissed her again, starting with her lips and then exploring, tasting, loving, until she shivered with release. And then he started all over again.

THREE DAYS LATER Nicole stood in the courtroom. She was ecstatic as she heard the jury's guilty verdict for every charge against Alvarez. Deliberation had taken a mere four hours. This was a victory Nicole felt on so many levels that she wanted to dance with joy. Next up would be Flores, but her boss was handling that one.

The minute she broke free of the chaos that followed the court's adjournment, her eyes found Constantine's, sharing a silent look of happiness with him. They'd done it. Alvarez would never hurt anyone again.

As for Carlos, the Bureau had tracked him down through an informant and executed the arrest perfectly.

Reporters and flashing cameras awaited them outside on the courtroom steps, and Nicole gave a short statement. Not soon enough, it was over, and she slid into the passenger seat of a car, Constantine by her side.

Nicole and her family would be safe. Everything about Constantine's plan had fallen into place.

Nicole couldn't wait to get to Greece—the pictures in the ads had been gorgeous. For once, she was living for the pure thrill of it, taking chances, and loving it.

Constantine held her hand as he drove the car away. Nicole smiled at him. Smiled because she was embarking on a new adventure, and she couldn't wait to see what came next.

She was happy.